HELL BOUND BOOK 2

WRATH

SARAH HEGGER

Cover: Deranged Doctor Design

ISBN: 978-1-990731-28-0
ISBN: 978-1-990731-29-7

Created with Vellum

PREFACE

If you're anything like me, dear reader, by the time you get to the next book in the series, you've forgotten some of the previous book. Never fear! I got you. Here's a brief recap of what has happened to get you up to speed. Happy reading.
   - Sarah

The Story So Far...

Resident stage manager to a community theatre company, Edme Ward, fails to prevent a production of *Macbeth* from being staged by the Paradise Players. The witch's curse in *Macbeth* starts the paranormal ball rolling, and Edme is soon knee deep in more trouble than a normal woman can handle. Because unbeknownst to just about everyone else in the world, the Paradise Theatre is a hell gate guarded by the women in Edme's family for generations, and the witch's curse in *Macbeth* has opened a portal to hell.

With the hell gate open, all kinds of dangerous creatures leak onto the earth plane. Not the least of which is the hell prince for lust, Asmodeus—or as he likes to be called, Shade. Initially infuriated that Edme (Eddie) has summoned him, Shade quickly finds himself needing her help. Hell is in an uproar and the normal balance is disturbed. Shade is a hell prince and fucking and fighting come with the territory. But this time, his nearest neighbor, hell prince Wrath, is not only warring against him, but trying to end him. There must always be seven hell princes and seven corresponding archangels. The loss of one will end in the destruction of creation, but Wrath is trying to end Shade, and Shade needs to get to safety so he can figure out why.

With Shade on the earth plane, his opposite and equal archangel, Uriel, arrives to keep the balance. Together they discover that Eddie is not entirely human and is, in fact, Nephilim. Long abhorred by both archangels and hell princes, Nephilim have always been hunted to extinction. Eddie's grandmother has been hiding her for all these years from both archangels and hell princes, and also from the third group who keeps creation balanced, the human guardians.

The human guardians are not playing nice. They find Shade at the theatre and shove him back to hell.

Encouraged by her grandmother and Uriel, Eddie stages a rescue attempt and discovers that she might be able to repair the seals.

Shade and Wrath finally stop fighting for long enough to figure out that the problems in hell go so much deeper. The seals to the deadly sins are breaking, and if they collapse, it will trigger the end of days.

The imbalance in hell is being helped along by a demon rebellion. All seven hell princes are reporting losses to their demon hordes and growing unrest and anarchy within their demesnes. Their corresponding archangels are worried because an end to one is an end to all of them.

In hell, Eddie makes a couple of key discoveries. Firstly, Nephilim are the product of a hell prince and a human, and her father is none other than Wrath. And secondly, because she holds the power of both hell and earth, she may be able to repair the seals.

Her attempt to repair Wrath's seal meets with partial success. The third element to complete the healing is heaven, and she has no access to that.

On the romance front, Eddie is falling for Shade, and Shade has fallen hard for Eddie. She's not sure she can trust him, as he is the hell prince for lust. She's also not sure that what she's feeling for him is real or whether it's a result of him being lust.

Shade is sure that Eddie is who he wants, and he decides an old-fashioned wooing is in order.

On their way from Wrath's seal to Shade's, Eddie is kidnapped by an army of rebel demons.

Sure that Wrath's brother Lucifer is behind Eddie's disappearance, Shade and Wrath return to the earth plane determined to find her.

Meanwhile, the impact of the failing seals is being felt on earth...

The story continues as Wrath hunts for Lucifer and his daughter, and the supernaturals and guardians scramble to prevent the end of days.

DRAMATIS PERSONAE

- **Apassionata**: Lust Demon. Second to Asmodeus.

- **Ashe**: Pride Demon. Second to Lucifer

- **Asmodeus aka Shade**: Hell Prince for Lust. Counterbalances Uriel

- **Beelzebub aka Zeb**: Hell Prince for Gluttony. Counterbalances Cassiel

- **Belphegor aka Belle:** Hell Prince for Sloth. Counterbalances Gabriel

- **Bianca Fiore:** Member Paradise Players. Human witch

- **Blot**: Avarice Demon. Imp

- **Calix**: Envy Demon. Higher order.

- **Chris Fellows:** Head of the Guardians. Human

- **Covet**: Avarice Demon. Mid order

- **Daniel Lee**: Hell gate guardian.Human

- **Deandra Ward**: Eddie's grandmother and hell gate guardian. Human

- **Edme Ward aka Eddie**: Resident stage manager for the Paradise Players. Nephilim

- **Gabriel:** Archangel for Diligence.Counterbalances Belphegor

- **Haziel**: Second to Ramiel. Seraph

- **Indolex**: Demon Lord. Evolving being

- **Isabelle Henshawe aka Issy**: Sick child. Human

- **Leafrot**: Avarice Demon. Woodland gnome

- **Leviathan aka Levi**: Hell Prince for Envy. Counterbalances Azriel

- **Lillian Hampstead**: Lead Actor Valley Players. Human

- **Lucifer:** Hell Prince for Pride. Counterbalances Raphael

- **Mammon aka Ava**: Hell Prince for Avarice. Counterbalances Michael

- **Matt**: Member Paradise Players. Actor *Macbeth*. Human.

- **Michael**: Archangel for Charity. Counterbalances Mammon.

- **Oliver**: Guardian. Human

- **Peter Hampstead:** Director and board member of the Paradise Players. Human

- **Raguel**: Second to Gabriel. Seraph

- **Ramiel**: Archangel for Patience. Counterbalances Satanus

- **Rapace:** Avarice Demon. Second to Avarice.

- **Raphael**: Archangel for Humility. Counterbalances Lucifer

- **Rodney Sykes**: Member Paradise Players. Human

- **Rosabella Ward**: Eddie's mother. Human

- **Satanus aka Wrath**: Hell Prince for Wrath. Counterbalances Ramiel

- **Uriel aka Sophia**: Archangel for Chastity. . Counterbalances Asmodeus

- **Vexia**: Wrath Demon. Second To Wrath.

- **Xerxes & Cronus:** Lust Demons. Hellhounds

- **Yesterday**: Wrath Demon. Imp

- **Zephon:** Patience Angel. Seraph

ONE

Haziel stood at her assigned place behind Ramiel. As his second in command, she was always where he needed her to be. From this angle she couldn't see the emerald glitter of his beautiful green eyes, or the sharp perfection of his bone structure. She made do with admiring the broad sweep of his muscular shoulders and the gleaming bronze glow of his nape.

Which made her officially the most ridiculous being in the room.

Although, not the most pitiable. That title was divided equally between Wrath and Shade. They were both absolutely gutted by the missing Nephilim, Edme. Wrath, her sire, paced the confines of the room that everyone called a greenroom but was mysteriously painted an unassuming beige. In fact, nothing in the room was green. Other than Ramiel's gorgeous eyes.

Sophia caught her eye over Ramiel's nobly shaped golden head and gave her a grimace of sympathy.

Haziel couldn't even pretend ignorance. Every being in

heaven, and judging by the smirk Avarice was giving her, a goodly portion of hell, were well aware of her infatuation with her boss.

Shade remained sitting beside Sophia, elbows on his knees, head slumped. One would be a fool to judge his mood by the dejection of his pose even though energy radiated from him in crashing waves that more than one being was struggling to assimilate.

She had no idea what Shade's connection to the missing Nephilim was, but if the looks Sophia was casting him were anything to judge by, he was in love with the Nephilim.

Poor Sophia. She'd waited years for Shade to spend one iota of the energy and attention he was currently spending on Edme on her. Haziel wrinkled her nose back at Sophia in sympathy. They were in the same leaky boat—in love with another who barely noticed them.

They were angels, divine beings with near immortal lifespans, and still, they could not conquer romantic love. Apparently, the hell princes hadn't done much better. Rumors abounded about Wrath and Edme's human mother, Rosabella, and how she'd rejected him.

Now, Haziel adored Ramiel, but objectively speaking, it was hard to picture any female rejecting Wrath. An inch or two taller than Shade and Ramiel with broad shoulders and the packed muscle of a born fighter. His face was more rough-hewn than classically handsome, but those blue eyes could blaze with the very fires of hell at a female. And the fires of hell burned *hot, hot, hot*. Then there was his mouth, the contradiction in the chiseled angularity of his face, full and sensual and hinting at another side to the bellicose hell prince.

Even thinking about Wrath in a positive light made her feel disloyal to Ramiel. As counterbalances to each other, Ramiel and Wrath were exact opposites. Ramiel was classically handsome with his silky blond hair and those melting green eyes in the flawless perfection of his aquiline features. And when he turned those eyes on her, most often when he wanted something, or when he had a task he could trust to no other, that brilliant jewel gaze would soften and his smooth, molten baritone would warm as he said, "Haziel, I need you."

Even thinking of him saying it made her shiver. She'd give her immortal soul to have him say that and mean something entirely different and a lot more intimate.

Shade looked up suddenly as if sensing the direction her thoughts were taking. Well, of course, he sensed the lascivious direction of her mental ramblings. He was, after all, the hell prince of lust.

The annoying head of the human guardians was on his feet again, staring at the room's occupants as if they'd personally bundled Edme up and handed her over to the demon, Ashe. Haziel recalled his name was Chris something or other. She guessed that it was because there were so many of them that humans needed both a name and a surname. It might get very confusing otherwise.

"You have lost the Nephilim," Chris thundered. "How could you have been so irresponsible?seraph

You, more than anyone, understand how powerful it is."

"How powerful *she* is." Shade didn't raise his voice, but waves of violence radiating from him made Haziel stiffen. It didn't take much to get a room full of hell princes and archangels fighting, and Chris's tone would do the job neatly. "She is not an it, and she has a name. Edme." Shade's tone softened. "Eddie."

"What he said." Wrath jerked his head at Shade. "And if you speak of my daughter in that way again I will—"

"Wrath." Ramiel's velvety voice rumbled a warning. As

Wrath's counterpart archangel, it fell to Ramiel to manage him.

She nearly snorted aloud. As much as anyone could manage Wrath. Of all the hell princes he was the most unpredictable. In terms of irascibility in any case.

The other hell princes had their own quirks. Avarice, or Ava as she preferred to be called—and who could blame her when she'd been saddled with the moniker Mammon—marched to her own drum and did exactly as she pleased. Dainty, China doll looking Belphegor—or Belle—never said much and was not often at these gatherings. She also refused most attempts to engage her. Beelzebub split his time between stirring trouble with his fellow hell princes and pursuing Leviathan, who was insistently independent. Haziel didn't know much about Levi. She was beautiful, aloof, and liked to irritate the archangels. Then there was Lucifer, currently absent from this meeting, and if Wrath and Shade were to be believed, the reason Edme was missing. The self-styled king of hell delighted in making life difficult for everyone.

"There is no cause for threats." Gabriel smoothed her already impeccable gleaming red hair. "If we're going to solve this crisis, we are going to need to work together."

Ramiel grumbled, and Haziel nearly snorted again. Work together? Archangels, demons, and guardians, all in one happy little pot boiling away together under the heat of this unprecedented crisis. Pressure, inflated egos, phenomenal cosmic power, and ancient enmity all bubbling around each other. What could go wrong?

"This is my child we speak of." Wrath stood and glared at the room.

Ramiel shuddered at the notion. Haziel had already listened to Ramiel's diatribe on the idea of having relations with humans. She hadn't said anything, merely listened and nodded, but Haziel didn't feel that humans were that distasteful. They had a charm about them that had always drawn her to them. They were fun and threw themselves into life with such enthusiasm. Of course, there were always the nasty ones, and the evil ones who gave the hell princes a run for their money in that department, but for the most part Haziel rather liked humans. She loved the children. Those were so sweet with their eager little faces and bright eyes. Yes, the children were delightful.

"We, understand, Satanus." Gabriel even looked like she might mean that. "But the guardian is correct about Edme being powerful, and we have not seen how her power has manifested yet. We certainly do not want it in the wrong hands."

"Christ!" Dee, Edme's grandmother, slapped her hands on her knees and stood. "All you do is talk, talk, fucking talk. And in all this jabbering, I've yet to hear one solid idea for getting Eddie back."

"Sit down, Deandra," Chris snapped. "You are only tolerated here because of your relationship to Edme."

Dee did no such thing and shot Chris a look so scorching Haziel expected his perfectly pressed suit pants to catch fire. "Bite me, fuckwit."

That there was one of the things Haziel liked about humans. They didn't back down, and they didn't give up, especially when it came to people they loved.

She'd give anything to have Ramiel speak to the others in this room about her like Dee had about Edme. Of course, she'd never done anything to warrant a spirited defense of herself, but the idea was enthralling.

"Your guardian status has been revoked." Chris—and she really should remember his surname. She'd wager Raguel,

Gabriel's second, knew it well—curled up his lip in distaste. "You are no longer under our protection."

"She doesn't need your puny protection." Wrath pounded one gigantic fist against his chest. "She has mine."

Well, judging by the breadth and depth of that chest on Wrath, Haziel had no trouble believing that would be more than adequate protection for any being. Another tiny shiver snaked down her spine. So inappropriate.

Shade looked up with death in his gray eyes at Chris. "And mine."

"And mine." Sophia raised her hand. "I like Eddie, and I like Dee, and if you guardians hadn't come charging in here like your asses were on fire, we might have had a chance to deal with this before it became critical."

Chris yelled, "What?"

"Sophia does not stutter." Michael broke his silence and yelled back. "And she speaks for me as well."

And the entire room disintegrated into chaos for about the four hundredth time. Dee was right. They did a lot of talking and not a lot of doing.

"Haziel?" Ramiel's soothing voice reached her through the hubbub. His warm breath caressed her ear and made her skin prickle. "I need you."

But not in the way I want you to. Still, she leaned closer and caught his unique citrus and bergamot scent. "I am here, Ramiel." *In any way you need.*

"Wrath is unpredictable." He scoffed. "More unpredictable than usual."

"He certainly does seem overly upset." Haziel let her gaze linger on Wrath. It was like looking at an unrefined version of her archangel. Ramiel had the same power and physical presence, but his didn't pound against you like a gigantic wave against a rock. No, Ramiel was polished, and sophisticated. Elegant.

"I believe he is going to try to find his get," Ramiel murmured. "I would follow him myself, but I am needed here to deal with the seal crisis."

Haziel was so lost in the way Ramiel's lips caressed the syllables of his words that it took a moment for their meaning to catch up with her. "You want me to follow him?"

Please, please, please let that not be what Ramiel wanted.

"Dear Haziel." He turned his gaze to her and smiled, and it was like the dawn breaking over the sea. "You always know exactly what I need. What would I do without you?"

Follow Wrath himself? Haziel's stomach twisted as she eyed the big hell prince. And she had to admit Ramiel was not far off in his assessment of the situation.

Wrath's blue eyes had gone flint hard, rivaled only by the impregnable set of his jaw. His huge hands were fisted by his sides, veins popping along his forearm.

"His power was bound by that demon of Lucifer's," Ramiel murmured. "He shouldn't give you any trouble."

Ashe must have bound Wrath when he took Eddie, and Haziel had not known that. She studied Wrath more carefully. For a being with his power bound, Wrath didn't look one iota less intimidating. It was probably the tremendous scowl creasing his rugged features. He might be quite handsome if he didn't always look so irritable. Not that Haziel would take her existence into her hands and tell him so. Then something more important occurred to her. "How will he get his daughter back if he has no power?"

"Now you comprehend why it's doubly important that one of us keep an eye on him." Ramiel flashed her another of his rare smiles, and Haziel wanted to bask in its glory.

"We believe you should reconsider your stance on Deandra." Gabriel nodded to Raguel, and he passed a tablet to her. "According to the treaty," Gabriel read, although Haziel was certain Gabriel had no need to read the treaty, she probably had the entire thing memorized chapter and verse. A little angelic humor never went amiss. Someone should tell Wrath that, and perhaps he wouldn't scowl quite so much. "The hell gate must have an active guardian at all times." Gabriel handed the tablet back to Raguel.

Haziel liked Raguel. They'd spent many hours keeping each other company whilst their respective archangels did whatever they did. Raguel had a great sense of humor and a near godlike ability not to get irritated by Gabriel. He also did a wickedly accurate imitation of Michael.

"The hell gate will have an active guardian," Chris snapped. "One is expected here imminently."

There was another one that needed to grow a sense of humor.

"What?" Dee gaped at him. "You can't just send someone into my home."

"This is a hell gate." Chris glared at her.

"But first it was my home," Dee scowled right back. "This theatre has been in my family for generations. Long before the hell gate was established here, and you can't march some stranger in here and expect me to house him."

"Your family ceded their rights to the theatre as a home when they became guardians," Chris said with a smirk.

"Not out of choice." Dee's eyes snapped with temper. "A fucking hell gate opened up in our basement. It's not like we could exactly ignore it."

Chris looked at Dee with open disdain. "That is beside the point."

"Bullshit," Wrath snapped. "That is precisely the point. My daughter's family behaved with honor when they took on the responsibility of the hell gate. A hell gate that they neither wanted nor had any hand in creating. You are shitting on their honor."

If Wrath had his power, Haziel was certain his wings would be out by now. Wrath had beautiful wings, glossy black with red and gold lights in the filaments. Her own wings were plain white, like a goose or a duck. She sent a mental apology to her wings for that thought. Wings were wonderful. She loved flying. And while hers might not be as beautiful as the other beings in this room, as a seraph, she had six of them.

"Stay out of this," Chris bellowed. "This is guardian business."

"We can't involve ourselves, Wrath," Gabriel said and smoothed down her skirt. "According to the treaty, we need to let the different realms manage themselves."

"Fuck the treaty. This is my daughter we're talking about."

Gabriel's cheeks went pink and her eyes flashed ire. "You can't say that about the treaty."

Yeah, Gabriel wouldn't like anyone being disrespectful about her beloved treaty. She probably tucked it into bed at night with a story and glass of warm milk.

"The only reason you have a daughter," Ramiel said, "is because you contravened the rules and lay with a human." His distaste for the idea loaded every syllable.

"Oh, please." Wrath sneered. "I'm hardly the first one of us to dodge that rule." He looked around the archangels and hell princes with contempt. "Now, am I?"

TWO

As the meeting descended into loud protestations and objections, Wrath reached his tipping point. If he stayed in the room much longer, he'd burn the whole fucking place down and everyone in it–without his powers. He'd go the human route of a can of gasoline and a match. With a nod to Shade, he turned and stalked out of the meeting. Fucking sanctimonious angels made him want to puke. As for his fellow hell princes, they could fuck right off as well. Hypocrites, the lot of them. Sitting there and pretending like nobody had ever made a little side trip to the human realm.

He stalked into the corridor outside the greenroom.

An attractive woman of middle years with long, dark hair stopped when she saw him, and her mouth dropped open. "Oh, hello."

He'd seen her around the theatre. She had something to do with the production currently happening. Neither in the mood, nor having the time to play nice, he nodded to her and sidestepped.

"Excuse me." The woman followed him, her sky-high heels clacking on the linoleum tiles. "I don't believe we've met."

Wrath ground his teeth as he turned. "No, we haven't."

"I'm Lillian." She held out one elegant white hand. "Lillian Hampstead." She giggled, a sound far more suited to a teenage girl than a grown woman. "Or Lady Macbeth currently."

That was right. She was an actress. Wrath vaguely recalled something about her being married to the director.

Her green eyes were giving him a thorough eye fucking, which pissed him off and made him want to take a bath at the same time. He took great delight in replying, "And I'm Satan."

She blinked at him in shock, and Wrath took the opportunity to take the stairs up to the living quarters above.

In the kitchen, he found a half empty bottle of white wine and took a swig. Alcohol was another of those human inventions that supernatural beings had copied. On the fridge, a shopping list was penned in Eddie's bold scrawl. Ashe had snatched her from right beneath his and Shade's noses. And he should have stopped it. As her sire, he was no use to his child if he could not protect her. All this power at his fingertips, and he'd allowed Ashe to siphon his power and take his daughter. If this weren't Eddie's kitchen, he would tear it apart to get some relief from his rioting insides.

Where the fuck was she, and what was Lucifer doing to her?

He should have ended his brother millennia ago. The fucker was an arrogant, useless piece of crap who thought the sun shone out his ass. Fucking king of hell. Jesus! Only Lucifer could cook something that ridiculous up.

"Hey." Shade entered the kitchen after him and took the wine from his hand. He grimaced when he saw what it was but took a swig anyway. "They don't have anything stronger?"

"Nope." Alcohol didn't do much for hell princes other than

soothe the sharp edges. It was extremely difficult for them to get drunk, and they recovered their senses quickly. Although, without his powers he couldn't say how anything would affect him, and he took another, longer swig from the bottle. No power also meant no wings, and he missed the freedom and the mind clearing space of flying.

Shade propped his shoulder against the doorjamb and looked at him. "I have to find her."

Eddie was his daughter, born of his body and his power. Having another hell prince interested in her, as Shade was, brought his simmering anger to a spitting boil. The only worse option would be if she had fallen for an archangel—Ramiel would be the shittiest case scenario. "She's nothing to you."

Shade gave him a long, measured look. "We both know that's not true."

"What do you want with my daughter anyway?" In the furor of the last three days, Wrath had almost forgotten Shade's ridiculous infatuation with Eddie.

"Everything." Shade shrugged. "I want everything she is prepared to give me."

Rage surged through Wrath. He needed an outlet for all the fury churning inside him. "You stay the fuck away from Eddie. You're no good for her."

"You're right," Shade said. "I'm as much of an asshole as you are, but I love her, Wrath, and I'm not going to stay away from her."

"Love?" Wrath nearly puked at the word. "What do you know of love? All you know is lust."

Shade's anger flashed through his eyes, but he took a careful breath. "Before I met Eddie, I wouldn't have argued with you, but she's different."

"Give me fucking break." He didn't want this horny fucker

anywhere near his daughter. Heaven and hell were littered with the broken hearts Shade had used and discarded.

Cocking his head, Shade folded his arms and studied him. "What would it take to convince you?" He raised a hand before Wrath could tell him to go fuck himself. "Not that you're the one who needs convincing. This is between Eddie and me."

"She doesn't trust you." It didn't give Wrath nearly as much satisfaction to say as he thought it would. He knew all too well how it felt to pine for a human woman who didn't love you. "And she doesn't want you near her."

"Then she can tell me that," Shade said. "And I'll respect it if it comes from her. But we're not talking about Eddie now. We're talking about you and me, and how you need to know my intentions are honorable."

Wrath's intentions had been honorable to Rosabella. He'd remade his castle to please her, would have hacked the wings off his back if she'd asked, even ceded power to his second and become human. But she'd said no, and then thrown the lacerating blow that she didn't love him.

Shade watched him. "Whatever you ask, it shall be done."

Well, if Shade was going to soft ball him in like that, Wrath was not above taking advantage. "Your obedience," he said. "You do what I tell you, when I tell you. And you use every ounce of your power to find her until I get mine back again."

"Done." Shade didn't even hesitate with his answer. "Just as long as one of the things you ask of me is not for me to stay away from Eddie. I've already told you I'm not doing that."

Shade looked serious. Hell princes never gave up control to another hell prince. It didn't matter. He still wasn't going to stand aside while Shade toyed with Eddie. He didn't trust Shade, but he was going to need help, and those useless fuckers downstairs were not going to do a damn thing. He didn't trust the other hell princes, and the archangels and guardians would only try to end Eddie if they found her first. "Accidents" happened all the time and faster than one could blink. "I need to find my daughter and my brother."

"You think Lucifer will be near her?" Shade looked doubtful.

Yeah, Wrath shared his skepticism. Lucifer knew Wrath would be looking for Eddie, and he wouldn't risk being close when Wrath came to find her. As twins, they could vaguely sense each other. Although, now that he had no power, the bond was muted like it was covered in several layers of leather. That had to be why Lucifer had insisted Ashe take his power.

Another thing he needed to know. What the fuck were those amulets? He'd never seen anything like them. "You ever see an amulet like the one Ashe used on me?"

"No." Shade shook his head. "I was going to ask you the same question." He studied Wrath. "And your power is definitely gone."

"Yup." He didn't bother to tell Shade that he could feel his power slowly regenerating inside him. It paid to have your enemy underestimate you.

"We should work together," Shade said. "We can split up and cover more ground."

It went against everything in him, but this was his daughter they were looking for. "I will take lead."

"Of course." Shade shrugged. "And you're the only one I would allow to do so. You want to find her nearly as much as I do."

Arrogant prick. "More than you."

"Whatever you say." Shade sneered. "And we find your fuckwit of a brother at the same time." He held out his hand.

Wrath stared at it. He'd never shaken hands with another hell prince, but he put his hand in Shade's. "Deal, but I get my brother when we find him."

"We can discuss that when we find him."

No way Wrath was giving up the pleasure of ripping Lucifer into pieces. "What happened to your vow to do as I command?"

Shade struggled with that for a moment before giving a stiff nod. "Very well. You can punish Lucifer first. Let's find Eddie. She's all that matters right now."

They stared at each other for a long moment, neither of them prepared to turn their back on the other. "Okay then." Shade nodded. "I'll stay in contact."

He turned, stopped short by a human woman standing in the kitchen doorway.

All the air rushed out of Wrath's lungs as he looked at her. He hadn't seen her since he'd left the earth plane without her. "Rosabella."

THREE

Rosabella? The name resonated with Haziel as she lurked in the corridor outside the kitchen. To be fair, she hadn't come upstairs with the intention to lurk. She'd been standing in the corridor outside the kitchen debating how to break it to Wrath that he now had a shadow —her—when the human had swept past her in a waft of roses and oranges.

She was a touch over medium height for a human woman, with a willowy shape draped in muslin. Shining honey brown hair reached her waist in a cascade of gentle curls. She'd moved past Haziel so quickly that she hadn't caught a glimpse of her face.

The look on Wrath's face held Haziel captive for a moment.

He looked like Shade had kicked him in the solar plexus.

Shade stopped beside the woman and eyed her as if he were trying to place her.

"Wrath," the woman said. Her voice was soft and husky like she was whispering delicious secrets. "You look good." She laughed and put a hand on his arm. "But then you always look good."

"Rosabella," Wrath croaked. He opened and shut his mouth a couple of times.

What Haziel wouldn't give to be able to render a hell prince speechless. Rosabella, whoever she was, clearly had some human sorcery because she had two hell princes staring at her in stunned silence.

"You're Eddie's mother," Shade said, and his expression hardened.

Oh, snap! The woman who had allegedly broken Wrath's heart. Haziel edged closer, fully prepared to indulge her vulgar curiosity.

Rosabella turned to him, tilted her head and smiled. "You must be Asmodeus."

"Must I?" Shade folded his arms.

Rosabella chuckled and mimicked his pose. "Uh-huh. Gorgeous, sex on legs and glaring at Wrath. Of course, you could be Lucifer, but he wouldn't be caught dead in jeans."

Haziel wasn't totally following Rosabella's reasoning. She was right about Lucifer and the jeans, but there were seven hell princes, and none of them were hard on the eyes. Then again, Shade did ooze sex, and not even angels were immune to that. Just ask poor Sophia. Rosabella's profile resembled Eddie's. They had the same straight nose and pointy chin. Same high cheekbones over peachy skin and full, gently curved mouth. Eddie kept her hair braided or in a ponytail, but Haziel was guessing they shared hair color as well. Rosabella didn't look much older than midthirties.

"You're here," Wrath went ahead and stated the obvious.

He was looking at Rosabella like he'd been in a drought, and she was a cask of water. Apparently, this hell prince was still nursing an infatuation for his human lover.

"My mom called me." Rosabella sashayed into the kitchen and closer to Wrath. She blinked up at him. "Mom said my Eddie has gone missing."

"Your Eddie?" Shade looked ready to spit lightning bolts. And not even an act of creation would move Haziel from her prying spot now. "Was she still your Eddie when you abandoned her and left your mother to raise her?"

Ouch! And also poor Eddie.

"Wow." Rosabella glanced at him and raised her eyebrow. "I must say, Wrath, I can see why you hate him. He's a judgmental prick, isn't he?"

Not entirely wrong, but Haziel bristled anyway.

"He's also right." Wrath moved his arm away from Rosabella's light hold. "You have some explaining to do."

Rosabella pulled a face. "Yeah. I suppose I do." She glanced at Shade again. "Could we talk? Privately."

"I'm leaving anyway," Shade said. "Going to find my Eddie."

"Your Eddie?" Rosabella chuckled, and it held a nasty edge. "Could it be that my daughter shares my fascination with hell princes? I should warn her about that."

"Why don't you do that?" Shade drawled. "But make sure you do it while you're hurrying out the door. I hear that's your power move."

Bam! Shade shoots, Shade scores.

Shade strolled into the corridor. Straight for her hiding place, which was not so much a hiding place as her trying to make herself small against the wall.

It was too late to move, and Haziel held her ground. When he drew abreast of her, he stopped and lowered his voice, "You skulking now?"

"No." Well, technically she was. "I came to find Wrath, and

she arrived before I could." Honesty compelled her to say. "So now I definitely am skulking."

Shade chuckled. "Keep an eye on him. That woman is a fucking bitch."

It seemed as if beings were tossing Wrath at her from all directions. "That's what Ramiel wants, for me to keep an eye on Wrath, so that's what I'm here to do."

"And you always do what Ramiel wants, don't you?" Shade's gaze was gentle and empathetic as he looked at her. "He doesn't deserve you."

"You're probably right." Ramiel had certainly never encouraged her unfortunate feelings for him. "Then again, do any of us really deserve those we love?"

Shade dropped his head and looked at the floor. He heaved a sigh that seemed to come from the depths of his immortal soul. "True that, gorgeous. Fucking true that."

Asmodeus, prince of lust and sexy times had called her gorgeous. Haziel was horrified to feel a blush stealing up her cheeks and had to repress the desire to giggle. Instead, she cleared her throat and tried to sound levelheaded. "Good luck finding Eddie."

"Thanks." He nodded and strode away.

In the kitchen, Wrath and Rosabella had taken positions at opposite sides of the small room. Wrath was presently jammed up against the fridge and looked like a demon with its horns in a trap. He folded his muscular arms and dropped his chin like a prize fighter staring down the contender. "You should have told me about Eddie."

"Told you when?" Rosabella propped her hands on the counter behind her and leaned back slightly. Her muslin skirt draped lovingly over her long legs. "When you were busy fighting one of your inane wars? Or maybe I should have crossed hell to find you and let you know you'd left a little something behind?"

"You sent me back there." Wrath growled. "You sent me back to my demesne when you told me you were done with me."

Rosabella sighed. "Don't be a fucking drag, Wrath. You didn't want a daughter any more than I did."

"Is that what you thought?" Wrath's expression was genuine confusion. "You thought I would abandon my child?"

"You walked away from me fast enough." Rosabella sniffed. "What was I supposed to think?"

Wrath took a deep breath, his huge chest rising and falling like it housed a working set of bellows. "You're rewriting history. You were the one who walked away from us. I wanted to try." He jabbed a thumb into his chest. "I was the one who would have done anything to make us work."

"Oh, please." Rosabella glared and tossed her head. "You were...are...a hell prince. I was never a priority for you."

"I guard the seal to wrath." He gaped at her. "It's an important job, but that didn't mean I never had time for you. I wanted you. I loved you."

Haziel suspected he might still love Rosabella. Her heart went out to him a bit. Unrequited love was totally shitty. And Wrath had lost a daughter when he'd lost his love as well. Watching him defy the entire treaty to assure Eddie's safety, Haziel had a feeling he would have made a great father. A scooch overprotective, but a good father nonetheless. Human girls needed a strong father in their lives. Fates alone knew, human girls had enough challenges to face and enough stacked against them.

"This is all ancient history." Rosabella flapped a hand. "And you know why we had to keep her a secret."

That much was true. Love Ramiel as she did, Haziel

wouldn't like to bet against the possibility that he might have eliminated a Nephilim if he'd known about her.

Haziel didn't get the abhorrence archangels had for Nephilim. It wasn't like Nephilim had any choice in their conception. And if Eddie was an example of Nephilim, Haziel couldn't agree with the elimination policy preached by the archangels. Eddie was lovely and sweet, also missing and in all kinds of danger.

"You should have told me about my child," Wrath said. "I could have kept her safe."

Rosabella's facade crumbled, and tears filled her blue-green eyes. "You're right. I should have told you." She wiped at her cheeks with her palm. "But I was frightened."

Wrath flinched. "Frightened? Of me?"

"You're so…" Rosabella's voice quavered. "You're so intense. So much. How did I know you wouldn't get angry and try to kill me and the baby?"

Now Wrath could be a bastard, and he certainly had a temper, but killing a pregnant woman? No. Haziel studied Rosabella a bit closer. She didn't want to be harsh, but she wasn't entirely sure the woman was genuine. If she'd been so afraid of Wrath, why had she become his lover?

"Rosabella." Wrath frowned at her. "Is this what you think of me?"

Yeah, that had to be a bitter pill to swallow.

"Please, Wrath." Rosabella held her hands out to him. "Find my baby girl. Find her and bring her home. Don't let your hatred of me color the way you treat her."

Wrath stared as he worked words out of his mouth. "I don't hate you, and even if I did, I would never punish Eddie for that."

"Please." Rosabella rushed from the kitchen.

As she passed Haziel, her expression of forlorn pleading

smoothed into a little smirk. She caught sight of Haziel and stopped. "And who are you?"

"I'm Haziel." It was the truth, and she didn't owe Rosabella any more than that.

Rosabella studied her with a sneer. "So, you're Wrath's latest."

"No." The idea of her and Wrath was just...well...ludicrous. She loved Ramiel and he and Ramiel were, if not exactly enemies, then opposing forces. "I'm not Wrath's anything."

"Hmm." Rosabella's gaze swept from her toes to her crown. "Take it from me, honey, you don't know what you're missing out on." She grimaced. "Then again, he may be hot, but he's a stage five clinger. Ugh!" She wrinkled her nose. "Nothing turns me off faster than a clinger."

Haziel had no idea how to respond to that, so she repeated, "I'm not Wrath's anything."

"Pity for you." Rosabella smirked. "Although, I don't know how much of him there's left." She leaned closer. "Now that I'm gone."

Well, wow! Haziel turned and watched her as she hurried down the stairs. Eddie did not deserve that mother of hers. She'd have been much better off with her father.

"What are you doing here?" Wrath thundered.

Oops. Haziel turned back to him with a sinking in the pit of her stomach. "I was looking for you."

"To spy on me?"

"No." But she had been spying, so she confessed. "But when I saw you arguing with Shade, I didn't want to interrupt, and then Rosabella came, and that didn't seem a good time to announce I was here either." And because she could never tell a half-truth because Ramiel had made sure she couldn't, she finished with, "And I was fascinated when I heard who she was."

Wrath tensed like an enraged bull about to charge. "You admit it."

"I admit everything." They may as well get this out of the way right up front. If they were going to work together, he needed to understand this about her. "In fact, I wouldn't tell me a secret because I'm incapable of keeping them."

"What?" He gaped at her.

Haziel stepped away from the wall she'd been trying to blend into and straight into the full-bore glare of Wrath. It was lucky for her that he didn't have his power, or she'd be angel dust by now. "It's my gift." If one could call it that. "Or curse, if you will. Truth. Always have to tell the truth."

With a head shake, Wrath studied her intensely. "You always have to tell the truth?"

"Yup." And how she wished sometimes she didn't. "And don't get me wrong." She risked a step closer to him. In his current powerless state, he wouldn't be able to hurt her too much if he lost it with her. And Wrath lost it a lot. Like most of the time. "I would love to be able to tell the odd half-truth, maybe a white lie, and there are definitely circumstances that call for an outright lie. This one being a case in point." She shrugged. "But I can't."

"So no lies?" The corner of his full, sensual mouth quirked. Those bluer than a summer sky eyes gleamed. "No evading the truth either?"

"Eh." She waggled her hand as a visual aid. "That's more nebulous. More of a gray area."

"Like?" He closed the distance between them and towered over her.

Goodness, he didn't look this tall from across a room and from her usual spot behind Ramiel. "I can choose not to speak and omit the truth with silence."

"Huh?" He ran a palm over his chin. "Let's put that to the test."

Why did this always happen to her? She'd lost count of how many times similar conversations had left her squirming. "I'd really rather not."

"Why are you following me?" His pitiless blue eyes bored into her.

"Ramiel said he wanted me to keep an eye on you."

His eyes flashed ire. "Why?"

"He's concerned you're going to try to find your daughter on your own."

Wrath leaned closer to her. From across the room, she also hadn't noticed that he smelled good. A sort of leather and tobacco scent that was intrinsically male. "You're holding out, aren't you?"

"Yup." Fuck it!

"Why is he worried about me going looking for my daughter?"

"Because of your emotional state." She cringed inwardly. He wasn't going to like this next bit. "And because you have no power."

Wrath straightened away from her. "Well, look at that. You weren't lying."

"I told you." Just once it would be nice if beings got the idea before making her squirm. "Always speak the truth."

He narrowed his eyes in thought. "What did you think of Rosabella?"

Oh boy, this wouldn't go well. "She's lying to you and manipulating your feelings. You're still in love with her and she knows it."

"Damn." He grimaced. "Remind me not to ask you questions I really don't want to hear the answer to."

That he wasn't ripping her head from her body seemed like a positive outcome. "What do you think of her?"

"I think you're right," he said. "I am going to find my daughter. But I'm not going to do so with you tagging along behind me. Go back to Ramiel and tell him that."

Haziel stood where she was as he stalked away. If only she could, but she wasn't going to let Ramiel down by failing to do what he'd asked of her. Ramiel needed her, and she wouldn't fail him.

FOUR

Dee looked at her daughter and was forced to admit something that would shock other mothers everywhere; she didn't like her daughter. Oh, she loved Rosabella and would gaze mistily at pictures of her as a child, but the woman she had grown into wasn't someone Dee could respect or take pride in.

Rosabella was selfish, petulant, a user, and sitting in front of her shedding crocodile tears for Eddie's safety. If Dee didn't send her updates, Rosabella would have no idea who Eddie was or what was going on in her life. She'd left before Eddie was properly off the breast and blew in every few years—generally when she wanted something.

And right now, it looked like one of those somethings might be Shade.

Rosabella was sitting on Eddie's bed as Shade gathered a few possessions and shoved them into a duffle bag.

Dee turned her attention to the being who had the best chance of finding Eddie. "Are you sure she's on the earth plane?"

"No." Shade grimaced. "But I have to start somewhere. I'm not so sure Wrath is right about Lucifer being behind this either."

"Eddie's very capable." Rosabella laid a hand on his wrist. "Wouldn't it be better to wait for her here?"

Dee managed to contain her desire to laugh. Rosabella was so transparent and so obviously barking up the wrong tree. She'd sashayed into the room a few minutes after Shade had come in. Dee had been sitting on Eddie's bed, breathing in the atmosphere that was so full of Eddie it was comforting. Panic squatted like a hulking toad in her chest. And guilt sat right beside it. It was her fault Eddie was in this position. She should never have left on that cruise with Jean-Claude, never encouraged Eddie to go to hell after Shade, and never left Eddie in charge of the hell gate. In her idiocy, she'd reasoned that the hell gate was stable, had been stable for years. What could go wrong?

Everything and anything, apparently. "If Lucifer is not behind this, then who is?" she asked Shade.

"I don't know." Shade sank onto the end of the bed.

Rosabella edged closer and put a hand on his shoulder. "You're so stressed."

"The thing that keeps nagging at me is when Lucifer helped us get out of hell," Shade said. "He had no reason to bring his chariot and get us out of there faster. He said it was to piss off Wrath, and he's certainly made a career out of that over time, but why rescue Eddie?"

Dee had to admit that Shade made an odd kind of sense. "Or why not kidnap her then? You and Wrath were injured, he could have taken her without much resistance."

"Right." Shade nodded.

"You're holding so much tension in your shoulders," Rosabella simpered.

Dee couldn't even say for sure that Rosabella had stopped long enough to consider if she even wanted Shade for herself. If Dee had to bet, she'd say it was part Shade didn't like her, and part Shade liked her daughter better. Neither of which Rosabella could stand.

"I'm thinking about Ashe as well," Shade said. "He was Lucifer's right-hand demon, his second, and they were close." He wrapped his fore and middle fingers together. "Like really close. Lucifer gave Ashe whatever he needed, and Ashe seemed to relish that trust."

Dee had to snort at that one. "Can you imagine having to work for Lucifer?"

Shade flashed her one of his gorgeous smiles and shrugged Rosabella's hand off his shoulder. "True that. But when Ashe took Eddie, he was powerful, Dee." He looked at her with his piercing gray eyes. "I mean, like way more powerful than he should have been, and the power felt...other."

"Other?" Upper demons were often imbued with the power of their maker. "Other than Lucifer?"

Shade nodded.

"I'm a massage therapist," Rosabella lisped. "Fifteen minutes with my magic fingers, and your tension will be history."

"Yeah." Shade rubbed his palm over his face. "I didn't recognize the power signature at all."

It must be a new experience for her daughter to be so thoroughly ignored, and Dee was here for it. "So, what's your plan?"

"The hounds are very bonded to Eddie," Shade said. "And they're demanding I let them track her."

Cronus and Xerxes had been dragging their furry butts around the theatre like a pair of lost puppies since Eddie's abduction. "Can they find her?"

"They'll end themselves trying." Shade stood and shouldered his bag.

Hell princes and humans together didn't often end well, but Eddie wasn't entirely human, and she also wasn't Rosabella. Still, Dee was a grandmother who adored her granddaughter. "And will you do whatever it takes to find her?"

He looked at her tenderly. "You know the answer to that, Dee."

And she nodded, because yes, she did. Shade would move heaven and earth—quite literally if he had to—to find Eddie. "Stay in contact." She patted his shoulder. "What do you need me to do?"

"Stay here," he said. "And let me know if there's anything I need to know about."

"Will do." A part of Dee wanted to be out there with Shade searching for Eddie, but keeping the candle in the window lit was the best thing she could do. She didn't command the hounds or have the powers Shade did. She was also on the guardian's shit list. If Eddie was in heaven or hell, then she had even less chance of finding her than she did on earth. So despite her need to take action, she would stay here and keep the business as usual going. "Good luck, Shade."

"Take care, Dee." He kissed her forehead, and she got a waft of the pure sex appeal that was the being who embodied lust. Her Eddie might one day be a very lucky girl...being... no girl. Eddie was her Eddie-girl, and she always would be.

"What a jerk." Rosabella threw herself back on Eddie's bed. "He just ignored me."

"He doesn't like you," Dee took an unmotherly delight in telling her. She could remonstrate with Rosabella about the inappropriateness and sheer shittyness of hitting on a being who was involved with her daughter, but Rosabella would shrug that off as inconsequential. All was fair in love and war as far as Rosabella was concerned. And only where she was concerned. Rosabella got to do what the hell she liked, and the rest of humanity was merely a supporting cast in the play of her life.

Rosabella rolled to her stomach and rested her head on her folded hands. "Don't be a bitch, Mom. You're just pissed at me."

Was she? Dee studied her daughter. She might have gone beyond pissed into numb several years ago. "What are you doing here, Bella?"

Rosabella yawned and closed her eyes. "I told you," she mumbled. "I'm here because you managed to lose my daughter."

WRATH COULDN'T SAY he disliked Haziel. She seemed a decent enough sort for an angel, and the honesty thing was funny as fuck, but he didn't want her as his watchdog. He didn't want any watchdog.

He stormed down to the greenroom where he sensed Ramiel was still squatting.

Ramiel looked up when he strode into the room. "Wrath."

"Call off your watchdog." Wrath really didn't like this archangel. He was a pompous, bigoted motherfucker who thought the sun shone out his ass. He didn't see why a decent angel like Haziel was wasting her energy on such a pile of crap.

Ramiel studied him thoughtfully for a long moment. "I'm not going do that, Wrath. You're out of control. Your seal is weakening, and your get is missing. Along with your powers. You are a loose cannon, and we cannot allow that."

"Allow?" Wrath breathed deep as rage rose inside him.

What his fellow supernaturals didn't understand was that for every time he exploded, there were another two hundred he kept a lid on it. The word allow was like a red rag to a bull. Angels were so fucking sanctimonious. Over the millennia, they'd begun to believe the bullshit humans spouted about them. "You don't get to allow or disallow me anything."

"Not this again." Ramiel rolled his eyes. "You're not a single entity occupying a closed system, Wrath. You're part of an alliance, and that means you are answerable to that alliance."

Fair enough, the fucker had him on a technicality there. "But you're not heading that alliance, and you don't get to control me." He'd like to see Ramiel try. Actually, he'd love to see Ramiel try. He'd relish the opportunity to beat the fuck out of him. Especially in his current mood. Which reminded him. "You refer to Eddie as my get again, and I'm going to rearrange your pretty face. Then I'll rip your pussy white wings off your back and shove them up your ass.

"Really, Wrath." Ramiel grimaced. "Must you make threats you can't execute?" Power crackled around Ramiel, setting his skin aglow and making his muscles swell.

In a fight between him and Ramiel, there would be no winner, but Wrath would enjoy the getting to stalemate. "Wanna give that a try?"

Ramiel sighed, an angel with the weight of the world on his shoulders. "I'm not going to indulge your desire for violence, Satanus."

"Oooh, my real name. I'm really scared now." Wrath added a little muscle flex to that one. He might not have his powers, but he could still toss some hurt around. "What's next, Mum? Will you send me to bed without any dinner?"

"Haziel is there for your protection as much as anything else," Ramiel said.

That right there made Wrath want to pound his pretty

fucking face into the linoleum. "I don't need protection from some low-grade, half-powered, feathered lightweight."

Ramiel laughed. "I would hardly call Haziel a lightweight." He cocked his head, those pond slime greens glimmering with amusement. "Tell me, Satanus, how did it work out for you the last time you miscalculated a lesser being's power?" He tapped a finger against his chin. "Oh right, silly me, you lost your daughter the last time you were arrogant enough to underestimate an underling."

Again, fucker had him on a technicality, so Wrath switched tacks. "Let's talk about sweet Haziel."

Ramiel's eyes flashed a warning.

Adrenaline fueled Wrath. "Such a pretty little armful." He imitated Ramiel and tapped his chin. "If she's going to be on my heels, I might take advantage of what you've been refusing." He sent a mental apology to Haziel, this wasn't about her. He was just using her to piss Ramiel off, and it was working.

Ramiel swelled to twice his size. "You will stay respectful of Haziel."

"Like you are?" Wrath reveled in the sore spot he'd found. "For a being who is so protective of her, I notice you don't hesitate to use her feelings for you against her."

"You know nothing of which you speak." Ramiel switched to angelic in his anger. "Haziel has value to me, and you will not touch her."

Wrath stepped right up to his swollen counterpart. "Or what?"

"I will end you," Ramiel growled and disappeared his ass out of there.

Wrath was taking that as win, although he was still spoiling for the fight the archangel pussy had denied him.

"Even for you, that was low," Haziel said from the doorway.

He repressed his guilt and turned to face her. Maybe it

would be a good time to find out how not lightweight she was. "Even for me?" he drawled.

"You're a dick, Wrath." She shrugged, cool as a cucumber. "We both know this to be true."

Motherfucker! These technicalities were like shackles. He was a dick. And because he was, he said, "You should be thanking me."

Haziel laughed, and it was such a pure, sweet sound, he nearly lost the edge of his hard riding anger. "I can't wait to hear this."

"For a being who treats you like a doormat, Ramiel is super protective over you." Wrath stepped close enough to catch the scent of her—lotus and rose—and lowered his voice. "Wanna use me to make him jealous?"

Her soft olive-green eyes crinkled in her tawny pretty face. "Oh, Wrath, you're impossible." Her giggle took the last of his bad temper away. She placed one long, slim hand on his chest. "You only want to provoke Ramiel."

Three thoughts hit him in rapid succession. One, her small hand felt so right against his chest. Secondly, it had been since Rosabella that he had shared his time and space, and his body, with a female. And thirdly, and strangest of all, he didn't feel rage anymore.

Sophia sat in the auditorium of the Paradise Players Theatre and stared at the dark stage. Humans really were the most ingenious species. Over the ages, they'd constantly amazed her with their ability to entertain themselves. For beings who had such a short lifespan, they seemed determined to extract every ounce of pleasure from their existence they could. She didn't like this particular age. Humans had lost contact with what they really were. They scurried around in isolation and ignored that their true strength lay in what they could achieve together.

She remembered when theatre had been a group of humble priests delivering religion to the masses. They had been so passionate about getting their message out, and so determined to deliver it in language that the masses understood.

Even then, she'd been drawn to theatre.

But before then, the Greeks had used theatre to bring their gods to humanity. Oh, the days of those amateurish spectacles. And the danger. She had seen more than one performer catch alight or get caught in some dodgy invention.

Now, humans had television and movies and the internet. An entire world on those little cell phones they were so bonded to. But they had forgotten this. She looked up at the banks of silent lights waiting to flood with electricity and shed the spectacle before them in shades of pure magic.

There really was nothing like live theatre. It was immediate, flawed, passionate, primal, and so innately human. The silent auditorium thrummed with the passion and laughter, the tragedy and the joy that had taken place here. A vortex of all that was most human.

Shade had left to find his Eddie. Perhaps he didn't even realize how much he loved her, but Sophia knew. She'd watched him over the ages, the beautiful play of emotion in his glacial eyes, and the way he looked at Eddie...dear universe. Sophia pressed her hand to her chest to soothe the aching. How she ached to have him look at her like that. It was like something in the very core of that hell prince had warmed and found life.

And Eddie didn't know it. Sophia ached for Shade as much as she ached for the fact that she would never be the being to bring him into the full flower of his existence.

"Sophia?" Lillian walked up the abandoned aisles toward where she sat. "What are you doing in here?"

Sophia, a name she'd chosen for herself meaning wisdom. It had been her tiny little giggle as she moved amongst humanity. So wise that she'd fallen in love with a being who wouldn't love her. How many plays had been written about that? She smiled at Lillian. "Just thinking. I love the quiet here."

"Yeah." Lillian slid into the seat beside her. "There's nothing like it, is there?"

Lillian had such a narrow view of the universe, limited by her humanity, but in this she was absolutely correct. "No."

Lillian nodded and took a deep sniff. "Nothing smells quite like a theatre."

A mixture of sweat, paint, and dust. Sophia nodded. This human woman saw her as a threat. In that, she was so much more aware than her compatriots, but not for the reasons she thought. "I'm not here to take your glory," Sophia said.

"Then why are you here?" Lillian turned in her seat and looked at Sophia fully. "I get the strangest feeling that I'm missing something."

Lillian was missing a great many things. Sophia answered as honestly as she could, "I'm not really sure." Initially she had come because Shade was here, and wherever he was, she had to be, to balance his power.

"Anyway." Lillian flicked her hair behind her shoulder. "You know our next show is *The Importance of Being Earnest?*" She touched her chest. "I will, of course, play Gwendolyn. And I think you should audition for Cecily."

Sophia opened her mouth to gently decline, and then stopped. She liked being at the Paradise Players, and she certainly loved theatre. Gabriel would bitch, the guardians would have a meltdown. Archangels did not involve themselves with the doings of humanity. And why not? They were here to help humanity and guide their souls to ascension. Yet, they remained removed from the very souls they were guiding. "I don't know if I can act."

"That's why you audition, darling." Lillian gave her a superior look. "Peter would never cast someone who couldn't act."

Sophia wasn't a totally rule abiding angel. She'd had her small moments of rebellion, but few and far between. She'd played chastity to Shade's lust for centuries. There was certainly nothing that had demanded she be chaste herself, merely guard the seal. Still, she'd stayed that way, the perfect counterpoint to Shade. She'd been waiting for him, waiting for

Shade to notice her and want her. And now Shade had gone to find his Eddie, and she was alone, untouched, and quite frankly tired of playing by the rules. She smiled at Lillian. "I'd love to. When are the auditions?"

WRATH STOOD in the theatre parking lot as Shade drove into the night with Xerxes and Cronus propped up in the cab of a dusty old pickup he'd found somewhere. No human would see the hell prince Asmodeus in the image he would present of himself. He'd taken the name Shade from his ability to blend in with the shadows, and he traveled like this to blend in with the humans. Shade was off to find Eddie, and Wrath had a whore weasel of a brother to track down.

Lucifer had somehow masterminded the disappearance of Eddie, and Wrath would not let him get away with it. The slimy little sludgeworm had managed to slip and slide his way out of the consequences of his actions one too many times.

The purr of an engine brought his attention back to the quiet road outside the theatre. At this time of night, the goodly folk of Clayton, Ontario were all safely tucked up in their homes, sharing a meal and watching their idiot boxes.

A single, bright light split the darkness as a large motorcycle eased down the road and into the parking lot in front of the theatre. Wrath liked motorcycles, although he didn't share Lucifer's obsession with speed. Humans had a few things he enjoyed. Although what they were doing to this rock circling the sun that they lived on defied sanity. They were as likely to destroy themselves without the seals breaking.

A man parked the bike and swung one leg over. Taking off his helmet, a man in his thirties, with conservatively cut hair and regular, handsome features, stopped and stared at the theatre, and then consulted his phone.

Wrath caught the tingle of awareness that indicated a guardian.

The bike rider shrugged out of his motorcycle jacket to reveal the standard black suit, white shirt, and uptight tie. Lucifer would have fit right in with them.

"Wrath?" The rider tucked his helmet beneath his arm and draped his leather jacket over it. He braced his weight evenly as if waiting for Wrath to charge like an enraged buffalo.

Wrath nodded and took his measure. Above average height, strong shoulders and chest without being overly bulky. Chris Fellows's choice of Dee's replacement was intriguing. Wrath had been half expecting someone more like Chris.

The guardian walked forward. "I'm Daniel Lee, guardian."

"Good for you." Wrath kept it noncommittal. He didn't like guardians, although this one didn't seem to fit the standard mold.

Daniel chuckled and stepped back to examine the facade of the Paradise Theatre. "This is a nice change," he said. "My last hell gate was in a gym."

"A gym?" The question got away from Wrath.

"Yeah." Daniel nodded and looked around the town. "They tend to put hell gates where the overflow of emotion won't alert people to the presence of the hell gate. Gyms are packed with insecurity, aggression, competitiveness, and hormones."

From what Wrath had seen of the Paradise Players, Daniel's gym didn't seem all that different. It was probably the longest conversation Wrath had had with a guardian outside of official business. "You're here to replace Dee?"

"Deandra." Daniel nodded and focused back on Wrath. "Deandra Ward, yes."

"Huh." Wrath let his gaze travel from the man's head to his toes. "You're not what I was expecting."

Daniel flashed him a friendly smile. "I get that a lot."

"I'm sure you do." Was he actually kind of liking a guardian? He jerked his head at the door. "You better go inside. Although I wouldn't get comfortable. Dee is not happy about sharing her home with a stranger." He stepped closer to Daniel to get his point across. "And if you make Dee unhappy, then you make me unhappy."

"Wow." A boyish grin broke over Daniel's face. "You really are as badass as they told me you were."

Wrath struggled against his own smile. He rather liked that descriptor. "Just remember that."

"Right." Daniel gave him an assessing look. "I'm not here to piss anyone off." That smile appeared again. "Unless I find a being where they shouldn't be."

"Then you're definitely going to be pissing beings off." Wrath took delight in telling him. "Because there are hell princes and archangels coming out the woodwork here."

Daniel sighed. "Great." He shook his head. "I knew there had to be a reason they sent me here."

Squaring his shoulders, he opened the door to the theatre and went inside.

Curiosity had Wrath following.

"So, you're my replacement." Dee stood in the middle of the passageway outside the greenroom with her arms folded.

Daniel held out his hand in greeting. "That's what they tell me. Daniel Lee."

"This is my theatre." Keeping her arms crossed, Dee tried to maintain her icy composure but in the face of the friendly smile she was getting, it was a pathetic attempt. "And I live above it. There isn't a room for you."

"That's fine." Daniel retracted his hand and looked around him. "This is an amazing building."

Dee defrosted a mite more. "It's been in my family for generations."

"Beautiful façade," Daniel said. "And this part must be where the work happens." He smiled sheepishly. "I don't suppose you'd be okay with giving me a tour?"

"The hell gate's in the basement." Dee jerked her head toward the door to the basement stairs. "That's all you need to know."

Daniel sighed. "Fair enough."

"Hi." Rosabella appeared on the stairwell from the living quarters. She'd changed into a flowy summer dress that clung to her curves all the way to her ankles. She looked fresh, and sexy, and beautiful. She approached Daniel with a coquettish smile. "Don't mind my mother; she's just feeling grumpy."

With a groan, Dee turned to her daughter. "Stay out of this Rosabella. This is guardian business."

"You're always telling me I should get more involved in guardian business." Rosabella blinked her sea-colored eyes at her mother innocently. "Why don't I get Daniel settled?"

Daniel flushed to his hairline and stared at Rosabella. "That's okay. I can show myself around. Like Deandra says, the only thing I really need to know is where the hell gate is."

"Nonsense." Rosabella gave him her husky bedroom chuckle and threaded her arm through his. "I'll show you everything."

With a triumphant glance over her shoulder at him and Dee, she sashayed away with Daniel in tow.

"Balls!" Dee watched them go with a scowl. "Whenever she appears, trouble is sure to follow."

Wrath breathed deep through the jealousy burning his soul. Rosabella would hardly look at him, said he frightened her, but she'd gone off with Daniel—a stranger—without a second's thought. "Why does she do it?"

"Oh, Wrath." Dee put a hand on his arm. "I wish I had a dollar for every time I've asked that question." She shrugged. "To piss me off. To piss you off. Because she can. Pick one. Pick them all."

Yeah well, Wrath wasn't about to stand around and watch Rosabella make a slave of Daniel Lee. He had better things to do, like find his fucking brother and exact some payback. Then he needed to find his daughter. And he was going to do all of that without the pretty little shadow Ramiel had assigned him getting in his way.

SIX

Wrath waited until the theatre was busy for the evening. He couldn't sense her nearby, but he didn't want Haziel popping up when he didn't need her. Auditions taking place on stage covered his exit as he slipped down into the basement and opened the door to the room with the hell gate.

"Wrath." Daniel appeared out of the murky basement and startled him. He hadn't even sensed the fucker near him.

He didn't have time for guardian bullshit, and he wasn't about to let some puny human stop him. "I'm going through," he told Daniel. He might not have his power back yet, but he could still take out one human.

Daniel studied him with careful brown eyes. "You're going to find Lucifer."

"And beat out of him what he's done with my daughter."

"Fair enough." Daniel nodded.

The silence stretched between them, and Wrath moved to edge past him.

Rubbing his nape, Daniel intercepted him. "The thing is, Wrath, what if Lucifer is not behind her disappearance?"

Of course Lucifer was behind Eddie's disappearance, and this human was in danger of losing a vital body part if he didn't move. "He is."

"He might be, or he might not be." Daniel held up one hand. "Just hear me out."

This was not the direction Wrath had thought a conversation with the new hell gate guardian would take—actually, he'd been looking for no conversation—but he'd listen. "What?"

"Something doesn't add up." Daniel grimaced. "All signs point to Lucifer, but according to Chris's briefing, Lucifer helped Eddie and Shade escape you. Why would he do that if he wanted to kidnap Eddie?"

It echoed what Dee had said to him. "Then who else?"

"I don't know." Daniel shrugged. "Lucifer just seems such an obvious culprit."

Wrath was so tired of explaining his brother to others. It felt like he'd come into being with excuses and explanations for Lucifer on his lips. "It was his second that kidnapped Eddie. A second he trusts implicitly. He's been missing since she has. And he would do anything to piss me off. Kidnapping my daughter would be an epic move on his part." He stepped into Daniel. "He seems like an obvious culprit for all those reasons and because he's a dick wart of epic proportions. He thinks he's the king of hell."

"Yeah." Daniel chuckled. "It does make you not like him." His laughter died. "But he's not stupid, and this is such an obvious finger being pointed at him. I would have thought if Lucifer had taken Eddie, he would have been a lot smarter about covering his tracks."

Wrath was really trying his best not to like this guy, but

Daniel Lee was so fucking reasonable and clear thinking. Lucifer was smart and cunning and never showed his hand until it was too late to do anything about it. He didn't want to give what Daniel said credence, but being this clumsy about abducting Eddie wasn't his brother's usual MO. Then again, he was as arrogant as he was smart, and he could be using the rebel demon hordes as cover. "What are you saying?"

"I'm saying, I totally understand why you're going to find him, it makes all kinds of sense. And I get why you are trying to rescue your daughter, but if you could keep a halfway open mind while you're down there, it would be useful." He jerked his head toward the portal. "See what else you notice. The one thing we're really missing is accurate information. From what Chris told me, there's a whole lot of maybes and what ifs floating around, and we need proper intelligence if we're going to combat what's going on."

"Okay." That wasn't too much to ask, and it was exactly what he would have done if he was planning a battle. "Anything specific you want me to look for?"

"Yeah." Daniel frowned. "These demons that are disappearing and the hordes that attacked you and Shade. It speaks to some kind of organization. Ashe is Lucifer's second for a reason. He's as clever as the hell prince he serves. He wouldn't do something impulsive or stupid, and one could argue that kidnapping the daughter of Wrath is both of those things."

Wrath wanted to get going, but Daniel had him intrigued. "So far nothing you've said doesn't point to Lucifer."

"But it does point to some kind of large-scale organization." Daniel shrugged. "I know Lucifer has called himself the king of hell for centuries, but have you ever noticed him care enough to actually make that come true?"

Wrath let that sink into his brainbox. "Yeah, he's a lazy turd."

"Right." Daniel clicked his fingers. "And whoever engineered the attacks on you and Shade and made them look like you were attacking each other is organized and strategic. Even kidnapping Eddie is the kind of thing that would destabilize hell. And I'm suggesting you consider that perhaps getting you to take out Lucifer could be part of that plan." He shrugged. "After all, if they can get one hell prince to end another, they can end us all."

That made Wrath's head hurt. "Why would anyone do that?"

"And that, Wrath"—Daniel snapped his fingers—"is the million-dollar question. The only party who would do that is one who either had an elaborate death wish, or one who had a contingency plan."

"What contingency plan?" Daniel was hinting at something so much bigger than warring hell princes and rebel demon hordes. "There is no contingency plan to the end of creation."

"That we know of," Daniel said with a weighted look. He held up his hands. "Look, the more I think about this, the more questions come up. All I'm asking you to do is consider the possibility that someone wants you to think Lucifer did this."

Universe alone knew Wrath wasn't looking for any reasons not to end Lucifer, but Daniel was making an annoying kind of sense. "You think he's being set up, and by extension, me as well."

"It's a possibility." Daniel shoved his hands into his pants pockets. "I think it's worth bearing in mind."

Wrath didn't want to believe this wasn't Lucifer, and that, in itself, was a problem. "Anything else?"

"Yeah." Daniel cleared his throat and flushed. "Any idea how to avoid Rosabella?"

Not that he had ever tried, but Wrath answered honestly. "Not a clue."

Having limited power made it easier for Wrath to avoid detection as he made his way across Shade's demesne heading for Lucifer's on the other side. His inability to use his wings made walking his only option. Slapping on a reasonable glamour as one of Shade's lot, he trudged toward Lucifer's demesne. Word picked up in taverns and from traveling demons was that Lucifer was missing, along with him and Shade. He'd also heard more than a few times that the news that he had lost his power was out. It would still take a brave or a foolish demon to take him on, but you could never underestimate the might of stupid.

And there was a lot of stupid happening across Shade's demesne. Shade's demesne was a mess. Even more of a mess than when he'd last been here. Bolder demons ran wild, taking advantage of Shade's absence. Those demons still loyal to Shade cowered in their dwellings, confused and frightened and staying out of trouble. He'd avoided more than one pack of roving demons made up from all seven hell prince's hordes.

He traveled through abandoned settlements, homes and livelihoods destroyed. Huge swathes of Shade's lush jungles had been hacked down and burned to charred remnants. It made him concerned for his own demesne. Some of his demons would stay loyal, but many, like he had seen here in Shade's territory obeyed only under the steady pressure of a boot on their throats.

Still, the level of chaos from Shade's short absence gave him pause. Daniel had asked him to look around and take notice of what was happening, and it was impossible not to.

Hell was descending into total chaos, and it bore no relation to the amount of time Shade had been missing. For this amount of mayhem to have taken over, a guiding hand might be behind it. Other than the higher demons, most demons were ugly cockhammer stupid. They lacked the brain cells to put something this widespread and quick into action.

He was passing through what had been a prosperous settlement. The riverside tavern still smoldered from a recent fire. A demon and his partner stood by the smoking ruins speaking quietly as Wrath approached them.

They both eyed him with suspicion as he asked, "Was this your tavern?"

The demon nodded.

"What happened?" Wrath indicated the debris.

"Fire." The demon spat.

His demoness eyed Wrath warily. "Who are you?"

"A friend of Shade's," he replied. A friend who'd like to pull the hedonistic shitgoblin's ass through his nose, but admitting that would get him nowhere. "I am checking on his demesne."

"Shade." The demoness narrowed her eyes at him. "Shade should be here."

"Agreed." Wrath nodded. "Who did this?"

The demon squared up to him, swelling to three times his size and answering Wrath's question as to how he had survived when his tavern had not. "You ask a lot of questions."

"Shade cannot be here." Wrath hunted for a good enough excuse. "He is chasing a rogue angel." That would work with most demons. The only thing they hated more than each other were angels.

The demoness nodded as if that mollified her.

Her mate was a tougher sell. "What angel?"

"Haziel," he improvised and sent a mental apology her

way. It was the only angelic name he could come up with in a hurry.

"Haziel." The demoness squinted her yellow eyes. "Is she not part of Ramiel's host?"

"Yup." The best lies needed a touch of truth. "Pretty little thing. Green eyes, lots of hair. Not a lot of brain."

The demon nodded as if he'd met Haziel. "What did she do?"

"Can't say." Wrath nodded.

"Can't or won't?" The demon still remained his impressive almost twenty feet.

"Can't." Wrath shrugged and toed aside a charred piece of wood. "Shade didn't say, and I know better than to ask. Hell princes are a cagey lot."

"Right." The demoness nodded and touched her mate's hand.

He immediately shrunk back down. "Still." He motioned the mess in front of them. "This wouldn't have happened if Shade had been here."

"He'll make it right." Wrath had no problem promising away Shade's fortune and power. "Send word to his palace and he will make reparations."

The demoness gaped at him. She might have been attractive had it not been for that third eye halfway down her cheek. All three eyes were currently staring at him as if he'd recently hatched. "You haven't heard?"

"Heard what?" And Wrath knew worse news was coming. He almost felt sorry for Shade.

"The palace is gone," she said. "Well, the building is still standing, but the same horde who did this attacked Shade's palace and ran off any demon who remained loyal." She growled and all three eyes narrowed. "Most of them joined the mixed hordes who attacked the palace."

"Mixed hordes." The demon shook his head. "I never would have believed I'd ever see a time when those of us from Shade rubbed shoulders with Wrath's scum. It seems like there are more mixed hordes every day, and more and more demons joining them."

Wrath chose to ignore the insult to himself and his horde. Shit on a stick, that made no sense. "How did they overrun the palace? Surely Shade's horde defended it."

"They tried." The demon shook his head. "Same as we tried to take care of our place. Bunch of them slunk through here yesterday. They were forced out and are running for their existence."

"You jest." It was his turn to gape. "How is that possible?"

"Do you call me a liar?" Big boy swelled like he was ready to take on some height again.

"No." At full strength, Wrath would have given the demon a demonstration of what real size looked like. "I am just finding it hard to believe."

"Well, believe it," the demoness snapped. "The ones that came through here said the demons in the horde that attacked the palace are strong. Much stronger than they should be. There has to be a hell prince behind them. No way they could be that strong on their own."

"But who?" Wrath played dumb.

"My guess would be that warmongering turd, Wrath." The demon spat. "His lot have been making free with this demesne. Almost like they own it."

The urge to defend himself rose, and he had to tamp it down. "Huh!" He looked around him. "What about Lucifer?"

"Oy!" A voice broke into their discussion from their left.

The demon and his demoness vanished.

An upper order demon staggered over from the treeline. Large, pointed horns stuck out on either side of his head, and he stood nearly eight feet tall. Muscles bulged and flexed beneath his gray skin.

At full strength, Wrath would have smashed him like the questionable crotchmonkey he was. He faced him. "What?"

"You ask a lot of questions." The demon came close enough for Wrath to smell his fetid breath. He tried to get a read on the power signature but with his power flickering in and out, it was nearly impossible. Maybe Avarice?

"Got a problem with that?" Wrath put his hand on his sword hilt. What was one of Ava's demons doing in Shade's demesne?

"Pretty pig sticker you got there." The demon sneered. "Get that while you were on your knees for Wrath?" He chuckled. "Word is he likes his demons on their knees."

Battle lust pounded in Wrath's blood, but he fought it down. There was a lot about this situation he needed to take note of. Firstly, the demon was an upper demon, so he should have been more wary of approaching another upper demon like his glamour depicted. Upper demons were justifiably nervous of each other because they all had nasty, hidden tricks. This posturing fucknut was oddly sure of himself. "Word is, you know that from firsthand experience."

A good fight was exactly what he needed to get his mind working again.

With a roar, the demon attacked. Prick was stronger than he looked, and his first blow connected with Wrath's abdomen and drove the air out of him.

Wrath ducked and pivoted, jumping back to give himself a moment of recovery time.

But the assnugget closed with dizzying speed. A knee to his balls drove Wrath to the ground. Bitchzilla had gone for the kill shot, and Wrath cupped his abused junk.

Hard hands grabbed his hair and wrenched. Wrath found

his face on the receiving end of a knee and blood filled his mouth. His nose cracked, and pain lanced through his scalp.

There was an outside chance he was going to lose this fight.

Wrath grabbed the sheepshagger's ankles and wrenched his feet out from under him.

The demon hit the ground with a *boom,* and Wrath lunged for him.

He rolled, and Wrath hit dirt.

A boot to the back of his head made him see stars.

Wrath rolled toward him, and crotch itch hit the ground again. This time, Wrath didn't fuck around, he drew his dagger and plunged it into flesh in one move.

The demon yelped. Black blood spurted from a hole in his thigh.

As Wrath staggered to his feet, the demon's wound healed, and his dagger popped out of the demon's flesh.

No way that should have happened.

His loss of concentration cost him, and a kick to his ribs sent him staggering back.

Having the crap beaten out of him sucked. It was not an experience he would recommend, and he stepped back to give himself room to assess and plan his attack. His opponent was strong, like the demoness had said, stronger and faster than he should be.

"Come on." The demon waggled his fingers at him. "Is that all you got?"

Wrath had to face the disturbing truth that in this moment, the demon might have gotten him on another of those sniveling technicalities, because that might be all he had.

Something whistled past his ear, and he jerked his head away from the sound.

A crystalline blade hit the demon in the throat, and he collapsed.

Haziel brushed past him, ripped the blade out of the demon's throat and plunged it into his heart.

With a pop and a burst of ash, the demon ceased to exist. A seraph should not have been able to do that, but Haziel wasn't any seraph; she was Ramiel's second, which meant if Ramiel ever got tired of being Ramiel, he could transfer his power to her, and she would become the next archangel. Haziel must be closer to Ramiel's power than any of them realized.

"Right." Haziel holstered her blade and brushed her hands off before turning to face him. "Not my favorite thing to do, but best we destroy the evidence." She studied Wrath. "Wouldn't be good for word to spread there was an angel in hell."

Surprise had him spitting blood while he tried to formulate a reply.

"You don't look great." Haziel stepped closer to him. "That should have healed by now."

"My power was drained." And it bit his ass that he had to admit that. "Healing will take longer."

"Hmm." She rubbed her hands together. "Let's see what we can do about that."

Bright white light glowed from her hands. Haziel slapped them against his chest and the light went through him like an electric enema.

"Motherfucker!" Wrath jumped back from her and her happy hands.

"You're welcome." She giggled.

"That hurt." But he could no longer taste blood, and his ribs didn't bitch with every breath.

"I'm sure it did." She twitched the hood on her cloak back over her face. "But you're still welcome."

Wrath dusted off his pants to give himself time to formulate a semi coherent reply. "You shouldn't be here."

"I know." Her big green eyes widened further as she looked around her. "And if you hadn't gone scuttling off like a cockroach, I wouldn't have had to follow you." She jammed her fists on her nicely rounded hips. "What were you thinking, Satanus?"

Universal tits, but he hated the full name thing. "I was thinking I didn't need a babysitter to do my job."

"Well, that's not true." She chuckled and motioned where the demon had been lying. "Otherwise, he would never have gotten close to beating you."

"I had it in hand." A bit of bluster never hurt, and if by in hand he meant he was about to see the wrong side of a fight, he was telling the truth.

"No, you didn't." She patted his chest. "And that's why I'm here."

"You shouldn't be here." He was really losing his verbal touch. It must be the shock of what had happened.

"We've been over this." She rolled her eyes. "But now that I am, what's the plan?"

"For you to go back." He fingered the rip in his shirt that must have happened during his fight. Dammit! He liked this shirt. It was a favorite. Which is why he had about twenty of them hanging in his wardrobe.

"Ugh." Haziel groaned. "Keep up, Wrath. Until this is settled, I'm your shadow." She winked at him. "And lucky for you that I am."

"You ended him with a heaven wrought blade." Wrath followed her curvy round ass out of the clearing. "That's hardly a fair fight."

She strode forward, pushing undergrowth aside as she

went. Stopping suddenly, she exclaimed and bent to her right to examine a flower. "Isn't this pretty?"

"Where are you going exactly?" And how did she seem to know her way around so well? But as she was currently entranced by some bright red flower thingy, he stuck to one question at a time.

Haziel stroked the petals of the flower and gave a happy sigh. "Mammon's demesne."

"Mammon's." She was on the move again, and he had to step lively to catch up with her. "I need to get to Lucifer's."

"Why?" She blinked at him. "If Lucifer is causing all this, that's the very last place you should go." Lowering her voice, she leaned closer. "Especially considering you have no power."

Not no power, just not enough to talk about yet, but he wasn't going to share with her interfering ass that his power was trickling back. Even if it was a rather fine ass. "Because if he has my daughter, I'm going to make him tell me where she is."

"Don't be obtuse," she tossed over her shoulder. "You can't face Lucifer in your current state. And you, more than any of us, should know that even if he is guilty and doesn't end you on sight, he's an accomplished liar."

"He's not an accomplished anything." Wrath followed behind her, simultaneously furious that he was and unable to do anything else.

Haziel looked around her and took a deep breath. "It really is quite lovely here."

"My demesne's better," he snapped, for no reason other than she got under his skin.

"Agreed." Haziel smiled, and two dimples popped up in her velvety cheeks. "But this is also beautiful."

It irked him him comfortable she was with hell. "How do you know how to get to Mammon's?"

"I have a map." She patted her pocket. "Just like you hell princes have a map of the heavenly realm.

She had him there. "Why are we going to see Ava?" And how had they become a we?

"We should see if Avarice's demesne looks anything like this." She gestured around her. "Let's see how widespread this damage is." She winked at him over her shoulder. "Plus, the way I hear it, Ava has her ear to the ground down here, and if anyone knows anything, it's her."

It did make a certain sense, and Ava did have her nose in everyone's business. Purely coincidentally, she would not be happy to see him. "I need to find my daughter."

"Wrath." She stopped suddenly and jammed her hands on her hips again. The motion drew her top tight against her pert breasts. She might be doing that on purpose to befuddle him, and it was working far too well for his peace of mind. "We both know Shade has gone after Eddie, and with his hounds, he will find her faster than anyone. Now stop asking inane questions and tell me instead how much of your power has come back."

SEVEN

Sophia liked Daniel Lee. He was a definite improvement over the bunch that had descended on the theater with Chris Fellows.

"The gate is stable." Daniel looked across the kitchen table at Dee and smiled.

Dee did her best not to smile back, but Daniel was a good-looking man and had an easy way about him that made it hard for even Dee to hold a grudge. She'd lifted her edict about him not being in her living space enough to let him eat with them. Sophia didn't think it would be long before he was rolling up his sleeping bag and leaving the basement for the guest room upstairs. Dee had offered the guest room to her, but she preferred the nice little B&B at the end of the road. They made wonderful French toast, which Sophia liked to slather with maple syrup.

"You mean since Wrath and Haziel went through." Sophia needed Daniel to understand that she may look harmless, but she was still an archangel.

Daniel chuckled. "Right. Since then."

Sophia appreciated that a guardian was sharing information freely and not taking their normal territorial approach.

"It hasn't registered any activity since Haziel went through," Daniel said.

Which was good news, because it meant no demons were trying to come through to this realm. "Any sign of the original witch who summoned Shade?"

"No." Daniel put his fork of mashed potatoes on his plate and raised an eyebrow. "Were we expecting there to be?"

"Perhaps." Sophia had given this a lot of thought. "Someone summoned Shade, and we know it wasn't Eddie. Then that someone disappeared, and it strikes me as strange that a witch went to all the trouble of summoning a hell prince and then did nothing about it."

"Hmm." Daniel picked up his fork and resumed eating. "You make a valid point. What do you think, Dee?"

"It's not my problem anymore." Dee sniffed, but her objection lacked weight as she frowned in thought. "But if it were my problem, I'd have to agree with Sophia. You don't summon a hell prince for shits and giggles."

"For nobody to notice this witch, she would have to be someone familiar," Daniel said. "Someone who is free to move about the theatre without raising any questions."

Dee raised her chin. "We have over four hundred members in the Paradise Players, not to mention our regular audience members."

"But an audience member wouldn't be wandering backstage." Daniel dug into his parmesan chicken.

"How would you know?" Dee snapped. "You're not familiar with how we do things here."

Daniel stopped chewing and stared at her. "You're right. My bad."

Dee huffed and went back to her dinner.

Sophia really liked Dee, but where Daniel Lee was concerned, Dee had a blind spot. She was determined to dislike a thoroughly likable young man. Dee's barriers wouldn't last much longer, but for the sake of all their digestion, Sophia changed the subject. "I imagine Haziel has caught up with Wrath by now." She didn't approve of Ramiel sending his second to track Wrath, and she'd told him so. Hell wasn't a safe place even for archangels, and a seraph would draw all the wrong kind of attention. As per usual, Ramiel wouldn't listen to anyone else's opinion and smiled and waved away any objections. According to him, Haziel was very powerful and could take care of herself. Sophia hoped he was right about that.

"But there's more bad news," Daniel said, and forked mashed potatoes into his mouth. That he ate with such gusto was in itself a miracle. Dee was a lovely woman, but her cooking was not a leading skill. "Word from HQ is that the other hell gates are also experiencing power fluctuations."

"Dammit." Dee added another piece of chicken to Daniel's plate.

Sophia grimaced inwardly on his behalf. The chicken was as dry as old boot leather, and the parmesan a burned offering on top.

"That means demons are coming through." Dee started and then wiped all expression off her face. "Not that it's anything to do with me."

Sophia hated to be the voice of doom at their cozy little dinner. "If demons are running amok on this plane, it's all of our problem."

"What about your lot?" Daniel chewed a mouthful of chicken and turned to Dee. "This is fantastic, Dee."

Dee hid her pleased smile and scoffed.

He looked like he meant it as well, and Sophia nearly

laughed. "What about my lot?" Sophia had a nasty suspicion she already knew what he was about to ask.

He turned back to her. "It seems to me that if the hell princes are needed at the seals, the archangels should be trying to do something about the demon infestation."

Sophia couldn't agree more. "They are trying not to get involved."

"Are you fucking kidding me?" Dee dropped her fork on her plate with a clatter. "How can they stay out of this?"

"Archangels are..." Sophia tried to put it politely. "They see their role as staying neutral."

Dee gaped at her.

Shaking his head, Daniel said, "I think the time for neutrality has come and gone. I have been watching the news, and it's not looking good."

"No." Depression settled on Sophia's chest. "And the other archangels are researching how to repair the seals. Since Eddie tried and was missing the heaven element to enact a full repair, we are trying to find something that might help." It was little enough in the current spiraling situation. She had been watching the news as well, and humans were definitely reacting to the weakening seals. Combine that with a stronger demon presence on this plane, and things were only going to get worse.

Gabriel had sent her a not so polite request earlier today for her to return to the heavenly realm. Her fellow archangels saw no reason for her to linger here.

She'd sent an equally not so polite response. Shade was still on the plane, and that meant she was staying. Hiding out on the heavenly plane and pretending what was happening on earth and in hell wasn't going to impact everyone was unmitigated stupidity. The weakening seals and busy demons on earth meant humanity was in trouble, and they were going to need all the supernatural help they could get. A spot of research was hardly a proportionate response. "I sent a message to Michael," she said. "I stressed the importance of us getting involved."

Dee cocked her head. "Why Michael?"

"He is not always in favor of Gabriel's policy of wait and see." She sipped her wine and was relieved that not needing to eat to sustain herself had saved her from Dee's cooking.

Daniel held his plate up for more.

"Michael is more of a fighter than a politician or a archivist. If I can impress on him how serious the situation is getting on this plane, he's the most likely to act," she said.

"Good idea." Daniel nodded and went at his second helping with gusto. "Have you heard from Shade?"

Dee stopped eating and stared at her intently.

"Not directly." Sophia touched her temple. "But I can sense him on this plane. He went north and is continuing to travel in that direction."

Dee's bravado crumpled. "He has to find her."

"He will." Sophia took her hand and squeezed it. She prayed she was right. Eddie's disappearance bothered her, and not only because it was gutting Shade, or that she liked Eddie, but more because it didn't make a lot of sense. "I thought maybe an archangel might have taken her," she said, voicing a fleeting suspicion. "But I checked with all of them, and there is no sign of them or their host having gone through any of the hell gates."

"But a demon took her." Dee frowned. "Ashe."

"Yes." And that was the part that made no sense to her. "But archangels can also be rather stubborn, and I wanted to cover that base. Eliminate the possibility."

"Fuck." Dee shook her head. "And we humans think archangels are the good guys."

Shade parked his dusty pickup in front of his cheap motel room. With the hounds, he'd chosen not to fly and had glamoured his power signature down to almost human. The hounds lay in the covered back, concealed from nosy humans who would, no doubt, freak out if they saw them. Three days of traveling and nothing.

Wrath was in hell, and if there was any sign of Eddie there, he'd pick it up. Unfortunately, the hounds didn't have their full power in the earth realm, but they were still the best option he had.

The hounds had him moving steadily north. Towns thinned out to smaller towns and finally just sparse outposts. He waited until there was nobody else around the quiet parking lot before opening the door to his room for the night and letting the hounds in. He hadn't slept since he'd set out, and it was time to get some rest.

Wherever Eddie was being held, it was probably going to involve a fight to get her out. The angels swore blind she wasn't in heaven, and as much as he didn't trust those sanctimonious fucks, keeping her in heaven would make no sense. No, if the angels had taken her, they would have been far more likely to kill her.

On that cheery thought, he opened his bag of fast food and unpacked the contents.

Being on earth made him more susceptible to human needs. Although he didn't need to eat and sleep as regularly as humans, he did still have those needs.

The hounds would need to feed soon, which meant he'd have to find some useless piece of human detritus and let them take its soul. Or a demon that was hanging out here when it shouldn't be.

He made short work of his burger and fries and flipped the television channel to a news station.

Cronus and Xerxes sprawled on the other queen bed in the room, their huge bodies eating up the space. Both hounds had their eyes closed, but they weren't sleeping. They were filtering out the input from their physical senses and letting their meta-physical senses take over.

Hounds fed on souls, which meant they could find souls, and they'd been hunting the ether constantly for signs of Eddie. Being bonded to her, they were particularly susceptible to the unique soul signature she gave off.

As much as he wanted to ask, he suppressed the desire. They would tell him as soon as they caught so much as a flicker of Eddie.

Shade concentrated on the news. If Eddie's hell gate was unstable, it could mean the others weren't faring much better, and the human news channels were his best source of information. Weak hell gates and missing demons didn't need a physicist to piece together. If demons were escaping into this realm, they would bring havoc with them.

He read the ticker tape running along the bottom of the screen. An African dictator was making noise about reclaiming land from a neighboring country.

The news went from politics to crime. The news anchor was one of those interchangeable plastic looking faces with a trust-me expression and a weighty way of delivering their script.

The word rape caught Shade's attention and he turned up the sound.

"...fifth rape and murder in as many days. London police are asking the public not to panic..."

Shade tuned the lacquered and painted anchor out.

Another article along the ticker tape caught his attention.

This one about a famous artwork being stolen from a museum. Human news was always bad, and Shade didn't know why they watched it. But there seemed to be more bad news than normal. A riot had broken out in a US city for no apparent reason, and a few people were dead, several more wounded. Negotiations had broken down between two large NATO allies, and the politicians were taking nasty swipes at each other over the media.

The effect of the breaking seals was most definitely leaking into the earth realm.

EIGHT

This bloody angel was going to be the death of Wrath, which might be a possibility for the first time in his eons-long life. Head held high, humming to herself, she marched their asses through the lush jungle like she was leading the heavenly host to Zion. Leaving him to tamely follow behind like he was carrying her fucking harp and trumpet.

"Isn't the river lovely?" She stopped a moment beside the winding, lazy, green river, slapped a delighted smile on her mug, and drew in a huge breath. Her breasts pushed against her tight white tank top as she did so.

What had happened to the old voluminous robes angels used to wear? Those were far less distracting. He nearly suggested she put her cape thingy back on.

"And there is the loveliest fresh breeze coming off the water." She turned her beaming smile his way. "Everything smells of flowers. And the colors are glorious."

"What are you wearing?" Angels were not supposed to be wearing form fitting white tank tops and flowy pants that the breeze molded to their long, shapely legs. The soft fabric stuck to her ass like she owed it rent.

"What?" She blinked at him and then glanced down at herself. "I thought this was perfect for the jungle. Not too tight, and natural fabrics. Linen is best in humid climates. I researched it."

He wouldn't know sod all about linen and humidity, but he did know what temptation looked like, and despite their day of tromping through the jungle, she didn't have so much as a speck of dirt on her. A fine sheen of perspiration had bronzed her dusky skin like the flesh of a ripe peach, and he wanted to take a great, big ball-curdling bite.

"You must be hot." She grimaced sympathetically.

"No." Sweating beneath his fighting leathers like the palms of an adolescent boy with a *Playboy* in his hands. Leathers were good for fighting and hiding weapons, good for protecting him from glancing blows from other weapons. Plus black disguised blood so much better than all that white could. He had no idea where she'd hidden her blade beneath that skimpy top or those translucent pants.

"Okay." She shrugged and strode off again.

And he kept right on following.

"So, your power is coming back?" She tossed the words over her shoulder as if his answer didn't matter to her. It damn well should matter to her, because him getting his power back might be all that stood between them and a horde of angry demons determined to add an angel's wings to their trophy wall.

What color were her wings? Ramiel's wings mirrored his in white, the filaments shot through with red and silver. As part of Ramiel's host, did her wings in any way mirror his? He liked the idea that they might have that in common.

Stap his vitals, but she had him thinking like a moony eyed

boy. Wing feathers! He was fantasizing about the color of her wing feathers.

She'd stopped and was looking at him expectantly.

Oh right, his power, she wanted to know about his power. "I guess we'll find out in a fight," he said.

Rolling her eyes, she sighed. "You know this would be so much pleasanter if you'd stop being so grumpy."

"I'm Wrath," he groused. "Grumpy goes with the territory. And what have you got to be so infernally chirpy about anyway?"

"I'm having a lovely time." She waved her hand at the jungle. "It's not often that an angel of my standing gets to journey to hell, and then only in the company of our archangel. And it's so vibrant here." She bent and cradled a flower in her palm. "Look at this gorgeous pink. Have you ever seen such brilliant color?"

No, he supposed he hadn't. He was probably going to earn himself another comment about his grumpiness, but perky angel tits needed a reality check. "There's a reason you don't come here without your archangel," he said. "Demons don't like angels and do their best to make sure angels get that message."

"I know that." She shook her head at him. "But let's not forget it was me who saved you from that demon earlier."

As if he could. A hell prince being saved by a seraph. Crap! He'd never live it down if any of his fellow hell princes discovered that.

"And anyway." She marched off again, lithe legs eating up the ground, rounded hips swinging. "I have you, and you're as much protection as an archangel." Glancing over her shoulder, she gave him a full body once over. "Maybe even more so, considering the location."

"Even without my powers?" Nothing could dent her optimism. He didn't know why he was trying. It wasn't making her any less distracting, and he felt like a big, bad-tempered bully.

"Oh, Wrath." She chuckled. "You'd be formidable as a human. You don't need your powers to be big, bad, and scary."

He wanted to ask her how big, bad, and scary but that seemed a little needy, so he shut his pie hole and dropped into place behind her. And the uninterrupted view of what he had to concede was one spectacular ass. How had he never noticed her ass before? Possibly because whenever he'd seen her, she'd been with Ramiel. And when he and Ramiel were around each other, admiring the scenery took a low priority.

They walked in silence for a long while. Around them, the jungle began to thin, more space between trees and less vegetation. Harsh sunlight pierced the leafy canopy and picked out red lights in her dark hair.

"If Ramiel was so concerned about me, why didn't he come himself?"

"He's very busy." Her shoulders tensed. "He has to deal with the seals breaking."

"And how's he going to do that sitting in heaven?" It irked him that Ramiel had her loyalty and her affection. That glittery glob of angelic goop treated her like an amenity.

"I don't ask all those questions." She kept her head facing forward, but the inflexible muscles of her back suggested his line of questioning was getting to her.

"So, you just do what he asks, when he asks?" Not even his dumbest demons gave him that kind of blind obedience.

"Ramiel relies on me."

And he'd bet she never let good old Ramiel down. He decided to give her honesty feature a little workout. "Word has it you're in love with him."

Her shoulders jerked. "Word has it right."

His laughter died in his throat. It bothered him that she

thought she was in love with Ramiel. Although she was annoying the creak out of his fighting leathers, Haziel was a good angel. Not one of those stuck-up butt plugs, but a basically kind and warm being. How that insufferable sphincter had managed to inspire such feelings in Haziel baffled him. "Why?"

Heaving a massive sigh, she stopped and faced him. "You know I have to answer you honestly."

He was counting on that, and he waited.

Her green eyes softened and gleamed. "Ramiel is courageous and good. He always puts his duty before his personal needs and takes wonderful care of his host. He's generous and kind and always—"

"He's using you." He'd had to damn well ask, hadn't he? The topic made him uncomfortable, so he switched it. "What's the plan when we get to Ava's demesne?"

And perhaps now might be a good time to mention that his welcome might be less than warm in that corner of hell. Then again, he didn't have any ridiculous honesty thing to deal with, and she hadn't asked. He would be on his way to Lucifer's if Haziel hadn't inserted herself into his mission.

"Not much of a plan." She resumed walking again. "I thought we'd ask her what condition her seal was in, and if she'd seen Lucifer."

"I wouldn't ask Ava about Lucifer." He smirked. "Not if you want to keep your head. They have history."

She stopped and looked around her, consulted her map, and then with a nod, set off again. "Bad feelings?"

"You could say that." Those had been a few good days when Ava had hunted hell with the sole intention of ripping his twin's balls off. Good thing Lucifer hadn't asked him to hide him, because Wrath would have delivered him to Ava with a ribbon around his neck.

Haziel frowned at him. "I thought you were the one who had the disastrous affair with Avarice."

He stopped in his tracks. Where the fuck was she getting all this information on him? "Who told you that?"

Waving her hand, she said, "Oh, everyone knows about that and how angry she was when you ended it over Rosabella."

Ava had spent a few scary weeks hunting for his balls as well. "Everyone knows this?"

"Mostly." She shrugged. "Of course, we didn't know that Rosabella had birthed a child. I'm glad we didn't know that."

"Why?" Fatherly protective instinct rose in him, and with it, his rage. Power tingled over his shoulder blades, as if his wings were about ready to reappear. Wings would be great right now and would cut down on a lot of this walking.

"Ramiel doesn't like Nephilim," she said so softly, it took him a moment to decipher her meaning.

"If Ramiel touches her, I'll rip his pussy white wings off and shove them up his ass."

"He won't hurt her." Haziel didn't look so sure of that.

"You don't know that."

"No." She chewed on her lush bottom lip. "He does seem to have very set opinions about Nephilim." She peered at him. "I understand why you kept her hidden."

"And now she might be the one being that can repair the seals." He took great satisfaction in pointing out that wee factoid.

"But she didn't repair yours." Haziel stopped and studied the landscape around them.

"No, but she improved it." His smugness vaporized. "It seems like we are going to need power from all three realms for a full repair."

"And such a being does not exist." She pointed to their left. "Ava's demesne starts just over that line of hills, doesn't it?"

"Yes." He gestured to the path they were on. "We're going to want to stay on this path if we don't want to stray into Lucifer's demesne. If he is behind Eddie's disappearance, he will have set wards to warn him if I cross into his territory."

She studied him with a small frown. "How do you know that?"

"He's my twin." As much as that galled both of them. "And it's what I would do."

On one side of the path, Shade's demesne sprawled in a fertile tangle. The other side belonged to Lucifer, all rigid lines and perfect symmetry. Perfection was an obsession with the urine-reeking obscenity he called a brother. It delighted Wrath no end to move things around and break the rigidly maintained order of Lucifer's demesne. Sometimes, he marched his horde over there just to mess shit up a bit. Violence thrummed through his blood as he thought of Eddie and what Lucifer had done. When he found his daughter, he would devote his existence to ensuring Lucifer never got another moment of peace.

They reached the hills and crossed to the other side.

Ava's demesne was a fascinating jumble of objects that resembled a giant magpie nest. The scenery was broken up by treasures Ava had managed to purloin from other realms. He had once spent months exploring the extent of her collection and barely seen a fraction of it.

Rare trees, rarer animals, geological impossibilities, and natural anomalies all clustered together in a fascinating tangle.

He'd been fond of Ava, and their time together had never been boring. She was sharp as a tack, endlessly curious, and impossible to predict. Ava was like trying to hold mercury in your palm. As they approached the border, a sizable group of upper order demons appeared on Ava's side. They glanced at Haziel and then focused on him.

"You're not welcome here." Ava's second and their leader, Rapace, squared his shoulders and puffed out his chest.

At first, Wrath thought he was talking to both of them, but Rapace's orange eyes were fixed on him. Rapace had never been his biggest fan when he and Ava were involved.

"We're here on important business." Haziel gifted Rapace one of her sweet smiles.

"Doesn't matter." Rapace glowered. "If you're with him, then you can't cross the border."

Wrath had no patience for this kind of crap. Rapace could go ahead and park his issues with him. He had a brother and a daughter to find, and an angel to get safely back to her realm. "Tell Ava it's about the seals and we really need to speak to her."

"Won't matter." Rapace shrugged and produced an obsidian sword. "Ava said we were to gut you like the miserable, lying worm you were if you tried to cross into her demesne. Whatever the reason."

Rapace took great delight in informing him of this, and Wrath recalled Rapace having a bit of a crush on Ava way back when. "Look." He gave reason a try. "I wouldn't bother her unless it was of the utmost importance. We really need to see her, and I won't be here longer than a simple conversation."

More demons materialized out of the air.

Without his full power, and with Haziel to take care of, Wrath didn't like the odds.

"Leave." Rapace pointed his sword in the direction from which they'd come. "Or we'll clip her pretty angel wings." Rapace smirked. "And we both know you can't stop us."

Frustration writhed in Wrath. He hated being bested by a mere demon, and in front of Haziel. But there was another of those fucking technicalities that were cursing him right now. He couldn't fight all those demons, and neither could Haziel. They couldn't end him, even without his powers, but in the hierarchy of things, angels like Haziel were expendable, and obsidian blades made the most final of all cuts.

Haziel turned to him and scowled. "Now what?"

And Wrath was very much afraid that he already knew the answer to her question.

NINE

Eddie had never felt so exhausted. Weariness had sunk into her bones and resided there in a constant dull ache. Every part of her hurt after Ashe and Calix had been at her again with the fucking pendant. Every time they came to her with the cursed thing, she felt like they sucked part of her being into it and left her a wrung-out husk without will or strength.

The door opened and dread tightened in her stomach. She couldn't handle it again, not so soon. She whimpered but didn't even have the strength to turn her head and see who had entered her cell.

"Eddie." Ashe crouched beside her cot. His voice was disturbingly gentle as he said, "This is tough on you, Eddie, and I'm sorry for that."

Not sorry enough not to hold her down while Calix put that fucking pendant over her head though. Her mouth was too dry to form words and she didn't have it in her to lean down and grab the bottle of water by her bed.

Ashe put a hand under her head and raised her. He pressed

the mouth of a water bottle to her lips. "Here, drink. It will help."

Cool, crisp water flooded her mouth and made her saliva glands tingle. "Why are you doing this?" she rasped.

"Your power." Ashe gave her more water. "We can use your power to amp up the other demons." He shook his head and dropped his gaze. "And your power, Eddie. It's like a shot of purest adrenalin straight to the muscle. You've no idea how much power you really have, or how to use it. But we do."

He offered her more water, and when she shook her head, he put the bottle down and lowered her back to her pillow. "There's a war happening, Eddie, and it's going to change everything we know and believe. You've become an unwilling participant in that war."

She nearly laughed at the look of regret in his eyes. "Collateral damage?"

He grimaced. "Something like that." He leaned closer to her. "But as bad as things get, Eddie, remember that you always have your dreams."

"What?" She stared at him. Now he was offering her Hallmark slogans along with hydration.

Ashe stood. "We'll see you soon, Eddie. Try to get some rest."

The water had helped, and Eddie stared at the door, counting the four locks closing. First one lower down, next a deeper more resonant click higher on the door, then a bolt sliding, and finally a bass clank as the last lock slid into place.

Another vaguely ghostly looking demon would come back later with a meal for her. They fed her regularly and well, and Eddie tried to eat everything they gave her. She needed to build what strength she could, because if they made one mistake—just one—she was getting out of here. Lately, though, even the effort of eating felt too much.

Exhaustion crept up through her limbs and weighed her eyelids down, and she closed them. Ashe's weird comment played back through her mind. *"But as bad as things get, Eddie, remember that you always have your dreams."*

Fucking dreams! What use were dreams to her in this heinous place? She had dreamed of Shade in the days before he had crashed into her life. Those dreams had been vivid and so real. As if he really could see her, he had turned to her in those dreams and spoken to her.

Her heart skipped a beat. Dream walking.

Shade had spoken to her. Even Wrath had looked right at her in those dreams, as if they could penetrate her mind and speak to her.

Excitement tingled through her, and her breath quickened. Would that work? Would she be able to reach out to Shade or Wrath in her dreams and tell them something about where she was? She didn't know anything beyond this room and Ashe, Calix, and Casper the unfriendly ghost.

Eddie closed her eyes and willed sleep to come.

SHADE WALKED down the sidewalk of another interchangeable Ontario town. Tim Hortons—check, Shoppers Drug Mart—check, LCBO—check. He hadn't even registered the name of this town.

The hounds had stayed in the truck, still trying to catch a hint of Eddie. All they could give him was the vague sense that they were moving in the right direction.

The image of Eddie flashed into his mind so quickly he stopped dead.

"Fucking hell." A person slammed into the back of him. "Watch where the fuck you're going."

Shade tossed a quick apology over his shoulder.

The man glared at him. "Asshole."

And Canadians were supposed to be polite. Shade hadn't found much politeness through his journey. He'd found increasing levels of aggression and intolerance. His daily scan of the news channels confirmed his fears. The seals were all leaking their noxious contents into the earth realm. Unsuspecting humans went about their daily lives with no understanding of why they were suddenly experiencing urges they couldn't control.

Eddie's face sparked through his mind again, and he stepped closer to a storefront and stilled his mind.

There it came again. Christ, she looked like shit and amazing all at the same time. Wrath said she was still alive, but Shade hadn't known how much he needed that confirmation until right this minute. His knees felt like rubber, and he supported himself with the brick frontage of the store. He turned his attention inward to her. "Eddie?"

A woman shot him a nervous glance and he realized he'd spoken aloud. He didn't care. This was his first contact with Eddie since she'd been taken from him. "Eddie?"

"Shade?" Her voice sounded weak and tired. "Is that really you?"

"It's me, sweetheart."

"I didn't know if this would work." Tears tracked down her ashen cheeks, and her chest rose and fell as she sobbed softly. "I didn't know if I could reach you."

"I'm trying to find you, sweetheart."

A couple of kids looked at him and jostled him with a sneer.

Yes, he was crazy. Crazy with worry, crazy with missing her, crazy to get her back where she was safe.

"I don't know where I am." She lay on a spartan cot in a featureless gray room. "They have me locked in this room."

Every muscle in his body tensed as he asked, "Are they hurting you?"

She hesitated and licked her chapped lips. A struggle played across the finely wrought lines of her face.

"Tell me, Eddie."

"They have an amulet, like the one they put on Wrath. They're draining my power."

"Fuck." Shade punched the wall. Four bricks crumbled beneath his fist, and the kids went pale and ran away. "I'm going to find you, and then I'm going to make them pay."

"Find me soon, Shade." Her voice trembled. Her big aqua eyes looked dull and desperate. Eddie's eyes should never look that way. Eddie was life and fire and strength.

"I will, sweetheart. This I vow." He forced himself to concentrate past the panic. "Can you tell me anything else?"

"Ashe said there's a war happening and that it will change everything. They drain my power to feed it to their demons."

Primal rage beat a drum tattoo through his soul. "Have you seen anyone else but Ashe?"

"Calix is with him and some weird ghost looking demon who brings me my meals."

"Lucifer?"

She shook her head and wiped her tears with the corner of her blanket. "Those are the only three I've seen. I seem to be in some kind of facility, but I can't even see outside this cell."

"Summon me to you, Eddie, like you did before."

She coughed and shook her head. "I don't even know how I did that."

"I felt your desire for me. Reach for that, Eddie. Reach for your lust and give it space to grow. Summon me, and I will find you."

"Don't get ahead of yourself." She gave a weak chuckle. "Nobody said I desired you."

"Eddie." He let his voice grow smoky and seductive. He needed her to hang in there for him, and he'd use whatever he could to do that. "We both know you're lying now."

His words brought color to her cheeks and a gleam to her eyes. "Don't make me punch you, Shade."

He'd take that punch and a thousand more if it meant being in the same room with her again. "I'm coming for you, Eddie, and in the meantime, keep dreaming of me, sweetheart."

"You wish." She scoffed and then grew serious again. "Come soon, Shade."

His heart constricted. "I'm on my way."

Once the connection was broken, he ran back to where he'd parked his truck.

Cronus and Xerxes barely waited for him to get into the truck before they spoke.

We felt her, master. We have a direction on the mistress.

TEN

Wrath's temper snapped and simmered under his skin as the demon behind him shoved him in the back with a lance and snarled. "Get moving."

His back burned with the desire to unleash his wings and rain retribution down on Avarice's horde.

Haziel looked across at him and shook her head.

Yes, he fucking got it. They needed to cooperate to get to Ava. They needed information from Ava, and shredding her horde wouldn't be an effective conversation opener. Ava was slow to anger, but her desire for revenge burned long and strong. He had no doubt she'd instructed her horde to make an example of him when they brought him in.

He'd known all this when he'd grabbed Haziel's hand and stepped over the border into Ava's territory.

After a frozen moment of shock and fury, the horde had grabbed both of them and bound their hands behind their backs.

Despite being tied up and gagged, Haziel stared around her, eyes alight with wonder and interest.

There was a lot to look at in Ava's demesne. Her collections of stuff littered the path they were being marched long. Even the vegetation sparkled and glittered, jewel bright and flashy.

Ava liked pretty and rare things, and her demesne was stuffed full of them.

Their guards marched them through a beautiful town at the base of Ava's stronghold. Picture postcard perfect with thatched cottages and gardens brimming with colorful growth. The residents gawked at them as they were marched through.

A couple of them hissed his name and spat, but most of the attention was reserved for Haziel as many demons stared at what was probably their first in-the-flesh angel.

The simmering resentment didn't seem to bother Haziel. Nope, little Miss Chirpy on his left, nodded her head at everyone who met her eye, and despite her gag, attempted to smile. That relentless cheerfulness might do worse to him than anything Ava had no doubt planned for him.

Haziel made a strangled gasp as she looked at the castle.

He could read the questions building in her eyes. Yes, it was plated in gold, and yes, the millions of gemstones glittering in the buttery sunshine were real. The guards around the gate were dressed in emerald green and gold, their epaulets blinking and gleaming in the sun. They saluted smartly as their party passed through the gates.

Inside the castle grounds, Ava's most treasured collections were housed in glass and steel cages. Magical beasts of heaven and hell, strange and beautiful plants and artifacts, all lovingly and carefully tended by Ava's horde.

As they entered through the large golden doors, Haziel's head swiveled from left to right, taking in the vast collection of beautiful artwork from the earth realm. Genuine masterpieces that the humans had either lost or never heard of. The rarer a thing, the more Ava sought to have it.

The throne room was resplendent in its gold and green opulence. Heavy swathes of green velvet drapery framed the glittering crystal windows. Thick, silk carpets adorned the cream-and-gold veined marble floor. And at the end, her gorgeous, opulent body draped in silk, Ava lounged on a gem encrusted platinum throne. Her gleaming black hair draped over her shoulder in a shining mass.

"Satan," she purred and stroked the arms of her throne. "You're looking well. Even without your pretty wings."

She motioned to one of her demons to remove his gag.

Wrath took his time working moisture back into his mouth before answering. "Hello, Ava."

"Hello Ava?" She raised one dark sculpted eyebrow. "That's it, and after all this time?"

The quarrelsome cow also liked to play games. Not willing to indulge her, Wrath just stared at her.

"And who is this?" Ava switched her attention to Haziel. Uncoiling from her seat, she took her time sashaying down the ten or so steps from the dais her throne rested on and approached Haziel. "She's pretty, Wrath. As always, I must commend your taste." She circled Haziel. "And a seraph."

"She can also speak for herself," Wrath said. Things would go a lot worse for Haziel if Ava thought he had an interest in her. Not that he did. Much. It had been so long since he'd felt anything for a female who wasn't Rosabella, he couldn't be sure that was what was happening to him.

"Hmm." Ava tapped a finger to her glossy, scarlet mouth. "I'll bear that in mind." She strolled over to him and stopped right in front of him. "I must say, I was surprised you decided to enter my demesne."

"No, you weren't." He hated the games and he didn't have

time to indulge her. "You knew if I was here, I was going to enter. Regardless of what your horde thought about it."

Her pitch-black eyes flashed anger at him for a moment before she composed herself. "Remind me what it was I said when you were last here."

"If I crossed your borders again, you would rip me limb from limb and let your horde feast on my entrails." Not that he gave her pathetic horde much of a chance of managing that. Even with his power only about two thirds restored. This lot wouldn't stand a chance if he got angry, which was the only thing keeping his temper currently in check. That, and the fact that he and Ava had been good together, and he hadn't done right by her. "Would a belated apology interest you?"

She threw back her head and laughed. He'd always enjoyed her laugh. Husky and warm like whisky and honey, and damn near irresistible. "I'm not sure," she said. "It would all depend on what brings you here."

Losing interest in him, she turned back to Haziel. Stopping in front of her, she removed Haziel's gag and stroked her cheek to soothe the marks the gag had made. "I know you."

"Yes." Haziel licked her lips, her voice dry and raspy. "I am called Haziel. We've met a few times. I am Ramiel's second."

"Yes." Ava nodded and smiled. "And you're hopelessly in love with your archangel."

Wrath wouldn't put it quite like that. Haziel was infatuated with the uptight slimy rectum.

Haziel's honesty issue had her nodding. "Yes."

"And you can't tell a lie." Ava's eyes glittered. "Can you?"

He shouldn't have been surprised she'd known that. Along with the exotic and rare, Ava liked to collect information.

"No." Haziel looked crestfallen. "It can be very inconvenient at times."

Ava chuckled. "Times like now?"

"Yes." Haziel grimaced.

"Oh, Wrath." Ava threw him a sparkling glance. "You have brought me a delightful little present."

"Leave her alone, Ava. Your issue is with me." He didn't like Ava toying with Haziel. She might annoy the shit out of him with her cheeriness and her positivity, but he reserved the right to toy with Haziel for himself.

Wait! What? And why did that make him think of other, and far more pleasant, ways he could toy with Haziel?

"Tell me, lovely Haziel." Ava smoothed Haziel's hair behind her ear. "What are you doing with Wrath?"

"Ramiel sent me," Haziel moved her head away from Ava's stroking fingers.

"Why?"

"To keep an eye on Wrath."

"Really?" Ava looked at him with keen interest. "Why?"

"Why what?" Haziel frowned.

Ava tossed her head and tutted. "Silly me. You cannot lie but you can evade a vague question because you are not sure what needs answering." She chuckled. "I shan't make that error again."

Slimy duck taints, but Haziel would hand Ava everything she wanted to know.

"Let me be more specific. Why did Ramiel send you to watch Wrath?"

Haziel gave him an apologetic grimace. "Because he is concerned that Wrath will go after his daughter, and he wants to know what he's doing. Wrath is unpredictable and also vulnerable with his power gone and his seal weakened."

"So, Ramiel sent you to babysit big, bad Wrath." Ava threw her head back and laughed. She turned back to him. "How demeaning."

Yes, well, there was truth in that. Another technicality there was no point in trying to dispute, so he shrugged.

Ava flung her arm over Haziel's shoulder and examined him with a hard, glittering gaze that scorched him from head to toe and back again.

"Tell me, Haziel." Ava leaned closer to Haziel. "What do you think of our Wrath?"

Haziel's tawny cheeks deepened to russet. "I like him."

"Oh, we all like him, my angel," Ava drawled. "Do you like all those muscles?"

"Yes," Haziel whispered, blushing even deeper.

"Do you like those beautiful blue eyes of his?"

Haziel cleared her throat and looked like she'd rather fly headfirst into a hurricane. "Yes."

News to him, and Wrath perked up. She liked his body and his eyes. He silently willed Ava to stay on her current line of questioning.

"What about those strong thighs?" Ava murmured. "Do you like those too?"

"I do," Haziel squeaked. "Wrath is very attractive."

Well, well, well, apparently, he wasn't the only one having inappropriate thoughts.

"You know," Ava whispered, "those strong thighs of his help him drive that thick, long—"

"Ava!" Crap, Ava was going to make him blush at this rate. "Is this really necessary? You know why she's here. You're angry with me, not her."

"You're right." Ava released Haziel and spun away from her and closer to him. "Sweet Haziel here has done nothing to me. Whereas you." She closed the distance between them and jabbed him in the chest with a sharp fingernail. "You made a fool out of me."

"No, he didn't," Haziel said.

Ava glared at her. "Yes, he did."

"No." Haziel shook her head, her face a study in honesty. "You're not a fool. Thus, nobody could make a fool of you."

Ava opened her mouth and shut it again. She stared at Haziel with far less malice as she said, "I think I like you."

"I'm likable." Haziel shrugged. "Unless you ask me if your ass looks fat in something and it really does, because then I'll have to tell you that." She flinched. "Not that your ass looks fat or ever could."

This time when Ava laughed it was genuine amusement. "I've changed my mind. I know I like you."

And with that, Ava's posture relaxed, her eyes lost their dangerous glitter, and her tone changed. "So, what are the two of you doing here?"

"Could you?" Haziel indicated her bound wrists. "We really do need to talk, and my hands are going numb."

Ava snapped her fingers.

Her demons leapt to obey, and Wrath found himself unbound and confused as fuck about what had just happened. One minute, Ava had been clawing at them like a cat with its favorite scratching post, and now she was motioning them to follow her out of the ostentatious throne room to what he knew was her much more comfortable sitting room to one side of it. Huh! Haziel might have her uses after all.

Haziel slid up beside him as they followed Ava. "You should apologize to her."

"What?" He already knew he should, but somehow Haziel telling him to do so made him want to do the opposite. Although, that was a fairly good example of how he handled most beings who tried to tell him what to do.

"You hurt her." Haziel turned those compelling green eyes on him. "And the least you can do is let her know you're sorry for doing so."

He didn't like how much sense that made, so he played for time. "Maybe I'm not sorry."

"Yes, you are." Haziel gave him a reproachful stare. "You're bad tempered, but you're not nasty."

"And you're so sure of that?" It irked him that she saw him so clearly.

Haziel smiled, and it made him want to thump his chest and strut around like a peacock. "I'm sure."

"And you're also sure that you like my body," he said. He wouldn't be him if he crumpled in the face of a challenge, and Haziel had been winning far too many of their verbal sparring matches for his liking.

"Yes," she said through a tight jaw. "And before you go there, I also like your blue eyes and your thighs."

Heat shot down his spine and curled around his abdomen. "What else do you like about me, Haziel?"

"I like your sense of humor." She grinned at him. "And I really, really like your ass."

ELEVEN

Haziel woke to champagne light filtering through the gauzy curtains of the room she'd been shown to after they'd had a long chat with Ava that had lasted well into the small hours. By the time one of Ava's demons had led her to a bed chamber, she'd been so tired it had been a struggle to keep her eyes open.

Being in hell was draining, and she grew as tired as the average human would on earth.

A virulently red bird fluttered to a perch outside her window and started a showy song to the morning sun. Ramiel's demesne was considerably less colorful, and she rather liked the contrast here.

The bed was amazingly comfortable, and she took a long, luxuriant stretch.

Somewhere in the palace, Wrath would also be waking up. He was very different from Ramiel, which was not surprising, considering they were each other's counterbalance. Being with Ramiel was soothing and calm. He revered order and reason and would never deign to flirt outrageously with her or force her to admit her attraction for him. He also didn't make her laugh like Wrath did. She felt guilty about her disloyal thought. Of course Ramiel didn't spend his time making jokes and trying to get a reaction out of her. He was busy, important, an archangel. Then again, Wrath was a hell prince. She took a deep breath and centered herself. Acknowledging her attraction to Wrath was healthy, sensible. Acknowledge, accept, and then move on. That's what she'd do.

Being attracted to Wrath didn't need to present a problem. She was a master at keeping her emotions in check and getting on with the task assigned to her. Once this mission was over, she would return to Ramiel's demesne with a bunch of new and exciting experiences that other angels of her station could only dream about. Her contribution to Ramiel's host would be more valuable with all that she was learning.

She got out of bed and padded into the adjoining bathroom.

A giant, crystal clawfoot tub took pride of place in front of towering bay windows. Beyond the pristine grass, a garden of insanely bright flowers competed for most garish color, yet somehow, blended in a delightful jumble. Large gold statues littered the garden and caught the bright sunlight in dazzling displays. Jewel colored ponds—blues, greens and even reds and yellow—nestled between the flower beds. So much color that it almost hurt to look at, yet Haziel enjoyed it.

She poured her bath and added lavender crystals from a platinum bowl thoughtfully placed beside the bathtub. Her clothing had been freshly laundered and sat folded on a chair close to the tub.

As urgent as their business was, Haziel lingered over her bath and getting dressed. She rubbed jasmine scented lotion into her skin. Tiny flecks of gold in the lotion turned her skin to a bronze sheen.

Ramiel would be horrified by the excess, but he wasn't here, and she decided to enjoy it while she could.

A demon waited outside her bedroom door and bowed low as she opened it. "Seraph," he murmured. "If you would follow me, the mistress is waiting for you."

"Have you seen Wrath?" She found it hard not to gape at the lavish paintings and tapestries clawing for space on the walls.

The demon cleared his throat. "Follow me, please."

She hoped Wrath hadn't been awake and upsetting Ava before she could get there and mediate. He had a way with words, did Wrath, and it wasn't a good way.

The room she was taken to had one silver and glass table in the center, with one chair, and one place setting.

"Breakfast," the demon said as he bowed his way out.

Haziel took a seat, feeling dwarfed by the open, airy space.

The door opened, and more demons entered with her breakfast. Fresh, plump berries that made her mouth water. A jar of pale honey and thick, creamy yoghurt with it. A bowl of nuts was carefully placed beside the other items. A platter of golden, flaky pastries joined the rest of her breakfast, along with a pat of bright yellow butter.

The same demon who had led her to the room bowed. "What else can we get you?"

Eyeing the feast in front of her, Haziel had to laugh. "I'm sure this will do perfectly."

"Very good," he said and disappeared again.

Wrath had probably already had breakfast, and for all her languid ways, Haziel didn't imagine Ava lounging around in bed for the entire morning.

She had finished her second bowl when the door opened, and Ava stepped into the room.

This morning she wore an indigo silk gown that clung to

the strong, lithe lines of her body and trailed along the floor behind her. Precious gems were woven through her lustrous dark hair piled atop her head. She smiled as a demon produced a chair for her and set it at the table opposite Haziel. "Good morning."

"Morning." Haziel waited for Wrath to appear. When Ava selected a berry from the bowl and bit into it, she took the initiative. "Is Wrath joining us?"

"Hmm?" Ava popped the rest of the berry into her mouth. "Funny you should ask."

And Haziel's belly fluttered uncomfortably. There was a glint in Ava's dark eyes that made her nervous. "And why's that funny?"

"Wrath left." Ava shrugged and helped herself to another berry. She dipped it in honey and dropped it into her mouth.

Haziel couldn't have heard that right. "Did you say Wrath left?"

"Yup." Ava winked at her and licked honey off her fingers. "Seems you and I now have something in common."

"Eh?" It was the best she could manage. This had to be one of Ava's games. Wrath would never have—actually Wrath may very well have. He'd made it quite clear from the start that he hadn't wanted her along with him. Outrage rippled through her. She was a seraph in hell. She couldn't be here without an invitation, and she wasn't safe without a hell prince.

"Yes." Ava ripped into a croissant and dipped a piece in the honey. "Don't you love honey?"

"Yes." A direct question always demanded she answer it. "When did he leave?"

"According to my house demon, he slunk away sometime in the early hours of this morning." Ava dunked another piece of croissant into the honey. She glanced over her shoulder and called. "There is no coffee here. Why is there no coffee here?"

The demon Haziel assumed to be the house demon bowed low. "Right away, mistress."

"There really should be coffee." Ava fixed him with a gimlet stare. "If I have to ask for it, then you have already failed me."

He bowed low enough to scrape the floor with his forehead. "You are right, your highness, as always."

Good grief. At least Ramiel had never treated her like that.

"Demons." Ava rolled her eyes when the demon had left. "You have to keep a very firm hold on them, or they get ambitious." Her expression darkened. "Especially lately. Like the other hell princes, my horde is molting demons."

Haziel didn't want to discuss demons, not the lower order ones anyway. "You said Wrath left early this morning. Without me?"

"So, it would appear." Ava laughed and popped another berry between her full red lips. "Take it from one who knows, angel. He's good at slipping away from a female."

The reality of her situation started to trickle through her brain. "But I can't traverse hell without him. I'm an angel."

"Yes, you are." Ava beamed at her like a proud parent. "And you wouldn't make it two steps outside the palace before a demon took exception to you being here."

No need to panic. Ramiel knew she had followed Wrath to hell. He wouldn't leave her here for eternity. "Perhaps I should contact Ramiel?"

"Good!" Ava beamed as the demon entered and put a tray of coffee in front of her. "I can't start my day without my coffee. Don't you think humans are ingenious at times? For all their faults, they certainly have a trick or two worth copying."

"I like humans," Haziel said. Ava seemed to be taking her unwelcome guest rather pleasantly. In fact, she seemed to be enjoying herself. "If we contact Ramiel, he'll arrange for me to leave here."

"Why would we do that?" Ava poured two cups of coffee and added cream. "When Wrath so kindly left you as my hostage."

"What!" Haziel was fairly certain she'd never shrieked in her life, but that was the only description she could find for the sound that catapulted out of her.

"Oh, yes." Ava handed her a cup of coffee. "He left a message for me explaining how he was leaving you here with me as a show of faith that would allow him to travel across my demesne." She grinned at Haziel. "Isn't he kind?"

"No." Haziel shot to her feet. How dare Wrath do this to her. "It's the very opposite of kind. In fact, I think we can say it's unkind."

"Hell princes." Ava smirked and sipped her coffee. "At least the ones with dicks. Welcome to them, sister. They're a prize bunch."

Now that Haziel looked closer at Ava, she noticed a certain grim acceptance to the hell prince. "I thought you were enjoying my discomfort, but you're not, are you?"

"Maybe a teeny bit." Ava showed her a small gap between her thumb and forefinger. "But only because that makes us sisters in the struggle." She grimaced. "And I really can be a bitch."

"He left me as a hostage." Haziel still couldn't quite believe it. She picked up her coffee and drank deeply. Ava was right. It really did help clear the fog in her brain. "Does that mean he's coming back?"

"Probably." Ava shrugged. "My guess is that he's trying to keep both of us occupied while he does whatever he wants." She leaned forward. "The penis contingent down here tend to think they can do whatever the fuck they like."

A few female angels complained of the same thing, and

what Ava said made too much sense for Haziel to ignore it. "I take it he's done this before to you?"

"Yes, indeed." Ava drained her coffee cup and poured herself another. "They're all the same, you know. Shade, Lucifer, even Zeb, and he's crazy about Levi and would stab himself rather than piss her off." She waved an elegant hand through the air. "They march around like having a penis gives them special dispensation to do whatever they like."

Haziel took a *pain au chocolat* from the basket. Humans had that right too. Chocolate was perfect for comfort eating. "Even with you female hell princes?"

"Oh, yes." Ava snorted. "Patronizing, condescending, entitled sons of whores, the entire lot of them." She rolled her eyes. "And don't get me started on the mansplaining."

Now that Ava mentioned it, Haziel could see some parallels. "Archangels aren't really any different."

"No?" Ava raised an eyebrow.

"Not really." As much as she adored Ramiel, she couldn't not see the similarities in what Ava was saying. "Michael postures around, thumping his chest and pretending like he singlehandedly invented war.

"Ugh." Ava wrinkled her nose. "You don't need to tell me about that one. He's my counterbalance, and somehow in his tiny little brain that translates to my superior."

"I can believe that." Haziel had seen the way Michael flexed in front of Ava. "And Cassiel will lecture anyone who stands still too long." Haziel dared dipping a toe in territory she had never gone before. "Raphael never bothers to explain but goes ahead and does whatever he thinks is best."

Ava cocked her head. "And Ramiel?"

Conflicted feelings writhed inside her. She didn't want to be disloyal to her archangel, but he had sent her to follow Wrath and set in motion this entire situation. "Ramiel can be a bit hard-headed and uncompromising. He tends to think he always knows better.”

“Right.” Ava thumped the table. “I mean, what does he mean by sending you after Wrath? He’s the one who should be shadowing Wrath. You can bet Wrath wouldn’t have managed to slip away from him, what with the way they can sense each other, and Ramiel would have been able to track him.” She growled. “Instead, he sends you down here, and honestly, anything could happen to you in hell.” She filled Haziel’s coffee cup. “I mean, you’re with me, so you’re perfectly safe, but he didn’t know that.”

Haziel felt uncomfortable with Ava’s criticism and even more so because she couldn’t outright deny the truth of what the hell prince was saying. “He probably didn’t consider the danger to me. He finds me very valuable and wouldn’t want anything bad to happen to me.”

“I’m sure he does.” Ava gave her an admiring glance. “But that doesn’t give him the right to toss you to the hell princes like a piece of prime rib.”

Righteous indignation burned away any lingering feeling of disloyalty. “No, it doesn’t. And I’m not a piece of meat.”

“We have to stand together.” Ava leaned forward and tapped the table with her forefinger. “We female supernaturals. Hell princes, archangels, even those guardians. We females need to stand together and remind the penis contingent that we are as powerful, and as important.”

“Yes, we do.” Haziel clinked her coffee cup against Ava’s. “Screw the patriarchy.”

“Screw it.” Ava clapped. Her expression grew crafty as she leaned closer. “And now, girlfriend, let’s fuck with them. Starting with...oh, I don’t know...Wrath.”

TWELVE

The niggling feeling sat in Wrath's chest like annoying vermin as he winged across the border into his brother's demesne. His full power had returned in the small hours of the morning, and with it, his ability to fly. There was nothing keeping him cooling his heels while Ava toyed with him. Haziel could stay and get any useful information from her.

He'd done the right thing, he assured the voice trying to tell him otherwise. Haziel was safer with Ava while he tracked down Lucifer. And he was going back for her as soon as he found Lucifer.

Lucifer's horde resembled their master; impossible to deal with and full of arrogance and bravado. Lucifer's demesne was no place for a sweet, trusting soul like Haziel. Lucifer's horde would feed on her soul first and ask questions later. He would be far more effective and quicker if he wasn't worried about protecting her all the time. No, he'd done the right thing.

He wasn't feeling guilty. Not even the tiniest of jots. Nope, he wasn't. His feelings were more like residual concern that Ava would take out her anger with him on Haziel.

"No, she won't," he spoke out loud. Ava may want to have him strung up by the scrotum, but she wouldn't hurt Haziel. If he knew Ava, she would merely show Haziel to the nearest hell gate in her demesne and send her back to earth, safe and sound, and probably well fed and watered. Ava had an excellent chef.

After the delightful jumble of Ava's demesne, Lucifer's looked even more constipated than it normally did. His twin had poured every ounce of his conceited self-importance into his area of hell. Even the fucking trees grew to precise heights and bordered roads that Wrath could put a tape measure to and they wouldn't deviate by as much as a fart. The whole place made him itch to fuck shit up. He took childish delight in letting his wings blow dirt onto the pristine paving of the road he flew above.

As far as plans went, his was simple. He was going to march right into the heart of this uptight, asshole squeak of a place and demand entry to the palace. Of course Lucifer had a palace. And one full of reflecting surfaces to remind the thunder cunt of his cum-filled sweaty sock of a face.

That was another reason he'd done the right thing in leaving Haziel behind. She really wouldn't like his language, and he'd have to tame it down in front of her. She could probably read his foul thoughts from his face. Plus, he was heading straight into—and with no small delight—a fight with Lucifer.

A bird sang a precise rising crescendo of notes from the forest.

He'd been flying for most of the day when it occurred to him that he should have seen at least one demon on the road. When nobody had challenged him at the border, he'd assumed he'd slipped through undetected, but in light of the unnatural nothing, his mind churned. Yesterday he'd told Haziel the border would be warded, yet he'd felt no confirming tingle as he crossed. As far as he knew, the road beneath him was the major thoroughfare to the palace, and Lucifer's sycophantic minions should have been on their way to worship at the crusty feet of their leprous master.

He entered an immaculate settlement of thatched, white-washed cottages. Flowers bloomed in the precise order of the color spectrum in the angular garden beds in front of each cottage. He bet there were precise regulations to height and type of bloom as well.

The silence was so complete it made his nape prickle. No smoke drifted from the chimneys either, and even the tavern door was shut with no sound coming from inside the yellow mullioned windows. The place was deserted.

It was the same in the next three settlements he passed, and it creeped him out.

His senses were on high alert as he approached the palace.

Lucifer's pennant snapped smartly and perfectly from the top of all twelve towers in a breeze that was neither too strong nor too weak.

Wrath had seen human storybooks, and the palace reminded him of something from a human fairytale in its gleaming white perfection.

Finally, a sign of life as he stepped up to the guardhouse.

A sentry in a smart black and white uniform stepped onto the road leading into the castle and stopped him.

Wrath's power crackled and spat beneath his skin, and he kept his wings unleashed.

The sentry eyed his wings nervously and said, "The master is not within."

"And I'm supposed to take your word for that?" Wrath let his stare linger on the demon.

Sweat broke out on the sentry's top lip. "The master left a message for you."

That shook Wrath out of his purpose momentarily. "For me?" And then rage surged through him. Lucifer had known he was coming. It was further proof that his brother had Eddie.

Wrenching the sentry aside, Wrath strode into the castle. He didn't want to end the demon, but if the fucktard followed him, Wrath wouldn't hesitate to let him know he wasn't going to be turned aside.

The great doors slammed against the wall when he threw them open. His boots resounded against the pale marble floors.

"Wrath." A demoness in a starched and pressed white gown glided down the stairs toward him. With her long, dark hair and flawless bone structure, she was beautiful in the way Lucifer insisted all his household demons be. She stopped in front of him and inclined her head politely. "The master is not here. He warned us that you would not believe the sentry and would enter anyway."

Her calm composure took the edge off his rising anger. "I'm looking for my daughter."

"I understand." She folded her long, elegant hands in front of her. "The master said you would be. He also said to tell you she is not here." She motioned the palace with a graceful sweep of her arm. "You are, of course, welcome to search without challenge."

Like he was going to take her word for it. Search, Wrath did, every inch of the place, and taking savage delight in leaving destruction behind him. He was looking for any clue to where Lucifer might be, or where he'd taken Eddie. It took him late into the night to finally admit the palace was clean of any trace of Lucifer or Eddie, or any hint of where they might be now. There was also no glimmer of Lucifer's energy signature that was more recent than a week.

He took one of Lucifer's chariots, again without opposition from the palace staff, and used it to search Lucifer's demesne. Passing time pressed at him, but he didn't trust anything where Lucifer was concerned. His brother was tricky and smart, and just because Wrath couldn't sense the fucker, didn't mean he wasn't hiding somewhere. Finally, days longer than he would have liked, he had to admit defeat and turned the chariot back to Shade's hell gate.

A week after he'd left Haziel with Ava, he was spat out into the basement of the Paradise Theatre, more pissed off than ever and thoroughly frustrated. He half expected Haziel to be waiting for him. Instead, Daniel appeared at the door moments after Wrath's arrival. "Did you find Eddie?"

"No." Failure made Wrath grind his teeth. His search had taken too long, and he'd returned here, hoping that Shade had found her while he'd been gone. Time they didn't have, and Eddie didn't have, was ticking by while Lucifer led the dance. "And I didn't find any trace of Lucifer either."

Daniel nodded his understanding and led the way out of the basement of the theatre. "Shade is not back yet."

"Have you heard from him?"

Daniel nodded. "He checks in daily. The hounds picked up a trace of her a few days ago, and he's following." Daniel's expression gentled. "But they haven't found her yet."

Worry whipped his simmering anger into rage. He pressed the agonizing possibilities of what was being done to his daughter into a mind box. "Is Haziel here?"

"No." Daniel stopped and looked at him. "Isn't she with you?"

"Wrath?" And, of course, his catastrophe of a journey wouldn't be complete without Rosabella waiting at the end of it. She leapt into his path as he stalked across the corridor toward the stairs leading to the living quarters.

"Where is she?" Rosabella scanned the area behind him. "Where is Eddie?"

Wrath didn't owe her any explanations, and the rush of anger he experienced as he looked at her took him by surprise. Brushing past her, he took the stairs two at a time. It had to be his constant worry about Eddie making him terse with Rosabella. Rosabella had been...was the love of his life. He stopped when he reached the upper level and turned. "I'm sorry, Bella. It was a waste of time."

"Wrath." Rosabella shrieked and clapped both hands over her mouth. "You can't tell me that. Where is my daughter? Why haven't you found her?"

"Our daughter," he snarled before he could stop himself. Taking a deep breath, he gentled his tone "She is our daughter."

Paling, Rosabella took a stair down and away from him. "Well of course she's our daughter. That's what I meant to say." Tears swam in her eyes, the same color as Eddie's. "You have to find my baby girl."

"Wrath?" Dee appeared from the kitchen. "You didn't find her?"

"No." He hated giving Dee his bad news. "I searched the entirety of Lucifer's palace and his demesne, and she wasn't there." Grim anger hardened in his gut. "And neither was Lucifer."

For an awful moment, it looked like Dee might burst into tears, and then she took a deep breath and regained her stoicism. "You think he's got her on the earth plane?"

"Lucifer has Eddie." Rosabella wailed and wrung her hands. "You have to stop him."

Only Dee's genuine upset stopped him from asking Rosabella firmly to modulate her tone. Her hysteria wasn't helping the situation. He kept his attention on Dee. "I saw

Mammon while I was in hell as well, and she hasn't heard anything either."

"You saw Mammon?" Rosabella ran up the stairs and stopped in front of him, so close he could smell her shampoo. It was the same one Eddie used and his heart clenched. Where was his daughter?

Rosabella's eyes glinted at him viciously. "Why did you see Mammon? She has nothing to do with this."

Wrath got the nasty feeling he was missing something because now Rosabella looked pissed off. "Haziel suggested that Ava might know something. If there's something going down in hell, Ava almost always knows."

Rosabella narrowed her eyes, her lips thin. "Are you sure that's the only reason you went to see her?"

And Wrath was caught gaping like a trout after a fly. He glanced at Dee but her look of disgust aimed at Rosabella didn't make things any clearer. "Why else?"

"Oh, I don't know." Rosabella tossed her hair over her shoulder. "Maybe renew an old acquaintance. Don't think for a second I've forgotten who Mammon was and what you had with her."

As he had left Ava for Rosabella, her anger baffled him. "What?" Stepping around Rosabella, he couldn't formulate words that made sense. He'd gone to hell to find their daughter. Why the fuck would he be there to start his relationship with Ava again? "Haziel suggested it. It was a good suggestion."

"Who's Haziel?" Rosabella forced herself between him and Dee. "Was she the angel I saw here watching you?"

"She's a seraph," he said. "Ramiel's second."

"Where is Haziel?" Dee frowned and looked behind him.

Rosabella scowled at him. "And that's all she is?"

"Yes." He looked at Dee for help. Given how Rosabella was

behaving, no way in creation was he admitting to liking Haziel. His conscience tweaked as he thought about how he'd left her.

"Stop it, Rosabella." Dee's voice sounded tired and strained as she stared at her daughter. "We need to concentrate on getting Eddie back."

"Don't you think I know that?" Rosabella wailed. "Don't you think I spend every waking moment in torment about where she is?"

"Honestly, Bella, I haven't got a fucking clue what you think." Sighing, Dee turned and went back into the kitchen. She grabbed a beer from the fridge, popped the cap and handed it to Wrath. "Shade hasn't found her either." She got herself a beer and propped her hips against the counter. "And I don't know if it's related, but Bianca has disappeared."

"Bianca?" He propped his hips against the kitchen counter and let the bitter bite of hops slide down his throat. "Who the fuck is Bianca?"

"Bianca?" Rosabella squeaked from the hallway. "Who's that?"

"She's a member of the theatre group." Dee flitted a significant look in Rosabella's direction and he got it. There was more but she wouldn't say so in front of Rosabella.

Rosabella flounced into the kitchen. "I want a beer too."

Dee motioned him to follow her.

"Where are you going?" Rosabella yelled. "Eddie is my—our daughter—and if you're going to talk about her, I have a right to know."

Daniel appeared at the top of the stairs and took the situation in with one quick glance. "Rosabella." He strode into the kitchen. "I can see how upset you are. This must be awful for you."

Wrath tuned out the sound of Rosabella pouring her woes into a receptive ear.

"Bianca is…" Dee sipped her beer and glanced about them. "I didn't know it at first, but now things are starting to drop into place."

He didn't have time for games, but out of respect for Dee, he waited.

"She's our witch," Dee whispered. "She has to be. The one who performed the summoning. She showed up here a few months ago and knew all about the hell gate. At the time, she offered to help me, and I trusted her. She kept her mouth shut and even offered to keep an eye on Eddie while I was away." Eyes wide, Dee leaned closer. "But she was behind the *Macbeth* thing. She suggested the play at the board meeting. Only a witch would know about the curse and how to capitalize on it."

Wrath got it. "She wanted to activate the curse so she could summon one of us."

"Right." Dee shook her head. "I should have known better than to trust a stranger, but she guessed what Eddie was, and she seemed so sympathetic and promised to help me keep her hidden from the guardians." Her voice wobbled. "I thought she was my friend."

He knew all about trusting the wrong person, and as a hell prince, he had no excuses. The biggest regret of his eternal life continued to weep and wail in the kitchen. "Witches are too good at hiding their true purpose."

"But now she's disappeared, and you tell me so has Lucifer." Dee cleared her throat and took a long swallow of beer. "I don't believe in coincidences."

It was bad enough when he thought of Eddie in Lucifer's hands, but the idea of a witch having access to the kind of power Eddie could produce made his blood freeze. "Tell me everything you know."

He felt Ramiel's presence moments before the archangel thundered his name, "Wrath!"

Like a virulent STD, Ramiel materialized in front of him. "You're back."

"Yup." Wrath wasn't going to waste his time explaining himself to this gutter guzzler.

Ramiel nodded politely to Dee. "You didn't find Lucifer."

Something about his tone made Wrath pay better attention. "You already knew that."

"Raphael says he can sense him on the earth plane, but he can't get a lock on him." Ramiel leaned closer to him. "Your powers are restored."

"Disappointed?"

"Don't be churlish." Ramiel gave him a chiding glance. "Where is Haziel?"

That was going to take some explaining but not to this sock worm. "Haziel is safe." And if Ramiel had really given a crap about Haziel's wellbeing, he should never have sent her after him.

Ramiel's wings released in a whoosh. "Where is she?"

"I told you, she's safe." Wrath released his wings and let his rage bubble to the surface. Ramiel was the perfect target for his fear and frustration.

Stepping into him, almost chest to chest, Ramiel asked, his voice silky with menace, "Where is my seraph?"

"Where you sent her." Wrath could go for a full-on battle right now. "In hell."

Ramiel's fist shot toward his face, and Wrath caught it and held it. Power for power, they were a match, and a fight between them would be exactly what Wrath needed.

"Stop it." Gabriel strode out of Dee's bedroom.

Was Dee housing the combined hosts and hordes of heaven and hell in her and Eddie's tiny apartment?

Gabriel clapped her hands. "There will be no fighting on this plane."

"He left Haziel in hell." Ramiel kept up the pressure of his fist in Wrath's palm.

"And you should never have sent a seraph to do a task that clearly fell to you." Gabriel straightened her mauve pencil skirt over her hips. "Fighting is only a possibility because neither of you have stuck to doing what you should be doing."

Raguel followed behind her. "Is Haziel okay?" His concern was genuine, which was why Wrath deigned to answer him.

"I left her with Ava. She'll be fine, and Ava will keep her safe."

"Fetch her," Ramiel grated. "Or I will not be answerable for the consequences."

Gabriel pushed between them with a sniff. "You really do need to fetch her, Wrath. Section fourteen, subsection twelve of the code states quite clearly that no angel can exist in hell without a valid purpose." She tapped his chest. "And as you are currently here, Haziel has outstayed her welcome in hell."

He wasn't going to waste his breath telling them that retrieving Haziel was next on his to-do list, so he settled for sneering at them.

THIRTEEN

A bar in London

ACROSS THE CROWDED happy hour rush, the women clustered together giggling at some shared joke. Their cheeks were flushed with the combination of liquor, excitement, and ambient heat.

Like a miniature sun in the middle of the bar's solar system, they drew the men around them into their orbit. They pretended not to notice, but they knew. He could see it in their smug laughter, and their self-satisfied smirks.

Whores and vicious bitches. Every last one of them. Laughing at the men around them, laughing at him.

Too tight, revealing clothing pressed their flesh and presented it for display. Their faces were painted to betray men into thinking they were prettier than they were. Deceitful, calculating liars, all of them. The dark one drew his eye the most. Her mouth was painted glossy and pink. She pouted and preened, tossed her hair, and flashed her eyes at every man here. An open invitation.

Her gaze passed over him and moved on, as if she had assessed him and found him lacking. As if she thought she was too good for him.

She would pay for that, just like the last one. Her screams had been beautiful to hear. The warm gush of her blood over his hands had been the ultimate high, and he craved another fix, but he had to go slowly. He'd already made the news. They were calling him a serial killer, but he was so much more than that. He was the equalizer, the balancing force. A hint of glee had wriggled into his chest and lodged there when he'd seen his work televised. *It's me*, he had whispered at the screen. *Here I am. Catch me if you can.* But he couldn't abandon caution. Others like him had been caught by giving in to the thrill of the chase and the conquest.

"Evening." The bartender cleared away his used glass as he replaced his beer. "Nice to see you again."

The bartender remembering him was not good, but it was a different bartender from the one who had protected the first dead bitch, so he forced a smile. "Yeah. This is my local."

"Good to know." The bartender lingered a moment, his eyes on the group of women. Leaning his palms on the bar, he shook his head. "I've never seen them in here before."

"No?" He would need to find a new hunting ground, which was a pity. He had the routes around this pub all mapped out, the darker alleys, the shortcuts, even the abandoned row of houses he used to perform his cleansings. Of course, he moved the bodies once he'd purified them. Meticulous attention to detail kept him safe from sharp-eyed coppers and their DNA testing.

The bartender sneered. "That lot is trouble waiting to happen."

Yes, they were, but then nobody knew how much trouble but him. He was the center of the storm, the spinner of trouble, the controller of destinies, the sword of justice.

"Somebody should deal with them," the bartender said.

Shock held him immobile for a moment. It could be a trap. Had his arrogance tripped him up like so many before him?

The bartender's dark eyes met his, and for a moment there was a distinctive red flash across his irises. "But not here," he murmured. "You have been seen here once before."

His mouth dried, and he guzzled his beer before he dared speak again. "I don't know what you mean."

"You're right." The bartender laughed. "You don't know what I mean." He winked. "And I've never seen you here."

The brunette stood and yanked her tiny dress over her thick thighs. Before he had slit the first one's throat, he had used her body for what she had begged him for, begged all the men here. But only he was man enough to do what she truly craved.

She passed by him on her way to the loo, close enough for him to catch a waft of her cloying, sickly perfume.

The thrill of the chase beat like a war drum inside him.

From across the bar, the bartender gave him a tiny, secretive smile.

~

Somewhere in Africa.

FUCKING SNIVELING COWARDS, they surrounded him, hemmed him in, tried to clip his wings. They called themselves his ministers, but they were nothing more than oxpeckers feeding off his living carcass.

"Mr. President." His minister of defense mopped his shiny bald head with a paisley handkerchief. No, not oxpeckers, more like vultures. That handkerchief was Hermès and paid for by the chances he took, the liberties he normalized for them. All around them and outside this room, people lost the struggle for survival in squalor and this coward spent enough to feed three families for a year on a rag to mop his flop sweat. "This will be seen as an act of aggression."

"Yes." He held the vulture's gaze. Let them see his resolve, let them see he was like Shaka Zulu of old—relentless, determined, powerful.

The minister for internal affairs slammed his fist on the table. "This is madness."

Madness? He'd never been saner in his life. An entire continent peopled by bottom feeders and weak, corrupt bureaucrats, and his for the taking. Where others saw misery, he saw only opportunity.

"Mr. President." His new secretary leaned over and refilled his water glass. So quietly, he barely heard it, the woman whispered, "Slowly now."

She had arrived a week ago, with an impressive resume, and his staff had hired her immediately. Beautiful enough to be distracting with her liquid dark eyes and her glowing, smooth skin, he had dreamed of her every night since she had taken up her position. She was like this continent: alluring, compelling, and a mystery waiting for him to unravel. Yet she focused him and grounded him. Had it been only a week?

"I understand your concerns," he found himself saying to his ministers. "And I share them, but let me present the facts to you. The historical facts written by our people and not by the colonizers who sought to rape this land for all they could."

He hadn't noticed his secretary dropping the dossier in front of him, but he opened it now, "Next order of business…" The information poured into his brain and out his mouth.

The atmosphere in the conference room eased, and a few nervously relieved glances slid around the table. He took a mental note of each look. They would bend to his will. He would make sure of it.

His secretary looked at him over their heads and smiled. *Soon*, she mouthed.

~

A private basement in Vienna.

AND THERE SHE WAS, so beautiful she took her breath away. Up until this moment, she'd been half afraid the sketch was a myth. So simple, yet so evocatively powerful that the reclining woman called out to her. Here was femininity in its glory and mastery. The powerful sensuality of those few simply dashed lines made by a master across canvas had called to her across all these years, and now it was finally hers.

She wanted to stroke the long, graceful sweep of her thigh to her hip, caress the gentle slope of her shoulder to her long, willowy arm.

Her assistant hovered nearby, his breathing an annoyance in her ear. "Lovely, isn't it?"

No thanks to him. He had reported back failure after failure in his efforts to obtain this Degas. Finally, she had stepped in and used the money earned from the four animals she had married and buried to get what she desired.

"And she's all yours." The tone in her assistant's voice had her turning and looking at him. Gone was the vaguely patronizing assumption of obsequiousness. He looked different as well, standing taller, his shoulders back, his stare as he held hers bold.

"Yes." Perhaps she had underestimated the elitist little toad. "I stepped in after you failed."

He inclined his head and smiled at her. "It was a pleasure to watch you work, madam."

Had she imagined the flash of color across his irises? Work, such an interesting word and so open to interpretation. It had taken a few well-placed enquiries on her behalf by a firm whose name nobody dared ask to discover the leverage she needed. That leverage was currently safely ensconced in an apartment in Zurich and would be released once she was sure she had made her acquisition cleanly and with no repercussions. Even the most avid of art collectors had a weak spot, and in this case, it was the bastard's children.

Of course, her assistant had been part of the distasteful business and the only loose end in a flawlessly executed plan. She despised the process of finding a new assistant. Why could people not remain loyal like they had in the days of her infamous ancestors?

"Shall we?" He motioned the artwork.

Earlier he had placed the necessary items to transport an object of such value out of this collection and into hers on the table behind her. She had been surprised by his forethought at the time. She did not let any of her thoughts show as she nodded.

She had not noticed before how attractive her assistant was. But she noticed now as his shirt defined the toned planes of his shoulders and back as he removed the artwork from the wall and laid it carefully in the traveling crate.

"She really is quite exquisite." He stepped back and studied the sketch. "I can see why you wanted her so much. She is the very essence of feminine mystique."

To hear her thoughts so neatly phrased surprised her for a moment, and she nodded. "Yes."

"And as such belongs with like." He flashed her a slightly mischievous smile as he began fastening the crate.

It had been years since a man had flirted with her, and she was slow to recognize the signs. His impudence both offended and intrigued her. "You risk much."

He didn't even pretend to misunderstand and chuckled. "I risk much for much." Straightening, he looked right at her. "Together, there is nothing we cannot accomplish."

Somewhere in the US

Life was about defining moments. The trick was in recognizing those moments when they presented themselves. But he saw his, like a neon sign blinking across the sky. In the days following him totaling the imposter's car in his parking space, he had held his breath, waiting for the call or the knock on the door that would announce he'd been caught. They hadn't come, and days had stretched into weeks. People in the offices around him had whispered and wondered about what could have happened until a new juicy office tidbit had snatched their attention away. He had gotten away with his vengeance, and now his path had become clear to him.

His immediate superior was jawing at him again. "We need to manage this outcome." The woman's helmet hair never moved, even as disturbed as she was. "This has the potential to go viral, and we don't want that."

"Indeed," he murmured. Another politician caught between the thighs of a woman he shouldn't have been anywhere near. It was all so damn tedious, all so pitifully predictable.

"I've prepared a statement." Helmet hair produced yet another folder from beneath her armpit and handed it to him. "Go through this with him, point out the possible pitfalls."

He nodded and looked interested, as if he hadn't done this a thousand times before.

"I've also prepared a list of questions and answers we can expect from the press." Yet another dossier appeared from the armpit maw. He was halfway convinced there was the entrance to a parallel dimension beneath that YSL suit. "Make sure you go over them carefully with him. I don't need to remind you what happened with the last incident's press conference."

Incident. Almost like a bus crashed into a streetlight. It hinted at something that was absolutely avoidable. Between their senator's libido and his staggering Napoleon complex, disasters like the one they were currently navigating were a certainty.

He had been born a forgettable man for a reason. Until he'd received his call to action in the parking lot, he'd never understood. He'd been resentful of his endlessly gray nothing life. But now his blinders were off, and his path illuminated in front of him. He would bring them all down. Quietly, unobtrusively, working away beneath their noses, he would right their wrongs and expose their rot.

Helmet hair, he refused to use her given name in the privacy of his thoughts, straightened her suit jacket. "I'm sorry I can't be here, but POTUS calls."

Marcia–there he'd said it–grinned smugly at the perceived glory of her new position. She almost skipped out of the office, which given her age, seemed obscene.

He looked at the dossiers in his hands and crossed to the shredder. Turns out, after a lifetime of always doing the right thing, he had a taste for anarchy that he loved to indulge. The caption on his high school yearbook: *Most Likely to own a Minivan by Thirty* no longer stung. Little gray men moved the wheels of power, and nobody ever looked at them when the giant engine ground to a halt—merely a harmless cog, a nothing, an inconsequential part of a greater whole.

FOURTEEN

"Oh my." Ava lounged on her throne and popped another chocolate whatever into her pouty mouth. "I don't see you for years, and now, here you are again." The grin she threw him made Wrath want to break shit.

After his confrontation with Ramiel, followed by a lecture from Gabriel, and then a quiet conversation with Dee, he was back in the avarice demesne. He didn't tell Ramiel and Gabriel that he had always intended to come back and fetch Haziel. They were so fucking annoying bitching at him, that he'd decided against it. Dee, however, was a different matter. As the grandmother of his child, he owed her respect and consideration, and so he'd let her in on the truth. He had always intended to fetch Haziel.

Still, he didn't feel like dancing a jig as Ava strummed her fiddle of resentment. He didn't have the inclination, and Eddie for damn sure didn't have the time. "Cut the crap, Ava. I'm here for Haziel."

"Haziel?" Ava frowned and tapped a forefinger against her chin. "Remind me who that is."

Wrath breathed deep and reached for his tiny store of patience. He needed to grab Haziel and leave. Lucifer wouldn't wait for Ava to finish playing, and he couldn't bear to think what was happening to Eddie right this minute. "You know exactly who she is."

Rapace stepped closer to her throne. Aside from the creepy orange eyes, he was a good-looking bastard with bronze muscles barely concealed by the scraps of white fabric he wore. "I believe Haziel is a seraph, your grace," he said to Ava as if Wrath wasn't standing right there. "From Ramiel's host. Pretty thing with big green eyes and lovely skin. Sweet as a peach."

If that fucker had laid one finger on Haziel, Wrath would end him. "Where is she?"

Ava looked confused and blinked at her second. "Can you answer that?"

"Alas." Rapace laid a hand on his overdeveloped chest muscles. Despite being a pretty fucker, Rapace could swing a sword like a master. Not as good as his Vexia, but certainly skillful enough for Wrath not to completely dismiss him. "I lost track of her earlier this morning. She mentioned something about being inconsolable." He uttered a theatrical gasp. "You don't think she might have..."

"Don't even think that, Rapace." Apparently, Ava was not immune to amateur theatricals as she clasped her hands in front of her chest and blinked at her second. When Wrath found his daughter, he'd make sure to mention they had two prime actors right in this demesne. Their talents would be put to much better use for the Paradise Players. The need to find Eddie lashed through him and reminded him he was wasting time dealing with Ava and her crap.

Ava fastened her gaze back on him. "What could be so bad as to drive an angel to such dire straits?"

Clasping his hands in front of him, Rapace lowered his head and gave it a sad shake. "Abandonment, rejection, desert—"

"All right, Ava." Wrath knew when he was outmaneuvered. Learning the right time to retreat was as much a part of winning the battle as knowing when to attack. "You've had your fun. I'm here to fetch Haziel and be on my way."

Clearly not done with him yet, Ava turned soulful eyes on Rapace. "Tell me what overset her so?"

"Her nails." Rapace heaved a sigh and shook his head. "Our darling seraph was horrified to discover the color did not compliment her skin tones."

Wrath suppressed the desire to bellow. His back burned where his wings were demanding to be released. He needed to retrieve Haziel and then get back to finding Eddie. But losing his shit wouldn't work with Ava. She had legions at her beck and call, and here in her demesne, she was virtually unassailable.

"Tragic." Ava shuddered.

"Enough," Wrath spat. "Just get her for me, and we'll be on our way."

Rapace managed to look passably apologetic. "Regrettably, hell prince, that is not within my purview."

"Then make it so," he snapped. Ava was one thing, but her dancing princess of a demon was another entirely. He wouldn't tolerate disrespect from that flashy popinjay.

"Oh, Wrath." Ava giggled. "You've made some fairly basic mistakes here."

He remained silent. Ava would have her say, and things would move faster if she did.

"Firstly, you mistake us for thinking we have the authority

to make Haziel do anything she doesn't want to do." She straightened on her throne and grinned at him. "When you made her a guest of this court, you gave her control of when she leaves." Leaning forward, she gave him a mischievous wink. "And to tell you the truth, I rather like having her here."

He ground his molars hard enough to make his jaw ache. Ava wanted him to lose his temper, and he refused to give her the satisfaction. "She's outstayed her welcome in hell. Ramiel has recalled her."

"Ramiel?" She went with that annoying chin tap again and turned a mystified glance on Rapace.

Rapace cleared his throat and leaned solicitously closer to her. "Archangel. Counterbalance to Satanus. Blond, green eyes, proverbial stick up the arse."

"Ah, yes." Ava clapped her hands like a delighted toddler. "Now I remember." Her face hardened. "Arrogant bastard who thinks he has the right to shift a female supernatural along the chess board of his asinine games."

Rapace grinned at Wrath smugly. "Indeed. It seems to be an epidemic."

"You've made your point." Wrath tried reason. It seemed to work for others of his kind. "I shouldn't have left her here. And Ramiel shouldn't have sent her with me. Lesson learned."

"Really?" Ava cocked her head. "You think it's that easy?"

Rapace clicked his tongue and shook his head at him.

"Do you want to know what I think, Wrath?" Ava leaned back on her throne and made a song and dance of crossing her shapely legs over the armrest.

He'd bite. "What do you think, Ava?"

"I think you've only begun to learn your lesson." She grinned, catlike and triumphant. "And I've only begun to have fun with you."

WRATH PACED the limits of the bedchamber a smirking Rapace had shown him to. After her last pronouncement, Ava had stood and sashayed out of her throne room. His bellow for her to get back to him and finish their conversation had fallen on deaf ears.

Rapace had left him with instructions to change for dinner. With the night now upon them, he would be better to wait until morning before he left. Demons came out with the dark, and Haziel would make a shining beacon for them. Three more demons entered in Rapace's wake and poured him a bath, then filled it with lavender bath salts. The final insult was the pale pink satin knee breeches and shirt that had been laid on the bed for him to wear to dinner.

Ava was relishing every minute of this. Granted, he shouldn't have abandoned Haziel here, but he'd only done so for her own good. He couldn't have taken her into Lucifer's demesne and kept her safe. As it had turned out, he needn't have worried, but he hadn't known that at the time he'd left.

He would explain all this to Haziel when he saw her. And being the extremely reasonable angel that she was, Haziel would understand precisely why he'd done what he'd done.

In the meanwhile, Ava was doing everything she could to stop that conversation from happening.

Stepping out of his bath, he wrapped a towel around his hips and walked into the bedroom. Evening light glinted off the satin of the outfit Ava had chosen for him. She really should know better than to think he would calmly submit to being dressed up like a doll for her to play with. Unfortunately, a quick survey of the room revealed that his clothes had been removed, and he was left with pale pink breeches, a towel, or naked as his options.

The image of Ava's gloating face if she saw him in those breeches decided matters for him, and he tucked his towel firmly around his waist and sat down to wait.

A soft gong sounded through the palace, and Rapace opened the door.

Eyes sparkling with amusement, he took in Wrath's towel. "The breeches didn't fit?"

"I will rip your arms off and beat you with them."

"Oh, my." Rapace chuckled and gave him a toe to top eye fucking. "But you do look delicious like that as well. Our mistress will enjoy this ensemble even more than the pink satin."

"And then I'm going to tear your cock and balls off and stuff them down your throat."

Rapace chuckled and bowed. "Dinner is served."

One day, Wrath would make Rapace regret every smirk and every drawled insult, but now was not that time. He motioned the door. "Lead on."

Arrayed in a sparkling black gown that clung to each dip and swell of her figure, Ava greeted him in a small private dining hall. "Good evening, Wrath." She motioned the table. "I have taken the liberty of having all your favorites prepared."

He should have known better than to expect Haziel would attend dinner, but he masked his frustration well. "Very kind of you."

"Have a seat." Ava motioned a chair with an elegant wave of her hand.

Eight courses later, and Wrath had to loosen his towel and thank his foresight for not squeezing into those delicate knee breeches. Through the interminable meal, Ava kept up a flow of inconsequential chatter. Any time he attempted to bring up Haziel, Ava neatly sidestepped his enquiry and kept right on nattering nonsense.

By the time dessert was served, with an accompanying wine and all its pomp, he was ready to rip the table apart with his bare hands.

Grinning all the way, Rapace returned him to his chamber.

Wrath paced the room as his mind worked. Ava had had her fun. It was time to end the game. Somewhere in her palace, she was keeping Haziel, and he'd played nice for as long as he could. Eddie needed him, and he was wasting fucking time, time none of them had.

Haziel was of Ramiel's host, right. And that meant he could tune into Ramiel's energy and find her.

Opening that part of his being, Wrath searched the palace for traces of Ramiel.

A clear signature pinged across his awareness to the left and Wrath tightened his bath towel around his hips and prepared to launch into battle.

ALL THINGS CONSIDERED, Haziel was having a lovely time in Ava's palace. The food was exceptional, and always available via hot and cold running demon, the company delightful, the accommodations sumptuous, and tomorrow Ava had promised to show her the rare collection of extinct species Ava had collected and preserved in her demesne.

Ava had a side hustle in preserving species that were about to go extinct on earth. Amongst her rare collection she had dodos, quaggas, and a Tasmanian tiger. According to Ava, she kept them safely breeding here until such time as earth could be trusted to respect its natural environment again.

She'd felt Wrath arrive this morning and had been expecting a visit from him. Still, she did want to see those rare animals, and Ava and she had a spa day planned for the day after that. Haziel had never had a pedicure or a hot stone massage, but she was sure she'd like them.

As Wrath's energy approached her suite, she took a long sip of her strawberry daiquiri. Working for Ramiel didn't allow any time for indulgences, and she was beginning to discover that even angels had needs. Still, if Wrath was here now, she couldn't in good conscience delay him any longer. Messing with him a bit, though, that she was looking forward to.

The pounding on her door was typically Wrath—demanding, impatient, and impossible to ignore. Still, she didn't get up from her comfortable velvet chaise with its beautiful view of the fountain garden. Classical music drifted in with the soft evening breeze. Water danced in the fountains to the tune of the music. It was all rather splendid and definitely relaxing.

She suppressed a sigh as she called, "Come in, Wrath."

"There you are." He appeared in her door like a summer thunderstorm—all force and implacable nature.

Haziel took another sip of her cocktail. "Here I am."

"Angel?" A demon appeared at her elbow. "Would you like another?"

Who wouldn't love being here? "I would." She smiled at Covet. The demons here were so helpful, it was hard to remember why angels had been at war with them since the beginning of time. "That would be lovely."

Covet twitched his thick, unruly red eyebrows. "Or perhaps you would like to sample a mango daiquiri. Our mixologist is a master with the mango."

She did like mango. Another thing she'd discovered since Wrath had abandoned her here. As she would be leaving soon, she said, "I would love to try the mango."

"Very good." Covet scuttled off, leaving a very disgruntled looking hell prince glowering at her.

Dressed in nothing but a short bath towel, Wrath was

almost a better view than the dancing fountains. Unless she could persuade him to dance, and then it might be a fair competition. "Do you dance?"

"What?" He frowned at her. "No, I don't fucking dance."

"Pity." No contest then, the fountains won.

Wrath took a slow, careful breath and stalked over to her. He had lovely, muscular legs, and the towel hit him mid bulging thigh. Maybe she'd overestimated the appeal of the dancing fountains. He wiggled his fingers at her. "Enough, Haziel. We're leaving at first light. I need to find Eddie."

Covet arrived with her mango daiquiri, and a charcuterie board. Creamy, mature cheeses, ripe figs, pickles, fresh honey, warm bread—Wrath could do what he liked. She wasn't going anywhere. Not at this particular moment anyway. "No." She took her time selecting the right combination of cheese and olive. "You are welcome to leave, but I am a guest here."

"You're an angel," he snapped. "And you have outstayed your welcome."

Ava hadn't said anything like that. "Did Ava say so?"

"No." His jaw went tight enough to break rocks. "I did, and Ramiel did."

"Ramiel knows I'm here?" Her heart gave a little flutter. Ramiel knew she was here, and he must be worried about her to demand she return. She sipped her drink. The mango was delicious. She might prefer it to the strawberry. "He's right, you know." She gestured to where Covet had disappeared. "The mango is very special."

"Haziel," he growled in a way that sent sensation skittering over her skin. "You need to come with me. My daughter is still missing, and we haven't found Lucifer."

"You left me here." She hated pointing out the obvious. Not really. It was rather satisfying. "You left me here where anything could have happened to me. And now—"

"I left you with Ava. You were perfectly safe." His gaze flicked over her clothing. "And clearly, very comfortable."

"Oh, yes." She looked down at her floaty, gauzy outfit. She'd taken to copying these from Ava. A cropped top left her midriff bare to the cooling breezes, and the overlapping panels of her long skirt revealed her legs. "Do you like it?"

Wrath gave her legs a searing look. "Don't ask stupid questions, Haziel."

"So, that's a yes?" After her embarrassing confession he'd forced out of her about his ass, she was due a little payback.

"That's a yes," he said. "But we still need to go."

"Sit down." She motioned to a nearby comfortably armchair. Night was not a safe time to travel in hell with roving demon hordes most active and powerful in the dark. "You're looming over me in a very disagreeable manner."

He raised that brow again but took a seat.

"Charcuterie?"

"No." His towel created a couple of minor difficulties, and he solved those by shoving it between his thighs.

"Have a drink." She studied his sculpted and muscular body without bothering to hide it. She'd already admitted to liking his form. "You're more muscular than Ramiel."

He sighed. "I don't want charcuterie or a drink. What I want is for both of us to get on with searching for my daughter. And you're drunk."

"Tipsy." She needed to clarify the drunk part, but he was right about their needing to find Eddie, Still, she could torture him a little more. "I am pleasantly buzzed."

"Right," he drawled. He looked a bit grumpy. "And when did you see Ramiel naked?"

For Ramiel's sake she needed to clear up any misapprehensions he was forming in his fertile mind. "I have worked under...I mean...with Ramiel for a long time. I have seen him sparring many times. And other things." She didn't feel like going into too many details, and especially not about how Ramiel liked to hold some of his meetings with her when he was in the bath. Those were particularly torturous for her, because unlike now, when she didn't have to hide her perusal of Wrath, when she was with Ramiel, she kept her eyes strictly on her papers.

Covet appeared with a piña colada and handed it to Wrath.

He took it with a growl and tossed the bright pink umbrella and hibiscus blossom on the floor.

"Fine, we'll play this your way for now, but only because I don't want to travel in the dark," he said and took a careful sip of his drink. He pulled a face, but she got the sense he did it more for effect than anything else. Who didn't like pina coladas? Coconut, pineapple, white rum—yummy.

"You're leaving in the morning," she said and drained her daiquiri.

"At first light." He fixed her with a gimlet stare. "So, you have your fun but I'm off to find my daughter and you can join me or explain to Ramiel why he has to get you out of Ava's demesne." He smirked. "You might also need to explain to him at the same time why you abandoned your mission to keep an eye on me."

Check-mate. Game over.

Covet reappeared.

"No." Wrath glowered at him. "She doesn't need another drink."

"Yes, I do." Haziel resented the end to her fun. She was also not enjoying the way he was taking charge of her and her drinking. "You abandoned me," she snapped. "You don't get to arrive here and start telling me what to do."

"I didn't abandon you."

"Yes, you did."

"Rosé All Day?" Her favorite demon smiled.

Just the thing. "Yes!"

"Haziel!" Wrath surged to his feet. "You have a job to do here. And that doesn't include getting shitfaced on cocktails and lounging around in skimpy outfits."

"You said you liked it."

He tossed his glass over the balcony and stomped over to her chaise. It was all rather thrilling with his dark, broody good looks and delicious muscles.

"We are leaving," he said. "In the morning." Leaning down, he put his face close to hers. "And don't mistake me for Ramiel. Next time you look at me like you want to touch, I'm going to take you up on the offer."

FIFTEEN

Sophia wanted to share her good news, but with Dee so worried about Eddie, she was forced to hug it to herself. She'd auditioned and been offered the part of Cecily. Peter had said she was a natural, and even Lillian had admitted she had talent.

If she'd known she would love acting so much, she would have done something about it centuries ago. All that time and all those wonderful parts that she hadn't played. But she was going to make up for lost time now. Gabriel would have a shit fit, but Sophia didn't care. Other supernaturals broke the rules with impunity and got nothing more than a slap on the wrist. She was going to act, and the rest of the heavenly host could get twisted about it.

"Uriel—I beg your pardon—Sophia." Daniel hurried down the corridor toward her. His clean-cut, handsome face wore a worried expression. "I've been monitoring the seals."

"You can do that?" The guardians had never admitted to being able to monitor what happened in hell.

Daniel flushed. "Yes, I'm not supposed to tell you but, in the circumstances, I think some of the rules need bending."

Exactly what she had been thinking. "The news is not good?"

"No." Daniel held up his phone and showed her seven bars of light. All of them either red or orange. "Each bar is one of the seals. Wrath is the most stable, lust still the worst, but avarice and pride aren't looking pretty either. I have a theory all the disruptions in hell are only adding to the problem."

"The red means danger?" Sophia studied the flickering lights.

"Yes." Daniel pointed. "The hell princes are going to get more unpredictable the more the seals deteriorate." He put his phone away. "Have you heard from Shade?"

"Not for a couple of days." And he was out there in the earth realm, broadcasting unadulterated lust as he searched for Eddie.

Daniel stared at his phone and frowned. "I understand what he's doing and why, but the situation is getting more precarious."

"Oh, dear." Her news took a definite back seat to Daniel's.

He put his phone away and looked at her. "Can you do anything?"

"I could find him and see how he's doing." Shade hated being checked on. "However, we need to get him back to hell where he can cause the minimum amount of damage to humans and try to contain his seal."

"Will he go?" Daniel chewed on his bottom lip.

"Not without Eddie." Sophia shared a concerned look with Daniel. She understood how Shade felt, but it was time to insist he went home.

Daniel nodded. "Maybe try to talk to him?"

Not that it would do much good, but she nodded. "I can sense him on this plane. I'll find him and see what I can do."

"Thank you." Daniel smiled at her, a nice smile, warm and inviting. "Oh, and congratulations on your part. You're going to be wonderful."

~

SOPHIA FOUND Shade in a crappy motel room with a bottle of cheap whisky tucked under his arm. He looked terrible with dark smudges under his bloodshot eyes. Actually, he didn't look terrible at all. He looked desperate and dangerous, and it was all alarmingly sexy.

"Sophia." He sensed her before she spoke. "What are you doing here?"

"Looking for you." She examined the bedspread for vermin before perching gingerly beside him. She needed to tell him about his seal, but her heart ached for him. Even though he was in this state over a female who was not her. "No luck?"

"The hounds are closing in on her," he said and swigged his whisky. He grimaced before swallowing. "They sensed her before I last called Dee. But just when we think we've got a lock on her, it goes dark again." He turned tortured gray eyes on her. "They're torturing her, Sophia, and with all my powers I can do nothing."

She pried the bottle from his fingers. Going full human in a crisis wasn't going to help the situation. "You don't know they're torturing her."

"Yes, I do." He watched her put the bottle on the nightstand with a dull gaze. "She can visit me in her dreams."

"Oh, Shade." Her heart constricted in her chest. She hated seeing him like this. It would have been easier if he didn't know how much trouble his Eddie was in. "Can I help?"

"Not unless you have some heaven magic that can find her."

The next words she spoke smarted, but she said them anyway, "You love her."

"Yes." He nodded. "She is my everything."

She dearly wished she could do something for him, but she had no heavenly tricks up her sleeve. "I have more bad news."

"The seals?" He reached for the bottle, then dropped his hand before making contact.

"They're worse than ever."

He nodded and clasped his hands in front of him. "I know. I can feel them."

"Then you know you're a danger to the humans who encounter you." She didn't want to kick him when he was down, but they both dealt in harsh realities.

"I know." He scrubbed at the stubble on his jaw. "I am doing my best to stay as far away from humans as I can, but it's not perfect. We both know that."

"Yes." They did know that, and their job was to protect humans from the emotions the seals guarded, not rampantly spread them.

He made eye contact with her, his gaze harsh and angry. "And you're here to insist I go back to hell."

"That's what I'm supposed to be doing here." She couldn't do it. Couldn't add to his anguish. "Instead, I'm going to stay with you. Mitigate the effect as much as I can and help you find your Eddie."

He blinked at her. "You'd do that for me?"

"Yes." And she'd catch all kinds of backlash for it, but they'd been partners of a sort for longer than the earth realm had been in existence.

Cocking his head, he studied her. "Even with the way you feel?"

That he knew startled her, and heat climbed her cheeks. It shouldn't surprise her. He was lust, and any romantic feelings toward him would be clear as day for him to see. "Even with that."

"Thank you," he whispered. "And if it hadn't been for Eddie, maybe…"

"Asmodeus." Her laugh felt like splinters through her heart. "We've never lied to each other before. Let's not start now." She stood. "Now get in the shower, because you stink, and let's get going. I have to be at rehearsal on Wednesday night."

EDDIE HELD BACK her tears as the door shut behind Ashe and Calix. They'd come to drain her powers again, and they'd left her wrung out and sick. She wanted to puke but couldn't even find the energy to turn her head.

Shade told her he was coming to find her, but night after night she left her dream to wake up in this metal box again.

She wanted to cry, but she wouldn't give them the satisfaction. The locks clicked into place on the door. First the one near the bottom, one close to the center, and then the bolt slid into place. Being in this silent, sterile space had honed her hearing. She waited for the deep pitched clank of the final lock.

They'd left the water bottle in her hand, and Eddie raised it to her mouth and took a careful sip. Any faster, and she would throw it up again. Ask her how she knew that. Sitting in her damp, vomit-stained sweatshirt until they brought her food and she could demand a change of clothing provided enough incentive to control her raging thirst and drink slowly.

She didn't know what time they brought her meals, but her body had grown accustomed, and her belly would remind her before Ashe appeared with her next meal. She only ever saw Ashe, Calix, and Casper. More often Ashe. Maybe she had early Stockholm syndrome because she was even starting to look forward to her chats with Ashe. Sometimes he stayed while she finished her meal. It was probably more a relief from the terrifying monotony of her days as she waited for them to come and drain her powers.

Something whispered at the back of her mind. A thing that was not the same as the endless sameness since she'd been here.

And she'd read that Stockholm syndrome wasn't even a thing. Not a syndrome so much as an emotional response of a captive to a capturer. She risked another small sip of water. As the water eased into her stomach, she catalogued her pain. She passed the hours after they'd drained her power by watching her pain recede. Initially, it felt like her entire body had been run over by a truck. Then the feeling receded first from her extremities and then traveled to her larger muscle groups. The pounding in her head was always the last to release its grip on her.

They didn't use the gas anymore before they came to drain her. She would like to believe it was a kindness, but deep down she knew it was because she was losing the will to keep fighting, and each time they drained her, they left her weaker than before.

That wrong thing pinged through her mind again. She stared at the solid metal walls, the sink and plain faucet, the toilet. Everything was much as it had been. Not a speck of dust marred the shining surfaces. The faucet didn't drip.

And yet, still, there was something. Something different. Something amiss. Something missing.

The agony had receded enough that she could roll her

ankles and wrists. Easing to her side, she replayed the last encounter.

Ashe had come in first. Her relief at seeing him had quickly been displaced by dread as Calix followed behind him. Then came the pendant that they placed over her head. The moment the crystal made contact with her, the pain started.

Calix's eyes gleamed as he watched her power drain into the amulet. At first, she'd tried not to scream, but she didn't even have the energy for that anymore. The louder she screamed, the more Calix seemed to enjoy it.

She dared not look at Ashe. If she saw signs that he enjoyed it, her one relief from this place would be tainted.

Once it was done, Calix lifted the pendant from around her neck and tucked it inside the leather pouch. He'd leave then.

As he often did, Ashe stayed for a while. Like before, he'd bent down and uncapped the water bottle. He'd lightly squeezed her fingers as he'd place it in her clasp.

Then he'd left, and she'd done as she always did and counted the locks.

The locks! The fucking locks!

She'd heard three clicks but not four. What did that mean? Nothing.

There were still three locks between her and freedom. Three locks keeping her confined in this miserable place. Each time they drained her, it hurt more, and it took her longer to recover. The time was approaching when she would no longer be able to recover and then what? She lay on her side, willing her body to recover, unable to move yet and stared at the door.

The fourth lock hadn't turned. That had to mean something, because it was all she had.

CHAPTER
SIXTEEN

Wrath woke with his heart beating like a war drum and blood surging through his veins. Rage pounded inside his chest, and he wanted to tear the world asunder. Blood surged to his muscles, and his wings ached for release.

Shit! His seal was weakening again, and he could feel the effects even in Ava's demesne.

Breathing deep, he wrestled it under control and stepped through the double doors to the balcony attached to his chamber.

Dawn was still hours away, and the need to act scratched at him. Fury prowled beneath his skin like a hungry predator demanding he let it out to hunt and gorge itself. His Eddie needed him, yet he waited here for Ava to stop playing her capricious games with him and for Haziel to sober up and join him. He could do as Haziel asked and leave her here. The moment the idea popped into his head, he ripped it aside. Haziel had come here with him, and she would leave with him.

It was because he didn't feel like the shitshow if he arrived on earth without her. Sure, let him continue to believe that was the reason. It beat the alternative, which was the primal insistence within him that they were now connected.

And that was pathetically stupid. Haziel was a seraph, not merely part of Ramiel's host, but his second. Seconds were vital and chosen for their strength. If there ever came a time when an archangel or hell prince wanted to pass on from this existence, they could transfer their power to their second. It had to be done willingly and didn't happen automatically on the death of the higher being, but it was an out for beings who might grow weary with their endless existences. There was no way she was now, nor could ever be, his. Still, her tawny skin beneath that floaty bit of nothing she'd been wearing last night rose in his mind—much as it had for most of the night. Haziel was beautiful and so very tempting. And she was far from immune to him. It all provided too much temptation.

Wrath pounded his fist on the balcony and got grim satisfaction when the wrought iron bent beneath his blow.

With his seal weakening again, the need to act became imperative. His emotions were skewing inside him and driving him to violence. The only way to control his urges was through action.

A fresh wave of fury washed over him, and Wrath threw back his head and bellowed.

He needed to act now. Making short work of getting dressed, he kicked open his door and charged into the corridor.

"Ava!" His voice reverberated off the domed ceiling. "Ava! Where the fuck are you?"

Wings beat the air, and there she was. Her eyes glittered with obsidian fury as she closed on him. "Wrath! You dare disturb the peace of my palace."

The air charged with menace as they faced each other.

"Leave," Ava hissed.

Wrath released his wings. "Not without Haziel."

~

"Angel." Covet stood by her bed and stared at her.

She blinked at the predawn view outside the window. "No cocktail, thank you. Not now."

"No, angel." His fork tongue shot out and he licked his lips. "You must come and stop them."

"Stop—"

A massive shout resounded through the palace, and then the sound of big things shattering.

"The hell princes." Covet's gaze shot toward her door. "They are fighting, and they will tear the palace down if they don't stop."

More crashing and thudding, and it felt like the entire building shook. "Which hell princes?" She stumbled out of bed and hunted for a robe. "Is Lucifer here?"

"No, angel." Covet held her pale yellow robe out to her. "He is not here. It is the mistress and Wrath."

Haziel stared at him, aware that her mouth had popped open, and she was gaping. "Are you sure?"

"Yes, mistress." Covet shook her robe to hurry her along. "The seals are weakening, and their tempers have flared. You need to control them."

"I can't control them." Haziel slipped into her robe. Fighting hell princes were way out of her weight class. She considered sending for Ramiel.

A thud reverberated through the floor, and then two more. It sounded like they were about to bring the walls down around everyone's ears.

Covet held her slippers out to her. "You must. You must use your angelic power to make them stop, or they will end us all."

Surely, they wouldn't...well, Wrath might. Who knew what that hell prince could do in the grips of his temper. But Ava—

"Wrath!" Ava roared, her voice barely recognizable through the battle lust pulsing through it.

Perhaps, Ava might. "I'm not an archangel." Stomach in knots, Haziel followed the demon to her door. Ramiel should be here, and from the sounds of it, Michael was needed to take charge of Ava. "I can't stop them."

"They will end us all." Covet tugged at her hand. "You have Ramiel's power, right?"

"Well." She followed him down the hall, the sounds of the battle growing louder as they went. "Sort of, but it's watered down."

Covet nodded. "I understand. We are the same with Mammon's power. But we are of her and not her counterbalance."

"We need Michael and Ramiel." Haziel didn't know how to get them to respond from here. Since she'd been in hell, she'd been unable to contact Ramiel at all.

Covet shook his head and tugged harder on her hand. "No time."

An enormous crash punctuated his statement and Haziel quickened her pace until she was running.

Demons stood in clusters along the hallways as they passed, whispering and flinching as each new sound reached them.

The doors to the throne room had collapsed into the grandiose foyer. As Haziel ran down the stairs, dust and fine particles of marble clogged the air and limited her visibility.

Wrath roared and another massive smash followed.

Then Ava made a sound so feral Haziel's skin prickled.

Glass smashed, and a marble pillar crashed to the ground. The roof creaked ominously.

Her slippers crunched over broken glass, marble, stone, and crystal as she reached the throne room doors.

Ava and Wrath were locked hand to hand as they hovered in the air, both of them easily ten feet tall. Wing feathers floated in the air like confetti at a parade. Both hell princes' eyes glowed red, and they bore bloody marks from their conflict.

They would crush her like a bug.

"Here goes nothing." Haziel sent a fervent wish to the part of her brain connected to Ramiel and released her wings. Maybe he would miss her when she was gone and regret the times he'd left her love unrequited. She hovered close to the pair. "Stop it. You need to stop."

The fighting hell princes pivoted in the air. Some grappling part hit Haziel and sent her careening through the air and into the wall. Her back hit the wall. The breath was knocked out of her, and pain seared through her wings.

Covet was there, helping her to stand. "Are you all right?"

"No." Haziel staggered to her feet.

A block of masonry crashed into the floor not three inches from her, and she leapt out of the way.

Putting every ounce of her Ramiel power into her voice, she reached deep within for her power well and bellowed, "STOP!"

Miraculously, they did both glance at her.

"Cease." Her voice caused plaster dust to rain from the ceiling.

"Angel," Ava snarled. "You are in the wrong place."

That stung, even though Haziel knew Ava was lost to battle lust. "Ava?" She softened her tone. "It's me. Haziel. You invited me to stay."

Ava blinked at her. Some of the red draining from her eyes.

"Wrath." Haziel fluttered closer to him. Massive and pulsing with power as he was now, he could rip her wings from her and dismember her in seconds. "Please, Wrath. You need to stop fighting."

"Haziel," he growled and launched himself at her.

Huge hands fastened around her shoulders, bruising her arms, and Haziel whimpered, "Please."

She'd never been frightened of Wrath before, but as he was now, he was terrifying.

"Wrath," Ava said, her voice no longer sounding like it came from the depth of depravity. "Wrath. Don't hurt her."

Wrath flinched and glanced down at his hands. With a yell, he released her and shot away across the room.

Haziel tapped into Ramiel's calm tranquility and tried to send it through the throne room. It hit the raging emotions of Ava and Wrath and dissipated.

The hell princes circled each other again, teeth bared and eyes gleaming.

"No." Haziel wouldn't consider herself a brave angel, which is why she didn't think about it as she launched herself between them. Holding out her hands, she tried again. "You need to stop. You're not yourselves. It's the seals. They're making you do things you wouldn't normally do."

"It's working, angel," Covet hissed from the door. "Keep talking."

And Haziel did. It was like standing between a tsunami and a towering cliff and words poured out of her. "The seals are weakening, and they're ramping up your emotions. You are not yourselves. You actually like each other. And you both like me. At least, you both seem to like me, and if you don't stop glaring at each other you're going to fight again. I'll be caught in the middle, and you'll both end me. I don't want to end. I'm a relatively young angel. As angels go. I have so much more I want to do before my time comes. And if I end here in hell, I don't know what will happen—"

"Haziel." Wrath took her by the shoulders, his touch gentle. "Stop."

"Nope." She screwed her eyes shut and gave every drop of Ramiel power she had to keep them apart. "If I stop talking, you're going to start fighting again."

"Haziel," Ava this time. "Open your eyes. We're calmer."

She dared to crack her lids. They were back on the ground, and both hell princes had receded to a more normal size. The throne room was a shambles, and both hell princes were bloodied and sweating.

Wrath gently stroked the flesh of her upper arms. "Did I do that?" He was looking at the red marks on her arms with real regret.

Haziel nodded. "But you were not yourself. You were in the midst of battle lust."

"I lost control." Wrath shook his head. "I've never lost control. Even at my angriest, I retain control."

"You weren't alone in that." Ava looked around her at the devastation and sighed. "I woke with this overriding desire to get you out of my palace."

Wrath nodded but kept his gaze on her. "My apologies, Haziel. I would never want to hurt you."

"I know." She nodded and stepped closer to him. "But I think we should leave now. Two hell princes this close together with the seals weakening can only spell more trouble."

SEVENTEEN

Wrath in the throes of fully developed regret was a different beast entirely to deal with. Haziel had to keep checking to make sure the meek and agreeable being following her out of Ava's palace was the same blustering warmonger who'd marched in with her.

"I know you didn't mean to hurt me." She gave releasing his guilt another try.

He looked at her with remorseful blue eyes and shook his head. "I could have ended you."

"Well, considering you've threatened to end us all on more than one occasion, I don't see that as something to torture yourself over." Wrath regularly liked to threaten to pull earth, heaven, and hell into an end.

The old Wrath razzle-dazzle kindled in his eyes and by razzle-dazzle she meant killing spree fury. "Careful, angel."

As she seemed to have abandoned careful days ago, Haziel gave him a wink and a cocky grin. "Lead on."

They reached Ava's cluttered courtyard.

"Psst!" A bush to their left quivered.

With a growl, Wrath dove into the bush and emerged dangling a small, yellow imp by a horn. "Yesterday." He gave the imp a shake hard enough to rattle his dark eyes in his over-size head. "I've been looking for you."

"I have information," Yesterday yelped, his tongue flapping out of his mouth.

Haziel took pity on the poor creature. Imps were notorious liars and trouble causers but this one was sort of cute. "Perhaps you should listen to him before you shake the brains out of his ears."

Studying the imp like he was a glob of goo, Wrath stopped the shaking.

"What information?" Haziel approached the imp. For a moment, she envied their ability to lie. What would it be like to open your mouth and trot out a lie? Just once, she'd love to say something untrue. Ramiel had slapped the truth telling gift on her when she'd risen to the rank of his second. He needed to be able to trust her, he had said. It had made sense at the time, but now she wasn't so certain that trust worked like that. Was it even trust if you had guaranteed honesty? Her wing throbbed, but she resisted checking the damage. Wrath was already remorseful enough.

Yesterday's left eye dropped back to facing forward in his eye socket, and he focused on her with a piteous expression. "He wants to end me."

"You lied to me and Asmodeus." Wrath gave him another shake. "You caused war between Asmodeus and myself, and then betrayed both of us." Wrath pulled him closer to his face. "And you endangered Eddie, and that I cannot tolerate."

That did sound rather damning. "To be fair, Wrath, you and Shade do rather enjoy making war on each other."

"Yes," Wrath snapped. "But this little turd burglar told

each of us the other was attempting to end us. He caused a struggle for survival."

And that was a good enough reason for her not to intervene further. Haziel stepped back. "Fair enough."

"Not going to beg me to save him?" Wrath raised one dark brow and smirked.

Yesterday gaped at her. "You're an angel. You are supposed to be all love and light."

"Not that kind of angel." Haziel shrugged and pointed at herself. "Ramiel's court. More of a keep the peace kind of angel." She felt sorry for him and softened her tone. "And right now, you sound like a threat to peace."

"That's why I'm here." Yesterday gave up on her and turned his attention back to Wrath with a pleading look. "To help keep the peace."

"I've had all that I can take of you." Wrath's wings flared behind him, and his power brushed over her senses. It had a similar power signature to Ramiel's but was rawer and cruder, like denim versus silk.

Covering as much of his huge head as his stubby arms could achieve, Yesterday squealed. "I have information on where Lucifer is."

Cocking his head, Wrath held the imp up to his eye level. "You're lying."

"No." Yesterday shook his head and pointed to his horns. "My horns aren't moving."

"You could have mastered that tell." Haziel had met very skilled imps in her time. The more they lied, the better they got at it.

Yesterday glared at her. "You're not helping."

"Oh, I am." Haziel moved closer to Wrath. "But I'm helping him not you."

Wrath's head snapped around and those blue eyes smoldered at her. "Are you, sweet seraph? Are you helping a cursed hell prince?"

His voice stroked across her senses and made her want to stretch and purr. "Ramiel wanted me to help keep you out of trouble."

The warmth in Wrath's eyes died, and he went back to glowering at Yesterday. "Tell me your information first, and then I will decide if you're lying." He gave Yesterday a shake. "And don't think of lying or bargaining with me. I still might end you even once I've heard your information."

"How is that fair?" Yesterday sputtered. "I bargain information for my life. That's how this works."

Wrath put his face close to Yesterday's and whispered, "Rule change."

He looked like a powerful, deadly predator as he toyed with Yesterday, and heaven help her, but she liked it. There was something appealingly primal about Wrath. Ava had said something similar. That part of Wrath's attraction, aside from that mouthwatering body and those penetrating eyes, was the way you felt safe when he was around. Safe in a way that made you want to melt into the shadows behind him and have him face all your fears and troubles.

There was a brutal honestly to him as well.

"Lucifer isn't in hell," Yesterday babbled. "He's been spotted on the earth plane."

"By who?" Wrath snarled.

"Demons." Yesterday twisted in Wrath's grasp like a wind-blown dandelion. "We talk to each other, and the rumor is that he has left hell for the earth plane and hasn't been seen down here. Not since you've been here anyway."

That made sense, but it might be a good idea to verify if Lucifer had been near his palace recently. "If he does have Eddie—" She kept her tone gentle. Wrath was especially hair trigger around the topic of his daughter. "Then it would make sense for him to be on earth." She pointed at Yesterday. "He's right, demons gossip worse than angels, and we would have heard something about him if he were here."

"I went to Lucifer's palace. He wasn't there and hasn't been there recently." Wrath glanced from her to Yesterday and then opened his hand and dropped the imp.

Yesterday wasted no time in using those stubby legs to exit himself from the courtyard.

Watching him scurry off, Haziel said, "You're going to show compassion?"

"I have been known to." Wrath pulled a wry expression. "Not often, but it has happened."

She laughed and resisted the urge to tease him further. "When did you go to Lucifer's palace?"

"Before I came to get you." He cleared his throat and stared over her head. "It was why I left you with Ava. I didn't know what I would find there, and I didn't want to put you between myself and Lucifer." He blushed. "Didn't want to put you in danger."

"I'm a seraph and a strong one." She didn't feel it was fair to remind him that she'd mere minutes ago been caught between him and Ava, so she changed the subject. "Earth?"

With a curt nod, Wrath opened his wings and took to the skies.

Haziel watched him climb with a wince. As a seraph she had wonderful wings, three sets of them in fact, which on a normal day made the seraphim more agile and faster in the air than even the archangels. But six wings meant a lot of delicate bones and cartilage to damage, and right now, her right wing was aching like a demon. When she'd smacked into the wall, she must have damaged something.

Taking a deep breath, she snapped open her wings. A

whimper of pain got away from her before she could stop it. Fortunately Wrath was too far ahead of her to hear and already stroking the air powerfully in the direction of Lust's demesne.

It was much quicker to fly than walk, and now that Ava knew they were leaving her territory, it was also safer.

And she didn't want Wrath feeling bad about her damaged humerus. The pain seared from her wing and down her back, necessitating the use of a wonderful curse she'd heard on earth. "Motherfucker!"

The thing about normally being able to fly faster than an archangel, or in this case hell prince, was that it didn't give an angel a true appreciation of how fast they were. This angel wobbling along like a lame duck was learning the hard way that hell princes could get some speed through their feathers. Haziel knew she could call out and ask him to slow down, but that would mean him getting to his daughter slower, and she didn't want him to feel guilty about her injured wing on top of his residual guilt about her bruised arms.

Pain, however, had different ideas and went from awful to searing, unbearable agony. It felt like the entire right side of her body was a torturous combination of numb and hypersensitive. She lost feeling in her right hand and cradled her arm against her chest as hot sparks prickled through it and brought tears to her eyes. Ahead of her, Wrath soared over the border between Ava and Shade's demesnes. He dipped his shoulder and took a long, lazy bank to the right.

And Haziel tried. She lowered her right shoulder and dropped like a stone.

Her injured right wing snapped back and fluttered uselessly amongst the other two on that side. She tried to flap her remaining wings, but her body was beyond responding and too busy hurtling her straight for the ground.

The fall wouldn't kill her, but it was going to fucking hurt, and she braced for impact.

A hard body appeared in front of her, and she smashed into Wrath's chest.

"Angel." He grunted as he took the impact and then his large wings tilted to create a backdraft and he lowered them to the ground. He touched down softly, but Haziel felt the slight jolt in every fiber of her being. She bit her lip to keep from crying out, but a guttural moan escaped before she could censor it. The world wobbled in front of her eyes. Blood drained from her head, and everything went dark.

She woke in a cave with luminous moss creating a soft indigo glow on the walls. She was lying close to a pool of shimmering iridescent blue water, and she was lying against Wrath. His big arm cradled her body against his chest, her injured wing draped gently over his forearm. And Haziel felt completely safe.

He must have sensed her wake, because he whispered, "Angel?"

She meant to say something blithe and bright, to allay the deep concern throbbing in his bass voice. What she said instead was, "Gargh." Or something close to that.

His large hand cupped her cheek and stroked hair away from her face. "Just rest, sweetheart," he murmured. "We'll have you better in no time."

"My wing." She dared not move for fear of starting the torment again. So far, her attempt to keep her injury quiet was going swimmingly.

"The humerus is broken," he said. "I splinted it and did as much healing as I could. I think if you keep it still for a day or two, it'll repair itself." He nudged her face up with a finger. "Here." He put a bottle against her lips. "Take a sip or two of water and then get some more rest."

"Thank you," she managed before taking a sip of water. "You should leave me here. Find Eddie." Sleep pushed her eyelids back together again.

"I'm not leaving you." Wrath muttered close to her ear, and she felt the soft press of his lips to her forehead before she drifted back to the place where it didn't hurt so much.

Warm breath huffed down her neck when she woke the second time. Her head felt clearer, and she could wiggle the fingers of her right hand without pain exploding through her. Her other wings must have retracted because her spine was pressed to Wrath's chest. The slow rise and fall of his deep breathing synchronized with her own and wrapped her in another layer of security.

Voice sleep raspy, he said, "How's the wing?"

"Feeling a bit better." She resisted the urge to give it a quick trial.

"Hmm." His arm tightened around her waist. "Care to explain why you didn't tell me about your injured wing."

And she gave him the honest answer. "No."

His thighs bracketed her legs and he shifted slightly, careful not to jar her wing. "Let's try a different question."

"Must you?"

"Yup." It was darker in the cave now, and she could barely make out the sharp play of muscle along his forearms. "Why didn't you tell me about your injured wing?"

"I didn't want to slow you down." Truth.

"And?"

Damn, shit, and bugger. "I didn't want you to feel bad about my wing getting hurt."

"Silly angel," he murmured. "Go back to sleep. Ramiel and I share opposite sides of the same power, so my healing should help. Did it?"

Her wing did seem to be feeling a lot better than it would without healing. "Yes."

"Give me the full answer."

Damn him for always going that extra mile. "But not as well as if Ramiel had healed it."

"Well." He chuckled. "That's a blow to the ego, but I'll take that it worked a bit." He pressed her head back against him. "Now go back to sleep and we'll talk about this not telling me business in the morning."

"I'd rather not."

"Tough shit. Now, sleep."

"You're very bossy." Wrath's heat wrapped around her, and drowsiness crept through her limbs. "And far too comfortable with using my unfortunate ability to always tell the truth."

"Uh-huh." He stroked her spine with one plate-size hand. "Sleep, angel."

Haziel pressed her forehead into the crook of his neck and did as she was told.

WRATH CLOSED his eyes and drank in the rose and lotus scent of the angel cradled against his chest. Her silky skin pressed against his throat. Her breath huffed softly against his chest. Ramiel's source power brushed against his, familiar and yet different from the signature of the archangel. Softer and lighter, lustrous and alluring, calling to him on a primal level.

When he'd first seen her falter in the air, his heart had lodged in his throat, and he'd almost shredded his wings getting to her in time to stop her plummeting to the ground.

She stirred things within him that he would rather were left dormant. Not since Rosabella had he felt the odd mélange of protective and possessive around a being.

The feathers of her injured wing tickled his arm. He'd wanted to puke when he'd seen the damage to the humerus. A simple break had become a complete longitudinal fracture with her insisting on flying with it. He'd been moments away from summoning Ramiel to help her, but his stubbornness had stopped him. He didn't want Ramiel close to her. Hated the idea of seeing the adoration in her beautiful eyes when she gazed at her archangel. He had poured every ounce of his own healing strength into the break, and it had sped up knitting her humerus. The effort had exhausted him, but thank fuck it had done something, because if it hadn't, he would have been left with no other option but to summon the feathery fartberry.

She murmured in her sleep and shifted against him. Her hip brushed his crotch.

His cock, the pig sniffer, took notice and stirred.

The lust seal was worsening, and here in Shade's demesne, the effects were shooting through his system. He wanted to move his hand up and cup the generous jut of Haziel's breast, strum the nipple until it stood hard and proud, and ready for his mouth.

Haziel made a soft moan and burrowed closer to him.

Not helping. The lust seal could be fastening its sticky tentacles around her as well.

His cock loved that idea so much, it offered up a salute.

He was getting confused. The seals were breaking and playing havoc with his emotions. He felt no tenderness for her. He didn't want to slide inside her and stay there until they were both satisfied. He didn't even like angels.

Yeah, the lust seal was the problem here. It had to be.

EIGHTEEN

"Haziel," Wrath rasped close to her ear. "Time to wake."

"No." She moaned her reluctance. Waking meant abandoning a delicious dream about Wrath pinning her to the wall of the cave, pressing his hard body against her, and pillaging her mouth with his tongue. Her nipples were hard and tight, and she throbbed between her thighs. She hadn't been celibate while she waited for Ramiel to notice her, but it had been a while since she'd had those needs met.

"Angel." He accompanied his words with a gentle shake. "You should be well enough to walk now, and we need to go."

And she'd been having an erotic dream about him. Heat bloomed in her cheeks as her reality dissipated the lingering fog of her dream. She had no business having dreams like that about any hell prince, and especially not this one. He was Ramiel's opposing force. Even dreaming of him made her feel like a traitor to Ramiel. She loved Ramiel and only Ramiel.

She'd adored him for centuries. Hell was known to play tricks on angels.

"Well, well," Wrath murmured. "I'd love to know what has your face all flushed."

As long as he didn't ask, she wouldn't have to tell him. Haziel hauled herself to her feet, gingerly testing her wing. It wouldn't be flying soon, but it had healed enough for her to tuck it away. She stood, easing residual stiffness from her legs and back.

"Good morning." Wrath greeted her with a smirk that, thanks to aftershocks from her dream, made her belly tighten. Gripping the back of his shirt, he hauled it over his head.

She tried not to stare, she really did, but all the smooth, hard muscle right in front of her made that near impossible. "What are you doing?"

"I thought I would take advantage of what is offered." He gestured the pool before unfastening his pants and shimmying out of them.

Holy wing feathers but the prince was beautifully put together. Rumor had it naked Shade was a sight to behold, but she didn't know how anything could beat the eye feast currently before her. Powerful slabs of muscle packed his shoulders and chest and then tapered into the slimness of his hips. His stomach muscles descended like a ladder into his waistband and made her want to walk her fingers up and then down.

He turned and provided her with a delicious back view of the taut globes of his ass with their deep indents on each side. Powerful thigh muscles tapered to his knees.

All the hell princes and archangels were beautiful. It stood to reason if you were assuming a form for millennia, you'd make it a good one.

She'd seen Ramiel naked plenty of times. He liked her to

take notes when he bathed and wasn't shy about stripping down in front of her. But she'd never once wanted to sink her nails into his ass, or even bite like she did now.

Wrath took his distracting form beneath the water, and she was able to draw a full breath for the first time in heaven knows how many minutes. Naked Wrath viewing had seemed to take hours, or perhaps that was merely wishful thinking.

Submerged to below his bulky shoulders, he turned to her. "Will you join me?"

Yes, please, yelled her inner angel. And because she was who she was, and Ramiel had cursed her with honesty, her outer angel opened its mouth and said the same thing, "Yes, please."

Wrath grinned and stroked the water with his arms. "You need to strip." He gestured to her body. "Unless you have something other than that to wear."

"I have a change." She motioned to her bag. Wrath must have carried it here when he'd brought her to the cave. Relief washed over her. Stripping down meant too many naked beings in one woefully small body of water.

Wrath crooked a finger. "Come on then."

Warm water lapped at her ankles as she ventured into the pool. Wrath must have removed her boots while she was unconscious because she inched forward with her bare feet.

He dipped backwards and dropped below the surface with a splash.

Haziel kicked off into the sensual relaxing heat of the water. It smelled sweet and musky at the same time and kissed against her overheated skin in a way that brought the flush back to her cheeks.

Emerging and shaking his head like a big dog, Wrath grinned at her. "It's the lust seal."

"What?"

"The lust seal." He nodded at her. "I'm guessing that's what making you look all hot and bothered."

As much as she'd love to deny his words, she couldn't, so she settled for dunking her head beneath the water. Below the surface, the pool was darker, and she could only dimly make out the darker shape that was Wrath.

He must be right; it was the weakening seal causing these unruly thoughts and emotions. Like if she drifted closer might she press herself against his powerful body and twine her limbs with his? Made her wonder how he'd react if she kissed the smirk off his sensual mouth. But even her thoughts wouldn't tolerate a lie, and she knew the weakening seal wasn't entirely to blame. She'd been having these thoughts about Wrath since they'd embarked on this venture together. When he'd left her at Ava's, she'd felt abandoned and rejected, and far too delighted when he'd come back for her. The image of him in nothing but a towel was going to linger in her mind for a while.

She broke the surface of the water to find him watching her.

He caught the thick rope of her braid and gently pressed her closer. "Would you like me to wash your hair?"

His hands on her would be too much temptation to bear, and she shook her head. "I don't think that's wise."

"No?" He wrapped her braid around his fist and brought her close enough for her limbs to tangle with his and their hips to bump gently together. His mouth was so close. Water droplets clung to his full lips and clumped his dark eyelashes together. His blue eyes blazed with heat. "Why not?"

"It's not a good idea." She wanted to capture the water with her lips and tongue. She wanted to lock her thighs around his waist and pull him even closer.

"And why's that?" He released her hair and cupped her nape in one warm, callused palm.

Her breasts brushed against his chest, and his erection nudged at her thigh.

Oh, this bastard. He knew she had no choice but to answer him. "Because if you touch me, I'm going to want you to touch me more."

Desire darkened his eyes to a deeper blue. "I'm still failing to see how that's a bad idea. We're both feeling the effects of the lust seal. Why not help each other to ease some of the strain?"

"It's not the lust seal." Her voice had lowered to a breathy whisper. She dared not move or she would barnacle herself to him and not let go until he satisfied her needs. "I mean, it's not only the lust seal weakening."

He inched her closer, their breaths mingling in the tiny gap between their mouths. "No?"

"No." She should move away from him, put some distance between them. His hold on her nape was light enough that she could break it easily, but she didn't want to.

Spearing his fingers into her hair, he whispered, "Tell me what it is then."

"It's you." She craved the taste of him. "I desire you."

Wrath groaned and pressed his forehead to hers. "Then let me give us both relief."

"No." It killed her to produce that one meagre syllable and even now she wanted to take the words back.

"Why?" he rasped.

And she had only one reason. "Ramiel."

"Ramiel." As he jerked away from her, his eyes turned hard and angry. "Because you think you're in love with Ramiel."

"I do love Ramiel." Centuries with her archangel had taught her that. "But that is not the only reason." She hated the way he was glowering at her now. She wanted the other look back, the one that had liquified her muscles and set her nerve endings tingling. "He is my archangel, and you are his opposite. It would be a betrayal."

"Fuck." Wrath lurched away from her and hauled himself out of the water.

His cock jutted thick and hard from between his legs.

Her desire for him awoke with a ravenous yell, but she forced herself to breathe deeply. "He has my loyalty."

"Does he deserve it?" Wrath dressed himself in sharp, angry motions, yanking his clothing over his damp skin.

"Not always." Ramiel could be capricious and spoiled at times, taking what he regarded as his due. "But his behavior is not a measure of mine. He has my loyalty like he has my love, and his worthiness of either is not the point."

Wrath growled at her. "You're a blind fool. He doesn't love you back. He doesn't even respect you."

His words cut deep, but again she could only speak the truth as she saw it. "But he is fond of me, and it is my feelings we are speaking of, not his."

"Your feelings." Wrath scoffed and gathered their possessions. "The same feelings that desire me?"

"Yes." She moved to the edge of the pool.

He held out his hand to help her.

When she didn't move, he made a rough sound of impatience and took her by the elbow. His grip was firm but gentle as he steadied her.

"Your feelings seem to contradict each other." He rifled through her pack and produced dry clothing for her.

Haziel didn't know whether to laugh or to cry. He was right. There was a storm happening inside her. She loved Ramiel, and she desired Wrath, and neither of those were hers to act on. The sound that escaped her was a mixture of tears and laughter. "Isn't that often the way with feelings?"

Wrath dropped his head, and when he looked up, he wore a wry smile. "Unfortunately, yes."

"Do you not love another?" She accepted his help in wrestling off her wet shirt and trousers.

His voice deepened as his gaze traced her body clothed only in underwear. "Love?" He tugged a dry shirt over her head and eased her arms through the sleeves. "I really don't know how to answer that, but I will return your honesty with mine. I have believed myself to love Rosabella for a while now, but I'm not sure I can still freely give my love to a woman who abandoned our child as Rosabella did."

His answer pleased her too much, plus her brief encounter with Rosabella had done nothing to endear her to Haziel. It hurt her to ask the next question, but she had to know. "But she broke your heart?"

"She did." Wrath nudged her leg to get her to step into her trousers. His hands on her skin made her shiver, but despite the heat in his eyes, he kept his touch impersonal like a nursemaid helping his charge. "I wanted her, but she didn't want me." He bent and eased her feet into her boots. "Much like you."

She didn't want to be compared to Rosabella. "But I do want you," she said as he tied her laces. "Only I won't act on that want."

When he looked up, the signature Wrath arrogance bathed his beautiful face. "Want to place a wager on that?"

And Haziel gave him the only answer she could. "Most definitely not."

NINETEEN

The closer they drew to Shade's palace, the stronger the effect of the lust seal became. Haziel wiped her brow with the back of her hand. They'd been walking for most of the day. Neatly tucked away, her wing continued to heal but she wasn't ready to fly with it yet.

As the lust seal made itself more prevalent, she found herself watching Wrath near obsessively. The flex and bunch of his powerful thigh muscles as he strode forward, that near perfect ass, the bulging muscles on his arms and back. Other things about him also played havoc with her already unsteady resolve. The way he would constantly check back to see if she was doing okay. He seemed to know without asking when she was tired and instead of making a fuss about it, would merely stop and unpack provisions for both of them.

His eyes were the purest form of blue she had ever encountered. The blue of a summer sky or blooming forget-me-nots, and he always met her gaze directly. She felt seen in a way that made her want to preen under his steady regard. She could cut steel on the firm, uncompromising line of his jaw. The plush perfection of his mouth made her forget what he was saying at times and stare at the shape of his lips, imagining what they would feel like pressed against hers, crave to feel his tongue against hers and draw his taste inside her.

"There." Wrath held aside the sticky fronds of a creeper for her to pass.

Shade's palace slumbered like a sleek goddess in the waning evening light. Pink from the sun stroked lovingly over the smooth arches and pleasing sweeps of creamy stone.

"It's beautiful," she whispered, momentarily dragged from her fascination with Wrath.

"That she is." Wrath winked at her and strode toward the palace.

The effect of the seal waxed and waned, and gave her moments of reprieve. Which she spent watching Wrath as well. The sooner she got back to Ramiel and his calm, soothing presence, the sooner she could put her fascination with this hell prince aside.

Wrath stopped suddenly, his boots crunching in the crushed seashell path leading to the palace. "No demons."

"What?" Haziel followed his gaze and looked around them.

"No demons." Eyes narrowed, Wrath surveyed the area. "Even though most of them left, there should be a few still here." His jaw tightened to granite. Granite she wouldn't mind nibbling on.

Gah! This had to stop. "None?"

She sent out her awareness and hit no demon energy signatures.

"There were some of his demons here when last we came." Wrath drew his gleaming obsidian broadsword. "I'm getting nothing. You?"

"Nothing." Haziel grabbed her bow and nocked an arrow with a heaven-wrought tip.

Unnatural quiet hung about the palace as if it was holding its breath.

"Even with Shade not here, his demons should be here," Wrath murmured as he moved forward like a prowling predator.

The gleaming wooden doors hung ajar. Carved into the doors, figures were doing things that brought instant heat to her cheeks and fresh fodder for her imagination.

Stopping, Wrath glanced over his shoulder. "Want to stop a minute and take notes?"

"Pfft!" She matched his teasing tone. "Perhaps you are the one who needs to take notes."

Wrath chuckled and edged the door farther open. "I've already made a detailed study."

The dying sunlight filtered through a domed glass ceiling and cast soft light on the atrium it sheltered. A large pool graced the center of the long, impressive chamber, and jewel-toned fish darted about its azure water.

Tall, graceful pillars draped in silk flanked the pool, and beyond them, shadowy alcoves beckoned to passersby to take a moment to sink into their silken depths and indulge their wants.

Haziel suppressed an image of a naked Wrath spread over crimson silk.

The lust seal pulsed virulently, and she had to dig her nails into her weapon to stop herself from tackling him into the nearest alcove. Her breasts ached, and her nipples pressed through her linen shirt. Moisture pooled between her thighs, and each beat of her pulse drummed in time to the lust seal.

Wrath cleared his throat and shook his head. "Balls! That thing packs a punch."

"Yup." Haziel clamped her teeth shut before a lurid confession escaped her.

His fighting leathers cupped an impressive erection. And Haziel barely suppressed a groan. She'd give two sets of wings to be that leather right now.

Stopping, Wrath tensed and whipped his head to their right.

Then Haziel felt it, the distinctive energy signature of a high order demon.

"Lord Wrath." A tall demon with finely cut features beneath gleaming onyx skin stepped into the atrium. The faint silver glimmer of a defensive shield shimmered around his lithe form. Clasping his hands before his chest, he bowed to Wrath and then her. "Seraph."

"Fallen." She kept her arrow nocked as she returned his bow.

The demon strolled closer, his silk lounging pants fluttering around his shapely legs. Of course Shade would populate his court with sensual and beautiful beings. The demon pressed a slim, elegant hand to his naked chest. "I am called Apassionata."

"Are you here alone?" Wrath lowered his sword.

Taking that as a good sign, Haziel eased the tension on her bow string.

Apassionata's shield shimmered and disappeared. "The others have all fled."

"Fled?" Wrath sheathed his weapon in the scabbard across his back. "Why?"

"There have been a series of attacks." Apassionata lowered his head. "Some from your realm, Lord Wrath."

Wrath reared back as if Apassionata had struck him. "My demons are forbidden from attacking this demesne."

Haziel's heart twisted. Wrath loved his daughter so much he had declared a truce on his perpetual enemy because of her.

He blustered, he fought, and he loved with such intensity. It was impossible to remain neutral about such a being.

"Forgive me, lord." Apassionata glanced at her. "I misspoke. The attacks have come from mixed hordes. Some of Lord Lust's joined before I could prevent them."

"Are you telling me that you are all that remains of Shade's horde?" Wrath glowered at Apassionata.

Apassionata smiled and it made his perfect face warmer and reflected in the honey of his eyes. "Not all joined our attackers," he said. "Some merely chose not to stay here and become targets. They have hidden and are awaiting the return of our lord." He shrugged, an effortlessly elegant gesture that Haziel wished she could imitate. "I have the means to defend myself and was elected to remain and protect the palace."

Haziel had fought enough high order demons to know that despite his suave exterior, if he was the only remaining demon, Apassionata had all kinds of nasty tricks he could deploy.

"May I enquire as to why you are here?" Apassionata managed to say those words without sounding like a challenge, but somehow making it clear that it was a challenge.

Heavens, but Haziel wished she could achieve that.

"We are merely passing through," Wrath said. "We are on our way to the hell gate, and I wanted to check on the condition of the lust seal."

As if in answer to his question, the seal sent out a hearty pulse that turned Haziel's blood to lava and her good sense to oblivion. Before she could stop herself, she inched closer to Wrath.

Apassionata gave her an understanding glance. "It weakens daily. Our lord should be here."

"Your lord is searching for my daughter." Wrath's tone turned to steel and ice.

Apassionata inclined his head. "As we have heard, Lord

Wrath. We are sympathetic to the quest of our lord. Love is such a precious rarity, is it not?"

Wrath growled, and to her surprise, Apassionata chuckled.

Time to step in before the blood flowed and the feathers flew. "Have you any news on how many of these rogue hordes are in the demesne?"

"Indeed, seraph." Apassionata frowned. "They are still plentiful, but if you will allow me a few hours, I can gather an escort to aid your way."

Wrath swelled to twice his size. "I don't need a fucking escort."

"I misspoke." Apassionata changed tack smoothly. "I merely propose such an arrangement for expediency. Our demesne is particularly beset by these hordes."

They had encountered trouble on the way through Shade's demesne to Ava's. It would help if they didn't have to keep stopping and fighting their way to the hell gate, but this was not her decision, so she turned to Wrath. "Wrath?"

"You have an hour," he snapped.

"How generous," Apassionata murmured. "Perhaps some refreshments while you wait?"

Wrath remained silent, so Haziel said, "Thank you."

"It would be my pleasure." Apassionata threw her a mischievous glance. "In hell, we are always ready to welcome travelers. Regardless of where they come from."

She couldn't help but like him, and Haziel laughed. This trip to hell had been the first time she had ever bothered to really speak to a demon. Most of her previous encounters with them had been decidedly bellicose. In Ava's domain, she had befriended Rapace with his wicked sense of humor and keen, incisive mind. She would always have a soft spot for Covet, and Apassionata made another demon she would like to know better.

Wrath turned when she laughed, a cold expression on his face. "We have to get to the earth realm. We've delayed too long as it is."

And that was because he'd come to fetch her and then she'd injured her wing.

"Indeed." Apassionata winked at her. "Rumor has it that your brother has been seen there."

Haziel couldn't resist his charm. "You seem remarkably well informed for a demon stuck in a palace alone."

"Ah, seraph." Apassionata looked wicked and contrite at the same time, and it made him roguishly handsome. "I catch but whispers in the wind."

"You'll catch my boot up your ass if you keep flirting with my angel," Wrath growled.

His angel. A wash of heat brushed Haziel.

"Indeed." Apassionata looked more amused than intimidated. "If you would follow me? I will show you to chambers in which you can wait, and I will bring you refreshment." He looked Wrath dead in the eye as he said, "For you and *your* angel."

They followed Apassionata up a sweeping marble staircase to an upper level with graceful arches and gleaming floors. He stopped in front of an arched door and opened it.

"Seraph." He opened the door and nodded her inside. "I think you will find everything you need within."

Wrath got his shoulder in front of Apassionata. "This will do for both of us."

"Wha—"

Wrath marched into the chamber, hands on his hips as he scowled at the interior.

Sharing a chamber while the lust seal played havoc on them seemed like an extremely dangerous idea to her. A tempting idea, but a very dangerous one.

"Of course." Apassionata's full mouth quirked. "You are, as always, Lord Wrath, an absolute delight."

Wrath glared at the door until Apassionata shut it behind him. "Shade needs to watch that one. Far too clever for his own good."

"I like him." Haziel examined the room. Through a bank of floor to ceiling glass, the jungle had been turned into a pirate's treasure of colors by the setting sun. The largest bed she'd ever seen graced the center of the room in a proliferation of jewel-colored hangings and pillows. The bed invited you to spend the rest of your days in its depth. And brought Haziel back to the first order of business. "I'm sorry about all these delays."

Whirling, Wrath closed the distance between then.

Her back hit the wall.

Wrath kept coming until he had her caged by his hard body in the front and his muscular arms on either side of her head. "I was the one who injured your wing."

"But I delayed you at Ava's." She should tell him to stop and step back, but she couldn't lie. She didn't want him to do either of those things. Whether it was the seal or her disturbing obsession with him, Haziel delighted in the sheer audacity of his presumption.

"I left you there. It was up to me to bring you safely back." He pressed closer until she could feel every hard line of him against her.

Her body delighted in the sensations. She drew in his scent of sage and leather. "Why are you doing this?"

"Because I can't help myself." Wrath lowered his mouth to within a breath of hers. "And I really don't want to anymore."

Neither did Haziel. She raised her chin and met his molten stare. "Kiss me."

On a groan, Wrath closed the distance between their lips.

Prepared for a full-frontal assault, she was surprised by the featherlight caress of his lips. Wrath took his time drawing her lower lip into the hot, wet cavern of his mouth. He released her lip with a moist plop. "You kiss me."

Pure, unadulterated lust swept through her. It could be the seal, or it could be her feelings for him, but Haziel didn't care to question. Gripping the back of his head, she took his tempting mouth like a marauder. Her tongue slid past his pillowy lips into the heated cavern beyond.

Wrath tensed and then he kissed her back.

Kiss was such a tame description for the way he took her mouth. He possessed her with lips, tongue, and teeth, taking and demanding, giving and surrendering.

His hair was like silk between her fingers; he tasted like pure temptation. Her body grew warm and pliant, and she pressed into his iron strength. His hard cock pressed into her belly in a blatant reminder of where a kiss like this led.

She wanted it all. All of him.

Holding her head, Wrath deepened the kiss until her head swum and she was a panting, writhing mess trying to get closer to him and all that he offered.

And then Wrath pulled back. Heat stained his cheekbones, and his breath came in harsh pants. "You're right," he rasped.

"What?" Haziel didn't want to talk. She wanted his mouth on hers, his body driving into her.

"This is a bad idea. This is not the right time." Wrath took a deep breath and stepped away from her. "And when I fuck you, Haziel, I want you to have no doubt about whether it's me acting because I want you, or that fucking seal making us both crazy."

TWENTY

Deep within the womb of creation, it stirred. So long dormant, the being did not recognize what was happening at first. Around it, its siblings still slumbered, but their eternal rest was fitful, as if they felt it too.

The summoning.

The awakening.

The end of days.

And the being remembered its name. It was Pestilence, and it rode its white steed with a crown upon its head, and a bow in its hands. It was the first of the harbingers of the end of days, and it felt the calling to it and its siblings—the breaking of the seals.

DEE DIDN'T WANT to like Daniel Lee, but her abiding sin was being a pushover for a pretty face and a kickass body, and Daniel Lee had both. As well as being a thoroughly pleasant and easy guest. She'd finally caved and cleared out the spare bedroom in the living area from years of old programs and posters and let him move into it. He already shared most meals with her, and bless his heart, ate her cooking as if he enjoyed it. So, it didn't seem too much of a concession to get him to pack up his sleeping bag and take over the unused bed.

As far as the guardianship went, he was winning points there as well. He consulted rather than sidelined her and often deferred to her experience. Unlike a lot of men she'd encountered, he was quite happy to take her advice as well.

They'd taken to having an unofficial meeting every morning in the basement to keep an eye on the hell gate together and decide between them on the best course of action. Most days, he made the coffee for their meeting.

Dressed in faded jeans and a snug white T-shirt, he divided his attention between the hell gate and the app on his phone. "It seems relatively stable."

"It did before it started coughing up rakshassa demons and imps." Dee had to work to keep the acidity in her tone.

Daniel threw her a sweet smile. "True. It's a tricky son of bitch to be sure."

Jean-Claude had sent her a message a few days ago. He'd found a group of people and joined a hike in Alaska. She shouldn't have been hurt by his defection. She certainly didn't love him, and was, at best, fond of him, but her ego smarted nonetheless. Dee left her men. They didn't leave her. After Rosabella's father had headed for the hills and taken her heart with him, she'd sworn never again. It had been surprisingly easy to keep her promise as well.

"You all right?" Daniel studied her.

Dee buckled into her emotional armor and wiped any expression off her face. "Of course. What would be the matter with me?"

"I don't know." Daniel shrugged, but kept that dark,

compassionate gaze on her. When Rosabella had first left Eddie with her, she'd been resentful. She'd raised her daughter and didn't want to be raising someone else's child. It had taken little Eddie mere days to help her overcome that. She adored her granddaughter and related to her in a way that she never had with Rosabella. Perhaps if she'd been closer to Rosabella, a better mother, Rosabella would have been different.

"With Eddie still missing, I can't imagine how difficult that must be for you," Daniel said.

The unwelcome worry and grief taking up residence in her chest gave a vicious twist. Rosabella being here wasn't helping either. With Daniel in the spare room, Rosabella had taken over Eddie's bedroom. It used to be hers when she still lived here, but Dee resented her presence in there. Mostly, she resented Rosabella's constant demands for information and veiled accusations that if Dee had done a better job of looking after Eddie, she wouldn't be missing now. Those accusations had wriggled beneath Dee's guard, and she lay awake at night tormenting herself with *what ifs*. What if she'd been more open with Eddie about the hell gate? Given her the information she needed. What if she'd told Eddie about her father? Maybe Wrath could have protected her better or even taught her how to use her Nephilim power. But like she always told Eddie, you can't change the past by wishing it that way. "Yeah. I'm worried sick about her. Wrath couldn't find her in hell, and we've heard nothing more from Shade. Sophia checked in to say she's traveling with him, but they have nothing concrete yet."

"This is all so hard on you." Daniel shook his head. "You were more like a mother to her than a grandmother." A roguish grin turned his face boyish. "Not that anyone would guess you are a grandmother."

Was he flirting with her? Well, he could cut that out. She

didn't have time for young, pretty diversions right now. All hell was literally breaking loose, and her granddaughter was caught in the vortex. When Sophia last reported in, it was with the tantalizing hope that the hounds were still on Eddie's scent.

But still no Eddie.

Bollocks, but she wanted Eddie back here, safe and sound, where she could first shake the life out of her for worrying her grandmother half to death and then hold her like she never intended to let her go.

She felt stripped to her soul by Daniel's compassion, and she needed to get away. "I'm going to...er...go and do my yoga. Meditate," she tacked on in case that sounded heartless. Not that she cared what this boy thought of her.

Nodding, Daniel went back to studying the app. "I'll check the deeper levels for activity before I come up."

"You don't need to tell me what you're doing," she snapped. "You're the hell gate guardian now." She instantly regretted her response, but Daniel kept his attention on the app. Something about the stillness of his posture stopped her. "What is it?"

"I'm not sure." Frowning, Daniel tapped his phone screen, and a new display appeared.

The hair on Dee's nape rose. Daniel was checking below the surface, way, way below the surface energy level. She'd never bothered to update her own app, but the thing was much more sophisticated now, and Daniel had the newest version. Another *should have* that she couldn't deal with right now. She moved closer and peered over his shoulder. He smelled of laundry detergent and herbal soap, but she dragged her attention back to the screen. "You're in the core."

"Yeah." Daniel's jaw tensed. "I've been checking on it every other day or so." He glanced at her, a chill in his gaze. "What with the seals cracking, it made sense."

It did make an awful, horrible, final sort of sense, and Dee licked her dry lips. "And?"

"Look." Daniel held the screen up to her. He was pale beneath his coppery complexion. "That can't be right, Dee."

She almost didn't want to look. She forced her gaze to the phone's screen. "Is that…"

"Yeah." Daniels expression turned grim.

One lone bar blinked back at her. "There's activity. I've never heard of activity at that level before." Her voice dropped to a hoarse whisper. "Not in all the years I've been a guardian. Not in all the years my grandmother's grandmother was a guardian. Of course, we didn't have all this sophisticated equipment, so maybe there has been activity before."

"Not according to any of the historical records the guardians have." Daniel swallowed loudly. "Dee, there's fucking movement down there now."

"But only one tiny shift." She knew she was reaching, but she couldn't stop herself.

Daniel took a deep breath. "Even that much is too much. We need to call a gathering."

They absolutely fucking did. She nodded. "Do it."

TWENTY-ONE

They hadn't come for her in what felt like days. Eddie had started a primitive clock by counting the knots on a thread she'd pulled out of her blanket by the beats of her heart. She was probably off by hours, but it gave her comfort to have even the loosest sense of time passing.

Her power built beneath her skin until she felt hot and swollen with it like a feeding tick. She'd never been aware of it until beings had used her like a power cow and milked it from her. But even as her power built, the rest of her body weakened.

Shivering, she pulled the blanket around her shoulders and resumed her pacing. The cold affected her more with the weight she'd lost. Despite them feeding her three reasonable meals a day, she couldn't find any appetite. The weight dropped off her, and her wrists looked skeletal where they poked out of her sweatshirt. How long had she been here? After they milked her power, she had no way of knowing how long she was out for. Her weight loss didn't augur well for time spent here.

Ashe had remarked on it the last time he'd left her food.

Eating had become too much of a chore when she needed what energy she had to keep breathing. The power draining left her in a haze of pain, and on those days, it became too much of a struggle to eat. Ashe had taken to sitting with her and making sure she finished her meals. It took hours some days.

On other days, she wanted to give up.

Shade wasn't coming. As much as she tried to keep the despondency away, the unescapable truth haunted her metal cell. Eddie wasn't even sure she had reached him in her dreams anymore. The Shade who had said such beautiful and tender things to her would have been here by now. Or perhaps her lack of trust in the sincerity of his emotions had been correct, and now that she was out of his sight, he'd moved on to someone else. Someone more willing. Someone who would give him their trust without question.

"No." She spoke aloud to beat back the aching alone. "You have to keep believing. He will find you. The hounds will find you."

Would Wrath look for her? *Maybe he never wanted a child,* whispered the constant doom voice that grew louder as time passed.

"He is looking for me," she said. "He told you how sorry he was not to have been there when you were a child. He promised he would do better."

Find me, find me, find me. The words kept time with the shush of her socked feet over the floor. *Find me, find me, find me.*

The door locks clicked. They didn't pump the gas into her chamber anymore. She was so weakened now that they didn't need it.

"Eddie." Ashe entered her cell, his penetrating silvery gaze sweeping her from head to toe. "You've lost more weight."

She managed a cocky grin. "Aww, Ashe, you noticed."

"Fuck," he whispered and shook his head. He jerked his head at the tray in his hand. "I brought your dinner. It's one of your favorites, fried chicken and mashed potatoes." His signature grin creased his handsome face but didn't quite dispel the concern in his silver eyes. "With green beans, of course. Can't have you skipping your veggies."

She eyed the tray without enthusiasm. Had she been here so long that they knew her favorite meals? "I'm not hungry."

"You have to eat, Eddie." Ashe put the tray on her bed. "Either you sit and eat with me, or they will force you to eat."

Her laugh had a rough edge to it. "Can't have the favorite power cow dying on them, now can they?"

"Please, Eddie." Ashe softened his tone. And if he hadn't been the one holding her down while Calix put the amulet on her, she might have even believed he did care about her with that gentle look on his face. "Don't make them do this the hard way."

"Fine." She stalked the distance to her bed and jammed her hand in the mashed potatoes. She shoved them in her mouth like a demented toddler, not bothering to swallow before she spoke. "Is this what you want?"

Ashe's mouth quirked. "Well, I was hoping for candlelight and little light repartee, but that will do."

A reluctant laugh escaped her. She might have hated him most of all for still being able to make her laugh.

He cut her chicken into neat bites, speared a small portion on the fork and held it out to her. "Most humans find the utensils help."

Eddie grabbed the fork and shoved the chicken in her mouth. She chewed and swallowed mechanically. The mash and chicken hit her belly, and she tensed as it threatened to revolt. Clamping her teeth together, she breathed deep.

"Slowly." Ashe stood and led her by the elbow back to the bed. "Take it slowly, Eddie. Cleaning up vomit is not in my contract, and it makes Calix super pissy to do it."

"Where is horse boy?" She opened her mouth obediently when he offered her another forkful.

"Eh." Ashe shrugged. "Probably out there trying on saddles for the perfect fit."

"Don't," Eddie snapped. Her control stretched thin. "Don't pretend you're my friend."

He stared at her for a long moment and then nodded. "Fair enough." He prepared another forkful. "But I am going to stay until you eat everything." He wagged the fork. "So the sooner you eat up, the sooner you can be rid of me."

She snatched the fork out of his hand and applied herself to the rest of the plate. Eddie only made it halfway through before her stomach rebelled and she couldn't take another bite. "Enough."

Ashe eyed her and then the plate before he sighed. "Okay. That will have to do." He frowned down at the remaining food. "Is there something you'd prefer?"

"My freedom."

He opened his mouth and shut it again. He then proceeded to finish the plate. She didn't know if he did it for her sake or his own, and she didn't care.

Once he'd cleaned the plate, he placed everything neatly back on the tray and stood. "Eddie..." He paused and lowered his voice. "I..."

"What?"

"Nothing." He cleared his throat and the cocky grin returned. "Until later. Your power is up. Calix and I will see you soon." His gaze was intent as he stared at her. "Really soon."

"Great." She refused to let him see the dread that swept over her. Her body was weak, and her spirit was faltering. She didn't know how many of those draining sessions she could take.

She listened as Ashe shut the door behind him and two locks clicked into place.

Once she was sure he was far enough away, she lay down. The effort of eating had exhausted her. Something cold and hard dug into her hip and she shifted away from it. Her cot wasn't made for enjoyment, and it was getting harder and harder to get comfortable. That and the cold made sleeping increasingly difficult.

The hard thing dug into her butt, and she reached down and pulled it out.

A key.

She stared at the metal object in her hand as her sluggish brain tried to make sense of what she was seeing. It was a key. It must have fallen from the bunch Ashe kept on a belt around his waist.

The lights flickered, and her cell was plunged into darkness.

It had been so long since she'd been in total dark that her eyes took long, agonizing moments to adjust. Even when she slept, they only dimmed the lights but never turned them off completely.

A plaintive, eerie howl penetrated the Stygian dark. It made the hair on her entire body stand on end. The power within her surged as if in answer to the howl. Was there another Nephilim here? She couldn't answer that. Shade, Wrath, and Sophia had told her she was the only living one of her kind. "Ugh." Her voice sounded unnaturally loud in the dark. She knew so little about her own power that she had no way of knowing what that surge truly meant.

The key pressed solid and cold into her hand.

It couldn't be the key to her cell door. Ashe would never have made that mistake.

Sounds came from outside her cell. With the light going, whatever had kept her in perpetual silence also seemed to have stopped. Raised voices, footsteps running past, and again, that soul searing howl that made her power leap.

Barely daring to breathe, she stumbled for the door. Her hands shook so badly, she had trouble getting the key into the lock. It fit.

Eddie suppressed a desperate sob. She couldn't believe. If it wasn't true, the dashed hope would kill her faster than the systematic draining of her power. It took all her strength to do it, but with a metallic snick, the lock opened.

It was too much to hope that the key would open a second look.

But it did.

And before she could process the fact, Eddie was staring into the deathly dark on the other side of her cell.

Noise buffeted her. Voices raised and shouting. And that howling. Over and over again, it echoed down the empty corridor.

Ashe's voice penetrated her fog. "Get those fucking lights on, and do it now."

"I don't know what happened," someone wailed.

"Are you going to explain to him how this happened?" Ashe asked. "He'll have your fucking guts for this. Get those fucking lights on so we can see where the prisoners are."

Prisoners, not prisoner.

"One of the prisoners' doors is open," the other yelled.

And Eddie moved into the corridor. Back against the wall, she edged away from the sound of Ashe and the other one arguing.

"Check him first," Ashe snarled.

"What about the girl?"

"Jesus! You want to tackle him or the girl?" Ashe's voice moved closer.

Eddie broke into a run. Her legs were lethargic, and it felt like wading through mud, but she forced them into action. Her breath sawed through her lungs, and she had to keep her hand on the wall to steady herself, but she shambled forward as fast as she could. With no idea where she was going, she focused on forward. One foot in front of the other and away from the voices.

"Mistress?" So faint that Eddie barely registered it in the escalating turmoil around her. Her head felt fuzzy and churned slowly.

She put everything she had into her reply. *"Xerxes?"*

"Keep thinking." Cronus came slightly stronger. *"Think about what you're seeing, just keep your mind open."*

Her pace quickened, her feet freezing against the rough floor. She snagged her toes on something, dodged and kept going, all the time keeping up a mental dialogue of whatever she saw or perceived, pure nonsense babble, but it kept the connection alive.

The hounds' voices seemed to grow stronger, or maybe she wished it so badly that it was all her imagination. Whatever it was, the hope kept her moving.

The wall beneath her questing palm changed, and she identified the outline of another door.

"There's a door. I don't know where it leads. I'm going to try the handle."

Something slammed into the door and rattled it in its jamb. A guttural snarl followed, and her power leapt. Eddie abandoned the idea of opening the door and pushed on.

"Follow our voices," Xerxes said. *"Keep following our voices."*

The lights flickered on, momentarily blinding her, and Eddie staggered but kept her forward momentum.

A metal spiral staircase appeared to her right, leading up.

"There she is."

She recognized Calix's nasal voice and took the stairs. She didn't know where they led, but as long as she was running she was still free.

Her breath labored through her burning lungs, and her legs threatened to collapse, but she kept climbing, one stair after another.

Footsteps clanged on the staircase behind her.

"Get her," Ashe bellowed. "If she gets out, Asmodeus will find her."

She was heading out. She had to be.

"Keep going," Xerxes said. *"We are close."*

A rough hand fastened around her ankle and sent her thumping into the metal staircase. Pain exploded from her knees as she hit the stairs.

"Got you," Calix snarled.

Eddie reached into a place she'd didn't even know existed. "No, you don't." With everything she had, she ripped Calix's hand off her ankle and shoved him back.

Calix's eyes widened before he careened back down the stairs. As he barreled into the pursuers behind him, screams, shouts, and thuds followed.

Eddie was moving again. She couldn't feel her left leg, and she dragged it behind her. The door loomed suddenly in front of her, and Eddie lurched for the handle. It turned under her palm, and daylight blinded her. Her eyes watered. The smell of air and growing things almost brought her to her knees, but she stumbled forward.

"Get her," Sophia yelled. "The hounds and I will deal with the demons."

"Eddie." Strong arms lifted her and cradled her against a chest. Honey and musk. Shade.

The door crashed open, and Xerxes and Cronus launched themselves at the demons spilling out of the door.

A blur of white wings and shining light shot past them and engaged the demons.

But Eddie was rising. Wings beat the air in a steady *whump, whump, whump.* Wind battered at her eardrums, and her clothes flapped around her limbs. She shivered, and Shade's arms tightened around her, tucking her closer to his body heat.

"Shade?"

"I've got you, Eddie. I've fucking got you."

Sounds of battle came from below them, and Eddie struggled against his hold. "My hounds."

"They deserve this," Shade said in a voice colder than the wind beating at her. "Let them have their vengeance."

SHADE HAD FORGOTTEN the sweet agony of emotion as he cradled Eddie in his arms. His powerful wings beat the air, putting distance between them and the place he had rescued her.

In his arms, she felt tiny and breakable. She'd lost a lot of weight, and she clung to him in a heartbreakingly un-Eddie way. But by the fire of hell, she was alive and with him. After all these weeks of searching, he finally had her.

Through their bond, he felt the hounds rip and sunder the demons who had pursued Eddie. Sophia's savage thrill as she handed out vengeance for both of them warmed his soul. He basked in their gory delight as the hounds and Sophia took their revenge on the beings who had held Eddie captive. As much as he wished he could enjoy the bloodbath with them, getting Eddie safe took precedence.

He buried his nose in her dusky hair and inhaled the rich, floral scent of her. Roses and cloves, and so dear to him it felt as if his heart would explode. Soon he would need to let Wrath and Dee know that he'd found her, but he had these precious minutes when she was his alone.

"Shade?" She stirred in his hold.

Hearing her say his name, even in that broken whisper brought tears to his eyes. The cold wind whipped them away as fast as they formed. "It's me, Eddie."

"You found me."

"Always, my love. I will always find you."

And then Eddie began crying. Each sob and tear ripped through his flesh and bone like the hounds' teeth. He would give his immortal soul to spare her this pain.

He, Sophia, and the hounds had been circling this area for days, the hounds catching hints and glimpses of her, but then having them disappear again. Only the hounds' steadfast conviction that she was here and Sophia's quiet but unwavering support had kept him waiting and searching. He hadn't slept in over a week, and neither had they. And their vigilance had paid off. He and Sophia had been running a routine sweep with the hounds covering the ground beneath them when suddenly Eddie's signature energy had surged up to him.

Like one being, all four of them had zeroed in on her location.

The sight of her pelting through that hidden door in the rock face had stupefied him for a moment. Thank hell for Sophia, because she had not hesitated, and her swift action had propelled him into motion.

Eddie's sobs subsided to the occasional shudder, and she shivered in his hold.

"Not long now, sweetheart, and I'll stop and get you

warm," he said, his voice rough with the emotion he could not contain.

"Shade?" She sniffed.

"Yes, Eddie." Not in all his years had he enjoyed hearing his name spoken by another being quite as much.

"I think my leg might be broken."

Fresh rage pounded through him, and he gloried in the carnage the hounds were wreaking behind them. "We'll fix it."

"I know." Her thin hand patted his cheek. "You're here now, and everything will be fixed."

TWENTY-TWO

Ashe threw Calix into the room, and his bloody form hit the floor in a wet squelch before Ashe lowered himself to the ground and pressed his forehead to the floor.

Shade's hounds and Sophia hadn't spared any of the demons who had pursued Eddie out of the bunker, and Ashe had fought hard to spare as much of Calix as he had.

Indolex's power washed over him in a hot wave of fury. His voice like metal over stone grated on Ashe's ears. "What happened?"

"She had the key, milord." Ashe kept his head lowered. "And as far as I can ascertain, this piece of shit gave it to her."

He felt Indolex move closer. No longer a demon, but something other and infinitely more powerful, the wash of his energy coated the back of Ashe's throat in a metallic taste and cradled his mind like a giant hand. The sweep of his robes penetrated the edges of Ashe's vision. "You are sure of this?"

"No, lord." Ashe kept his forehead pressed to the hard

concrete floor. "The cameras were not working during the incident, but only he and I had access to the key to her cell."

"I see." Indolex nudged the top of Ashe's head with his foot. "Look at me when I speak to you."

It was always a crap shoot with this fucking being, and whether you were looking at him or not, you were always guaranteed to be doing the wrong thing. Raising his torso, Ashe met the limitless black of Indolex's gaze. Once a high order demon like himself, Indolex had gorged himself on the power of the Nephilim until he was what he was now—deadly and undefeatable and terrifying. His power rivaled that of a hell prince now, and in a showdown, Ashe would put his money on Indolex. The bastard was driven by a soul-deep viciousness Ashe had never encountered in another being. For the first time in his long life, Ashe was truly afraid of a being. Lucifer at his angriest had retained some shade of reason. Indolex was pure evil purpose.

Indolex gazed at him, his unbroken black eyes drawing Ashe into the void of his soul. It was like looking into the face of chaos. "Then I have only your word that it was Calix and not you that gave her the key."

"This is true." Ashe held that fathomless stare. "But you know what is at stake for me."

"Yes." Indolex's raspy chuckle was like a cheese grater to his nerve endings. "We both know what keeps you chained to my service."

Ashe forced down his own rage and shrugged. "I would not risk them."

Indolex cocked his massive head, overhead lighting gleaming off the silver tips of his deadly horns. "You are a clever one, Ashe. I would not put it past you to play a deeper game."

He chose not to answer that.

In the next two minutes, Indolex would let him know the decision Ashe was certain the giant being had already made. Nothing he said would make any difference.

Indolex loomed over a moaning Calix.

Calix's lids fluttered open. His eyes widened in panic when he saw who was standing over him.

Ashe held his breath.

Bending, Indolex grabbed Calix by his throat and held him dangling five feet off the ground. "You have betrayed me, Calix."

Calix shot a panicked look at Ashe. "No, milord. It is—"

Closing his fist, Indolex crushed Calix's skull. His face expressionless, he then ripped the heart out of Calix's chest and ate it.

Calix's body dissolved into thick, gray ash and drifted to the floor.

On a low, disturbingly sexual moan, Indolex absorbed Calix's power. His body beneath the robes shuddered like he was climaxing.

The door behind Ashe opened, and demons poured through.

"You may not have betrayed me, Ashe." Indolex wiped the dust that had been Calix on his robes. "But you failed to stop the betrayal."

Ashe lowered his head and nodded. "Yes, milord."

"And for that you will pay."

This was going to fucking hurt. "Yes, milord."

UNENCUMBERED BY CARRYING ANOTHER BEING, Sophia flew ahead to the theatre. It still took the remainder of the day to reach Clayton. The hounds tracked Shade from the ground and remained close in case he needed them. Sophia had kept her senses wide as she tracked Shade's route in her wake. Sophia hadn't seen much of Eddie in those few seconds before she had ripped into demons, but she had gotten a fleeting impression of a thin, pale Eddie, barely able to hold herself upright.

Beside her, Dee couldn't contain her restless energy and paced the small parking lot outside the stage door. Trying to prepare Dee for what she might see, Sophia stopped the other woman with a hand on her arm. Mellow orange streetlights cast macabre shadows over the empty space as they waited. "Dee. Shade is carrying Eddie, and we must be prepared for her to be injured."

Dee paled. "What do you mean injured?"

"She's been held for a while now." Sophia counted her words carefully. "She may be in compromised health."

Tears filled Dee's blue eyes. "Oh, God."

"But we will heal her." Or drain themselves trying. "And Wrath should be on his way back. He is the best person to heal her. Ramiel will help him." Or Sophia would snap his fucking wings.

"Did you call the gathering?" Daniel stood beside her and watched Dee with a frown.

Sophia nodded. "I did."

"They should be arriving soon." Daniel shoved his hands in his pockets. His concern for Dee simmered beneath the calm, implacable mask he wore.

Sophia did enjoy humans and their shifting cauldron of emotions. She wished she could assure him that everything was all right, but until Shade arrived with Eddie, she could guarantee nothing.

Eddie had been hurt. The seals were weakening. The horsemen were stirring. Nothing would be alright until they could turn the tidal wave of bad back.

Dee's circular route brought her closer to them. "What's taking so long?"

"He covered a lot of distance looking for her. Now he's flying above the cloud cover," Sophia said and tried to put as much assurance as she could into her tone. "It won't be long now."

Dee threw her a fulminating stare. "You've been saying that for twenty fucking minutes."

"Shade loves her, Dee," Daniel said. "He will only do what is safest and best for her."

There would come a time when those words would not shred her innards, but that was not this night, and Sophia breathed deep through the pain. Being with Shade these past weeks, watching his desperation as he searched for Eddie had driven the point home that he could never be hers. She had waited centuries, sure that Shade would eventually turn to her. And now he belonged to a Nephilim, who Sophia really, really liked. Eddie was a special soul. One that deserved the being who now called her his. Envy turned a soul to dust. Sophia didn't know how Leviathan dealt with it all the time.

Shade's power built inside her. "He's nearly here."

"Thank, Christ." Dee stopped pacing and stood beside her. "Did he say how Eddie is? Did he tell us if she's all right?"

A winged figure shot through the thick, autumnal night and arrowed for the parking lot. "You can ask him yourself," Sophia said.

Shade backwinged, sending dust and debris swirling around them, and then he was before them, Eddie tenderly cradled against his chest. "Get Wrath," he rasped. "She needs his healing."

"Yes." Ramiel strode out of the shadows. "By all means, get Wrath. I would like to know where he has disappeared to with my seraph."

Sophia was not prone to violence, but at that moment, she could have cheerfully consigned Ramiel to oblivion.

The stage door burst open, and Wrath strode into the parking lot. "Nobody needs to get me." His gaze focused on Eddie lying like a broken doll in Shade's arms. "My child is here, and that is where I will always be."

"She's so thin." Shade's granite demeanor cracked as he looked at Wrath. "She's barely holding on. Her leg is broken, and she's close to giving up." Moonlight glinted off tears on Shade's cheek.

Dee stepped forward, her face creased with concern. "Eddie-girl?"

"She can't hear you," Shade said. "She passed out about forty-five minutes ago, and I haven't been able to rouse her."

"Oh, Wrath." Haziel stepped out from behind Wrath, her hand on his shoulder, her compassionate gaze on Eddie's inert form. "She will be well. Shade got to her in time."

Wrath seemed to draw strength from the contact, and his shoulders straightened. He held out his arms for Eddie. "Give her to me."

Struggle played across Shade's beautiful face as he looked from Wrath to Eddie.

"Please, Shade." Dee touched his arm. "Wrath can help her."

Shade's internal battle tightened his features, until with a sigh, he held Eddie out to Wrath. "She needs you."

"She's my daughter." Wrath cradled Eddie to his chest. "There is nothing that I will not do for her."

Sophia felt like an interloper as the silent battle took place between Wrath and Shade. They both loved this Nephillim so much, and neither of them could trust another with her.

"I vow to you," Wrath said, his voice quiet and gruff. "I will do all that I can."

Shade finally nodded. "I wish I could do more."

"You have done everything." Wrath gave him a curt nod. "I am forever in your debt."

Shade watched Wrath stride into the theatre with Eddie, and Sophia almost didn't catch his quiet words, "As I am forever in your debt."

"Haziel," Ramiel thundered, his wings out. "You will report to me."

Haziel stopped in the doorway where she'd been following Wrath and bowed to Ramiel. "Archangel."

And Sophia refused to hold her tongue any longer. "Shut the fuck up, Ramiel. We have much bigger things to worry about than your dented ego." She nodded to Haziel. "See what Wrath needs and make sure he gets it."

Ramiel sucked in a breath and straightened his shoulders.

She didn't give a fuck. Ramiel was a pompous blowhard who should spend less time strumming a harp on his cloud and more time dealing with the world.

Sophia stared him down and finally, Ramiel nodded.

On a hastily suppressed gasp, Haziel followed Wrath and Shade into the theatre.

Once they were alone in the parking lot, Ramiel rounded on her, wings flared and gaze threatening retribution. "You have no right," he thundered.

"Yeah, yeah, yeah." Sophia was so tired of the male presenting archangels assuming they were in command of her. She could match them power for power. She could blow their egos and their petty bullshit right out of the sky. "Tell someone who gives a shit."

"You countermanded me." Ramiel glowed like a midday sun. "You countermanded me before two hell princes, a guardian and a human."

"Let's not forget your seraph." Sophia let her wings flare

behind her. She refused to play subservient to these arrogant pricks any longer. "And I did so because you were out of line."

Ramiel eyed her wings and scoffed. "Out of line. Wrath has disappeared with my seraph for weeks, yet you defend him."

"The seraph you commanded to stay by his side. You sent a seraph to hell with only a powerless hell prince for protection." Sophia was not inclined to play nice. Nice got you nowhere. Nice got you consigned to underling. "If she has come to prefer his company, you only have yourself and your unmitigated arrogance to blame."

Ramiel stuck his chin out. "You have no idea of which you speak."

"Really?" Sophia called his bullshit. "Haziel went with Wrath only under your command, and now she recognizes what you fail to." She stepped into his space. "That the love of a father for his child exceeds all other concerns." She met his gaze and held it. "And I suggest that you start to develop an iota of empathy before you lose more than you're prepared to."

TWENTY-THREE

The sights, sounds, and smells of the theatre wrapped around Eddie like a cozy blanket as Wrath carried her up the stairs to her bedroom. She didn't know how long they'd been flying because she'd drifted off at some point, but night had fallen.

Shade's face showed no signs of exhaustion as his face hovered behind Wrath's shoulder. Wrath held her in a strong, sure grip that made her feel safe.

And then Wrath was laying her down on her bed. The old springs of the cast-iron frame gave a familiar creak, and the waft of her normal detergent was achingly familiar on the linens.

"Eddie?" Dee's face wove into sight above her. Tears spilled down Dee's cheeks and fogged up the lenses of her glasses. "Oh, Eddie-girl."

She could count on one hand the times she'd seen Dee cry. When Rosabella had left the first time, she had a dim memory of Dee wiping away tears. Tears of pride on Eddie's graduation and other special occasions, the wistful mistiness of Christmases and Birthdays. But she had never seen Dee too overcome to speak, sobs shaking her slim shoulders and tears running down her cheeks.

Gently cradling her face, Dee cried.

"It's okay." Eddie's voice sounded rusty and disused. "I'm okay, Dee."

Mutely, Dee shook her head and kept right on bawling.

Shade looked at someone over her head. "She needs something to drink. She's exhausted."

"Apple juice," Lillian chirped. "I have some in my tote."

The *Macbeth* rehearsal had been ending when Eddie had arrived, and a few had followed them upstairs.

Shade nodded. "That will do fine."

"Should we call a doctor?" Peter, *Macbeth's* director, spoke from somewhere near her doorway. "Better yet, take her to a hospital."

Eddie didn't want to go anywhere, and she tried to struggle into a sitting position. "No."

"You're staying right here." Shade pressed her down gently. "Wrath will take care of you."

There were so many figures in her room that they all blurred into a cacophony of words and images. Her head began pounding.

"Right." Wrath's voice cut through the chatter. "Everybody out. You can see Edme when she's rested, but right now, she needs quiet."

Lillian spoke up, "And apple juice. I have her apple juice."

"And apple juice," Wrath said softly. "I'm going to need you to take everyone downstairs. She's overwhelmed."

"Of course." Lillian's voice grew sergeant major strong. "Everybody but immediate family out."

There was more bustle and then silence.

Her bed dipped as Wrath sat down beside her. "Daughter,"

he whispered hoarsely. His big hand smoothed hair back from her face, calloused, strong, and tender. Moisture gathered in his blue eyes. "You don't look your best."

"I've had a bad few weeks." And the laughter was exactly what she needed to ground herself.

Her bedroom door flew open, and Cronus and Xerxes muscled their way into the room.

The hounds crawled onto her bed and took up position either side of her.

"Be gentle," Wrath said to them.

Both hounds gave him a fang flash and low growl.

"They won't hurt her," Shade said. "They adore her." His gaze caressed her face. "We all adore her."

Nodding, Wrath placed his hand on her chest. A warm glow emanated from the contact of his palm against her skin.

He frowned and glanced at Shade. "I will need to heal her." Then his tender blue eyes were back on her. "What did they do to you?"

"An amulet, like the one they put on you." Eddie shuddered as her mind flooded with terrible memories. "They drained my power."

Xerxes growled and pressed closer.

Wrath nodded. "Close your eyes."

Eddie did and comforting heat flooded from his palm into her. Her eyelids felt too heavy to open and she kept them closed.

Her bed dipped, and Cronus moved, and then Shade was there, holding her with her head against his chest. His hand stroking her spine. "Sleep, Eddie. we will be right here until you wake. Nothing will get past the hounds and me."

～

W RATH POURED AS MUCH of his power as he dared into Eddie's frail body. What he discovered through their connection threatened to break him in two. Eddie's lifeforce had been dangerously depleted, and whatever had happened to her while she was taken from them had attacked her mind, body, and spirit. He wanted to rage at the world that had hurt his precious child.

"Enough," Shade whispered from his place holding Eddie. "We don't want to do more damage trying to help her."

It took everything in him to remove his hand from Eddie. "I could do more if I had Ramiel's balancing power."

Eddie's eyes were closed, and a faint flush covered her gaunt cheeks. Fury pounded through him, and his wings sprung from his back.

"Don't." Shade shook his head. "Take that out of here."

Dee sat in an armchair beside Eddie's bed, the odd tear still trickling down her cheek.

He needed to get out of here until he could control his wrath.

Haziel was standing in the hallway outside Eddie's room. "How is she?"

"Not good." Being near her made him feel less like breaking the world. "She needs healing, and I'm not sure how long it will take. I need to..."

"I know." Haziel touched his hand. "Go and burn off some emotion. Shade and Dee will not leave her, and the hounds are here." She gave him her gorgeous smile. "And I will not leave until you return."

He didn't know why he trusted her like he did, but he found himself nodding. "When I find them..."

"You will do what needs to be done." Haziel's green eyes filled with the same fury he felt. "But for now, your anger may do more harm than good." She motioned the door to the theatre. "Stretch your wings. Find your balance, restore your healing energy, and then return here and help her."

He nodded. "How is your wing?"

"Don't worry about me." Her sweetness touched a place deep inside him. "My wing is great."

She actually drew a smile from him. "I thought you couldn't lie."

"Not technically a lie because five of them are great and one is a mite sore, but it will be fine." She cupped his cheek with her hand. "You took good care of me, and you will take even better care of your daughter."

HAZIEL CLOSED the back door behind Wrath and released the sigh she'd been holding. The summons for the gathering had reached them as they were leaving Shade's palace, and shortly on its heels had come the news that Shade had found Eddie.

They'd flown at full speed for the hell gate, with her forcing her injured wing to keep working. Wrath's healing had worked, and other than some residual stiffness now, she was going to be fine.

"That was a big sigh." Ramiel emerged from the greenroom.

The theatre company had all left for the night. She didn't know what they thought of the new beings drifting around the theatre, or even what explanation had been given for their presence.

"Ramiel."

He looked as beautiful as ever. His green eyes, almost the same shade as her own, glowed as he looked at her. The ever-present soft white light surrounded him like his own full body halo.

Ramiel motioned to the door she had shut. "You seem to be getting along famously with our bad-tempered hell prince."

"We get on fine." She felt suddenly guilty for all that had happened between her and Wrath. She prayed Ramiel wouldn't ask the sort of questions that would force an honest answer from her.

He stroked his smooth chin and tilted his head. "Fine? From what I saw, you and Wrath are getting along a whole lot more than fine."

If it had been any other being, she would have thought he was jealous, but despite every opportunity she'd given him, Ramiel had never shown that sort of interest in her. "Well, yes." Heat flooded her cheeks. There were words she could use that were not a lie. "We have spent some time together. He has taken good care of me while we were in hell."

"He abandoned you in Mammon's demesne." Ramiel folded his arms over his muscular chest. "I insisted that he fetch you back."

"Ava." The correction came automatically. "She doesn't answer to Mammon and prefers Ava."

As sure as she was that Ramiel would have been angry about her being left with Ava, she wasn't sure he was telling her the entire truth. Or not the truth she would love to believe. Her heart whispered that if he had insisted Wrath fetch her, it wouldn't have been out of fondness—not the sort of fondness she craved from him.

Like all archangels, Ramiel was stunning, even down to the small imperfections that stopped him from being too beautiful. In Ramiel's case, a small bump marred the bridge of his strong nose. His biceps wore a few small scars that he'd gotten from sword fights. The flaws only made him better looking, but her heart did not miss a beat like it did when she looked at Wrath's brutal beauty.

He studied her face. "You look different."

"I injured my wing." She longed for a mirror to see what Ramiel was talking about.

"And Wrath healed it for you?"

"Yes." Guilt flooded through her again. Ramiel would be horrified by what had transpired between her and Wrath. He would see it as a form of betrayal. She was a terrible seraph to entertain feelings for a being who was the arch nemesis of the angel she had always claimed to love. She needed to change the subject. "They need your help with her." She pointed to the ceiling that separated them from Eddie's room. "Your power is so similar to Wrath's, but gentler and more inclined to peace than war." As she spoke her enthusiasm for her idea grew. "If you worked with her sire, she would heal faster and better."

Ramiel pursed his perfectly formed lips. "You're right. I could help her."

"Will you?" Hope rang painfully clearly in her voice.

Ramiel stepped closer to her. He took her braid and wrapped it tenderly around his fist. He seemed to be studying the individual strands of her hair. "I rather think that depends on you."

"I don't understand." She'd seen Ramiel in many different moods, but this was a new one for her, and she felt adrift as she tried to navigate it. Perhaps it was her own guilt about the secrets between them that made her view him differently. She had never kept secrets from Ramiel. Until now.

"You see, Haziel. I know you." He tugged on her hair and brought her closer to him. Heat radiated from his hard body, but it didn't make her want to press into him like it did with Wrath. She didn't know what to make of that but the look in Ramiel's eyes kept her frozen; half speculative, and cunning. "You cannot lie to me, so if I ask you a direct question you will be forced to give me the answer."

"Please don't ask it," she whispered, her heart in her throat.

"And that, in itself, is an answer." He looked at her with profound disappointment, dropping her braid as he stepped back. "There is more between you and Wrath," he said. "And you are dangerously close to him." He shrugged. "I blame myself for sending you on a mission with him. I didn't think, however, you would be foolish enough to fall for a lout like him."

Haziel burned to defend Wrath, but Ramiel's unreadable mood kept her silent. She had fallen for Wrath, that much was true. But she had no idea how far or how deep.

"I will help the Nephilim." Ramiel sighed and stepped back. "And in return you will leave this theatre on a mission for me, and not tell Wrath that you have gone."

"Why?" She tried to glean the answer from his eyes. "Lucifer is still missing. The rebel demon hordes are growing. Our work in hell is not complete."

"Yours is." His eyes went emerald hard. "You will put distance between yourself and Wrath. You will go and investigate the stirring of the horsemen. And in exchange, I will help with his daughter."

Haziel gaped at him. She had never seen Ramiel's cunning streak turned against her. It felt like a kick to her chest. She was momentarily robbed of breath. "Why are you doing this?"

"Haziel." He shook his head. "You are so naive and it falls to me to protect you. Do as I ask, and I will help his daughter. And once you are finished, you will return to my demesne and remain there. I gave you my trust, and you have not proven worthy."

That hurt, and she barely suppressed a flinch. But Ramiel spoke only the truth. She had come dangerously close to betraying Ramiel in deed, and she had betrayed him in thought.

Then she thought about Eddie and the shock of seeing her lying drained and depleted in that bed. The horror Wrath had concealed from his daughter about her condition. The heartbreak written clear across Shade's face. And as much as she wanted to remain here, there really was no choice. Wrath loved his daughter, and perhaps if she hadn't delayed him in hell, they would have found Eddie sooner. If ensuring Eddie healed completely would spare Wrath the pain of watching her struggle, then that's what she'd do. "When would you like me to leave?"

"Now."

"I promised Wrath I would stay until he got back."

Ramiel's smile didn't reach his eyes. "I will explain that you have gone." He spread his arms. "The choice is yours, however." He smirked as if he already knew her decision.

And for the first time in the thousands of years she had served him, Haziel did not like her archangel.

TWENTY-FOUR

Eddie woke to her bedroom door creaking open. The hounds were bookending her, but Shade wasn't there.

"The master has to attend the gathering," Cronus said without opening his eyes. *"But your hounds are here."*

"Eddie?" A woman whispered.

"This one smells like you, but is nothing like you," Xerxes said.

"Eddie are you awake?" Rosabella slipped through the door crack. "It's Mom."

Her mother was here. Nobody had said a word to her about that. Easing herself into a sitting position, Eddie said, "Hi." She couldn't quite manage the mom and didn't want to hurt Rosabella's feelings by using her name.

It had to be weird that her first thought wasn't joy about her mother being here, but more along the lines of what Rosabella wanted.

"Oh, Eddie." Rosabella pressed a hand to her mouth. Her aqua eyes swam with tears. "You look awful."

Okay, putting that one down to shock, Eddie said, "It's been...rough."

"I told my mother she shouldn't get you involved in this guardian shit." Rosabella perched on the side of her bed. "Look what it's done to you."

There were so many counterarguments to that statement, but Eddie didn't have the energy. Some time in their brief interactions she'd given up on contradicting Rosabella's version of reality. "I'll be fine. Wrath and Ramiel have been healing me, and Shade says I need to rest."

"What happened?" Rosabella patted her cheeks dry. "Nobody will tell me, and I am your mother."

In the loosest and purely biological sense, that was true. "I don't really want to talk about it."

"Of course." Rosabella nodded and looked stricken. "I shouldn't have asked." Her eyes teared up again. "I just had to see you to make sure you were all right."

Flashes of moments when Rosabella had not been there went through Eddie's mind—the time she had broken her arm falling off the stage, the time she had come home crying from the park because none of the children would play with the "weirdo from the theatre," her first heartbreak. "I'm going to be fine."

Cronus pressed his huge body against her. *"You will be. The master and your hounds will make sure of that."*

"I don't know what's going on around here," Rosabella wailed. "But nobody will tell me anything, and now there are archangels and hell princes all over the place." She sobbed and swiped at her cheeks. "And they're all meeting and waiting for the guardians, and they won't let me attend. Of course, my mother is allowed to attend." Rosabella's face hardened. "And I don't know why she's allowed to attend when she isn't even the guardian anymore. That idiot Daniel has taken over from her, and officially she wasn't even the guardian before he arrived. I was."

"Hmm." Eddie kept it noncommittal. But she didn't believe you could claim the title of guardian without having been near the hell gate in years.

"Anyway." Rosabella heaved a big breath and squared her shoulders. "That's nothing for you to worry about." She patted Eddie's legs through the covers. "You need to rest up and recover, and the last thing you need to worry about is me."

Eddie's head gave a dull throb, and all she wanted to do was go back to sleep. She didn't have it in her to deal with Rosabella right now. "I am very tired."

"I'm sure." Rosabella squeezed her leg. "After what you've been through. I mean, after what happened to you…" She gave Eddie a look brimming with hope that Eddie would fill in the blanks.

"I could make her leave," Xerxes said.

A warm swell of appreciation washed over her. *"No, it's fine. I've found the best thing to do is let her have her say."*

Cronus eyed Rosabella. *"And you are certain of this course?"*

"Ugh!" Rosabella flapped a hand in front of her nose. "I'm sure these smelly beasts on your bed are not helping."

"They're helping." Eddie put a hand on each ruff. Having them here was almost as comforting as having—Nope! She couldn't think like that. The last few weeks all felt like too much, and she only had to close her eyes to see those metal walls closing around her, smell the astringent bite of whatever they had pumped through the air vents, feel the soul-tearing agony of that amulet draining the very essence of her.

Cronus put his mammoth head on her lap. *"We are here."*

"I saw Wrath was back." Rosabella tucked a shiny fall of hair behind her ear. "We chatted."

"Right." Despite all her questions, Eddie didn't want to discuss Wrath with Rosabella. Of the two of them, only one had never lied to her—not that she knew of, in any case. As soon as the caveat popped into her mind, she dismissed it. Wrath was nothing if not brutally honest.

Rosabella pursed her mouth and tossed a hand in the air. "Of course, he hates me now." She rolled her eyes. "I honestly don't know what he expected me to do. I was alone, young, pregnant by a demon—"

"Hell prince," Eddie said.

"What?"

"Hell prince. Wrath is a hell prince and not a demon."

"Whatever." Rosabella flapped her hand again. "Hell prince, demon, they're all the same thing.

Xerxes growled. *"I could show her the difference."*

A chuckle got away from Eddie before she could stop it.

Eyes gleaming, Rosabella assumed Eddie was laughing at what she'd said and leaned forward. "Am I right?"

"I'll speak to him," Eddie said, more out of a desire to have this conversation over than anything else.

Rosabella beamed at her. Her mother really did have a lovely smile. Broad and wide, a flash of white teeth and a crinkle around dancing blue-green eyes that invited you to share the joke. "Thank you, darling. Whatever Wrath thinks of me, I am still your mother, and the bond between mothers and daughters is a special thing."

If a distant one in their case. Eddie gave her a vague nod.

"And as your mother"—Rosabella took a deep breath— "and a woman who has made the mistake you're about to, I want to warn you."

A knot tightened in Eddie's belly. Rosabella was the last person she wanted to have a conversation with about Shade. "It's all right—"

"No, Eddie." Rosabella tilted her head and held up one hand, the sage voice of reason in a vortex of cray-cray. "I'm your mother, and I can see the way the wind is blowing. And if you'll pardon the expression, you are farting against a thunderstorm with this one."

"Eh?" All the wind metaphors were getting confusing.

"God knows they're pretty enough." Rosabella smoothed the lap of her sparkly maxi skirt. "They're gorgeous enough to make a smart woman want to do really stupid things." She pointed to herself. "And in my case, a smart woman did a really stupid thing."

Hmm? Would we say smart?

Cronus chuffed and gave her a doggy grin.

"But he said he loved me." Rosabella heaved a tremulous sigh and squeezed a tear out of her right eye. "And I believed him. I gave him my innocence and my trust."

According to Dee, both of those had disappeared long before Rosabella had met Wrath. "It's okay, I—"

"No, Eddie." Rosabella gave her what passed for her best maternal expression of concern. "I need to have my say. I've not always been allowed to be a mother to you, but nobody can stop me from warning you from making the biggest mistake of your life." She leaned closer. "Don't fall in love with a hell prince.

According to Wrath, Rosabella hadn't loved him, but the relationship between her parents was not one she wanted to wade into. "Shade and I aren't...that."

"Asmodeus is a demon." Leaning forward, Rosabella went eye to eye with her.

Hell prince.

"A fallen angel." Rosabella punctuated that with an eyebrow raise. "It's in his nature to lie and deceive and take advantage of innocent women."

Eddie didn't see any of those in this bedroom, and her headache grabbed her head in a vice grip.

"Ah, Rosabella." Shade strolled into her bedroom, every

inch of him looking like the warning Rosabella had tried to impart. He smiled at Rosabella, but it was not the same smile he gave to Eddie. It didn't touch the clear gray of his eyes. "There you are. Dee was looking for you."

"What for?" Rosabella looked concerned.

Probably because Dee was an expert in getting Rosabella to do shit around the theatre.

"She didn't say." Shade shrugged and draped himself on the bed beside Eddie.

Cronus grumbled on a stink eye directed at Shade and shifted to the floor.

"But Dee is on her way up here." Shade put his arm around Eddie.

Immediately something unknotted in her belly, and the pressure in her head eased. Maybe he had some kind of healing magic in his skin, or maybe it was just having him close?

Rosabella shot to her feet. "Well, then. I think I've said everything I came here to say." She shot Eddie a loaded look. "I'll go and find my mother."

Shade watched until Rosabella had disappeared, and her feet clattered down the stairs.

"I don't think she's going to find Dee," Eddie murmured. Shade was so warm, and her body seemed to nestle itself into him without her brain being one hundred percent on board with the idea. Then again, she had a headache, so her brain was probably on the fritz anyway. He smelled amazing, honey and musk with that sensual jasmine undertone. He smelled like safety and comfort, and other things her body had no business reminding her about. "Don't you have a gathering happening?"

"Eh." He shrugged. "We supernaturals are not known for our time keeping skills, and there are still a few key players missing." He smoothed her hair off her forehead. "The lads told me she was upsetting you."

She shot Cronus a look.

He yawned.

"Yeah." She kept it casual, not wanting to relate the conversation about Shade to Shade. "But she's Rosabella, so I'm used to it."

"You should let Xerxes eat her." Humor warmed Shade's tone.

Xerxes drew his lips back and licked his chops as if he'd tasted something nasty.

Eddie laughed, and Shade's laughter rumbled through her ear pressed against his chest. He kissed the top of her head. "Are you okay?"

"Yep."

"Liar," he murmured and tucked her into his side. "Let me guess." He hummed. "Rosabella would like to warn you about the dangers of hell princes." Cocking his head, he studied Cronus and then chuckled. "Sorry, demons. That we are not to be trusted and will break your heart without breaking a sweat."

"Well...yes." Heat climbed up her neck and over her face. With her mouthy hounds, he would never need to eavesdrop.

"She wanted to warn you not to make the same mistakes she did," Shade continued, his big palm caressing her arm from wrist to shoulder. "And that ultimately you should kick me to the curb."

"Would that be possible?"

"Kicking me to the curb?" Shade adjusted his position to look at her face. "I mean, you could try. Like I've said before—"

"Nephilim are rare and thus unknown."

He hugged her tighter. "And here I thought you weren't really listening."

"I listened." Eddie found comfort in the steady beat of his heart.

"Did you also listen when I told you that I had already lost my heart to you?"

Everything in her wanted to believe that, but she still harbored that bit of doubt. If she gave herself fully to Shade, he had the power to destroy her. And not only in the world ending kind of way. He would end her world if he left her. "You also said you would court me."

"This isn't courtship?" He cocked his head and met her gaze, humor dancing in his eyes.

"There's a concerning lack of flowers." Eddie loved this playful side of him. It called to something in her that wanted to come out and play. "And bringing me meals on a tray is not the same as wining and dining me."

"Hmm." Shade made a show of thinking over her words. "The lads have clearly been leading me wrong."

Cronus grumbled and closed his eyes again.

"I get it, Eddie." His tone turned serious. "You're not ready, and that's fine with me. I have time on my hands, and you are worth every moment of waiting."

TWENTY-FIVE

Wrath took a seat in the greenroom as far away from Ramiel as the small room would allow. The theatre humans were busy doing something in the bigger rehearsal space, which would have been better suited to all the thundering egos about to trap themselves in a plasterboard box.

He hadn't seen Haziel since they'd returned, which was odd because she'd said she would be here, and it wasn't like her not to do what she said she would. And he knew all too well that she couldn't lie. Still, he'd been preoccupied with Eddie and getting her healed. Ramiel had helped with that, their joint powers merging and packing more healing than his alone. If Ramiel hadn't done it with the air of a sanctimonious bible thumper, Wrath might have found it in himself to say thank you.

"How is Edme?" Ramiel smirked.

"Recovering." Wrath met his stare and held it, proud that he didn't use his fists instead. Haziel should be trotting along any moment now. Whither goest Ramiel and all that crap. If he accomplished one thing before he and Haziel parted, it would be to convince her how far beneath her she was punching. Ramiel didn't deserve any part of that female.

"Fuck me," Leviathan said in her throaty drawl as she stood in the doorway in all her tall, willowy, kickass beauty, and for a moment, Wrath wondered if that was an invitation or an expression of disgust.

Ramiel was eye humping her in a way that made Wrath want to make him eat his teeth. He had a brief and delightful mental of Ramiel shitting his own chicklets. Everything on the normal then.

"Wrath." Levi's pouty, red mouth split into a pure sin smile. "You're looking delicious as ever."

"Back at ya." He winked at her.

Levi chuckled and sashayed into the room.

Before Zeb had staked his claim, he and Levi had enjoyed a delightful no strings kind of connection. Unlike Ava, Levi didn't want to hand him his wedding tackle for their affair ending. Wrath wished Zeb luck with trying to stamp his mine-all-mine on Levi. The hell prince was the defining free spirit and wouldn't be tied to any being.

She dropped on the sofa beside him in a soft chuff of leather and air. "How many more of these fucking gatherings are we all going to have to endure?"

"Good afternoon." Gabriel clippity-cloppitied her way into the greenroom on her high heels. She pinned Levi with a head-mistress lip purse. "And you are aware that a gathering would not have been called unless under the direst of circumstances."

Levi stretched her long, leather-clad legs in front of her. "Super."

As Wrath had suspected he would be, Beelzebub followed hot on Levi's trail. He clocked her sitting beside him, and his jaw tightened. "Wrath."

"Zeb."

Zeb's face softened, which in the case of this particular hell prince, was like granite easing into quartz. "Levi."

"Hey, handsome," Levi rasped.

Flushing, Zeb wedged himself on the sofa on the other side of Levi and draped his arm over the back.

Wrath grinned at him to let him know he saw his bullshit and didn't give a crap.

The arrival of the other archangels chimed inside him, and he tensed along with Zeb and Levi.

Looking like a fucking Abercrombie & Who's-a-little-bitch commercial, they strolled into the greenroom in a six pack. Michael headed the flexing and radiating prissy posse.

"Jesus." Levi rammed a pair of Ray-Bans over her eyes. "Can you turn down the lightshow?"

Gabriel consulted her tablet. "We are still missing Belphegor, Shade, Mammon, and Lucifer from your side."

"Present and accounted for." Shade strolled into the greenroom, smelling like Eddie and looking like a being with a lot on his mind. As much as Wrath wanted to hate the thing between Eddie and Shade, he had seen the way she clung to Shade. He'd also noticed the way Shade didn't want to be any place other than close to Eddie. And he owed Shade for doing what he hadn't been able to: finding Eddie.

Still, he'd only just found his daughter, and it now looked like he might need to share her with another. The years he'd missed with Eddie sat like old porridge in his gut. Even with all the power in this room, they couldn't turn back time and give him what he'd lost.

"How is Edme?" Zeb glanced at him.

And it gave the sweetest relief to say, "She's recovering well."

"Oh my." Ava strutted in, her hips going like she had a pair of bongo drums laying down a slick track in her head. It was a good look on her. Even though he wasn't going there again, he could see why he had. She let her gaze do the walking over Michael. "We should totally do this more often."

Michael stiffened.

Shade chuckled. Yeah, they didn't need the lust hell prince to read the play on that one.

He almost missed Belle cruising Ava's wake and making herself small near the microwave. Easily the physically tiniest of the beings in the room, Belphegor liked to stick to herself and keep her opinions between her teeth. She reminded him of a tiny, sparkly sprite with her shiny waves of platinum hair and big blue eyes. Sending her a nod, he got a small smile in return.

"So." Gabriel tapped at her ever-present tablet. Wrath was convinced that thing was fused to her soul as well as her hand. And speaking of fused, Raguel joined them, whispered something in Gabriel's ear and then made like a ghost. Poor bastard. He'd really drawn the archangel short straw with that assignment. "Still missing Bel—I beg your pardon. Just Lucifer."

"You know, you could look around the room instead of consulting that infernal device." Michael shifted the broad sword between his shoulder blades.

Wrath's spine crawled, and then Lucifer appeared in the doorway. "Am I late?"

Red washed over his sight, and fury surged through his body. He'd kill him.

Wrath lunged for his twin, only to run into the brick wall of Michael, Raphael, and Ramiel.

"No fighting," Gabriel snapped. "We cannot afford to be divided at this time."

Wrath didn't give a fuck. Lucifer had been responsible for Eddie's kidnapping, and the torture they'd put his child through. He would have his vengeance in flesh, sinew, and blood. "He ends now."

"Stop," Michael grunted. "We can't let you end him."

Through his wash of rage, Wrath noted that Michael didn't deny his right to wreak his vengeance on Lucifer.

He threw his strength against the triumvirate of muscle between him and his target.

"Listen to him." Despite panting from his effort of holding Wrath back, Raphael managed to sound calm and rational. "I have spoken with Lucifer, and you should hear him out."

"Fuck off." Wrath pulled on his power. His wings released.

Michael, Raphael, and Ramiel pulled their power to hold him.

The mirror shattered, faucets exploded, cupboard doors wrenched from their hinges and flew around the room. The furniture buckled and slammed into walls. The lights exploded.

"Nope." Ramiel gritted his teeth, perspiration dotting his forehead. "Stop now, or I'm gonna have to shut you down."

And only Ramiel could do it. His check and balance, his countermeasure.

"Breathe." Shade touched his shoulder, then leaned closer and whispered, "Let's hear him out first, and then we end him. When these fuckers aren't around."

He'd always hated how tricky Shade could be, but right now, Wrath appreciated it. As an enemy he could drive you to destruction; as an ally he was a cool, measured head.

"I'm good." Wrath dragged a breath into his lungs.

Michael, Ramiel, and Raphael kept their hold on him.

"Get your fucking hands off me."

Ramiel stared into his eyes. "Are you calm?"

"Go fuck yourself."

Ramiel chuckled and glanced at his fellow archangels. "He's angry, but he's got a hold on it now."

Michael and Ramiel stepped back but kept themselves between him and the hell prince who was about to meet extinction.

"I love these little get-togethers," Belle murmured.

Lucifer's gaze met his over Raphael's muscled shoulder. "I didn't take her, brother. I vow it."

"Tell him who did." Raphael kept his focus on Wrath.

"Ashe." Lucifer's jaw tightened, his characteristic insouciance missing. "He was one of mine, but this was not under my instruction. Fucker went rogue, and I haven't seen him in months."

Wrath's temper lashed its tail within him, and Shade tightened the grip on his shoulder. "I don't believe you."

"I'm aware." Lucifer raised an eyebrow. "But think, Satanus. What reason would I have for kidnapping your daughter?" He pressed a hand to his chest. "My niece."

"Like you give a fuck about that."

Lucifer smirked. "Strangely enough, I do." He flicked his fingers between them. "Whatever issues I have with you, do not extend to Edme."

Shade snarled. "Get her name out of your mouth."

"This is why Nephilim should not be allowed." Gabriel pursed her lips.

"Shut up," Raphael snapped at her. "Go back to alphabetizing your Spotify playlist."

Gabriel's pinched expression tightened. "Raguel has already taken care of that for me."

"I agree with Raphael." Michael glared at her. "Shut the fuck up."

Moving closer to Lucifer, his wary gaze still on Wrath, Raphael said, "Tell them what you've found out."

"I've been looking for Ashe, tracking the hordes of missing demons." Lucifer snapped the cuffs of his priggish shirt. "As we're all aware, the horde is made up of demons from all of our hordes." His dark eyes swept all the hell princes. "And as anomalous as that is, they seem to be cooperating. I suspect we have a rebellion on our hands, and they're powerful, united, and using Nephilim power to increase their strength." He met Wrath's gaze. "That's what I suspect they are doing with the amulets. We have all noticed they are more powerful than they should be."

His words clanged like a dropped anvil into the destroyed greenroom.

Gabriel recovered her composure first. "That's impossible."

"As much as it pains me, I have to agree with you. It shouldn't be possible." Lucifer stepped into the greenroom. "But impossible or not, it's happening." He looked at Wrath. "Ashe betrayed me. No doubt about it, the duplicitous fucker is with them, and given his powers, I would not be surprised to find out he's the one leading them."

Wrath had heard Lucifer spout some crap in his life, but this took the cake. "You're lying."

"I don't think he is." Raphael came to Lucifer's defense. "After Lucifer and I spoke, I did some sleuthing of my own. I can confirm that Ashe is no longer a member of Lucifer's horde. I can also confirm that there seems to be a high level of cooperation and organization amongst this rebel horde." He shrugged. "You have experienced the power drain through the amulet. That has to be happening for a reason."

"You've been to my palace." Lucifer risked a step closer to Wrath. "You know the place is just about abandoned. I've lost almost my entire horde, and from what my spies tell me, Shade is no better."

"A rebel demon horde?" Michael shook his head. "They must be exterminated."

For once, Wrath agreed with the meathead.

"There's simply no precedent for this," Gabriel muttered, her fingers flying over her tablet. "This is not a possibility we accounted for."

"And not your biggest problem." Daniel entered the room. He looked about at the wreckage and shook his head. "You need to clean this up before Dee sees it." He turned to address the assembled beings. "I requested this gathering, and I went to a lot of trouble keeping it from my superiors, because quite frankly, I believe they'll make a bad situation worse." He took a deep breath. "The horsemen are awakening."

The room exploded into denials and expletives, and Wrath even forgot his mission to kill his twin as the news sunk in. The only being who didn't react was Ramiel. Had he already known and not shared the information with the rest of them? They all hated the gatherings, and cooperation was anathema to them, but withholding this was tantamount to courting creation's destruction.

"It makes perfect sense." Lucifer's voice rose against the uproar. "And provides one of the missing pieces to this puzzle."

It took a while for the room to quiet enough for him to continue.

Lucifer paced as he spoke, his loafers squishing and crunching through the debris on the floor. "It's the one thing I couldn't figure out. Why would these demons band together like they are when they know the chaos will weaken the seals?"

"Because you treat them like shit?" Michael scoffed.

"They're demons." Lucifer gave him a look of scrotum withering scorn. "Do you really think offering them daycare and a pension plan would keep them in line?"

Despite himself, Wrath wanted to laugh. He despised his twin, but the fuckwaffle had a way with words.

"We're tough on them because we need to be," Lucifer said. "Their entire purpose is chaos, and we were given the job of keeping that chaos contained."

"Angels are difficult to contain as well," Ramiel groused.

And speaking of angels, Wrath still didn't see Haziel. Now that he'd calmed out of his homicidal rage, he didn't sense her near either. She'd promised to wait until he returned, and Haziel did not lie. The only thing that could have compelled her to break that promise was a direct instruction from her archangel.

"If what Lucifer says is true—" Wrath was not the only one to scoff at Daniel's remark.

"If what he says is true," the guardian continued. "We are looking at a demon rebellion. And they took Eddie to boost their powers."

Lucifer nodded. "And it looks like my former second is leading them, which makes him my top priority." He turned to Wrath. "Think about it, brother. Why would I send my second to kidnap your daughter, knowing it would point the finger right at me?"

What Lucifer said echoed a lot of what Daniel had before Wrath had left for hell. Lucifer wasn't stupid or suicidal. "Let's assume I believe you," Wrath said. "And that's a big assumption. What are you planning to do about Ashe?"

The temperature in the room lowered under the lash of Lucifer's anger. "End him and any who follow him."

Gabriel raised her hand. "Excuse me, but I do believe the horsemen are an even bigger concern."

"Are they, though?" Raphael shoved his hands in the pockets of his gray slacks. "The entire thing is connected.

Demon rebellion destabilizes the seals, the horsemen sense the seals failing and are triggered by the end of days."

"Raphael's right," Lucifer said. "We need to attack this on multiple fronts if we have any hope of succeeding."

The strange thing for Wrath was the doomsday scenario paled in significance to where the hell Haziel had gone.

TWENTY-SIX

Haziel didn't know what Ramiel had told Wrath about her absence. Wrath hated broken promises as much as she hated breaking them. Her archangel, however, had sent her on a mission, and she could not refuse.

Her mission was simple; find out what was going on with the horsemen and how dire the situation was. Only not so simple. The horsemen were powerful beings. How powerful, nobody knew for sure because nobody could remember ever encountering them. What she did know was that they were too powerful for her to mess with, so caution was needed.

She flew through the night, taking it easy on her injured wing. Ramiel's power helped her fold time and destinations, and it took her only a fraction of the time it would have taken a mortal to journey halfway around the world to the resting place of the horsemen.

It was winter in her new location. Landing at night in a secluded corner of a hotel's garden, she changed into regular human clothes. For this mission, she would be going incognito, and she muted her angelic aura and powers. She wondered how humans would react if they knew how often supernatural beings moved amongst them. Still, people were always drawn to her angelic aura, and she had never had any trouble finding an ally or a temporary friend amongst people.

She brought into being the things she would need to go human: identification, a driver's license, and that most powerful of human gods, money. In this time, in the form of a credit card.

The hotel was quiet in the early evening hiatus between lunch and dinner, and she had no trouble securing herself a room for the night. The hotel gift shop was still open, and she added to her necessary supplies with toiletries and a change of clothes. She wouldn't be able to visit the site of the horsemen's underground lair until morning, so for tonight, she had a rare opportunity to be human.

Haziel had always appreciated humans, and her favorite assignments were the ones involving the earth plane that allowed her to mingle as one of them.

After finding an empty table in the hotel bar, she ordered a glass of wine and some appetizers and settled in to people watch. A middle-aged couple strolled into the bar hand in hand and took a seat near her. Haziel sharpened her hearing and listened in as they discussed their daughter, the possibility of selling their house now that their children had moved out, and then drifted on to a dream holiday they wanted to plan. Their conversation spoke of intertwined lives, a shared past that was both a comfort and a security, their mutual love and enjoyment of each other even after thirty years of marriage. These were things she would never have, and she drew a strange comfort from eavesdropping on a life that wouldn't be hers.

"Hello." A child stood beside her dressed in jeans and a

jersey, her small feet tucked into brightly colored sneakers. The clothes hung on her delicate frame, and a floppy hat shadowed a young face that bore the signs of a weight no being this young and fresh should carry.

Haziel discovered this sweet soul was not long for this plane, and her heart broke.

"I'm sorry." A harried mother hurried over. "I tried to stop her, but she insisted on talking to you. I hope she's not disturbing you." Grief hung over the mother like a noxious cloud that seemed to eat the life from within the woman.

"It's fine." Haziel gave her a reassuring smile. "I'm always happy to meet a new friend."

"See." The girl smirked at her mother. "I told you she would want to talk to me."

"It really is fine." Haziel skimmed the public areas of the mother's mind. "I was lonely anyway."

The child gave her mother a surprisingly adult look. "Why don't you go and call Dad?" She pointed to a bank of potted plants. "And you can watch me from over there."

The mother frowned. "Well, I don't—"

"It's fine." Haziel pushed a tiny amount of compulsion at the mother. "Your daughter and I will have a chat while you speak to your husband. We'll stay right here so you can watch us."

With a nod, the mother turned and walked toward the plants, already dialing.

"She doesn't want me to hear her conversation," the girl said and pulled a face. She settled into the padded chair opposite Haziel. "It's about me."

"I know." Haziel offered the girl some of her appetizers.

The child took a chip and dipped it. "Thank you."

"You're welcome."

"I don't have much appetite," she said, crunching into the chip. "It's the treatments."

"I know." Haziel sipped her wine and waited.

It took the girl a moment longer to find her courage. "You're an angel, aren't you?"

"What gave me away?" Humans faced their lot with such heartbreaking courage. She wished she had the power to change things, but the noninterference rule was unbreakable. A small tweak to the elaborate fabric of creation here could create a massive rip somewhere else.

"The wings. They kind of shine behind you." She squinted behind Haziel's shoulders. "They're pretty and there are a lot of them."

"I am seraphim," Haziel said and offered the girl another morsel to eat. "I have six in total."

"Wow." The girl's eyes widened, and then she giggled. Leaning closer, she said, "That's a lot of wings, and I don't think my mom can see them."

No, she wouldn't be able to. Only souls on the cusp of their transition into the next life would be able to see her wings. "I'm sorry you're sick."

"Yeah, it sucks." The girl sighed. Her brown eyes were direct and uncompromising as they met Haziel's. "Are you here to take me?"

"It doesn't work like that." Haziel nodded to a hovering waiter to refill her wine. If only the alcohol could wash away the tragedy of this child's rapidly dwindling existence. "What's your name?"

"Issy." She made a face. "It's short for Isabella but nobody calls me that."

"Hi, Issy." Haziel held out her hand. "I'm Haziel."

They sat in a silence for a moment longer.

Across the lobby, Issy's mother was crying as she spoke

into her phone. Her shoulders were slumped with a defeat too great for them to bear. The end was near, and human doctors could offer little help anymore.

"How does it work?" Issy cocked her head. "I mean, if you're not here to take me."

"You'll just drift away," Haziel said.

"Will I be scared?"

"No." Haziel took Issy's skeletal hand in hers. "Not then, you won't. You'll feel really peaceful, and you'll be ready."

Issy looked over at her mother. "My mom is not going to be all right."

"No, she won't." Even if she could, Haziel wouldn't taint Issy's trust with lies and platitudes. "She will miss you every day, until your souls meet up again."

"But they will meet up again?" Issy stared deep into her. "Won't they?"

This Haziel could tell her for sure. "Yes, they will. Your soul and your mother's are joined. You have traveled many lifetimes together, and you will travel a few more before you're done."

"Good." Issy nodded. "Can I ask you a favor?"

Haziel wished with everything in her that she could give Issy an unqualified yes. "I can't heal you."

"No, not that." Issy shook her head. "Nobody can heal me anymore. It's about my mother. Could you maybe, I don't know, visit her after I'm gone and let her know I'm all right?"

If she had to tie Ramiel up and lock him in a cupboard. "I will do that. I won't be able to appear to her as I am now, but I can send her a message that she knows is from you."

"Thank you. We've been bird watching since I got too sick to go to school. My favorite bird is the European bee eater. They're such pretty colors." Issy stood. "She's finished her call. She'll need a minute to make herself look like she hasn't been crying. She does that because she thinks I don't know."

A mother's love was one of the purest forms of love in the universe, and Haziel ached for the woman with a smile on her beleaguered face as she made her way back to them.

Issy turned to her. "How long?"

"Three days," Haziel said.

"Will you come for me?"

"No, but I will see you once your soul is freed from your body." She took Issy's hand. "In your next life, you will get to grow up and get married. You will have children and a wonderful future, and your mother in this life will be one of those children."

Ramiel would lose his shit if he heard what she'd said, but Haziel didn't care. Humans suffered so much tragedy and pain. If she could spare this child one moment, it was worth it.

"Good." Issy giggled and looked at her clothes. "I'd like to stop shopping in the children's section at some point."

Haziel watched her walk across the lobby toward her mother, and the two hugged. She needed another glass of wine —STAT.

"Ramiel would shit himself if he heard what you told her," Wrath said.

She whirled to find him standing beside her table dressed like a human male in jeans and a snug T-shirt with a plaid shirt framing his gorgeous chest.

"I didn't feel you approach." Her heart thumped against her breastbone.

Wrath smirked and pulled out the chair Issy had vacated. "Because I didn't want you to."

At a cursory glance, he looked like a human male, but if you looked closer, those clear blue eyes gave him away as other, not to mention the low-grade aura of power that hung around him. He'd muted it, but it was like trying to turn the sun to low.

Several people in the bar watched him, their expressions caught between intrigued and admiring. You could take the prince out of hell...

So many questions spun through her mind that she had trouble picking one. The wheels spun and landed. "What are you doing here?"

"Finding you." He smiled at the starstruck waitress who had appeared beside their table. "I'll have whatever the lady is drinking, and another for her."

"White wine?" The waitress blinked.

"Perfect." Wrath flashed his pearly whites at her.

"You were looking for me?" She shoved a handful of nachos in her mouth to stop her pick-me why from spilling out.

Wrath tilted his head and studied her. "You look good as a human."

The compliment warmed all kinds of stuff inside her. "Why were you looking for me?"

"Well." Wrath stretched his long legs out beside her chair and got comfortable. "I thought I'd make it easy for you to keep an eye on me."

"Liar."

He laughed. "You know, demons have been ended for less than that."

"Not a demon and not scared of you." She tried to suppress her answering smile.

Wrath's laugh was infectious, a deep bass rumble that made you want to share the joke. "Why are you here?"

Dammit with the direct questions! "Ramiel sent me."

"Why?"

She was the one who was supposed to be asking the questions, but she couldn't get control of the narrative, not with her heart pounding and a flush of pleasure that he was here controlling her good sense. "He wanted me to check on the horsemen and assess the damage."

Wrath sat up and frowned. "And he sent you? A seraph."

"He…" She wanted to say that Ramiel trusted her, but their last interaction had made her question that, and she couldn't say it. "He thinks…" Nope, she couldn't say that Ramiel even believed she could handle herself, because seraph versus horseman wouldn't go well for her. And she was down to the truth. "He wanted me away from you."

"Ah." Wrath smiled his thanks as the waitress put down their drinks. "Ah, Misty." He stopped her before she could leave again. "I know this is going to sound weird, and you don't know me, but the answer is yes."

Misty looked confused. "What?"

"The question that's bothering you." Wrath sat forward and leaked a tiny amount of his power. "You should leave him. If you don't, he will do it again." He took her hand and brushed a gentle finger over the bruise on her inner wrist. "He's an asshole and bad to the bone."

"How did you—" Misty frowned. "I didn't…"

"I'm psychic." Wrath shrugged. "I know shit."

Haziel stared at him. "Ramiel would definitely not like what you just did."

"Don't give a crap." Wrath sipped his wine and gave a happy sigh. "Humans and their wine. They really do know their way around a grape. These South African whites are particularly good. I've been trying to replicate them in my demesne, but I haven't got the composition of the soil quite right."

Her head was spinning with the information overload. Wrath cultivated wine. Wrath giving advice to human women. Wrath being here at all.

"Is Eddie okay?"

His face softened. "Yeah. She's doing great. Ramiel helped me heal her, and that sped things up a lot."

"Good." So Ramiel had kept his side of their bargain. But Wrath being here now could complicate things. "Does Ramiel know you're here?"

"Nope." Wrath finished his glass and picked up the wine list. "I think I want to give this sauvignon blanc a try. I like the vineyard."

"So he doesn't know you're here."

"Unlike you, sweet Haziel." Mischief made his eyes dance. "I don't have to report to Ramiel, and I'm here because I want to be."

"Why?"

He chuckled and motioned for Misty. "That is an entirely different discussion." He placed his order with the still mystified waitress. "Now, tell me why you told that child what you did."

Issy and her mother had left the lobby, but the story crashed into Haziel again. "She's dying, the little girl."

"I know." Wrath's gentle tone brought tears to her eyes. "But you know she's going to be all right. It all works out in the end."

"I do know that." Haziel had never spoken of her feelings to a fellow supernatural. Most of her peers barely noticed the human souls they shepherded from one incarnation to the next. "But humans...some of them go through so much in a lifetime, and they face impossible challenges."

"Yeah." Wrath sat forward and took her hand. "But you know why they do."

"I know." She sighed and enjoyed the warm comfort of his grip. "I know it's what each soul chooses before it enters this incarnation, but the person living through the reality doesn't know that. All Issy's mother knows is that her little girl is dying, and all Issy knows is that her mother will be shattered by her loss."

Wrath nodded and raised her hand to his mouth. "And it really sucks while they're going through it."

The warm press of his mouth against her fingers made her breath catch. "I suspect I said something to Issy for the same reason you told Misty about her violent boyfriend, because we'd like to give them what little help we're allowed."

"You like them. Humans." Wrath studied her with a heart clenching tenderness.

Haziel nodded. "I do."

Wrath's smile was open and sincere. "Yeah, me too."

And it didn't matter to Haziel anymore why he was here, only that he was.

TWENTY-SEVEN

Wrath closed her hotel room door behind them. He was so large and present that he shrunk the size of the room merely by being inside it. "So."

They'd enjoyed a few more glasses of wine, which had expanded into dinner before he'd followed her up to her room. Their conversation had stayed light and off the topic of what he was currently doing in her room. Or what they were both about to do in this room.

Now all the things they hadn't spoken of crowded into the room behind him.

Haziel faced him across the mouthy presence of the large bed between them. "So."

"I know you can't lie, so to keep things fair, I'm going to give you my honesty." Wrath stalked closer and stopped on the other side of the bed. "Here's how I see our situation. I'm a hell prince, and you're seraph." He motioned between them. "Your archangel doesn't want me anywhere near you because he senses what's happening between us, and he doesn't like it."

"I'm not sure why he cares enough to send me away from

you." Haziel hadn't been able to find a good answer for that question since Ramiel had dispatched her.

Wrath grimaced. "Okay, whatever does or does not happen here tonight, let's keep Ramiel out of this room as much as we can. He has no place between you and me."

"I don't see how we can avoid him being here." Even if she had the ability to lie and prevaricate, Haziel would rather keep things honest between them.

"Choice," Wrath said and pointed at her. "Yours."

"Explain." The mellow amber glow from the bedside lamp caressed his strong, harsh features. All these centuries she had seen only Ramiel's perfection as the pinnacle of male beauty but there was something fierce and primal in Wrath that called to a part of her she'd never known existed.

"I want to lie with you Haziel." Wrath spoke in the ancient tongue of angels and hell princes. "I want to lie with you as a male lies with his female and lose myself in the joys of your flesh." He stepped around his corner of the bed. "And I believe you desire the same."

"Yes." Her body flushed with how much she shared his sentiment. Her muscles softened and prepared to cleave, but her mind still held some semblance of sense. "Tell me of my choices."

"Whatever happens here this eve, you will have no choice but to tell if asked." He kept coming, eating up the space between them, making her blood pound faster. "Thus, the decision must be yours without coercion or influence." His eyes blazed into hers. "Yea or nay, Haziel?"

And there really was only one answer. "Yea."

Wrath closed the gap between them and stopped before her, close enough for her to feel the want radiating through his large body. He tucked a strand of hair behind her ear and reverted to English, "Yes."

She nodded.

"I need to hear you say it. There will be consequences for you, and I need to know that you are both aware and willing to take those consequences."

"I am aware." She closed the small distance between their bodies. "And I am willing."

There could be no other choice for her. Resting her palm against his chest, she gave herself a moment to experience the heat and the solidity of him. Tonight, she would take him onto that bed and into her body, and there would be consequences and truth to be told if she were asked, but she had never felt surer of anything.

Wrath slid his broad, calloused palm beneath her hair and caressed her nape. "Haziel," he whispered as he pressed a soft kiss to her lips. "I can make you no promises after this night."

"I know." She arched beneath his tender touch. "And I can make you none in return."

"So beautiful." His blue gaze caressed every inch of her face. "And so fucking desirable."

"You talk a lot." She focused on the plush pillow of his mouth.

"You scare me." He chuckled, deep and low. "I stand before you choking on my desire for you and terrified all at the same time."

It had always been honesty between them. "And you scare me, but if you don't kiss me soon, I might have to show you how powerful a seraph can be."

"Also, so bossy." He tutted and brushed his mouth against hers. His warm breath hit her moist lips like a touch. "Perhaps you need a lesson in how powerful a hell prince can be."

He was like liquid gold in her veins and she almost purred. "That's what I was hoping for."

And he kissed her. Not a demanding assault as she had

been expecting but a gentle, careful exploration of his lips over hers.

On a groan, he slid his tongue into her mouth.

Haziel's world dipped and slid around her as the rich, masculine taste of him marauded through her senses. He tasted of war and power, of strength and eternity. He tasted perfect, and she allowed her corporeal body to take over.

They kissed for what might have been years or merely seconds, but with a total engrossment in each other that made the kiss a destination within itself. She never wanted it to end, yet she craved what came next with each thud of her heart and each breath she drew.

Her fingers discovered the silk of his hair and wove through the strands, pressed into his skull and invited him deeper, to take more, to take all that she was and all she had to offer.

He gripped her hips and tugged her closer to him. "Let's make this worth the consequences." He pressed hard and demanding against her.

It had been so long since she'd been touched with desire, touched by desire, and she shoved his shirt off his shoulders. She wanted skin to skin contact, and she grabbed the back of his T-shirt and tugged.

Their mouths pulled apart long enough to get the T-shirt over his head, and then he was back, kissing her as if he wanted to leave no part of her mouth unexplored.

The press of her breasts against his chest sent heat flaming straight to her core. He was hard where she was soft, and there was something delightfully elemental about that sensation. Her shirt was in the way, so she unbuttoned it and dropped it.

And then there was only her bra between their skin, and she pressed herself closer to him. She spread her hands over the hot, taut expanse of his back. Power tingled from the place his wings would appear, and she paused a moment to enjoy a power that was so similar to hers and so very different.

Wrath groaned as she stroked his wing roots. He slid the straps of her bra off her arms, his blue eyes blazing. "Why would you wear this thing?"

"Human women do."

"Human women hate them." He nipped her shoulder. "And I can confirm that males of all species see them as a useless impediment."

Haziel laughed, thrilled by the lightness and heaviness of what was happening between them. They were going to join bodies in the most basic way, and that was a weighty matter, but Wrath made it a joyful thing. "That's because most males don't have breasts."

"No." Wrath unfastened her bra and dropped it to the floor. He stepped back and stared at the flesh he'd revealed. "And therefore, I'm going to have to conduct a thorough exploration of yours." He cupped the weight of her breasts in his hands, his thumb stroking the tight bud of her nipple. "And for the sake of accuracy, this exploration will need to take place in several phases."

"Phases?"

"Uh-huh." He bent his head, his hair shockingly dark against her skin. "First there is sight." His breath skated hot and moist over her nipples. "And then comes touch." His huge hands cupped almost the entirety of her breasts as he gently plumped them. "And then comes taste."

Haziel's breath caught as his hot mouth fastened over her nipple. "Ah, gods."

"Not quite." Wrath chuckled. "But as they're not here, I'll have to do my best."

"You're terrible." But she didn't even manage to convince herself, not with the steady draw of his mouth on her nipple.

"Comes with the hell prince thing," he murmured, switching his attention from one breast to the other.

Closing her eyes, she sank deeper into the sensations beating a pounding rhythm through her and raked her nails over the tight planes of his waist. She spread her fingers wider, trying to capture as much of his flesh as she could reach.

He hissed when she dragged her nails over his nipples. Drawing his head back, he gazed down at her slumberously. "Angels aren't supposed to scratch."

"No." He needed her mouth on his skin. "And they're not supposed to bite either." She nipped the hard slab of his pectoral then soothed the bite with her tongue. His skin tasted of musk and dark spices. It was the kind of taste a female wanted to lose herself in, wanted to have in every part of her.

"Right." Sliding his hand down her thighs, he split her legs around his waist. "Time to teach a bad angel what happens when they fuck with a hell prince."

"So you keep saying." She shrieked as he tossed them both on the bed. His cock landed at the juncture of her thighs. His weight knocked the breath out of her. She undulated her hips against him. "I'm starting to get an inkling of what you mean."

"An inkling?" He reared up on his arms above her and scowled at her. "I'll have you know that I am offering you so much more than an inkling."

"And you are still doing too much talking." Haziel cupped him through his jeans. He was hard and huge in her hand.

"Fuck!" Wrath reared back as she stroked him. "Go easy, angel. It's been a while."

"You mean absolute control doesn't come with the whole unlimited power thing?" Haziel squeezed the head of his cock before undoing the button at the top of his jeans and lowering his zipper.

His cock sprang free. Clearly Wrath didn't feel the need to add human underwear to the rest of his human clothing.

He pulsed silky and hot in her hand.

"Haziel," he growled as she pumped him.

"Wrath," she growled back.

"Fucking angels." He hissed. "So mouthy and not nearly as good as they should be." Catching her wrist, his blazing gaze met hers. "You asked for this."

"Repeatedly." She laughed from the sheer exhilaration of this much powerful and potent male between her thighs.

On a growl, Wrath ripped her jeans clean off her. Her chaste white cotton panties were all that stood between Wrath and those hot eyes.

His lips quirked as he looked at her panties. "Now that's more what I expected." He gripped the sides of her panties, and they went the way of her jeans. "But they're going to have to go." He pressed her thighs apart. "Are you wet, angel?"

She felt no awkwardness as he looked at her intimate flesh. "Yes."

"How wet?" His hands were warm and rough as he stroked the inside of her thighs toward her core.

Not close enough. "Find out."

"I think I might." Lowering himself to his knees beside the bed, Wrath yanked her closer to the edge. He pressed his nose against her and breathed deep.

His low rumble of pleasure made her flesh prickle.

He flattened his tongue against her slit and licked.

Haziel arched off the bed at the simultaneous onslaught of hot, silky, and wet against her core. She dug her hands into his hair and pressed him closer. She needed more.

Wrath growled against her, and even more pleasure shot through her. She wondered if she wouldn't be able to hold out long enough.

But Wrath was in no hurry. He teased, he licked, he drew closer to her clitoris, then retreated after little more than a gentle touch.

"Wrath," she panted, writhing her hips to increase the pressure and the contact. She tightened her fingers in his hair.

"Yes, angel?" His blue eyes blazed at her over the length of her body. "Did you want something?"

"You know what I want."

He licked her clit on a lazy swipe. "Say the words."

"Make me come." Even if she could lie, she was way beyond that.

"My pleasure." He made that animal rumble again and fastened his lips around her clit.

Haziel's climax coiled through her belly and thighs. She flew over the precipice with a mindless scream.

Wrath rose and crawled up her body. It was like being stalked by a predator, and Haziel felt too boneless to protest.

His erection brushed against the inside of her thighs.

He lowered his full weight on her and bracketed her face with his hands. "Hey." His smile looked remarkably like a smirk as he brushed her tangled hair away from her sweaty face. "Nothing to say now?"

Sometimes words were largely overrated, and Haziel reached between them and palmed his cock. "You're not done yet."

"No?" He pressed into her hand.

Haziel shook her head. "Not even close."

He sucked her bottom lip into his mouth. "So beautiful when you come." He pressed a soft kiss to the corner of her mouth, her jaw, over the pulse in her neck, and nipped her earlobe. "What do you need?"

A fresh ache of need washed over her. She felt empty inside where she wanted him the most. "All of you."

He lowered one hand and parted her flesh. The sight of his big hand gripping his cock almost threw her over the edge again. And then his broad head was at her entrance. With a powerful thrust, he sheathed himself inside her.

Haziel arched off the bed as he filled her.

"And you're not done yet," he growled as he pushed deeper into her.

Haziel felt full, but he pressed home until he was fully seated.

He rested his weight against her for a moment. Their skin was slick with perspiration as they breathed together.

And then he started to move. Slow deep thrusts that reached deeper inside her than she'd ever experienced before. It was hard to tell where he ended and she began.

Raising to his hands, he gained better leverage, and his thrusts grew more powerful, stroking in and out of her. He gripped her thigh and wrapped it around his waist. "Give me everything, angel."

Haziel tilted her hips and took him even deeper.

A deeper orgasm bloomed inside her, and Wrath increased his pace.

The bed creaked and groaned beneath them, but he drove on relentlessly, thrusting them both toward the inevitable.

Pleasure spread over every inch of Haziel.

Wrath dropped his head and watched the slick slide of his flesh into hers.

Her climax arrived in a rush, and she dug her nails into him, the only solid point in her careening universe.

On a shout, he buried himself to the hilt inside her and froze as he came.

The aftershocks went on and on, shuddering through both of them in gradually gentling waves.

He lowered himself to his elbows and did that thing she

was beginning to like way too much. He gently held her face and looked deep into her eyes. For an endless moment it felt like there was everything and nothing between them. An intimate vacuum in which words were not needed, and in which they were together in a way that shook her to her soul.

He kissed her, softly and gently, before rolling to lie by her side. His fingers found hers and tangled them together.

A tear trickled down her temple and into her mussed hair. That had been so much more than she could have expected or imagined, and she was in so much trouble now.

TWENTY-EIGHT

In all his thousands of years of existence, Shade would have laughed at anybody who suggested he could derive such pleasure from lying beside a woman and watching her sleep. But here he was. And Eddie snored, not a loud sawing, but a gentle kind of huffy growl on her exhalations.

He spared a brief moment to mourn the passing of his lust hell prince rep, and then let it drift away in the sheer joy of knowing she was here with him, and he could protect her.

She was so beautiful and so utterly unaware of it. Her beauty went deeper than her peachy skin, or those arresting aquamarine eyes, into the stubborn, courageous, resilience of her being.

He wanted to touch her and assure himself that she really was lying beside him, but he also didn't want to wake her.

Her breathing hitched, and she sighed. Her eyes remained closed as she said, "You're staring."

"I know." There wasn't another being in existence who would blame him. She was perfect.

"Psst!"

Shade sensed a demon was near, and he drew his power. If he hadn't been so busy admiring Eddie, he might have noticed sooner. "Show yourself."

He sorted through the impressions.

"No," the demon whispered. "I don't feel safe."

Wrath's horde. Low order. Imp. Led him to only one conclusion, and that meant ending the imp. "Yesterday," he growled.

Eddie's eyes shot open, and she frowned. "He's here?"

"Fucker is hiding." Shade let his senses widen. He regretted sending the hounds back to hell the night before to have a little nose around. Needless to say, they had not been happy about leaving Eddie, and would now be giving him shit for not being there to catch Yesterday.

"I need to explain first," Yesterday whined. He had masked his presence, but not very well.

Shade lay still as he zeroed in on where the fucker was. He didn't need to move a muscle to kill an imp.

Yesterday was cowering in the air-conditioning ducts. He yelped as Shade hit him with a blast of compulsion.

Eddie gripped Shade's arm. "Don't kill him."

"Seriously?" He had to look at her to verify she wasn't shitting him. After all the crap the asshole had set in motion, she was pleading for his existence.

She wrinkled her nose at him, which made him want to kiss her nose and cuddle her...aaaaand give her anything her heart desired. "Seriously," she said.

The AC duct grate flew across the room as his power yanked Yesterday into the room.

"Eeeyooooow!" Yesterday slammed into the wall beside the bed, slid down, and dropped headfirst to the floor.

Shade towered over him, making no effort to turn down the menace. If this little asshole had led to Eddie being abducted in even the smallest way, Shade would end him and hand his ashes to Wrath. "Speak."

Eddie was looking at him with an arousing mixture of impressed and a tad turned on. *Wooing*, he reminded himself harshly. *Not seducing*.

"That was very hostile." Yesterday sniveled. "And after all I've suffered on your behalf."

Well, he'd tried. Ending it was.

"What have you done on our behalf?" Eddie pushed herself to the edge of the bed and studied Yesterday.

Shade let the power fizzle in his palm but kept it active.

Yesterday threw her a pitiful look. "I am truly very hungry."

Shade let his palms light with extinction fire.

"Not that hungry." Yesterday yelped and leapt onto the bed beside Eddie.

He needn't think that would keep him safe. The thing with wielding power for thousands of years was that your accuracy was pinpoint. "You betrayed Eddie to Wrath."

"Would we say betrayed?" Yesterday scooted behind Eddie. "I mean, he was her sire, and he would never have hurt her."

Eddie grabbed him by an ear and hauled him out from behind her. "I would say betrayed covers it."

"What happened to you?" Yesterday's eyes widened as he stared at Eddie. "You used to be so sweet and trusting."

"And gullible," Eddie said.

"Okay, okay, okay." Yesterday held both palms out. "I did tell Wrath where to find you, but I already knew he was your sire."

"And stole the heaven wrought blade." Eddie locked her glare on Yesterday.

"That too, but I gave it back." Yesterday nodded so vigorously it looked like his oversize head might snap his scrawny neck. "You have to understand I was desperate. Wrath was out to end me, and I needed a little something to keep me safe." He sniveled. "And you went to hell. You saw how the demons are out of control. I'm just a little demon." His lip quivered. "A small imp and so easy for the bigger demons to end."

Eddie crossed her arms and gave Yesterday a no bullshit look that Shade found incredibly sexy. Mind you, he found just about everything about Eddie incredibly sexy.

"I could have been killed without that blade," Eddie said.

"But you weren't." Yesterday held up a finger. "You were fine, and I gave it to you when you needed it the most."

He had done that, and they wouldn't have escaped with an incapacitated Wrath without Yesterday tossing Eddie the blade. Still, the imp irritated him. "I haven't heard anything from you to dissuade me from ending you."

"I've been spying." Yesterday focused on the extinction fire in Shade's hand and swallowed. "Gaining information for you."

"Why?"

"Because I knew that you wanted to end me." He whimpered. "And I knew I would have to give you something to persuade you not to end me."

"I mean"—Eddie shrugged—"that is his consistent MO. He gave us up to Wrath to save himself."

Yesterday threw her an adoring gaze. "I knew I could rely on you, Eddie."

"I wouldn't go that far," Eddie snapped. "And you better have found something useful, or I'm going to ask Shade to teach me how to end a demon." She leaned into his space. "And we'll be using you as practice."

"Lucifer is telling the truth." The words rapid fired out of Yesterday's mouth. "He was not behind your kidnapping. He has spent the time since you were taken trying to find Ashe."

Eddie got there before Shade could. "And how do I know you're not lying for Lucifer?"

Yesterday opened and shut his huge mouth, frowned, and then twitched. "I don't know," he said and scratched inside his ear. "I don't have any way to prove that."

"What makes you so sure Lucifer is telling the truth?" Shade didn't want to believe the fucker, but he was starting to lean in that direction. Self-preservation was the only motive you could trust with the imp.

Yesterday stuck his chest out. "I followed him." He grimaced. "And it was not easy following that chariot of his."

Shade stared him down.

"He visited all seven demesnes." Yesterday's confidence wavered. "And he spent time at all seven seals."

Eddie got to her feet. "That doesn't prove he had nothing to do with my kidnapping."

"No." Yesterday's bravado crumpled completely. "No, it doesn't." He dug in his ear. "I thought maybe it would, but now I see that it really doesn't prove anything." He brightened. "But he did have trouble with those mixed hordes, same as you did."

Shade moved closer to Eddie, ready to provide physical support if she needed it.

She threw him an exasperated glance. "And it was a mixed horde who provided the distraction so Ashe could spirit me away."

"Something he shouldn't have had the strength to do." Shade hovered near her. He couldn't help it, so she could glare at him all she wanted.

"In fact." Yesterday took a strut to the wall and back. "He was almost beaten by one group of mixed demons and only the speed of that chariot saved him."

"Hmm." Eddie hobbled toward her bathroom. "So maybe

he isn't working with the mixed hordes." She looked at him from the far side of the door. "Then what is he doing?"

The door shut in Shade's face. "That is the question."

"Shade," Yesterday whispered and tugged on his pants leg.

"Go away, imp." Or Shade would do his best to forget his promise to Eddie.

Yesterday tugged again. "There is more I need to tell you."

"What?" Shade made a mental note to create no more imps.

"I knew you wouldn't want her to hear." Yesterday glanced at the bathroom door. "But I have heard whispers of a meeting on earth." He beamed at Shade, bloated with self-importance. "A meeting of some of those traitor demons."

Shade's brain tripped into overdrive. A meeting where he could find out what the fuck was going on here. "Are you lying to me?"

"No." Yesterday took a step back. "Or I swear you can set those hounds on me, and I will merely stand still and let them feast."

It could still be a trick. Imps were masterful liars and the longer they existed the better they became. Still, a chance to find more information on who had taken Eddie was not to be overlooked. He crouched eye level with Yesterday. "You will find out where and when this meeting is to take place." He held up a finger to stop Yesterday's reply. "And you will not tell Eddie what you find."

Yesterday nodded.

"And if this is a trick, you will pray that the hounds find you before I or Wrath do."

Sophia sat in the silent theatre as the other actors left for their homes and lives outside of *The Importance of Being Earnest*. As Lillian had played Gwendolyn several times before, they were rehearsing Sophia in as Cecily. The play would take place once the run of *Macbeth* was over. Sophia did love acting, and from what everyone was telling her, she was good at it as well.

Of course, they probably didn't realize they were responding to her angelic glamour. So she could be useless without having any idea.

A human male entered the auditorium and shifted into the light. The telling whisper of power told her he was a guardian.

She mentally braced for another unpleasant conversation with Chris Fellows. He had arrived earlier that day with a contingent of guardians and been incensed that they had missed the gathering.

"Sophia." He made his way down the central aisle to where she sat and took the seat next to her. "About earlier." He cleared his throat. "I apologize for my anger."

It took a moment for her brain to decode the words. She had never thought she would hear Chris Fellows apologize, and to a supernatural. And in fairness to the treaty, she had to admit, "We should have waited for you."

"Yes." Chris shrugged. "But after recent events, I suppose I can understand why you didn't."

She turned and examined his face. Some of her angels could detect human lies, but she didn't have that ability. "Does that mean you're going to reinstate Dee?"

Chris chuckled. "Like we could ever get rid of Dee." He indicated the auditorium. "As much as it galls, her family name is on the deed to this place."

"Right." Sophia had trouble understanding the human desire to own bits of land and call it their own, when all life was so interconnected that every place belonged to every life. "But Daniel seems to be a competent guardian."

"He is." Chris nodded. "He has a tendency to make up his own rules, but he does the job."

He stared at the silent theatre. "I'm keeping Daniel here to assist her. With the action this hell gate is seeing, we have no way of anticipating what nasty surprises might come through it."

"Then why not simply tell Dee that?" Sophia studied his face, trying to discern the truth.

Chris threw her a speaking glance. "Would you tell Dee that you left a guardian here to help her?"

Sophia had to smile. He had a point there. Dee with her fierce independence would not take kindly to being told she was being assisted.

They sat in an awkward silence. She had nowhere to go, so she waited him out.

Chris shifted in his seat. "I saw you earlier." He cleared his throat. "Acting."

Ah, here it came. The lecture about how she should not be engaging in human pastimes.

"You're very good," Chris said. "Very talented."

Her mouth dropped open and she snapped it shut. Pride kindled a happy glow in her middle. "Do you really think so?" It was probably the surprise that kept her confession going. "I do love it, and all the others tell me I'm good, but they would have to."

"The angelic glamour." He hummed and nodded. "But I am not affected by it, and I am saying you are good."

"Thank you."

"You're welcome."

The silence felt a bit easier now, so she asked, "Do you like the theatre?"

"I do." He smiled. "My late wife and myself used to make a point of seeing live theatre."

Her heart went out to him. Humans had to endure so much loss in their lives. "Is your wife..."

"Four years ago." His face bore the lines of grief carved around his eyes and mouth. "Cancer."

"I'm so sorry."

He gave a humorless chuckle. "Yeah. Me too." He clapped his palms on his thighs and stood. "Anyway, I didn't come to speak to you to share my life story." He dug in his jacket pocket and drew out a pale blue box tied with a sparkly silver ribbon. "I came more by way of apology and to smooth the way to future cooperation." Color stained his cheeks, and he kept his gaze on the box. "It's silly really." He looked pained. "But we do need to work together, all of us, to contain this threat. And I thought..." He cleared his throat. "Well, I mean, we humans often use this as a gesture of apology."

Sophia eyed the pretty box. "What is it?"

"A gift." Chris held it out to her as if he didn't quite want to hand it over. "A peace offering if you will. Chocolate."

"Chocolate?" Now Sophia was definitely interested. Of course she'd heard other angels and demons talk about chocolate, but she'd never indulged. "Is chocolate in there?"

"Yes." Chris's smile was genuine and changed his stern face into something a lot more attractive. "But if you don't..."

"Oh, I do." She took the box with embarrassing enthusiasm. "I've never had chocolate."

"Then you're in for a treat." He grinned. "And maybe we could turn over a new leaf? Clean the slate as it were?"

"That's a lot to expect from a bonbon." Sophia unwrapped the ribbon and took the lid off the box. Four little balls nestled inside some tissue paper.

"Ah." Chris's eyes twinkled. "But it is chocolate."

She selected one with nuts and sparkly paper over the top and popped it into her mouth. The flavor burst over her tongue in a decadent combination of sweet, bitter, aromatic, and rich. "You're right." She was already reaching for a second. "It is chocolate."

TWENTY-NINE

Haziel woke to sunlight streaming through the open curtains and on her bed. Her corporeal form felt wonderfully relaxed, her muscles strong and pliant. The pillow beside her still bore the imprint from Wrath's head. A better angel would feel guilty about what had happened between them—all six times—but she wasn't that seraph. Ramiel would be horrified if he found out, but if he never asked the question, she would never have to answer it.

Drumming water from the shower in the attached bathroom provided the answer as to where Wrath was. She'd half expected him to have left already but was glad he hadn't.

Wrath had followed her here. She had kept her deal with Ramiel—sort o. Stretching her arms over her head, and reaching for the bed end with her toes, she relished the delicious snap and crack of her muscles and sinews.

"Good morning." Wrath appeared in the bathroom door with a white towel wrapped around his waist. His dark hair was wet and slicked back from the rugged planes of his strong face. Muscle along his shoulders and torso flexed and gave her a private dance as he moved in that graceful prowl toward the bed. And he was smiling.

Wrath had a gorgeous smile. She didn't see if often, but it was all the more arresting for its scarcity.

"Morning." She tucked her hands behind her head and enjoyed the show. She believed human women had a weakness for a man in a white towel, with water droplets glistening over the defined slabs of muscle and creating small rivulets down the fascinating dips. That and gray sweatpants. Maybe she should ask Wrath if he owned a pair?

Wrath perched beside her hip on the bed. "You look very comfortable."

"I am." She toyed with the idea of luring him into the bed with her. Last night should have sated her need for him, but this morning she was discovering that it had done little more than whet her appetite.

Wrath hummed, his eyes taking careful inventory of her face. The sheet pulled taut over her breasts and the outline of her body beneath the covers. "I ordered breakfast."

"With coffee?" She had a weakness for that bit of human genius.

He chuckled and leaned down to kiss the tip of her nose. "With coffee." He smelled of evergreens and lavender from the soap he had used, and his voice dropped to the husky drawl that had lured her into more than one repeat of his first performance. "And now I'm thinking of a perfect way to spend the day."

It physically pained her to shake her head. "I have a task to perform, and Ramiel is waiting for me to do so."

"Ah, yes." His expression grew shuttered. "The estimable Ramiel."

He stood, leaving an empty place beside her and a small

ache in her chest. "He is my archangel, and I am tasked with serving him."

"Yes." The towel clung to the taut dents on either side of his spectacular ass. "The horsemen."

It wasn't a betrayal to admit as much. "He wants me to assess how close the horsemen are to waking."

Wrath turned and dropped the towel. He stood gloriously naked with his hands planted on his hips, glaring at her. "And he sent you?"

"Yes." Her ebullient mood popped courtesy of Wrath's sneer. It was not her favorite expression of his. "I am seraph."

"Exactly." Wrath turned and grabbed his jeans. He thrust his legs into them as if they owed him three years rent. "He should have come himself."

She agreed, but she still defended her archangel. "He has more important matters to attend."

"More important than the four horsemen of the apocalypse waking?" Wrath scoffed as he fastened his jeans and grabbed his T-shirt.

"We don't know how critical the situation is here." She climbed from the bed. "Hence, me being here."

His wicked blue eyes took shameless advantage of the opportunity she'd presented him, and his sneer softened into a sensual perusal that had her pulse pounding all over again. "Well," he drawled, closing on her. "If the situation is not yet critical..."

"But it could be." His interest delighted her into laughter. "And I need to deal with it this morning."

"Pity." He cupped her breast. "Go and shower so we can get this done and get back to more pleasurable activities."

"We?" Haziel stepped away and put some necessary distance between her and the distracting hell prince. "You are not tasked with this. You should not be here." And now that her brain was sort of working again, she added, "In fact, shouldn't you be trying to locate Lucifer?"

"Mmm." He trailed his forefinger between her breasts and down her stomach. "There have been developments with Lucifer, and I am going with you to assess the horsemen situation."

"Developments?" Heat trailed the path of his finger over her skin.

He smirked and kissed the top of one breast. "I really don't want to talk about my brother while I'm doing this."

"Then you need to stop doing that." Her breathy, needy tone didn't convince either of them. However, Ramiel would definitely not be happy about Wrath being with her. His deal with her to help Eddie had hinged on her putting distance between herself and Wrath. Last night he had appeared without her having any prior knowledge, but if she allowed him to come with her this morning, it would be reneging on Ramiel. She steeled herself and stepped away from him. "You can't come with me."

"Can't?" Up went one eyebrow, and his expression was pure, unadulterated arrogance. "Who says I cannot?"

"Ramiel." She had to move carefully around the truth. Wrath would react badly if he knew all Ramiel's instruction to her, and they didn't need more discord between the two of them. "He sent me to do this alone."

"And you will." Wrath shrugged. "I too have come here alone to assess the situation, and we ran into each other." His gaze grew slumberous. "Unless you'd like to delay our visit?"

It was ridiculous how much she wanted to do exactly that, and she hurried to the bathroom before her willpower broke. Wrath's reasoning was sketchy, but it was enough to quiet her guilt, and she wasn't about to look that particular gift horse in the mouth.

WRATH RENTED them a car to drive to the site where the horsemen had rested since way before humans had walked the earth, when the gas and dust particles orbiting a new sun had first formed a planet. They had been here before archangels and hell princes, and even before the old gods. No being she had ever encountered knew where they had come from or how they'd been formed. The horsemen just were. Everybody was clear on their purpose, however. They would bring about the end of days—meaning life as all current beings of heaven, hell, and earth knew it. Once they were roused, getting them to subside into their dormant state would be a monumental task.

She and Wrath could have flown to the site, but discretion was always the better option, and especially in this age where information moved at such a rapid pace. You never knew when someone with a cell phone was recording you. It also gave her more time to spend with Wrath, and she wasn't about to argue against that.

Wrath—not surprisingly—suffered from road rage, so Haziel drove. It was a crisp, clear Southern Hemisphere winter day as they passed dormant savannah beneath an achingly blue sky.

"So, what exactly does Ramiel want you to do?" Wrath had donned a pair of sunglasses and looked like a remarkably handsome human man in his jeans and oatmeal colored sweater.

"Since we first caught that stirring on the monitoring systems, there hasn't been further action. He wants me to ascertain how serious the threat is or if it's merely an anomaly."

Grunting, Wrath glared out his window. "And if it's not an anomaly, what exactly are you supposed to do?"

"Report back to him." And after that, she was to return to Ramiel's demesne and remain there. No more humans, no more adventures, and no more Wrath. If she hadn't known all too painfully well that Ramiel felt nothing more for her than familial affection, she would have thought he was jealous. Maybe he was jealous, but not in the way her foolish heart would have longed for. Ramiel saw her as his, a possession, a tool, and he did not share well with others.

"Hmm." Wrath turned in his seat and studied her. "You do know that their power will affect you?"

"Of course." She tried to keep her concerns hidden. As long as he didn't ask the question, she wouldn't have to admit her apprehensions. "That is why he sent a seraph. We are more sensitive to the powers of other beings, and if any being would sense more than a power anomaly or a temporary shift, it would be me."

"He should have come with you." Wrath's jaw tightened. "The horsemen are the most powerful force we know of, and anything could happen. He should be here to assist you should you require it."

"I assume he had other things, more important things, to do," she said. She hadn't asked Ramiel why he couldn't do this task, because she'd known that her mission was more about separating her from Wrath than anything else.

Wrath stared at her, and then shook his head. "You always give him the benefit of the doubt, don't you?"

"He is my archangel." And that meant more than she could put into words. She had come into being from Ramiel's power, created to serve him and do his bidding. His will was hers to obey, and she had always been happy to serve. Until a certain hell prince with a bad attitude and a beautiful smile had made her wonder if there were other ways to exist, ways that filled her aching, lonely heart and made her crave more.

"Fuck." Wrath stretched his arm over the back of her seat. "Let's not talk about that dickwad." He gestured the area outside the car. "It's a beautiful day after a great night." He winked at her. "And I don't want to be in a bad mood."

And that was fine with Haziel. Soon she would have to leave, and she had no idea how long it would be before Ramiel allowed her near Wrath again. It made more sense to enjoy the time they had. "Perfect."

THIRTY

The next morning, Eddie managed to persuade Shade she was well enough to be up and about. He didn't look happy about it as he trailed her through the theatre. He mumbled at her back about her needing time to rest and recover.

"I'm fine," she said, because she was. She didn't want to snap at him but this overprotective streak of his was making her edgy. She got the feeling he would bundle her in bubble wrap and stuff her in his pocket if he could. And while she appreciated the concern, she wasn't used to being swaddled and cosseted. Dee had always raised her with a much more get-on-with-it style of parenting. "As you've told me countless times, I'm Nephilim, and that means half hell prince."

Shade stuffed his hands in his pockets. "It's not that half I'm worried about."

"Me neither." She gave him what she hoped was a reassuring smile and took the stairs down to the theatre. *Macbeth* had a preview tonight, and she wanted to make sure everything was ready. At least, that was the excuse she'd given

Shade to get him to let her out of her bedroom. Her real reason for being up and about, she'd rather not share with him.

"You're up to something," Shade grumbled.

Cronus and Xerxes appeared from the workshop and flanked her. They'd returned from hell late the night before, and Eddie had missed them.

"*Where are we going?*" Cronus did his best to look nonchalant, but the expression didn't work on a hell hound. These two were almost as bad as Shade in trying to protect her.

"Do you know where Sophia is?" With all the skulking these two did around the theatre, it was a safe bet they did know. "And shouldn't you two be staying out of sight?"

"*The mortals cannot see us.*" Xerxes' long tongue lolled out of his mouth.

That stopped Eddie in her tracks. "Wait. What? You can do that?"

"*We can do many things.*" There was a ton of smug in his tone.

All this time she'd been worried people would see them, and they could make like a ghost. "You could have told me."

Xerxes gave her a look that stated clearly that she could have asked.

"Sophia," she snapped. "Do you know where she is?"

Shade came up behind her, close enough that she could feel his heat. "Why are you searching for Sophia?"

It wasn't like it was some big secret, but she got the distinct impression trying to bring up her request with Shade would end up in charming and well-considered objections. As a female archangel, as well as being the most approachable of the supernaturals, Sophia was Eddie's choice to take her request to. "I need her help with something."

"What?" Shade looked a little hurt. "What can Uriel help you with that I can't?"

"She prefers to be called Sophia." Eddie sidestepped his question and stared at the hounds.

"*She is in the basement,*" Cronus said.

"Good." Eddie headed off in that direction.

Shade followed.

"Look." She stopped and turned to him. "I want to talk to Sophia. Alone. I won't be in any danger, and I promise I will not leave the theatre without letting you know."

The hounds looked at Shade, and Eddie got the sense they were having a private conversation.

She gentled her tone as she took Shade's hand. "This is nothing dangerous. It's more of a woman-to-woman thing."

He searched her face for a moment and then nodded. "I worry, Eddie." He cupped her cheek in his palm. "The last time you were out of my sight terrible things happened to you."

Gah! This guy. He'd found her when she needed finding, taken care of her like she was the most precious being on the planet, and kept saying sweet things. And not once had he brought up their last conversation before Ashe had kidnapped her. She wasn't remotely ready to talk about them, and he seemed to know that, but there was an endless patient quality around him that reassured her he'd suffered no change of heart. "I just want to talk to Sophia quickly. I promise I will tell you about it after I've spoken to her."

"Then I shall wait right here until you are done." He pointed to the floor outside the basement door.

"Right there?" Eddie raised an eyebrow at him. "Won't your ass get cold?"

He flashed her the signature Shade smirk. The one that took her knees out in a twinkle of gray eyes and quirk to the side of his beautiful mouth. "You could always warm it for me."

"Keep dreaming, handsome." She patted his cheek and

scurried into the basement before she took him up on the offer. Shade did have a spectacular ass. Actually, Shade had many, many things that could be described as spectacular, and she'd seen all of them.

"Hello, Eddie," Sophia called as Eddie descended into the quiet gloom of the basement.

The archangel appeared out of the dark wearing jeans and a plaid shirt. A faint glow framed her, and Eddie was smacked in the head by the archangel's beauty. Blond, blue-eyed, peachy skin adorning perfect bone structure, and if that wasn't bad enough, Sophia was sweet and kind.

"You're looking well." Sophia smiled. "I didn't want to bother you, but Shade has been letting me know how you were doing." She glanced behind Eddie. "Where is Shade?"

"Waiting for me upstairs." She jerked her thumb to the stairs. "I wanted to speak to you on my own."

Sophia raised one of her sculpted brows. "Oh?"

Now that she was here, Eddie felt a bit silly, but she'd been thinking about this off and on since Shade had brought her back. "I need your help with something."

"Really?" Sophia looked delighted.

"Yup." Lying in bed recovering had given her all kinds of time to think, and all kinds of time to realize how vulnerable she was. "I wondered if you could help me with my powers."

Sophia cocked her head. "I don't understand."

"To control them." The few times she had used her power, Eddie had found it to be more of a battering ram than a precision instrument. But she'd watched the way Sophia, and Shade, and even Wrath could wield power like a finely crafted tool. How they knew what they were capable of. "To be able to use them effectively."

Taking a seat on a plastic storage crate, Sophia patted the space beside her. "Talk to me, Eddie. Why?"

"When I was taken—" Eddie was still not comfortable bringing those memories to the fore. "I felt so vulnerable, useless. I keep thinking if maybe I'd known more, been able to do more, I might not have been so much at their mercy."

"Oh, Eddie." Sophia took her hand and pressed it between hers. "From what you and Shade have told me, I don't think even I would have been able to free myself. They drained your powers, and that left you weaker than an infant."

"I know, but..." And this was the reason she'd chosen Sophia to speak to and not Shade. "As women, we're always aware of our own vulnerability. I don't want to live that way for the rest of my life. I know there will always be times when I can't do anything, but I want to know, that if I could do something, I would be able to."

Sophia nodded and her gaze was gentle. "You know, your world is not so different in that respect to ours. We that identify as female archangels or hell princes, we share the struggle of human women to be treated with the same respect, and to be measured by a fair yard stick." She shrugged, and her expression grew colder. "It matters not what powers we possess, or what acts we perform, we are always seen as somehow less than our male identifying counterparts."

"But you're just as powerful, aren't you?"

"Oh, yes." Sophia chuckled. "And in some cases, more so. You should speak to Ava about this." She shook her head. "She has much to say about the patriarchy and her resentment of it."

"Ava?" Eddie went through her mental files on supernaturals. "That's Avarice, right?"

Sophia nodded. "Her real name is Mammon, but nobody dares call her that."

"Who is her counterpart archangel?"

Sophia grimaced. "Michael, and he's…a little backward in his attitude toward females."

Michael hadn't impressed her much when Eddie had met him. He seemed to do a lot of chest thumping and threatening.

"So." Sophia squeezed her hand. "What would you have me help you with?"

"These powers I have." Eddie rubbed at her chest instinctively. She didn't know for sure, but her chest seemed to be the place they resided. "Help me understand them and use them."

"I can certainly do that." Sophia grinned at her, blue eyes dancing with mischief. "But I can do even better than that. Why don't I teach you to fight as well?"

"Like fight, fight?" Eddie had sudden visions of herself dressed head to toe in kickass leather and handing out bitch slaps.

"Like that." Sophia smiled. "You find yourself in a new reality, Eddie. And one where the stakes are incredibly high. It would be my honor to help you prepare for that reality."

Eddie needed to get this straight before her imagination went wild. "When you say fight, you mean like you did with Shade that time?"

"That and more." Sophia stood and brushed the seat of her pants. "Knives, swords, bow and arrow, whatever you like." She leaned closer to Eddie. "When Wrath returns, you could ask him to help you as well. Don't tell Shade I said this, but there is no finer warrior in heaven or hell." She winked. "And whatever you do, don't tell Michael. He'll take it as a personal invitation to prove you wrong, and Wrath will hand him his ass."

Eddie's insecure little girl chose to put in an appearance. "Will Wrath help me?"

"Oh, Eddie." Sophia's smile was pure sweetness. "Wrath is desperate to be of use to you in whatever manner you will allow him. And he really is the best one to help you with your specific power."

She hadn't seen Wrath in a couple of days. "Where is he?"

"I'm not sure." Sophia shrugged. "We're not very good at keeping each other informed, but if I had to guess, I would say he's gone to wherever Ramiel sent Haziel."

"Really?" And who didn't like a spot of tea. "Are he and Haziel a thing?"

"Not officially." Sophia's expression went mischievous. "But judging by the way Ramiel is looking like he wants to pee on Haziel's leg, and Wrath disappeared shortly after she did, I would say there is something going on."

Eddie had only met Haziel briefly, but the angel had seemed lovely. And it would do Wrath no good to pine after Rosabella. He deserved more than that. "How would that work, an angel and a hell prince?"

"I really don't know." Sophia frowned as she thought it over. "It's not something that happens often, as I'm sure you can imagine."

Not an overstatement judging by the tension that happened when the heaven and hell teams met.

"Back to you." Sophia clapped her hands. "We will start your training immediately."

"Now?" Eddie hadn't gotten past asking the question.

Sophia looked at her quizzically. "Why not now?"

Why not indeed, and Eddie stood. "Let's do this."

THIRTY-ONE

Haziel felt the horsemen's power while they were still a hundred kilometers from their destination. It began as a low vibration at the base of her brain.

Wrath rubbed his nape. "Are you feeling that?"

"Yes." She rubbed her own nape to alleviate her discomfort. "It feels very...other." The vibration increased to a sharp drilling that set up base in her nerve endings. Her vision wavered, and a dull whooshing blanketed her hearing.

"Yeah." Wrath looked at her. "Are you doing okay?"

"Not really." She pulled the car to the side of the road. "I think perhaps you should drive."

Leaning closer, Wrath cupped her chin and turned her to face him. "How bad is it?"

"Not terrible." But not good either. Saliva flooded her mouth, as if she was going to be sick. Something tugged at her chest insistently, and she began to sweat. "But it would be safer if you drove. It's going to get worse as we get closer."

"Fuck this." Wrath's eyes went glacial in his fury. "You shouldn't be doing this in the first place. Let's turn back."

"No." She had made a deal with Ramiel, and he was already disappointed in her. "I said I would do this, and that's what I'm going to do."

Wrath growled but threw open his door and stomped around the car. He pulled open her door and motioned her to get out. "I can see you're going to be pigheaded about this, and if you're insisting on going—"

"I am."

"—then I'm going to make sure we both get there safely."

She checked the clock on the dashboard. They still had at least another hour of driving before they reached the site, and already she could feel the effect of that other power. She was suddenly grateful Wrath was there. And he was right. Ramiel should have come with her. "Thank you."

As they drove closer, the tingling in her skull developed into a full-blown headache. The pain in her head radiated in dull throbs that made her teeth ache. She reached for her power to block it out. The pain in her chest increased to a sharp ache, but when she tried to draw her power, she found she couldn't. Low level panic unfurled in her belly as she tried again to draw her power. The horsemen had her power and were using it against her.

Their grip on her power tightened, a steady, merciless tug that she was unable to stop.

"Wrath," she whispered. With the pain shifting into her neck and shoulders, she found speaking difficult. Her back muscles went rigid as she tried to fight the pull.

Wrath glanced at her. "What is it?"

It was hard to form words over the roaring in her head. "I can feel them. They're compelling me closer."

He yanked the car to the side of the road. "Fuck this. We need to go back."

"Please." She didn't know who she was begging to stop.

Wrath turned the wheel, ready to turn the car around.

The pain became unbearable, fastening cruel, raking claws through her chest. "Stop," she panted.

The agony subsided slightly.

"We have to keep going." The horsemen were not going to allow her to turn back.

"Haziel." Wrath gently turned her face to him. "We have to go back."

"I can't," she managed. "They've got me, and they're not letting me go."

"Fuck!" Wrath pounded the steering wheel. "That fucking dipstick of an archangel needs to get here and help you. Now."

Haziel felt Wrath call for Ramiel through their bonded power. It was something all hell princes and archangels could do with their counterpoint. A sort of cosmic paging service that linked the balancing forces.

The horsemen's power swelled in her brain, insisting she obey. It overwhelmed her thinking like a massive invader in her brain, and she had no choice but to answer the summons.

As if from a distance, she watched her hand reach for the door handle and open the door. She had lost all control of her body. Deep within her own brain, she was aware that none of this was right, that she was not in command of her actions, but she was also unable to resist.

"Haziel." Wrath grabbed her arm.

Her own power surged and was amplified through her until it threw him back. He exploded from the car as if launched by a rocket and landed several meters into the bush on the roadside.

Inside, she screamed for him, she wanted to see if he was okay, apologize for using her power against him, but she couldn't. It was like her being had shrunk into a tiny kernel within her, trapped by a force greater than she could imagine. If she didn't obey, it would tear her apart.

Her wings unfurled, and she took to the air. Her body moved of its own accord, another master at the helm. The speed of her flight increased, straining her muscles and wing bones until she felt like she might break into pieces, but she couldn't slow down, and she couldn't control the flight.

She became aware of Wrath trying to catch up with her. But seraphim were faster in the air, and at the speed she was going, he could never reach her.

Hurt throbbed through her entire body. She felt like an open nerve ending being constantly pummeled. The pressure in her head increased, and a trickle of blood escaped her nose and was swept away by the speed of her flight.

Sharp pain seared from her wings where feathers were ripped off, and she veered in the air, not able to control her trajectory. Stress fractures ribbed along her wings, compressing the hollow center of her wing bones.

And still the horsemen had her under their control, tearing her forward at whatever cost. For the first time in her long life, Haziel knew debilitating fear. They would kill her before it was done. Her vision blurred, darkening around the edges. At the same time the force was pulling her, it was also drawing from her in great, greedy gulps.

"Release your power," Wrath shouted, dim over the distance between them.

She tried to tell him that she couldn't, but her mouth wouldn't form words, and they screamed silently through her head.

And then she was veering toward the ground, traveling too fast to stop in time. Her body collided with the earth, snapping bones as she made contact. The pain from her body, however, was nothing, compared to the sheer agony of the horsemen pulling her.

Wrath landed beside her. His great black wings sheltered her, and then his beautiful face was hanging over hers.

The dreadful pulling stopped, but her power was being leached out of her in steady draws.

"Haziel." Carved face creased with worry, he knelt over her, pulling her body against his. She felt the wash of his power. So different, yet almost the same as Ramiel's.

Some of the agony eased, and she was able to draw a full breath.

"My wings." She wept for her beautiful, broken wings radiating agony through her entire body.

"I know." Wrath smoothed the hair from her face. "We will fix them, angel. Ramiel comes, and we will fix them."

"They're taking my power." It was hard to form words through the constant hurting. "The horsemen are drawing my power into them."

Wrath looked up suddenly, his expression turning feral with rage. "It took you fucking long enough."

"Satanus." And Ramiel crouched by the other side of her. His green eyes were laden with sadness as he stared at her. "The horsemen are using her power to awaken."

"Stop it," Wrath snapped. "Make it fucking stop."

"I cannot." Ramiel shook his head and looked over his shoulder. "I am not powerful enough on my own."

"Use me," Wrath snapped, his face tight with fury.

"And me." A nimbus of light turned Gabriel's hair to flame as she leaned over Haziel. "I told you this might happen."

"You knew." Wrath bellowed at Ramiel. "You knew, and you let this happen?"

No. Somewhere deep within Haziel, the hurt beat back the

constant agony of her power drain. Ramiel had known this might happen, and still he had sent her.

"I'm sorry." Ramiel reached for her.

With a snarl, Wrath drew her back against his body. "Don't you fucking touch her."

"Wrath." Ramiel looked at her mournfully. In some tiny still functioning part of her brain, Haziel registered that this was as close to a real emotion as she had ever seen the archangel wear. "We had to know how real the risk was, and how close they are to waking. That would only happen if we brought a being of power close enough for them to want their power."

"And you sent Haziel." Red flames flared in Wrath's eyes. "You could have come yourself, you piece of shit. Instead, you did this to her."

"I agree with you, Wrath, but Ramiel couldn't." Gabriel shook her head. "If an archangel was caught in this power flux, that would be the end of one of us, and you know that can't happen."

"So, what?" Heat prickled against her skin as Wrath's anger turned incendiary. "You thought she was expendable? You thought you'd use her like a fucking canary with a gas leak?"

"Now we must break the connection," Ramiel said. "Gabriel and I are here to free her from them, but we must act quickly, or they will take too much."

Their voices had gone weaker and weaker, and Haziel could barely hear them. The heat from Wrath was her only tether on reality. She was tired, so very tired, and she wanted to close her eyes and submit to the inevitable.

"Angel." Wrath shook her eyes open. "You stay with me now. I'm going to break their hold."

Gabriel shook her head. "You can't do it without us."

"I can't do it without help," Wrath snarled. "But you

fuckers can fuck right off if you think I'm letting you near her. You did this to her, and you don't get to save her."

"Be reasonable, Satanus." Ramiel touched Wrath's shoulder.

Haziel could have told him not to.

Wrath lashed out with a pulse of power that sent Ramiel careening backwards into Gabriel. The two of them were thrown against a large rock outcropping and crumpled to the ground.

"Stay with me, angel," Wrath whispered. "I'm getting some help."

"Wrath." Shade appeared behind him. "This had better be fucking important—"

"Help me," Wrath said. "Help me break the lock they have on her power."

"Hells!" Shade knelt beside Wrath. "The horsemen?"

Wrath nodded. "They are pulling power from her to help them rise."

"Fuck!"

Shade's power washed over her, foreign and from hell.

And then Sophia was there as well, her power joining with Shade's.

More power signatures joined theirs. Hell princes and archangels, until Haziel could no longer identify them as individuals.

Inside her, the parasite writhed and fought, drawing harder, as if it sensed it was about to lose its source.

Her vision grew darker, noises muffled. Her breathing slowed, and her heart stuttered and then gave a thready beat.

And then everything stopped. The leach was wrenched out of her. In its sudden absence, she became aware of the ringing silence. Her entire body felt numb and her brain like mush.

"You need to give her to me," Ramiel said. "I need to take her to my demesne to heal her."

"You can fuck right off," Wrath said.

"Haziel," Ramiel said.

She forced her eyes open to focus on Ramiel hovering above her.

His gaze bored into her. "Your vow. Honor it."

And her will imploded like a soft cloud within her. She had given her vow to her archangel. Forcing her gaze to meet Wrath's, she whispered, "I will go with Ramiel."

Wrath frowned, fury and confusion blending on his face. "Did you miss the part about him knowing what would happen to you?"

She had no more strength, and she simply whispered, "Please."

⌇

"Wrath." Shade touched his shoulder, but Wrath shrugged him off.

He sat there like a puppet as Ramiel scooped Haziel's broken body into his arms.

The impact with the earth had shattered her wings and broken several bones in her body. And Ramiel was to blame for each and every injury. He had knowingly exposed her to the risk, and now she was going with him.

This was so fucking wrong. Every part of him wanted to snatch her away and take her to his demesne and heal her there. Ramiel had knowingly placed her in harm, yet Wrath sat here on the ground and could do nothing but watch the archangel take her from him. And all because of one word, please. Nothing could have persuaded him to give her up but Haziel herself. He would have fought the combined forces of

269

heaven, hell, and earth if they had tried to take her from him against her will, but she had asked him to let her go.

A sharp pain reverberated through his chest, and he had to put his fist against the bone to assure himself his chest hadn't cracked wide open.

"I will take care of her," Ramiel said.

Shade stepped between them. "Just fucking go."

Wind from Ramiel's wings washed over his face, and still Wrath couldn't move. The desire to protect Haziel pounded through him like war drums, but she'd asked him to let her go. He would not dishonor her. It was all he could do for her. And somewhere deep inside him, he remembered another female who had also begged him to let her go. You could not make a being stay with you when they did not want to be there.

"What happened?" Sophia was facing off with Gabriel.

"We had to see if the horsemen were really waking." Gabriel looked at Sophia as if pleading with her to understand. "The only way to truly know the extent of the problem was to expose another supernatural being to their power."

"You're a bitch." Sophia's slap echoed around the clearing.

Gabriel's hand flew to her reddened cheek, but eyes wide, she nodded. "I deserved that. I should never have consented to Ramiel using her like that."

"Why did you?" Michael stood beside Sophia, condemnation written over his features.

Wrath didn't give a shit. All he could feel was the aching void inside him left by Haziel.

"Let's go." Shade put a hand on his shoulder. "Let these assholes deal with Ramiel and Gabriel."

And Wrath hauled himself to his feet. There was nothing for him here now.

THIRTY-TWO

Eddie may not have known Shade or Wrath for long, but she knew they were hiding shit from her. Three days ago, Shade had up and vanished on her—literally *poofed* it out of there. One minute, they'd been sharing eggs and bacon—with maple syrup, of course—when Shade had sat upright and his eyes had gone glassy. A blink later, his fork had hit his plate with a clatter, and it was no more hell prince in her kitchen.

An interrogation of the hounds had turned up that Shade had gone to help Wrath with something, and that poofing was a thing with hell princes and archangels, and she shouldn't worry about it. She'd tried to track down Sophia, and—surprise, surprise—Sophia was nary to be found. Seems the theatre had suffered from an all-hands-on-deck poofing event, and Sophia had a rehearsal that night and needed to poof her ass back to the theatre before it started.

Sophia had arrived in time for her rehearsal, looking grim and not wanting to answer any of her questions. Shade had appeared next, looking furious and exhausted, and then Wrath had arrived, looking like he wanted to rip the world off its axis. She'd tried to talk to him, but his answers had been monosyllabic and terse before he'd stepped through the hell gate and disappeared on her.

Eddie had waited outside rehearsal for Sophia, but she had disappeared immediately after, and when Eddie had shut down the theatre and gone upstairs, she'd found Shade fast asleep in her bed.

For the first time since she'd known them, the supernaturals had circled the wagons and had not told her anything.

The next morning, Shade and Sophia looked concerned about something, and Wrath had reappeared looking devastated, which being Wrath, meant grumpy as fuck. If she'd known him better, she might have pushed for answers, but in that mood, he'd been way too intimidating for her to dare.

And Eddie had let it go. She didn't like people prying when she had shit on her mind, so she didn't pester them. Secretly, she'd been harboring the hope that one of them would share sooner or later. It hurt more than she liked to admit that they had excluded her.

Two days later, she was out of patience, and none of them were breaking the cone of silence. She went for the weak underbelly of the three, and the hell prince who would tell her anything—Shade.

He was in the workshop hammering nails into God alone knew what but doing it with an enthusiasm that spoke of a being with shit on his mind.

Eddie propped her shoulder on the workshop doorjamb, crossed her arms and waited. He was the one who had forced himself into her life. He didn't get to shut her out anymore, not after all they'd shared and all the beautiful things he'd said to her. She was worried as fuck about Wrath, as well.

Looking up, he gave her a tight smile that she didn't buy for a second. "Eddie."

"Shade." She gestured to the pulverized wood in front of him. "Whatcha doing?"

Shade frowned at the wood and then the hammer in his hand. "Hammering nails?"

"Uh-huh." When wrangling divas, it was important to give them the space to fill the silence. And as far as Eddie could ascertain, hell princes and divas shared a lot of characteristics. One being their inability to leave a silence uninhabited.

Shade tossed his wood victim on the pile at his feet and grabbed another.

Bam, bam, bam.

He punched a four-inch nail into the wood before glancing at her. "Are you okay? Do you need something?"

She strolled, super casual, over to his workbench. "I was wondering the same thing."

"Huh?"

He did great confused, but she was on to him. "You disappear from my kitchen and come back with something on your mind. You've spent the last two days hiding in corners and whispering with Wrath and Sophia. I think you might be the one who needs to talk."

"Eddie." He got his growly hell prince thing on.

Damn, that was so inappropriately sexy, but she needed to focus. "Yes?"

"You should be resting." He folded his arms in a bicep-bulging smoke show.

"And you should be talking." Eddie removed the hammer from his hand. "Not punishing innocent pieces of wood. And not pushing me away." She leaned closer to him. "I don't like it."

Shade growled.

Her ovaries fluttered, but she kept her steely stare locked on him.

"The four horsemen are waking." He sighed.

"And?"

"That's bad." He braced his hands on the workbench and dropped his head. "Very fucking bad."

"End of the world bad?"

"Yup."

Okay, now she was getting somewhere. "Is that where you and Sophia went the other day?"

He looked at her, those gray eyes tender. "Eddie, you are recovering from an ordeal. You should not be thinking about this."

"Shade." That he cared enough to try to protect her soothed some of her nasty tendrils of rejection, but they weren't going to build any trust between them with evasions and lies. "If you want me to trust you, you're going to have to trust me, and my resilience."

He stared at her.

She held his gaze.

"Fair enough." He blew out a long breath and leaned his hip against the workbench. "Have you read Revelations?"

"Bits and pieces." As in, not actually read but heard and seen here and there.

"For the most part it's a fairytale." Shade shoved his hand through his hair. "But there is some truth to it. The four horsemen of the apocalypse are a real thing, and they bring the end of days."

Eddie needed some clarity on the details. "And this is linked to the seals, right?"

"Yes." He sighed. "The weakening of the seals heralds the end of days and wakes the horsemen. With what's been going on in hell, the horsemen are stirring."

That did not sound good. "Does that mean they're waking up?"

"Yes." Shade strolled around the workbench to her, and as if he needed the contact with her, he drew her close to him and tucked her back against his front. "That was what we were uncertain about. They're ancient beings. From time to time, they shift or move."

"This has happened before?" Eddie was happy to be tucked in close to his warmth. It felt like home in the most elemental way.

"We've managed to keep it from the guardians, but every now and then, in a millennia type of way, it has." He tightened his arms around her. "We always check it out. Just in case."

"And?" She already knew she wasn't going to like the direction this conversation took.

"Ramiel sent Haziel to check it out." Shade's tone hardened, and she felt the tension in his body. "And he shouldn't have. Seraphim are strong, but they're not archangels. The horsemen are tuned into celestial or hell power, and the minute they sensed it, they drew on it. They use it to fuel their wakening."

"So why go near them?" It seemed fairly obvious to her that if a fire needed wood, don't toss logs on it.

"It's one of those things that we need to check, but do so carefully," Shade said. "A hell prince or an archangel has enough strength to resist the draw of the horsemen. At least while they're in this dormant state. Once they waken, there is no stronger power in the universe."

"So Ramiel sent a knife to a gun fight?"

Shade huffed a laugh. "Pretty much. Wrath found her and went with her, but once the horsemen caught her power signature, they latched on, and Haziel didn't have the strength to break free."

"So Wrath helped her?"

"He tried." Shade tucked his head into the crook of her neck. "But it's like a nuclear meltdown. The more power the horsemen get, the stronger they become, and it grows incrementally. Wrath couldn't stop the draw. He could only hold it at a certain level."

Eddie put the pieces into place. "So you and Sophia left to help him."

"Yes." He leaned them both back against the bench. "And we got her free. But it didn't stop there."

"Tell me."

"There is a lot of fucked up to this situation."

"Tell me."

"First," Shade said, "Ramiel should never have sent Haziel, and if any of the arches or princes had known about it before he did, we would have stopped it." He shook his head. "Except for Gabriel, who saw it more in the light of a litmus test."

"Because it could kill her?" He was right. That was seriously fucked up.

"Yes." Shade kissed the top of her head. "And also, it fuels the horsemen and brings them closer to waking."

Eddie had never warmed to Ramiel on the handful of occasions she'd met him. The archangel seemed sneaky. "So why did he do it?"

"That, my sweet Eddie, is an excellent question, and one I don't have an answer for."

She knew Shade better than that. "But you have a theory."

"I do." He chuckled. "And so does Sophia. We think Ramiel was unhappy about what is developing between Wrath and Haziel, and he sent her there to separate them."

Eddie remembered Haziel for her quirky smile and her sweetness. "That is fucked up. Ramiel risked the end of days because he was jealous?"

"Basically." Shade growled. "We may be near immortal, but that doesn't always prevent us from behaving like asswipes."

"Is Haziel okay?"

Shade nodded. "She is, but she was badly injured." He cleared his throat. "And she went back to Ramiel's demesne to heal."

"Wait." Eddie wriggled around to face him. "But he's the reason she's injured."

"I know."

"And she went back with him?"

Shade gave her a loaded stare. "Exactly."

"Why?"

He shook his head. "That is the question that haunts Wrath, I believe."

Eddie pictured her father's face. He'd looked tortured. "Surely Wrath tried to stop her."

"He did." Shade pressed his forehead to hers. "And she begged him to let her go."

That fucking sucked for Wrath, and Eddie's heart felt heavy for him. "Is that why he's so grumpy."

"Yes."

"Poor Wrath." He had the worst luck with women. First, he'd fallen for Rosabella, and now, Haziel had walked away from him. "So he has feelings for Haziel."

Shade nodded. "It certainly looks that way. To be honest, I'm not sure even he was aware of them until this all went down."

Her heart hurt for him, and she said again, "Poor Wrath." And then there were the bigger consequences to consider. "Surely someone is going to do something about what Ramiel did."

"The arches are dealing with Ramiel." Shade grinned. "And don't call me Shirley."

"And he makes crappy jokes." And they still made her laugh.

"Hey." He jostled her gently against him. "Leslie Nielsen was a comedic genius."

"You're so old."

"You have no idea."

She took a moment to bask in the tender warmth of his smile. And then it was back to business. "So what's the plan now?"

"Plan?"

Yeah, if this thing between them was going anywhere, he needed to learn that she was on to his bullshit. "The plan you, Sophia, and Wrath have been whispering about for the past two days."

Groaning, Shade dropped his head back and stared at the ceiling. "Eddie, why can't you be like most of humanity and wallow in blissful ignorance?"

She poked his stomach to get his attention—and holy ab overload. "What are you three cooking up?"

"It's unrelated to Haziel."

Not good enough. "Try again."

Shade's eyes gleamed silver. "There are far more interesting things we could be doing than discussing this."

Holy shitballs. She'd almost forgotten how powerful his lust thing was. It hit her in the core like a promise of Nirvana... but she was on to him, and she breathed deep and punched him. "Stop that shit and tell me."

Later, she promised her rioting woman parts.

"Eddie." He tugged her against him. "Please don't ask this of me. Please don't ask that I expose you to danger again."

How could you simultaneously want to hug and smack a

male? "I think the time for shielding me flew out the window when Ashe abducted me."

"Exactly." Shade drew back far enough to meet her gaze. "You suffered, and I would not have you suffer again."

"I'm in this. I want to help." She nestled against his chest, needing the connection. "I didn't choose this, but it is what it is now, and pushing me to the sidelines hurts like hell." She looked up at him so he could see her truth in her eyes. "And I'm tired of being a victim."

His struggle played across the finely made bone structure of his face and settled in the silvery depths of his eyes. "I never want you to suffer again."

"Then give me the knowledge that empowers me." He needed to understand this, or there was no future for them. "Give me choices."

THIRTY-THREE

Yesterday—who probably wouldn't see tomorrow if Wrath had anything to do with it—had produced a date and time for a rebel demon meeting. Since his return minus Haziel from the horsemen's resting place, he had thrown himself into activity. He didn't want to think about the gnawing ache in his chest, so he drove himself to get to the root of what was happening with the demons and the seals. Still, in those quiet moments when he rested, sparkling green eyes, velvety dusky skin, and a sweet laugh chased him back into action again. She'd gone with Ramiel. Worse than that, she'd begged him to let her go.

And he, like the fucking idiot he was, had let her. When was he going to learn around females? They all fucking left sooner or later. The ones that made him feel things did, in any case. One glimmer of a silver lining in this whole clusterfuck was that his loss of Haziel had put in perspective any lingering fondness he might have felt for Rosabella.

She was constantly around, batting her lashes at him and pouting in a way that used to make him want to move hell for her. Now her heavy-handed attempts at ingratiation made him want to punch shit. Actually, he pretty much wanted to punch shit as a default right now.

Just when Wrath was warming up enough to Shade not to want to eviscerate him on sight, they stood outside the theatre with Wrath unable to believe he was looking at Eddie standing there beside Shade. And Shade would do as his first punching bag.

"She asked me to let her make her own decisions." Shade shrugged. "To give her choices."

"Choices?" Wrath spat. Choices that could very well get her dead. Haziel had made a choice, and it hadn't been him. Rosabella had made that same choice. Now Shade wanted him to condone him sending his daughter right into the belly of the beast.

"Yup." Dee slid out of the backstage door and joined them. "We all need them."

And Wrath's night slid into his top three worst ever. Fucking choices! This was the problem with humans. They always insisted on choices in matters they were woefully ill-equipped to make decisions about. For the sake of his budding relationship with his daughter, he kept the rancor out of his tone. "These are not matters that involve humans."

"Beg to differ there, big man." Dee thumped his shoulder. "This affects all of us. You go *boom*, and we all go *boom*."

"Dee?" Eddie frowned down at her grandmother. "What are you doing here?"

"Me?" Dee's eyes went all innocent and wide behind her pink zebra print glasses. "I thought we were infiltrating a secret demon meeting. That's what I'm doing here." She shrugged and grinned at Eddie. "But if we're just going for a burger and a beer, I'm down with that too." Hauling a heaven wrought blade out from under her sweatshirt, she grimaced.

"But I'll probably leave this behind if we're doing the burger and beer thing."

Wrath felt the growl building in his core, and he closed on Shade. They'd agreed—him, Shade, and Sophia—that they would handle this quietly and on their own. He refused to be like Ramiel and send others into danger. "Did you tell everyone?"

"Eddie forced the information out of me." Shade grinned down at Eddie, his expression softening. "She can be very persuasive."

"Stop it." Wrath pounded his arm. He did not want to hear any of that about his daughter. "Don't do that. Don't think that. Don't even imagine that."

Eddie smiled and stepped closer to him. "There is nothing like that going on."

"Yet," Shade murmured.

Aaaand that was enough for Wrath. He threw a punch that sent Shade flying across the parking lot and into the side of the large trash containers at the far end.

"Satanus!" Sophia snapped and shoved his chest. "There is no need for that."

There was every need. "You heard what he said about my daughter."

"Standing right here." Sophia glared at him. "And I told Dee about this outing."

Wrath gaped at her, not sure he'd heard right, or able to make any sense of what she'd said in case he had heard right. She had been right beside him as they'd snapped the hold the horsemen had on his broken Haziel. "Why?"

"Because she's the guardian." Sophia smoothed her hair back into the braid she'd contained it in. "And she deserves to know."

"Ex-guardian." Daniel Lee stepped around the corner and

made an apologetic face at Dee. "Sorry, Dee, but officially you're no longer the guardian."

Dee stiffened and glared at Sophia. "What's he doing here?"

"The same thing you are." Daniel winked at Dee. "Either we're infiltrating a secret meeting or going for a burger and a beer. Personally, a cheese and bacon burger with fries and a micro IPA would be my vote, but I'll go with the crowd."

Wrath's head felt like it might explode. He wouldn't risk one more person he cared about. He couldn't see another being that meant something to him damaged. Breathing deep, he forced the image of Haziel's horrific injuries out of his mind.

Eddie put a hand on his chest. "Dad."

And everything in him stilled. All the anger, all the frustration, all awareness of anyone around him. His mind even took a break from the mental replaying of Haziel bleeding and broken in his arms. Eddie had called him Dad, and nothing else existed in that moment. His child had acknowledged their blood bond, and tears burned behind his eyelids.

"Dad," Eddie said it a second time. "Look, I know you wanted to keep this between you, Shade, and Sophia. But I can help. I'm Nephilim, and after what those fuckers did to me, I want to see them. I want to look my enemy in the eye and be part of bringing them down."

"Whoa, whoa, whoa!" Shade had made it back from his dumpster dive. "There will be no bringing down tonight, Eddie. We go, we observe, and we gain information. Then we leave and do the burger and beer thing."

Wrath barely heard him. All he saw was those aqua eyes of his little girl staring up at him, begging him to understand. How the fuck did human fathers ever deny their daughters anything? If she'd asked him to rip the moon from the skies and give it to her as a night light, he would have done it. If she'd asked him to wrap her in the entrails of her enemies—one entrails comforter coming right up. "I don't want you to get hurt again." Not like Haziel. Yes, Ramiel had sent her there alone, but Wrath had ridden in the car beside her. Been right there when the horsemen's power had latched onto her and refused to release her. The need to touch Eddie overcame him and he cupped her cheek. "I can't let you get hurt."

"I know." Eddie held his hand against her cheek. "And I appreciate that. But who's going to hurt me with you and Shade there to keep me safe? Is there even a being in this universe who could?" Her eyes beseeched him. "I have to do this. I have to not be their blind victim anymore."

She made an excellent point this being of his blood and heart. "Okay." His voice was gruff with the emotions he could not put into words. "But you stay by me or Shade the entire time. No going off on your own. No heroics and don't speak to anyone."

"We've already been through this." Shade gave Eddie a loaded glance. "She sticks by me, or you, and she keeps her head down."

At least the fucker was good for helping him try to keep his daughter safe.

"Oy!" Sophia jabbed a thumb at her chest. "One archangel, standing right here and not at all incapable of taking care of Eddie."

"Sorry, Sophia." Eddie took her hand. "I know you're just as kickass as these two." She looked at him and Shade. "And Sophia has been teaching me how to control my power and to fight."

He turned, in perfect unison with Shade, and glared at Sophia.

"What?" She shrugged. "You like to forget that we female

beings have as much power and an equal ability to leverage it. Eddie deserves to know what she can do."

She had him there, and the glance Shade shot him confirmed as much.

Shade nodded to Sophia. "Sorry."

Wrath knew he'd lost the battle against Eddie and turned to Dee and Daniel. "What about them?"

"We're nonnegotiable," Daniel said and slung an arm over Dee's shoulder. "We come or we blow the whistle on this entire operation."

Wrath did not appreciate being threatened by a mortal, and he got right into Daniel's space. "I can make it so you are incapable of doing so."

"Dad?"

Ah, fuck it! There she went again. Hell! Let his enemies never discover the size of this particular chink in his armor. Still, he could hold out on this at least. "What?"

"We're in this together." She waved her hand to encompass the entire party. "And nobody tells Dee what to do. Also, Daniel can report what he sees to the guardians."

"They won't even know we're there." Daniel dug in his pocket and produced two glowing vials of pale pink liquid. "I had a local coven do us up a little something to help us blend in."

It was no wonder demons were running rampant with as much control as hell princes exerted. He could not even control his small party in this shadowy parking lot. He had for damn sure not been able to protect his female.

"What local coven?" Eddie glared at Daniel.

Shade raised an eyebrow. "I'm guessing the same local coven that has been summoning hell princes."

Eddie turned to Dee. "Dee?"

"Never mind that, Eddie-girl." Dee patted her cheek. "Let's get this done first, and then we can talk."

"But we are talking." Eddie folded her arms and fixed her grandmother with a glare. "I am getting fucking tired of people not telling me shit around here."

"I'll stick with Dee and Daniel," Sophia said, using the soothing tone she normally reserved for Shade on a rampage. "You two keep Eddie safe."

Wrath felt his sigh down to his boots. "Okay, but we might need a glamour for Eddie. We can't take the chance that one of those fuckers tonight recognizes her."

Eddie grinned at him. "Did I not say Sophia had been teaching me a trick or two?" She snapped her fingers, the surge of her accessing her power tingled through him, and in the place of Eddie stood a demoness who looked a lot like Vexia.

Worry and pride warred inside him for a moment, and then he bowed to the inevitable and shifted his shape.

Shade chose an incubus shape and Sophia, rather unimaginatively in his opinion, went with succubus. He couldn't stop himself from wondering what shape Haziel would have chosen. Hells! Ramiel had better be taking good care of her. Better than good care.

And the gang was all there and ready to go. All they needed was their guide.

Wrath put some strong compulsion out there and the imp appeared like he'd been yanked out of the ether—which he had, so no surprise there.

Yesterday gaped at their party. "All of you are coming?"

"Problem?" Wrath channeled all his impotent frustration over their increased party size into one word as he glowered at the imp.

"No, lord." Yesterday almost smacked his forehead on the pavement as he bowed. "No problem, lord. Follow me."

At least one being knew their place. Even if it was a lying imp. Wrath was taking the win.

Because of the humans, they were forced to drive to their destination. Dee loaded them all in her mom wagon, and three hours—and twice as many arguments about directions—later, parked on a quiet suburban street outside of central Ottawa.

Wrath spared a moment's thought for all the residents of this nice neighborhood, going about their lives with no idea that all hell was literally breaking loose on their doorstep.

"Why here?" Eddie clambered out the back of the SUV.

Daniel joined her on the sidewalk. "Proximity to several hell gates and also, who would suspect Ottawa of harboring anything like this?"

The power signatures of many gathered demons hung in the night air like tar. Wrath identified signatures from his demesne, Shade's, Levi's, Belle's, and Lucifer's.

"Ugh!" Sophia winced, her archangel sensibilities particularly fine-tuned to demon activity. "This is quite the get-together."

"Told you." Yesterday puffed up his chest. "Demons have been chittering about this loud enough for a clever and industrious imp to hear."

That bothered Wrath. On principle, he cuffed the imp for his impudence, but it niggled at him that Yesterday had been able to pick up chatter about this particular meeting. For however long these demon hordes had been congregating, not one of the hell princes had picked up a thing. Were they growing brazen or was this a trap? He moved closer to Eddie.

She glanced up at him. "What's wrong?"

In demon form, she would be more susceptible to his

emotions. Especially since she'd chosen a demon form from his demesne. "I don't know." He shook his head. "Doesn't it seem a bit convenient that we've been able to discover this meeting now, when we weren't even getting a hint of this before?"

"I was thinking the same thing." Shade narrowed his eyes as he stared down the empty street.

Daniel appeared at his elbow. "You think it's a trap?"

"There's always that possibility." Dee held her hand out to Daniel. "Give me one of those glamours. No use standing here jawing about it. If it's a trap, let's spring the fucker."

THIRTY-FOUR

Eddie's new body took some getting used to. She was bigger and stronger, and her senses were sharper. Her vision peeled back the dark like it was daylight, and details became sharper, if somewhat monochromatic. And dear God, her enhanced sense of smell was not a plus this close to other people. It made her feel an all-new level of appreciation for dogs. Part of her wanted to test out this new form and see if she'd inherited Vexia's neat trick of disappearing into thin air, or maybe she could flip that minivan parked outside a neat bungalow. Options.

Shade flowed beside her with languid grace, his skin a pearlescent white that somehow made her want to stroke it. On her other side, Wrath had taken the form of one of those enormous Rhino-boys and towered over the rest of them casting a shadow like a dump truck on the road. She didn't have a name for what Dee and Daniel were supposed to be, but they looked disconcertingly reptilian. The glamours worked a bit like a TikTok filter, and if either of them shifted too fast, there was a slight lag before the glamour caught up.

Sophia was giving them both a stern lecture on how to move wearing a glamour. None of which Dee was taking seriously as she skipped along beside Daniel.

Looking over, Dee caught her eye and gave her a wink. Her eyes gleamed with delight. She was enjoying the crap out of this.

More demons slunk around them as they drew closer to the end of the street. None of the other demons made eye contact, and that was fine with Eddie. She moved closer to Shade. "Won't there be some kind of password?"

"Him." Shade pointed at Yesterday. "His blood will get us in."

So not reassuring, and Eddie really hoped this was not another time when Yesterday had a spot of betrayal or double dealing in mind. Nerves fluttered in her belly as they approached a small crowd of demons gathered around a door.

"Breathe," Shade whispered to her. "If it all goes sideways, you have enough power by your side to flatten this neighborhood."

It was odd what you considered romantic when you were being wooed by a hell prince.

Two high order demons guarded the door, looking nearly human. One of them had the same horn structure as Ashe, and for a moment, her heart stopped. Then he turned to glance about him, and she breathed a sigh of relief. This demon wasn't as handsome as Ashe, his features coarser.

Yesterday joined the cluster of demons waiting to be admitted.

The Ashe lookalike glanced at Yesterday, paused, and then studied him closer. "You." He pointed at Yesterday. "Imp."

Wrath tensed and shifted his shoulder in front of hers.

"Me?" Yesterday did a classic double take and look behind him combo.

The demon growled. "Don't try my patience, imp."

"Hello, Coal." Yesterday bounced up to the demon. "I told you I was coming, and I would be bringing friends."

Coal's dark eyes skimmed their group. He paused on Dee and studied her closer. "What demesne?"

Dee opened her mouth to reply but Yesterday got there faster. He pointed at Dee and Daniel. "Sloth." Then at Sophia. "Lust." He jerked his head at Shade. "That one too."

The demon moved closer to Dee and Daniel. "They don't smell like Sloth."

"What does?" Yesterday rolled his eyes. "Sodding hell prince is too lazy to even imprint her horde."

Grunting, Coal leaned forward and sniffed at Eddie and then Wrath. "Wrath."

"Yup." Yesterday bounced on his toes. "Can we go in?"

"Blood mark," Coal snapped, his gaze still locked on Wrath.

Growling, Wrath flashed a scary amount of fang.

"Fucking wrath demesne." Coal shook his head. "You try any of your aggressive crap inside, and I will personally end you."

"He's fine." Yesterday patted Wrath's forearm and then bit into his index finger and held it up for Coal.

Still glaring at Wrath, Coal licked the blood. "Seems good." He glowered at Wrath. "I don't like you. You make me twitchy."

"I don't like you either." Wrath's voice sounded like boulders grinding together. "Pride scum always makes me want to bite heads off."

Eddie tensed.

But Coal didn't seem to find anything wrong with the possibility of losing his head to Wrath's enormous gnashers and jerked his head. "I'll be watching you."

"Mmmh." Sophia glided closer to Coal and stroked her fingers over his cheek. "I like being watched." She licked her full, sensuous mouth. "Maybe you bring a friend later, and you can all watch if you like."

Coal lurched back. "Get off me." He snarled. "Fucking succubus. Don't try your tricks here."

"Or what," Sophia purred. "You'll spank me?" She giggled. "I enjoy a good spanking."

"Get in there and shut up." Coal shoved her through the narrow doorway.

Shade sidled closer to him. "Maybe—"

"Fuck off." Coal pushed Shade after Sophia.

Inside, demons filled a large, open space, and the combined smell assaulted Eddie's sensitive nose. Wrath led the way, shouldering other demons out of their path. A few turned around and snarled or snapped, but one look at the size of him, and they grudgingly gave way. They couldn't risk much conversation in such a confined space, so Eddie concentrated on looking around.

The array of demon shapes and sizes was dizzying. Some of her worst nightmares seemed to drift around the space. There was everything from the almost humanoid to the barely there mist variety of demon. She struggled not to stare.

Sophia was given a wide berth. Demons seemed united in their dislike of succubae. Eddie wanted to know why and added it to her mental tally of questions when they got out of here.

Wrath and Shade kept very close to her. Not allowing any other demon to get between her and them. Dee and Daniel stuck to Sophia, both of them taking things in like Eddie was.

The atmosphere in the room shifted, and a hush fell over the demons.

Eddie felt a power signature prickle over her skin, and she glanced at Shade.

He gave her a barely susceptible nod. Something was going down.

Coal stepped to the front of the room and mounted a small, raised platform. "Shut the fuck up," he shouted.

Silence followed.

Movement rippled from the back of the room. Eddie craned her neck to see what was happening and made eye contact with Ashe. This time there was no mistake. It was really him. Her heart leapt into her throat, and sweat broke out all over her.

Wrath growled and Shade tensed.

There were a lot of demons between them and the door if Ashe recognized her.

But Ashe made his way to the front of the room as demons parted for him. He passed close enough to Eddie for her to touch him, and she shrunk back against Shade.

He put a hand on her hip, warm and reassuring.

Power prickled and snapped from Wrath, turning his skin a darker shade of blue. Other demons started murmuring and side eyeing him.

Sophia wrapped her arms around his neck, pressed her body to him, and whispered in his ear.

He took a deep breath, and the power subsided to a manageable level. Between them, Shade, Wrath, and Sophia could level this gathering, but then they'd be working as blind as they were now. Information was what they needed most.

Coal bowed low to Ashe and gave up the platform.

All eyes turned to Ashe. Eddie could almost taste the excitement in the room.

"Pride is ours," Ashe said. He didn't raise his voice, but it carried to the corners of the silent space.

A murmur broke out.

Coal growled, and silence fell again.

"As is Lust," Ashe said. "Their lords are missing, and we are to take full advantage. The seal of Wrath remains stronger and should be a priority to destabilize."

Waves of fury drifted off Shade, and Eddie put her hand on his arm.

Sophia pressed even closer to Wrath.

"We are to continue to gather our armies." Ashe's gaze swept over them. "And to ramp up our destabilization of the seals before the hell princes figure out how to repair them."

Eddie's heart stopped as his gaze seemed to stick for a moment, and then he was speaking again.

"The master needs more demons, and it is your task to get them for him," Ashe said. "More rebel demons means more pressure on the seals, and we need those fucking things to break."

Nods of assent happened all around them.

Eddie nodded along but kept her eyes trained on the feathered back of the demon in front of her.

Coal held up his hand. "What of the amulets?"

"Production of amulets has slowed," Ashe said. "But the master has plans to correct that soon."

Another demon hand went up.

Ashe's gaze snapped in that direction. His voice dropped silky with menace. "You have a question?"

"No, Ashe." The hand disappeared again.

"The horsemen wake," Ashe said. "They sense the chaos we are creating. The master wishes for that to escalate. With the hell princes focusing on hell, we can continue to generate more anarchy on this plane." His gaze swept the room. "That is all. You know what you must do."

He stalked out of the room, and it wasn't until he'd gone that Eddie drew her first full breath.

"What are you?" A demon snarled close by.

The hair on Eddie's nape rose.

A large bull-like demon was focused on Dee and glaring at her.

"You know what I am." Sophia undulated in front of Dee. "And now you have my attention."

"No." The demon shoved her out of the way. "What the fuck is that?"

More heads swung their way.

"Time to go," Shade murmured.

"More than time to go." Another demon appeared beside Wrath. "You shouldn't even be here."

Wrath growled and went for the demon.

"Not now," the demon snapped and started herding them toward the door.

There was something familiar about the demon, but Eddie couldn't put her finger on it. She was certain she'd never seen him before, with his equine features and grace, but he felt familiar.

"It's a human!" Bull demon bellowed and lunged for Dee.

And pandemonium broke lose.

Demons lunged for Dee.

Sophia hauled her over her shoulder as if she weighed nothing and surged for the door.

"This is going to get fucking messy," Shade whispered.

Demons were pushing and shoving toward Sophia now, as she fought her way to the door.

With a bellow, Wrath transformed into himself.

"Wrath!" Someone screamed.

"Fuck it," whispered the strange demon. Light shimmered, and suddenly Lucifer was there.

Now the tide turned from trying to get to Sophia to trying to get to the door.

Demons shoved, screamed, punched, and climbed over each other to get out of the building.

"If you can't beat them." Shade shrugged off his temporary form.

Demons got jammed in the door trying to leave, and Shade scooped Eddie into his arms.

Lucifer grabbed Daniel and tossed him over his shoulder.

Power washed through Eddie, and she knew it was Wrath.

With a boom that hurt her ears, the demons, the room, and the house exploded.

Demon parts flew through the air, blood spattered everywhere, bits of brick, mortar, piping, and electrical clattered to the street.

"Subtle, brother," Lucifer drawled. He glanced around them at the carnage. "Do you think they'll know we were here?"

Sophia ran up to them with Dee still cradled in her arms. "We need to get out of here. I've called for my host to do clean up."

Car alarms blared and lights blinked on in the houses all around them. A thick dust cloud blanketed the area.

Shade grit his teeth. "Damage control," he said.

His power felt completely different to Wrath's, but calm drifted over the war zone street.

People peering out of windows, dropped the curtains and stepped away. Doors that had been hung open closed and the groans of dying demons silenced.

Up until this moment, Eddie had known she was hanging out with all-powerful beings, but seeing it in action nearly blew her mind into as many pieces as the former house.

A soft shushing sound made her look up, and angels appeared in the sky above them. Their white wings sending warm drafts of air down. Eddie had to blink away tears as she watched them. They were so beautiful and graceful and nearly silent.

One of them approached Sophia and they spoke for a while.

"Let's go." Wrath grabbed her arm. "We need to make a quick exit."

Shade nodded and scooped Eddie into his arms. "We fly." He turned to Lucifer. "Cloak us."

With a smirk, Lucifer tapped two fingers to his forehead in a mocking salute. "Your wish, oh mighty one."

Wrath grabbed Daniel, whose glamour seemed to be disappearing faster than the debris around them, and took to the air.

With her clasped to his chest, Shade hovered in the air above Sophia until she had lifted Dee with her.

"What about my car?" Dee's head whipped around as she tried to see past Sophia's wings.

Lucifer shot her a wicked grin. Did he have any other kind of smile? "I'll meet you at the theatre." He glanced at Shade and Wrath. "We need to have a little chat."

Nodding, Wrath swept his great red and black wings and shot high over the buildings.

"The keys." Dee dug in her pocket.

"Oh, ye of little faith." Lucifer winked at her. "Enjoy your flight, Dee."

As Shade lifted Eddie higher, angels worked their magic, and the house, the dead demons, and the damage started disappearing.

THIRTY-FIVE

Wrath stared at his brother, not bothering to mask his loathing. He might have been persuaded that Lucifer had not been involved in Eddie's kidnapping, but he still didn't like the troll fucker. "What were you doing there?"

Smoothing down the front of his black button-down, Lucifer smirked at him. "Why, brother, I am well. I'm so happy you asked."

Yeah, he wasn't going to bite. Well, not in the sense of rising to the bait, but his teeth breaking Lucifer's skin still held dizzying appeal.

"Why were you there?" Sophia folded her arms and propped her hips against the greenroom counter. Behind her, the kettle came to a boil and hissed.

"Tea first." Dee bustled at the counter putting bags in cups and pouring hot water over them.

Wrath could say with certainty that he did not want a cup of tea, but Eddie had seconded Dee's suggestion when she'd made it, so he would choke down a cup of fucking tea.

"Ashe." Lucifer's face went stony, and retribution chilled his eyes to pitch. "He is mine."

He could respect that sentiment. If Ashe had been part of his court, Wrath would take his defection personally and want to take care of payback himself. "Why didn't you take him when you had the chance?"

"Because, unlike you," Lucifer drawled, "I like to think before I act." He accepted a mug from Dee with a smile of thanks. "Ashe was my best demon. Him being part of something like this makes no sense. I wanted to know more before I end him." He smirked. "And I was there incognito. Until you decided to blow the place to shit, that is."

Wrath took his cup and cradled it between his palms. The warmth did provide a measure of comfort, so maybe there was something to this infernal tea drinking of humans. "What if you don't get another chance to capture him?"

"I'll get another chance." Lucifer's voice vibrated with malicious intent, and Wrath didn't doubt him for a second. He knew from experience exactly how vengeful his sibling could be.

"There's something bothering me," Eddie said and rubbed at her nape.

Shade rubbed her back. "What is it?"

"Ashe." She frowned into her teacup. "There were a couple of times in that meeting when I swore he saw me but then... nothing."

"He can't have seen you." Sophia spooned sugar into her mug. "Or he would have called out."

"Not necessarily." Shade's palm moved slowly up and down Eddie's spine.

The only thing that kept Wrath from ripping Shade's hand off his daughter was the comfort Eddie seemed to draw from the contact. She swayed into the touch in a way that made Wrath grind his molars.

"Beg to differ," Lucifer snapped. "The only reason that self-serving piece of shit kept quiet was because he knew she wouldn't be there alone."

Eddie's frown deepened, and Wrath sensed she had more to say. "What is it, Eddie? We're listening." He shot a glare around the room to make sure everyone else was onboard.

"I don't know." Eddie sipped her tea. "When I was a captive, it was mainly Ashe I saw."

Wrath's mug disintegrated in his fist, and tea sloshed on the floor. Before anyone could get pissy about it, he vanished the mess.

"And he was...well there were times when I felt like he was trying to help me." Eddie shrugged. "I don't know, because he was also always there whenever they were going to drain me. So maybe I'm suffering from some kind of Stockholm syndrome or something."

Shade watched Eddie as if he was being paid to do it. "What do you mean tried to help you?"

"Well, he was the one who said something about dreams before I reached out to you in yours."

Lucifer scoffed. "Coincidental."

"Let my daughter speak," Wrath snarled. It didn't matter that the same thought had crossed his mind as Lucifer spoke.

Shrugging, Lucifer winked at Dee.

Dee rolled her eyes at him, but she did it as she giggled, so it lost a lot of its scorn.

"And then he was the one who locked me in at night," Eddie said. "And he started leaving some of the locks open."

"He could be careless," Sophia suggested gently.

"Not Ashe." Lucifer shook his head. "Before he turned into

a traitorous shit, he was my best demon. The sort of demon I could leave to get something done and know it would be done."

Sophia wrinkled her nose in thought. "So, out of character then?"

"Completely." Frowning, Lucifer nodded. "To be honest—"

"That would be a first." Wrath wasn't going to let that opportunity slip.

"To be honest." Lucifer grinned at him. "This entire thing with him is out of character."

"Demons are demons." Shade glanced at him. "They're not known for their loyalty."

"But some are," Dee said. She looked at Wrath. "I mean, you trust Vexia don't you?"

"Yes." He was forced to admit. Also; that Apassionata prick from Shade's demesne had been straight up helpful and still in the palace long after the others had disappeared into the sunset. He allowed the possibility of what Eddie was suggesting to grow in his mind. He turned to Lucifer. "But Coal was one of your higher order demons as well."

"Coal is a dumb shit." Lucifer growled. "He'll be a pleasure to end. Never did like the fucker. But Ashe"—his mouth tightened in a grim line that didn't bode well for Ashe—"him, I liked. Trusted."

"And tonight," Eddie continued. "He seemed to work in the word master to his speech. It's like he was telegraphing that information. Trying to tell us there was someone else in charge." She scrubbed her face with her palm, and her shoulders slumped. "I don't know. None of this sounds like anything relevant when I string it all together. I'm probably imagining the entire thing."

Lucifer's expression screamed that's exactly what he

thought, and Wrath was inclined to agree with him—not out loud, mind you. He'd noted a few of his own in that crowd tonight, and he was planning to enjoy teaching them the error of their ways.

"He also spoke about the seals." Lucifer looked at Shade and then Wrath. "And from what he said about needing to keep the pressure on them, he inferred there is a way to repair them."

Shade stiffened. "Eddie is not that way. She tried with Wrath's, and the best she could manage was a partial repair. It took everything in her to do that much."

Wrath shifted closer to them. He hated the glint in Lucifer's eye. He was with Shade on this. If there was a way to repair those seals, Eddie wasn't going to be the guinea pig.

"But you never tried her on Shade's seal." Lucifer never knew when to fucking quit.

"And we're not going to now." Wrath wouldn't allow another female in his life to be used up and discarded as if she didn't matter. The horror of watching Haziel in the horsemen's grip threatened to overthrow his mind. "But if there is a way, we need to find it."

Eddie took a deep breath. "I could try—"

"No." Shade shouted her down at the same time as Wrath.

"There you are." Rosabella stood poised in the doorway, one hand on her outthrust hip and the other on the doorjamb. "I've been looking for you."

She wore a figure-hugging red dress that thrust her breasts over the top and ended well above her knees. Her hair was a tousled, sexy mess around her perfectly made-up face.

Lucifer straightened and stared.

Sophia growled, and Eddie shrunk against Shade.

Sashaying into the room, hips rocking like she was working

for tips, she said, "Nobody has the right to take my daughter away without telling me first."

"Everybody out," Wrath snapped. There was a conversation that had been a long time in coming. He caught himself before Dee and Eddie reacted. "If you don't mind."

With a glare at her daughter, Dee left the room, and everyone followed behind her.

Rosabella watched them go with a smirk before turning to him. "Wrath," she purred. "If you wanted to spend time alone with me, all you had to do was ask."

"Stop it." He stayed where he was, with his shoulders propped against the wall. Not too long ago, that look on Rosabella's face would have had him crossing hell to find her; now, he couldn't even be bothered to cover the handful of strides that separated them.

Cocking her head, Rosabella closed the distance between them and put her hand on his chest. "Come on, babe." She pouted up at him. "You can't stay mad at me forever."

"You're forgetting what I am." Her hand on him felt like an invasion, and he took it away. "I am Wrath, getting and staying mad is my thing. And I have nothing but time."

"All right." She crossed her arms, and her breasts threatened a breakout from her dress. "Get it out of your system. I've been a bad girl."

"No, Rosabella." It was kind of surreal to see all that cleavage and not be even slightly tempted by it. To be honest, it was good cleavage. Rosabella had always had, and still did have, a banging body. But she didn't have Eddie's courage and strength, or Dee's fortitude and determination. And her eyes for damn sure didn't grow warm and soft like she was seeing the best version of him, unlike those clear, emerald greens of Haziel's. But like Rosabella, Haziel had left him. She'd taken all her serenity and joy with her. And he fucking missed them.

Missed her. "You haven't been a bad girl; you've been an asshole."

Rosabella gaped at him. Temper kindled in her eyes and tightened her lips. He cut her off before it could burst into flame. He wasn't in the mood for one of her tantrums. "You left me, and that was your right." The ever-present tightness in his chest was gone. "But you should have told me about my daughter."

She scowled at him. "I—"

"Be quiet. I am speaking now." He put a thrust of compulsion into his tone. Her justifications might move him to violence. "I lost years with her. And I know we have time now, but I've lost all her firsts, and there is no fucking way I can get those back. Her first word. Her first step. Her first day of school. Her first boyfriend." He hauled his thoughts up before he lost it completely. "She is my daughter, and I barely know her."

Rosabella's face twisted into a grimace as she tried to fight the compulsion.

"And then you abandoned her." No shade on Dee, she'd stepped up and done a great job raising and loving Eddie. "Dee was her mother and gave her all the love you didn't, but that's not a credit to you. That's all Dee. She did what she had to do, and with all the love in the world. But still you left scars on my little girl, and I'll never forgive you for those."

Tears pooled in Rosabella's eyes and slipped down her cheeks.

Wrath had seen it all before. Rosabella wielded tears like an onyx blade, deadly and irrevocable.

"Now, I'm going to do what I can to take those scars away and make her know that she is loved and wanted and the best fucking thing in this entire universe. Scars may fade, but they never entirely go away." He leaned closer to her, making sure she got his meaning. "What you're going to do is make sure you go away. You have no rights here, and you don't belong here. You did that all by yourself with the decisions that you made, and you have nobody to blame but yourself. And if you don't—" He gave it every ounce of menace he had, and that was a fuck ton. "You're going to find out how Satan is the hell prince of Wrath, and there is no place you can hide from me."

THIRTY-SIX

Time passed differently in heaven, and Haziel lost track of how many days had passed on the earth plane. Her time became a blur of pain and healing and Ramiel. Always Ramiel, by her side and pouring his healing energy into her until he nearly depleted himself. Always Ramiel, sitting by her bedside when she woke, ready to give her whatever he could. Except for the thing she needed most, and that was a grumpy hell prince who had thrown himself between her and harm.

The pain in her body healed, but the gaping emptiness in her chest merely deepened. The trust she'd had for Ramiel was shattered, and no number of delicate treats to tempt her to eat or selfless healings could paste the pieces back together again.

When Ramiel had brought her back, he hadn't taken her to the infirmary, or even to her old quarters, but brought her to his and laid her in his bed. He'd brought in healing seraphim to help her between the times when he could heal her, and then sat by her bed and waited, those brilliant green eyes on her constantly.

Haziel wanted to scream at him to go away and leave her alone.

"Haziel." Ramiel stood from the armchair beside her bed and leaned over her. "You're feeling stronger."

Connected to her as he was, he would know, so she barely even bothered to nod.

"Right." Ramiel shoved his hands in the pockets of his lounge pants and dropped his chin to his chest. "We should talk."

She didn't want to talk. Or think. Not that her wishes mattered to the constant barrage of images playing through her mind. Top of them was Wrath's face as she'd begged him to let her go with Ramiel. She'd seen in his eyes the same betrayal she'd felt when she'd realized how callously Ramiel had sent her to the horsemen's resting place to die.

"I'm sorry." Ramiel perched on the side of her bed. "I should never have done it."

"Why did you?" Her voice sounded rusty and hoarse. Even as she asked, she didn't know if his answer would matter. Centuries of love and devotion she'd showered on Ramiel, and he had used her as if she was expendable.

He reached for a glass of water and handed it to her. Even the water in heaven tasted different, pure, essential and of nothing but the atoms that made it up. On earth, the water tasted of the place it sprung from, and all the pipes and mechanisms humans used to bring it to people.

Ramiel sighed and clasped his hands. Leaning his elbows on his knees, he dropped his head. Light gleamed off the golden strands of his hair and accentuated the broad expanse of his shoulders. For so long, it was a sight that would have struck her dumb with longing. "There isn't a simple answer for that."

And Haziel wanted to laugh at his words. Because unlike

her, he could choose whether to be honest or not. The irony of the truth imperative Ramiel had imposed on all his close circle, but not himself, had never felt sharper to her or cut deeper. She had loved this being for countless millennia. Content to merely bask in his shadow and gather the crumbs of affection he tossed her away. Until he had sent her to follow Wrath, and she had known what it was like to be treated as if she mattered. Even after he'd abandoned her to Ava in the early days of their time together, Wrath had come back for her, insisted she came away with him. She wouldn't have known any of that if Ramiel hadn't sent her on that mission. She could have thanked him for that.

Until he had knowingly set her a task that would end her. If Wrath had not been there, she would be no more.

Wrath. A fist constricted around her chest. His blue eyes filled with hurt and then bitterness haunted her.

Ramiel took her hand. "Haziel?"

"What?" No accompanying thrill followed his touch.

"Are you listening to me?"

"You're sitting within arm's reach of me." And way too close. She pulled her hand away. "I cannot but hear you."

"Indeed." Ramiel took a deep, careful breath. "I have earned your anger."

He had cursed her with this truthfulness, and she saw no reason to spare him. "Yes, you have."

Anger flashed in his brilliant green eyes, and his face hardened.

She met his stare, daring him to get angry with her, challenging him to pull his archangel crap on her.

He sighed and his shoulders drooped. "I was jealous."

"Eh?" That shook her out of her righteous anger.

"I was jealous." He reached for her hand and then stopped. "The way matters have been between us for so many years, I had grown accustomed to you always by my side, always putting me before all others."

"By matters, you mean me loving you?" Haziel couldn't spend countless more millennia dancing around the truth and pretending what existed between them didn't.

He cleared his throat. "Yes, that."

"Then let me put your mind at rest, I no longer feel the same."

Flinching, Ramiel stood and shoved his hands in his pockets. "You are angry, and you say things that will wound. I understand."

"No, you don't." His condescension enraged her and made her head pound. "You made it so I could never lie to you. I am not spewing venom in my anger; I am speaking my truth."

"Your truth at this moment," Ramiel said. "Your truth as you believe it to be."

His arrogance was beyond insufferable. He'd always been this way, but it had never made her want to punch his perfect face like it did now. "Are you implying that I don't know my own feelings?"

"No." He held up one hand as if to pacify her. "I do not doubt that at this moment you despise me and are furious with me." Regret clouded his eyes. "And I have deserved all that and more. I knowingly put you at risk to get you away from the influence of that hell prince."

"Wrath." She took delight in speaking his name. "You mean Wrath."

"Yes...Wrath." He sneered. "It never occurred to me for a second when I paired you with him that you would not continue to see him as you always have. That you would not despise him."

"You despised him." Haziel didn't see the point to this conversation, but Ramiel had effectively trapped her here with him, and she was done tiptoeing around his sensibilities. "I always liked Wrath. You were the one who despised him."

Stilling, Ramiel frowned at her. "Always?"

"Yes, always. He was kind to me, in his gruff and forthright way." She shrugged. "And yes, he had a temper, but he's Wrath. It's not like his seal was going to allow him to be any other way."

"Kind to you." Ramiel tapped his chin. "Yes, I suppose he has been. I should have seen that before now, but I suppose I saw only what I wanted to see."

She didn't need to respond to what was patently obvious. "I did what you asked me to. I went to hell with him, kept an eye on him, and for the most part kept him out of trouble." Barring that fight with Ava.

"And you fell in love with him." Ramiel cocked his head and studied her. "There is no use denying it, I can sense it in you."

As if she could deny what was true, so she stared at him.

"I've been a fool." Sighing, Ramiel dropped his chin to his chest. "A fool that only saw that he wanted a thing when it was lost to him."

A ringing sound started in Haziel's ears. She couldn't have heard him right. "What?"

"You see, I always knew you loved me, but I became complacent in that love, sure that it would always be mine. You are such a creature of constancy, Haziel. For as long as there was me, there was you beside me, loving me. And then that love was gone, and I finally understood how precious a gift I had squandered."

If he hadn't looked so crushed, the irony of it might have made her laugh. How many times had she fantasized, longed for him to say these things to her. And now...

Now she understood that love was not a thing of awe and

hero worship. Love was vital and primal and messy and glorious. It was in the tiny things like the way Wrath's eyes crinkled when he smiled. Or the way he very rarely laughed, but when he did, it came from the depths of him and made her want to hear it again and again. In the way he touched her, at times reverent and at times raunchy, sometimes both together. No, love was not a distant pining for an illusion, but a soul deep understanding of another being that made you feel like you were home.

Ramiel was staring at her. "Say something."

"I don't know what to say." For the sake of their history and their future, she would not tell him what she was thinking, but she could only ever be honest. "My feelings have changed."

"I understand." He cleared his throat. "But we have been together for many years, Haziel, and on the basis of that, I would ask something of you."

"What?" Tension and dread knotted in her stomach.

"For the sake of the love you once felt, and its duration, I would ask that you not reject me out of hand. Stay here, recover, and think about what I have said. You are not one to lightly change how they feel. If there is a chance that what you once felt for me is there inside you, buried beneath your anger, I would ask that you give it a chance to flourish again."

He had called her back to his host. She could not leave. "To what end?"

"To us being together." He gestured between them. "Being mates here who work and love together. Who rule my host together."

She opened her mouth to tell him it was pointless, but he held up his hand.

"I know you believe you won't change your heart, but for the sake of the love you bore me, at least give it a chance to wake again."

"And if it doesn't?"

Ramiel gave her a grave smile. "Then we will find a way to work together as close friends. But I vow to you that whatever your decision, I will never knowingly put you in harm's way again, and I will never take you for granted. If I have lost you, then I will bear that as I must, but regardless, you are owed a deep and heartfelt apology for what I did. I can only hope that somewhere within that huge, beautiful heart of yours, you can forgive the unforgivable."

He left her then, closing the door to his bedchamber behind him.

All his actions since he'd brought her back here spoke of his regret, putting her in his quarters, caring for her himself. She had never seen him take such actions for another being in all her time with him. And now it meant so little to her.

How long had she ached to lie where she was, and now she couldn't bear lying here.

The room was as cold and monotone as the rest of Ramiel's palace. Where once she had seen all the gleaming white as pure and clean, now she only saw a soulless lack of color. Ramiel had leaned hard into the archangel aesthetic when he had created his palace. Everywhere she looked, it was white. White floors and walls, white furniture, white pillars holding up a molded white ceiling. The only break in the white was a change in texture. Not even the merest hint of blush or beige ever made it past Ramiel's keen eye.

She longed for a bright pillow, even a pastel one to break the monotony.

She longed for Wrath.

THIRTY-SEVEN

Sophia stood by the hell gate as Wrath said goodbye to Eddie.

"I'll be back." He kissed Eddie's forehead. "And if you need me, you have but to call."

Eddie looked woebegone and so much younger than her years as she stared up at him. "But why can't you stay?"

"My demesne is in shambles." He gently took her hands. "As much as I would love to stay here with you, I need to see what order I can establish. I also need to find out if there's another way, other than you, to repair those seals." He glanced at Shade. "And I will also check on Shade's demesne while he remains here with you. In the end, I am a hell prince, and I need to serve my purpose."

"But Shade is staying." Eddie blinked back tears. "If he can stay, why can't you?"

Sophia's heart broke for both of them, and she decided to help Wrath out. "With Wrath going back, it is easier for Shade to stay." She had never thought she would see Wrath sacrifice his needs for another. But then, she had never seen a hell prince or an archangel acknowledge a child and then seek to preserve their relationship with that child. Always they had hunted Nephilim to extinction, called them abominations and condemned their existence. From what she'd seen, Nephilim brought out the best in a supernatural being.

Eddie blinked up at Wrath. "You're going so he can stay?"

"Partly, but there also is a lot that needs doing, and quickly." Wrath shot a look at Shade that promised endless retribution if Shade did not prove worthy of what he did today. "But the bond between us is alive now, and all you need to do is call me to you, and I will come."

Voice almost childlike, Eddie whispered, "Promise."

"I vow it." Wrath pressed their joined hands to his heart. "There is nothing that could keep me from you." He forced a smile. "And when this is all over, perhaps you could spend some time in my demesne." His jaw tightened. "With Shade, of course."

"I'd like that." Eddie swallowed. "And if you need me, you have to promise you'll call for me. That bond works two ways, you know."

"Yes, it does."

Sophia swallowed her tears at the infinite gentleness in Wrath as he bid his child goodbye. He would be back soon, and if she were a betting angel, she would lay money on sooner than even Eddie expected him.

Wrath enfolded Eddie into a hug. "Keep practicing with Sophia. Make yourself safe."

Over Eddie's head, he looked at Shade and nodded. Grief was carved into his handsome face and shadowed the cerulean of his eyes. It wasn't only leaving Eddie that had etched sadness into Wrath, and Sophia ached for him. Perhaps she felt an echo of her own pain and regret in Wrath's. In the lonely hours she spent in her cozy room at the local B&B, questions taunted her. What if she hadn't waited and spoken to Shade? Would he have loved her like he did Eddie? Probably not. And that was the most depressing thought of all.

Stepping closer to them, Shade put his arm around Eddie's shoulder. "Come on, Eddie. Lillian is threatening not to perform tonight, and you know you don't want me to get her to do it my way."

"Okay." Eddie stepped back with a sniff and a nod. She jabbed her forefinger at Wrath. "Soon."

"Soon," he said.

He watched, his expression unguarded as Eddie and Shade left the room and climbed the stairs up to the theatre.

"He will take care of her." Sophia stuffed her maudlin thoughts back in their box. She had been waiting for a moment alone with Wrath. Love shouldn't be squandered or left untended. Love required the courage to risk self in its pursuit. If only she'd use her own wisdom.

Wrath growled. "He had better." His expression hardened. "In the meantime, I will see what I can discover about who leads this rebellion. The demons have been taking advantage of our ignorance, but that is over now."

Sophia pitied any demon who crossed Wrath in his present state of mind. "Try to leave some of them alive."

He barked a reluctant laugh. "You are staying on this plane?"

"Shade is here." Sophia shrugged. "And for as long as he is, I must remain."

Wrath cleared his throat. "You will watch her too."

"Of course." If she hadn't known he would probably toss her across the basement, Sophia might have hugged him. He definitely looked like a being in need of a hug. Humans had that right about the hugs and the comfort. "While you are in hell, Shade and I will see what we can discover on this plane. My fellow archangels are looking into repairing the seals, Lucifer is hunting Ashe, and we will keep an eye on all of that too."

"And those fucking guardians." Wrath's eyes sparked red. "If they so much as breathe in her direction, I want to know."

"You'll be the first to know." Which wasn't strictly true, so she amended. "Well, one of the first." Because if the guardians moved against Dee or Eddie, she and Shade would not hesitate to remind them of the power of the immortals. That was another situation that had gone too long unchecked and unmanaged. But that was not the reason she'd lingered to speak to Wrath, and she got to it now. "Haziel is almost recovered."

Wrath stiffened but nodded. "Good."

"You know." She had to proceed with utmost caution. This was Wrath she was dealing with. "You could always request to visit her."

Jerking his head back, he stared at her. "Go to Ramiel's demesne?"

"You've been there before," she said.

Wrath narrowed his eyes and studied her. "What are you not saying?"

For an archangel who was renowned for her diplomacy, Sophia found herself floundering. "Just because a hell prince and an angel have never been together before, does not mean it cannot happen."

"You know better than that." Wrath scowled at her.

"I know that it has never happened in the past." Sophia spoke quickly before he lost patience with her, and she went basement air surfing. "But there has also never been a living Nephilim, and the horsemen have also never stirred this strongly before. We have also never had a demon rebellion before."

He scoffed. "What does that have to do with anything?"

"Everything." The cold look on his face was irritating her. "We are in uncharted territory now. Shade will stay here with Eddie, and the gathering has agreed to that. Why should Shade and Eddie be the only beings entitled to their happy ending?"

For a long, tense moment, she was sure Wrath was going to attack her, and then his shoulders slumped. "Even if that was true, you forget one pertinent fact."

"What?"

"She went with him." Wrath's voice dropped to a low, tortured rumble. "I offered her sanctuary, and she chose him."

The Wrath she had known for time beyond counting would never have been able to show his weakness like he did now. She risked her wings and put a hand on his forearm. "I don't think that means what you think it means."

He stiffened and glared at her offending hand on his person. "Speak plainly."

"I saw Haziel's face when she was with you. I was there in that moment, and I don't think she went by choice."

Wrath's expression grew thunderous. "You are saying Ramiel forced her?"

"I am saying that matters are not always as they seem. And that you should not let your experience with Rosabella cloud your judgment when it comes to Haziel."

Something painfully akin to hope flared in Wrath's eyes and then disappeared behind his habitual ire. "Even if what you say is true, it merely proves that she will always be bound to Ramiel."

"Ramiel is not all bad," she said.

Wrath growled.

"Grant you, he behaved like a complete prick sending Haziel to the horsemen, but I believe it's more a case of him behaving badly than a case of him being an unmitigated asshole."

"Beg to differ." Wrath shifted away from her light touch. "He will never let her go. Even if what you say about a different set of rules governing this time holds, it all means nothing, because Ramiel will never let her go."

Sophia held his furious stare. "How do you know if you don't ask?"

"I'm not going to ask." He crowded her back. "Because even if I did, she went with him. She looked me in the face and chose him." His voice dropped to a low growl. "You say I should not allow my experience with Rosabella to cloud my judgment. I would argue that I would be a fool not to. Two beings I have offered my heart to, and two beings have walked away. The trouble is not our rules, or even Ramiel and his possible motives." He pounded his chest. "The problem is the heart I offer is a corrupt and vile thing that is worth nothing."

He stepped through the hell gate before she could even shake her head in denial.

"Oh, Wrath." Sophia sighed and walked back up the stairs to the theatre. Her own loneliness pressed down on her. Had she not also wondered if the reason Shade had chosen Eddie was because he had seen some flaw within her? She wanted to laugh at herself. The advice she had given Wrath was useless because she clearly was not using it herself.

"Sophia." Dee stopped her outside the rehearsal hall. She held a brown paper package wrapped in a bright silver bow out to her. "This was left at the door for you."

Sophia eyed the package. "For me?"

"That's what it says." Dee tapped the handwritten note on the front. She winked at her. "It looks like you might have a secret admirer."

She waited until Dee had bustled off before she opened the package. The handwritten note was taped to the top of a small box of chocolates.

The love of chocolate transcends all barriers.
- Chris

THIRTY-EIGHT

Eddie locked the front door of the theatre behind the last patron. Already the Paradise Player volunteers were clearing away glasses and coffee and teacups from that night's performance. The buzz was unanimous: *Macbeth* was a hit. It was ironic how the patrons crowding the theatre night after night had no idea of the chain of events the play had set off. Which reminded her, that she still hadn't gotten a clear explanation on the witch's curse and how the entire thing worked. That little detail had gotten lost in the shit tornado that had followed.

She did her check of the bathrooms, calling out before entering the men's. It was the sort of thing you made sure to do after you'd made that mistake once. To this day, she didn't know who'd gotten the nastier shock, her or the octogenarian still taking care of business.

Footsteps sounded behind her as she checked the stalls. The low hum of Shade's presence was like a warm stroke against her senses. "I'm in here," she called.

"I know," Shade replied. "That's why I'm here."

She didn't know what to make of where things stood between them at the moment. Shade didn't sleep in her or Dee's rooms. In fact, he'd taken a room in the local B&B, in the room beside hers according to Sophia. No surprise that the two women who ran the B&B were twisting themselves like air puppets to make sure he had everything he needed.

She knew he wasn't using his lust thing on them because he'd promised her he wouldn't. Shade was many things, but he wasn't a liar.

He helped her check the final few stalls. "Lillian makes an amazing Lady Macbeth."

"She does." Eddie shared a smile with him. With all that had been going on, they weren't alone together often since her recovery, and she found herself feeling shy and breathless around him.

After the men's bathroom, she walked across the foyer to the women's.

Shade followed her in.

No point in telling him he shouldn't be here; there was nobody around. They completed the check in silence.

Back in the foyer, one of the younger volunteers batted her lashes at Shade. "Hi, Shade. Did you watch the show tonight?"

"From backstage." He returned her smile.

She leaned closer to him, her cheeks flushed. "Wasn't Lillian amazing?"

"Amazing," he agreed and took the tray of glasses from her.

The girl giggled. "I can manage."

"Of course you can," Shade said. "But I'd like to anyway."

"Oh, okay," she breathed.

Even without him doing the lust thing, people were drawn to Shade. Matt got so tongue-tied around him, he barely managed much above the occasional syllable.

It would take a being with a strong sense of self to be his partner. Could that be her?

She strode into the servery and loaded glasses into the dishwasher. The volunteers did their best, but they often forgot that last load for the night. Eddie wanted to leave everything clean and ready for tomorrow's matinee.

"Is that it?" A young volunteer poked her head around the servery door. Gaze locked on Shade, she said, "Because I can stay and finish if you like."

"Thanks, Dana." Eddie added detergent and turned the machine on. "We're all done."

Dana stared at Shade. "Are you sure?"

"Yup." She turned and chivvied Shade out of the servery. "Thanks for tonight. We'll see you tomorrow night."

"Right." Dana blinked at Shade.

Eddie snapped the light off. "Good night, then."

"Yeah." Dana shook her head and cleared her throat. "I'll see you tomorrow." Then she whispered, "Good night, Shade."

"Goodnight, Dana. Sleep well."

"I promise I will," Dana said and scurried away.

The poor girl was smitten. Eddie didn't blame her, and she couldn't fairly blame Shade either. He didn't flirt with any of his fan club, but they remained fascinated.

"Have you always had that effect on humans?" She motioned with her head to the door Dana had disappeared through.

Shade watched her with an unreadable expression. "I'm not sure how to answer that."

"With the truth." Eddie had to laugh as she flipped foyer lights off. "And why wouldn't you answer truthfully?"

"If I tell you yes"—Shade's voice came out of the darkness toward her—"you might hold it between us."

"And if you say no?"

His teeth flashed white in the gloom. "You'll know I'm lying to you."

Eddie's heart beat erratically as she took the passage between the foyer and the backstage area. The statement about her holding it against him was as close as he'd come to any reference to what he'd said in their conversation before she'd been taken hostage.

Since then, he'd been attentive when she was sick, kind and caring—she might even say loving and gentle—but he'd made no move on her and never said a word further. She wasn't sure how she felt about that.

Aaand she was a dirty, rotten liar. Inside, she was a mixed bag of anxiety, disappointment, and hope. But she didn't have the courage to bring it up herself.

The backstage was quiet with most of the lights already turned off. Eddie climbed the stairs to the dressing rooms. A light gleamed beneath the women's dressing room door.

"Sophia is in there," Shade said as he followed.

"How does that work?" She glanced over her shoulder at him. The dim light of the stairwell carved shadow beneath his cheekbones and highlighted his perfect bone structure. "That sensing each other thing."

"We have the same root power." He touched his chest. "And I can sense when she's near."

"But you're opposing forces?"

"Two sides of the same coin." He nodded. "And what we sense is the coin in each other."

Nodding, Eddie pushed open the dressing room door.

Sophia was tidying up the row of dressing tables, and she turned to look at them as they entered. "Time to go?"

"I'm shutting up for the night."

"Good." Sophia stood, her movements so effortlessly

graceful that Eddie felt like a lumbering heifer. "It was a good audience tonight."

"And they loved Lillian." Eddie didn't have to stretch the truth with Sophia. "And they'll love you as Cecily."

Sophia shrugged and blushed. "*The Importance of Being Earnest* is an excellent play, and the cast is all very talented."

"Modesty, Sophia?" Shade drawled.

Laughing, Sophia shoved his shoulder. "Shut your mouth." She shrugged. "I do love acting. I should have started years ago."

"Does Gabriel know?" Shade leaned his shoulder against the wall beside her mirror.

Sophia gathered her things in a bag. "I've made no attempt to conceal what I'm doing."

"Then, no," Shade said.

Blue eyes flashing retribution, Sophia glared at him. "I don't have to get anyone's permission. I am doing no harm."

"Still." Shade smirked. "I'm betting there's a regulation somewhere in Gabriel's files about it."

"Undoubtedly." Sophia laughed. She looked from him to Eddie. "I spoke to Wrath before he went back."

It surprised Eddie that she could miss someone she barely knew, but she did miss her father. *Her father.* Just the ability to be able to say those words and apply them to a living being made her heart skip a beat. All through her childhood, her father had been a mystery figure who would swoop in and save her from whatever misfortune had beset her. Turns out, she'd been right. Her father was more than capable of saving her from just about anything. "Is he okay?"

"Not really." Sophia sighed and shouldered her bag.

Shade straightened. "Haziel?"

"What else?" Sophia shrugged. "I don't mean to offend, Eddie, but your mother really did a number on him."

Rosabella had done a number on anyone close to her. "I know." Come to think on it, Rosabella had not been around the theatre for the last couple of days. Eddie was so accustomed to her fly-by visits that she hadn't bothered to keep tabs on her. "Do you know where she is?"

Sophia and Shade shook their heads.

Shade said, "I know Wrath and her had a conversation before he left, but I haven't seen her since then."

"He loved her." Sophia's voice had softened and the look on her face was breathtakingly gentle. "He loved her for years."

"He had quite the reputation before her," Shade said to Eddie. "But after he met your mother, he became more reclusive and cleaned up his act."

Eddie trod carefully. There might be things she did not want to know about her father. "Reputation?"

"Best not to ask." Shade grinned at her. "But let's say that despite what one might think, I was not the biggest man whore in hell."

Sophia frowned at him. "You weren't a man whore at all. You never have been."

That was news to Eddie, and it unsettled her. She had assumed with his ability that he would have plenty of beings ready to take up his offer.

He caught her looking at him and winked. "Surprised?"

"Yeah." There was no point in verbal evasion when her face was doing the talking.

"Shade embodies lust," Sophia says. "That does not mean he indulges."

Shade gave her a roguish smile. "And what does that say about you and chastity?"

Giggling, Sophia went all shades of red and slipped out of the dressing room.

Eddie turned off the lights and followed her and Shade downstairs.

They got to the outside door and stopped.

"I'm concerned about Wrath," Sophia said. "He seems very sad."

Groaning, Shade shook his head. "And that's going to make him grumpier than ever."

"Is that even possible?" Sophia grinned and then slid through the door into the parking lot. "Good night, Eddie."

"Good night." She didn't like to think of Wrath being sad. "Is it even possible?" She turned and looked up at Shade. He was closer than she'd thought, and her body reacted to his proximity. She wanted to lean into him, stand on her toes and press her mouth to his. She remembered the taste of him— honey and musk. Words made themselves impossible to catch in her mind, and she had to breathe deep. "Is it possible for Wrath and Haziel to be together?"

"Anything's possible, Eddie." Shade shifted closer, and her breasts brushed against his chest. The heat and want in his gray eyes made her pulse pound. "Just because a thing hasn't happened before, doesn't mean it cannot."

Were they still talking about Wrath and Haziel?

He cupped her cheek with his palm. "Hell princes can fall irrevocably and completely in love."

"Is Wrath in love with Haziel?" Her voice went deeper and raspier. Her heart raced.

"You'd have to ask him." He leaned closer and pressed a soft kiss to her forehead.

Disappointment soured in her belly. For a moment there, she'd been sure he was about to kiss her. Properly kiss her and not a chaste peck on the forehead. "Shade?" She didn't know what she was asking, but the moment felt heavy, and she needed clarity.

"Would you like me to check on Wrath for you?"

"Please."

He nodded and stepped back. "I will leave in the morning."

Checking on Wrath meant he would be gone from her. "Won't it be dangerous?"

"Eddie." He flashed a grin. "I am a hell prince. I am well able to take care of myself."

She remembered several occasions when that hadn't been true. "Maybe, but take the hounds with you."

"No." Shade's face hardened. "They stay here to watch you."

"I wasn't the one who was stabbed the last time we were in hell." She didn't want to play dirty, but she would feel much better if he took Xerxes and Cronus—as much as she would miss them.

"But you were abducted." Shade crossed his arms. "The hounds stay, or I don't go."

"Ugh!" He could be so frustrating when he got his hell prince face on. "I have Sophia here to watch over me and Dee and Daniel."

Shade merely stared at her.

"You're saying you won't go unless the hounds stay here?"

He nodded. "That's exactly what I'm saying."

"Then I could go and check on my father." Dee was back. The theatre would be fine without her.

"You're not going to hell." He glowered at her. "Need I remind you what happened last time you did?"

"We could go together."

He didn't move.

"You're such an asshole."

Not a twitch.

"I don't want you to go and get hurt."

His face softened, and he walked back to her and slid his

hand to her nape. "Eddie, I will be fine. I can move faster without you, and I am on my guard now. I won't be caught out again."

The image of Shade after he'd escaped hell with a mortal wound flashed in front of her. "I take it back; I'll call for Wrath and see how he is."

"Let me go." He pressed his forehead to hers. "It will be quicker, and I can check my demesne and my seal while I'm there. And keep the hounds here because I will be distracted with worry if they're not with you." His eyes twinkled. "And if I get distracted, I might get hurt."

That was him playing dirty, and she glared at him. "That's not fair."

"Maybe not." He straightened away from her and dropped his hand. "But that's the way it's going to be."

He strolled away from her into the night and suddenly it hit her that he wouldn't be around tomorrow. "How long will you be gone?"

Turning, he walked backwards as he said, "A day or two at most. Will you miss me?"

"Maybe."

He grinned. "That's a definite improvement. I'll take it."

THIRTY-NINE

The impact of his weakening seal hit Shade as he crossed through the hell gate into his demesne. Lust pounded through his system like a steady heartbeat reminding him he needed to find a way to stabilize the seal.

The jungle lay quiet around him, and he sent his senses out to detect any demons. There was nothing around, and he unleashed his wings. It occurred to him that he was relying on Wrath's goodwill not to have him shot out of the sky as he crossed into that demesne. For all he knew, Wrath's horde could still be instructed to shoot him from the sky.

By air, he could take a direct route, and it was about half of those hours that Eddie counted so obsessively before he crossed into Wrath's demesne.

No demon rose to challenge him. No bolts shot from the ground to bring him down.

All good thus far.

Part of him had to laugh at what he was doing. He was willingly entering the territory of his archenemy to make sure said enemy was okay because the Nephilim he loved to distraction had asked it of him. The truth was humbling. He would do this and so much more just to make her smile.

Hell felt wrong, like an uncomfortable grating against his senses. There were also far fewer demons going about their lives as he flew over than there should be. He cursed his inattention. An entire rebellion had been spawned and executed beneath the noses of all the hell princes, and not one of the seven had noticed.

All-powerful beings tasked with a sacred duty, and they'd all fucked it up.

Wrath's demesne felt more stable, probably because of the repair Eddie had done to Wrath's seal. It wouldn't hold, but it seemed to be sounder than his seal. The heaven component had been missing from Eddie's fix, and in all the excitement, he hadn't given that much thought. Did that mean an archangel needed to help fix the seals? It would be lucky if it was that simple, but nothing about recent events suggested luck was with them. The archangels were researching solutions and he hoped they were doing better than they'd thus far managed in their research into ending war on earth.

Vexia was waiting for him in the forecourt as he back-winged into Wrath's fortress.

"My lord." She clasped her hands to her chest and bowed. "We were not expecting you."

He nearly laughed. No, they absolutely wouldn't have been. He and Wrath had never popped in on each other for a beer and a chat. "I mean no harm by my visit."

"I am aware." She bowed again and motioned him to follow her.

Wrath's demons eyed him suspiciously as they milled about the courtyard. According to Wrath and Haziel, his own palace was virtually deserted.

"How many have you lost?" He jerked his head at a cluster of demons staring at him with their hands on their sword hilts.

Vexia glanced at them and made a motion for them to stand down. "Too many."

He followed her up the stone stairs and through the door to the inner courtyard. The two central fountains sparkled and gurgled beneath the clear sky. Vexia had been Wrath's second for centuries now. When she took off those gowns and donned fighting leathers, he knew from personal experience, she was a magnificent fighter. The demon could make magic happen with a sword and a pair of daggers. "There's something that's bothering me."

She stopped and tilted her head as she waited for him to speak.

"Did you know?" He stepped closer to her.

She was a beautiful demon with her ivory skin and gleaming red hair.

Her golden eyes flashed as she considered her answer. "You are asking if I had any knowledge of the rebellion before it became noticeable?"

"Yes." Apassionata had said nothing to him, and he had to believe his second would have informed him if he'd known. Lucifer must have thought the same thing, only to be betrayed by his second. They all needed to be a lot more alert to what was happening around them.

"A fair question." Vexia inclined her head. "And one that I have asked myself repeatedly."

"And?"

"Hindsight is so exacting, isn't it?" A small smile teased at the corners of her mouth. "I was aware of groups of our horde speaking amongst themselves. I can even recall a conversation I had with an under demon, which given where we are now, would seem to suggest they were trying to ascertain the depth of my loyalty." She sighed and shrugged one shoulder. "But demons are demons, and it is in their nature to be malcontent."

That was true, and he nodded.

Vexia turned and led them into the foyer. She stopped suddenly and took a breath. "But it is good that you have come."

"Why?"

"My lord is not himself." Vexia's elegant hands twisted together. "He is...angry."

Shade had to laugh at that. It was a bit like calling the sky a sky. "Is he not always?"

"Indeed." Vexia almost smiled, but then concern clouded her features. "But this time, it is different. Always before his rage was a living thing."

As he'd seen evidence of that aimed against him, Shade nodded and motioned for her to continue.

"And now it is silent and...tortured."

That didn't sound good. "Eddie sent me to check on him."

"I thought as much." Vexia nodded. "Or else I would have had you brought to ground the moment you crossed the border."

THE MOMENT SHADE entered his throne room, Wrath shot to his feet. His heart beat uncomfortably in his chest. "Is it Eddie? Is she safe?"

"Eddie is well." Shade sauntered around the fire pit and approached him. He cocked his head and studied Wrath. "She is concerned about you."

That ignited a warm spark in his chest, but also guilt. Eddie should not be worried about him. He was the sire, and he was the one who should be worried about her. His voice was brusque as he said, "There is no need for her to worry. I am fine."

"But are you?" Shade stopped at the bottom of the three stairs leading up to the dais on which his throne sat. He put one foot on the bottom stair and stared up at him. "Because you look like shit."

Even his familiar need to wipe the smirk off Shade's face failed him. "Thanks."

"Eddie is worried about you," he said. "And we all know I'm a pushover for your daughter, so I'm here to check on you."

He hated the idea that Eddie might fret. "Tell her I'm fine."

Vexia cleared her throat as she came closer.

He sent her a glare to let her know exactly what he thought of her opinion on the matter. She'd been uncharacteristically verbal with him since his return, always checking on him, questioning his state of mind, daring to suggest that all was not well. She was right, but fuck that anyway.

"Let's pretend for a minute that I believe you." Shade looked around him. "And maybe we can sit and chat about what's going on down here."

Vexia compelled a large chair toward him, and Shade took a seat.

Talking about the situation in hell felt safer, and the knot in his chest unraveled enough for him to speak freely.

"Your palace remains deserted." It felt wrong to perch above Shade in this manner, so he motioned Vexia for another chair for him.

She placed it beside Shade's.

Wrath took a seat and ignored Shade's raised eyebrow. "There are still members of your horde in the villages, but there has been some definite thinning. Those that remain are fearful."

"Fuck." Shade rubbed his jaw. "And Lucifer's demesne?"

"Worse." Wrath had flown for hours and seen not one demon. "It seems like most of his horde has followed Ashe."

"Ava?"

Wrath grimaced. "Ava is not happy with me and did not allow me access."

"Is she ever?"

Wrath had to smile. "But she did send a message that her seal is compromised, and her demesne grows more unstable. She is also bleeding demons."

Shade frowned. "Belle?"

"Silent." Wrath had been unable to reach Belphegor, but as she was determinedly reclusive, that hadn't raised any immediate alarms. "Zeb and Levi report much the same as Ava."

Vexia appeared with refreshments and placed them on a low table that had materialized between them. Wrath would be bereft without her and had an inkling about how Lucifer felt about Ashe's defection. Seconds were vital to the running of a demesne, but they served a second, and as important, purpose. If a hell prince tired of their long existence, their power and their essence could be passed to their second, thus sidestepping the catastrophic results of a hell prince ending. The choice of a second was not made lightly. Which was probably part of the reason Ramiel had been so territorial over Haziel. He shoved that thought away. He had survived Rosabella's rejection, and he would survive this. There were more vital matters that demanded his attention. But speaking of Ava reminded him of Haziel and how comfortable she had been in Ava's palace. Unlike most seraphim, Haziel had exhibited no discomfort around demons.

Fuck! He would stop his every thought from straying in her direction. "Ava, Zeb, Levi, and I have reached an understanding in recent days. We are sharing information and all hostilities between us end until we have this under control. When I get hold of Belle, I'll be sure to get her cooperation."

Shade nodded and sipped the wine Vexia had brought them. "That's good. I think we're all going to have to get over our crap with each other and work together if we want to stay alive."

Hell princes working together was enough of an imagination stretch that he almost laughed. He was not given much to laughter, but it felt as if nothing had felt worthy enough of laughter since—

He would control his thoughts!

"Belle would not allow me access to her demesne either," he said.

Shade made a face. "Is that any surprise? She's viciously private."

She always had been, and Wrath nodded. "I shall send another emissary to her court. As you say, working together is vital if any of us are to survive." Then he asked what he most wanted to know. "How is Eddie?"

"She's well." Shade smiled the smile of a truly besotted being. As much as he disliked the hell prince, if one had to trust one's child with another male, to have one who adored your child like Shade did Eddie softened the blow. "She tried to come with me."

"No." His gut tightened.

"I have the hounds watching her," Shade said. "They will protect her and let me know if she makes any move to head in this direction."

Like he thought—besotted. "Good."

Shade stretched his legs out in front of him and looked about. "I've always liked this hall of yours."

"Even when you were bleeding on its floor?"

Shade grimaced. "Less then, but it's very appealing."

"Why are you really here?" Wrath did not for a second believe Shade was here to swap interior design tips.

"I told you." Shade held his palms up. "I came to check on you for Eddie."

"And now you've done that—" The thing with immortal beings is that they knew each other far too well. "You can return and tell her I am well. Or you can say your piece, and then return to her and tell her that I am well."

Chin resting on his palm, Shade studied him. "But you're not really well, are you?"

"Don't I look it?" For good measure, Wrath thumped his chest. No, he was not well. He felt as if his insides had been scooped out and laid in the sun to dry.

Taking his sweet time, Shade selected a snack and then took another sip of his wine before sitting back and dropping his head to the back of his chair. "Emotions are not really my thing." He crossed his ankles. "Urges," he shrugged. "Totally my thing. But emotions...eh."

Here it came, and Wrath waited.

"You're a coward," Shade said.

"Pardon?" Wrath had to lean forward to make sure he'd caught Shade's correctly. Shade would never throw that word in his direction. Shade! The being above all others who knew he was the very farthest thing from a coward.

Shade popped a handful of nuts into his mouth and grinned. "You're. A. Coward." He yawned. "Or to use an Eddie colloquialism—a little bitch boy."

"Did you just..." Words failed him. And he did what he always did when words failed him and reached for a weapon. Only to find his dagger not at his waist and the scabbard over his back empty.

Vexia stood behind Shade with both weapons clutched to her chest. "I think you should listen."

"He called me..." Wrath couldn't even speak that phrase.

She nodded. "I heard, but I still think you should listen."

"Have you turned rebel?" His voice thundered through the echoing space.

She raised an eyebrow at him. "You know better than that."

He did, and he huffed. "Fine." Ever since Dee and Eddie had visited, Vexia had grown a personality to match her fighting skills. Most of the time, he appreciated the change. Now? Not at all. He turned his glower on Shade. "But if you call me that again, I'll cut your—"

"Yeah, yeah, yeah." Shade stirred the air languidly with his hand. "Cut off my balls. Eviscerate me. Rip off my head and shit down my throat. Blah, blah, blah."

The situation was careening out of his control. "I mean it."

"No, you don't," Vexia murmured. "Because Shade is beloved of Eddie, and you would never hurt what she loves."

"Well I—" No, he wouldn't, and he subsided into a stew of outrage and impotence. "What the fuck do you want?"

"What the fuck do you want?" Shade sat forward and pinned him with those irritating eyes.

Vexia whispered one word, and it hung in the hall like a death knell. "Haziel."

"Exactly!" Shade snapped his fingers and pointed to her. "You want that angel. And what are you doing about it?" He glanced at Vexia.

She crossed her arms. "Nothing."

"Two out of two." Shade threw her an approving look. "Except maybe a little brooding, and it's not a good look on our boy."

The two of them infuriated him, and Vexia's betrayal stung like salt in his wound. "She chose to return with him."

"Yes, she did." Shade nodded. "But when has Satanus, the hell prince of wrath, ever let a thing like an archangel stand in his way."

Vexia was right there with the answer. "Never." She sighed. "Until now."

FORTY

Wrath cursed himself for being all kinds of an idiot. He'd been in this position before, and it had cost him his heart and his pride. Still, he entered Ramiel's demesne and waited at the portal for Ramiel's host to recognize his presence.

A seraph appeared, wings out, sword brandished. "What are you doing here, hell prince?"

Wasn't this going swimmingly? "I've come to see Ramiel." Wrath held the angel's stare. Feathery fuckwit had best think long and hard about his future if he sought to challenge him.

The seraph landed before him but kept his wings extended. "Ramiel is not expecting you."

"Well." See, this was the problem with angels—arrogant and entitled, every last one of them. Well, maybe not *every* one of them. Suppressing the desire to rip off all six of the seraph's wings and shove them up his tight ass, he played nice. "It wouldn't be a surprise visit if he did."

The seraph eyed him suspiciously. "Wait here. I will check if he will see you."

Yeah, nope, that wasn't going to happen. Wrath released his wings and took to the air.

"Oy!" The seraph yelped and followed him. "You. Hell prince. Stop."

Nope, he wasn't going to wait around like some supplicant at his master's gate while an underling sought permission for him to enter. The seraph may be able to keep up with him flying, but if it came to a fight, the ponce was seriously outclassed.

Another three seraphim popped into the air beside him. And then another twenty.

Well, now the odds were looking a little more even. Not much, but hey, he was feeling amicable. He'd give them a few free blows before he showed them why lesser beings did not mess with a hell prince. Especially not a hell prince on a mission.

Seven of the seraphim formed an attacking position and dived for him.

Wrath blasted them out of the air. Not hard enough to end them, but certainly hard enough to leave a mark. He spat white and silver feathers out of his mouth and kept flying for Ramiel's palace.

The palace was no big surprise, given the tightwad who owned it. Low and sprawling, it lounged in glaring white across the top of a green hill. Built of flowing, pleasing lines and perfectly symmetrical, it made him want to take a shit on the walls, just to put something out of place.

Ramiel appeared on a balcony central to the complex and stared up at him.

He must have given some instruction to his angels because they kept pace with him but there were no more attacks.

Back winging, he landed on the balcony beside Ramiel.

The air stirred as seraphim landed all around them. Vexia had wanted to come with him, but he'd refused. He wasn't here to make war. Not yet, at least.

"Satanus." Ramiel raised a brow. "Nice of you to drop in."

Wrath gestured to the seraphim around him. "Get rid of the pigeons."

Waving a hand, Ramiel dismissed his host.

The one who'd met Wrath at the gate gave him a glare as he went.

Wrath flashed a grin at him. Yeah, food chain, shithead. And he was on the top.

"How is your seal?" Crossing his arms, Ramiel studied him.

Wrath was okay with getting the pleasantries out of the way first. "Eddie's repair is holding, for now, but we need to find a permanent solution."

"Hmm." Ramiel pursed his lips. "And the other seals?"

"Shit."

Nodding, Ramiel said, "We are making some headway into researching seal repairs, but nothing definite yet."

"Not going to invite me in?" Wrath gestured to the open glass doors behind Ramiel.

"I'm considering it." Ramiel shoved his hands in his pockets.

It had taken Wrath a few days to arrive at his determination to come here, and he wasn't going to be turned back now. He strode for the doors.

Ramiel stepped into his path with a growl. "Wrath."

"You know why I'm here." He met Ramiel's gaze. "And after what you did, you owe me the courtesy of listening to what I have to say."

Ramiel chuckled grimly. "Or what?"

"Or I level this place around your ears." Wrath didn't make

the threat lightly. He was here to see Haziel, and he wasn't leaving until he did.

"Try it." Ramiel scoffed. "You think I'm going to stand by and let you do that?"

"I think you'd try to stop me," Wrath said. "But it doesn't have to come to that."

A long, tense moment passed as Ramiel stared at him. Finally, he nodded and motioned Wrath to follow him inside.

The inside was as white and antiseptic as the outside. All this white would give him a ball ache before today was over. He couldn't picture Haziel in this sterile environment. She was so full of life and fire. She was color, vivid and fascinating.

Ramiel surprised him by foregoing the ostentatious white throne on its white marbled dais—Ramiel really had committed to the theme—and led them to a smaller seating area to the right. He lowered himself into one of the three—you guessed it—white armchairs and motioned Wrath to take the other.

An angel appeared and put refreshments in front of them. The color of the biscuits, cheeses, and fruit seemed almost garish against everything else. Thankful he didn't have to choke down a glass of milk, Wrath accepted a glass of ruby wine from the angel.

"I can guess why you're here." Ramiel crossed his legs and leaned back in his chair. He held his glass of wine up to catch the light. "But why don't you tell me anyway?"

"I want to see her." Wrath sipped his wine and was surprised by Ramiel's excellent choice of vintage. The Cabernet Sauvignon rolled across his tongue in a burst of blackberries and tobacco.

Ramiel tilted his crystal goblet and studied the red refraction of the wine against the crystal goblet. "Why?"

"There are things I must say to her." Wrath wasn't going to

have this conversation with Ramiel. Haziel wasn't some kind of medieval serf who required her lord's permission to speak with him. Neither was she some female chattel that he needed to approach through her nearest male relative. "There are things that I would say to her and her alone."

Ramiel hummed and sipped his wine. "You see, Wrath, we're at a bit of an impasse here."

"What?" It made his butt clench the way angels always had to make word games of a conversation and couldn't come right out and say what they were thinking.

"I'm going to guess you're here because you have strong feelings for her." Ramiel gestured around them. "I can count on one hand the number of times you've been here, and those were only because we had urgent matters to discuss. The serious intent behind your visit is not lost on me."

Didn't that make Ramiel a super brain. Irritation had him finishing his goblet before he tossed it at the fucker. "If I speak to my feelings, I will speak those words to Haziel."

"Fair enough." Leaning forward, Ramiel topped up his glass. "But let us speak first." He took a careful breath. "What I did to Haziel, putting her at risk like that, it was wrong."

"Damn fucking right it was." Wrath would still like to rip Ramiel's head off his shoulders over that. Actually, he pretty much always wanted to perform a beheading on Ramiel. "If I hadn't been with her, she would have..." He couldn't say the words. The idea of a being of such light and joy ending did not bear even considering for a fleeting moment.

Ramiel met his angry stare. "You're right. I fucked up, and I have no excuse, other than that I am a jealous ass."

The open admission caught him wrong footed, and it took a moment for him to catch up with the meaning.

"Jealous?" Vexia had suggested as much to him, but Wrath had never really believed it. How could Ramiel be jealous? He'd had Haziel's love and devotion for centuries, and he'd done nothing about it. Hells! Wrath had only experienced it for a handful of days, and now he would do anything to get it back.

"Sadly, yes." Ramiel grimaced and sipped his wine. "It does not reflect well on me that I have known I had her love for all this time, and it was only when I sensed that love slipping away that I did anything about it."

Fury lashed its tail inside him. "And killing her was your idea of a grand romantic gesture?"

"I never meant for her to be hurt." Ramiel's tone sharpened. "You may not believe it, but I didn't. I merely reacted in the moment. I wanted her away from you, and I grasped at the first opportunity to do that."

Wrath leapt to his feet. End of the world be damned. This fucker had almost killed Haziel because he got his dick in a knot. "You're a fucking asshole."

"Yes." Ramiel glanced up at him. "I've come to that unfortunate conclusion myself."

Wrath had been dealing with Ramiel their entire existences, and he found himself lost. This was not the archangel he was accustomed to dealing with.

Ramiel indicated he take a seat again.

And Wrath sat. "What are you saying?"

"I love her too." Ramiel shrugged. "And it's my stupidity that made me squander the gift of her love."

Wrath found himself struggling to keep up. He didn't know what to make of a humble and contrite Ramiel. As much as he didn't want to admit it, the archangel seemed genuinely regretful about what he'd done.

"You know what it's like." Ramiel studied his wine. "We have all this power and beings who fawn over our every need. It becomes ridiculously easy to believe that one is as special as one is led to believe."

He wanted to deny Ramiel's words and fling them back at him, but he couldn't. When he'd fallen in love with Rosabella, it had never occurred to him that a mere human woman would reject him, find him wanting, choose her freedom over him. After all, he had offered her himself and the world. Then she had said no.

It was a humbling thought that he and Ramiel were not so very different. If he had never encountered Rosabella and never had to face failure and the harsh truth that one being did not find him worthy of their love, he would have been the same. He couldn't think he would ever have sent Vexia knowingly to her death, but it would have stung to know that he was no longer the most important being in her existence. "You're saying that you love Haziel."

"Yes." Ramiel sighed. "It would have been extremely beneficial to all of us if I had extracted my oversize head from my ass sooner, but alas, here we are."

Weariness washed over Wrath, and he leaned back in his chair. "Where does that leave us?"

"I have declared myself to Haziel." Ramiel met him stare for stare. "I have thrown myself at her mercy, as it were."

Gorge rose in Wrath's throat. Haziel had loved Ramiel for most of her existence. She had finally gotten what her heart had desired for so long. He couldn't sit here and stare at the fucker who'd gotten the gift of Haziel's amazing heart. He wasn't a big enough being for that. Wrath stood.

Ramiel blinked at him. "Where are you going?"

"You want me to wish you well?" Rage simmered inside him like live flame.

"I wish that you could." Ramiel chuckled, but the sound was forlorn. "But she does not want me."

Wrath's knees felt weak, and he sat again. "What are you saying?"

"I offered myself to her." Ramiel waved his hand about him. "All that I am and all that I have. Haziel is a generous soul, and she agreed to give me a chance to plead my case, but even in my arrogance, I can see that her heart is already given... elsewhere."

Needing to hear it spelled out for him, Wrath kept his seat and stared at Ramiel.

"Do you need to hear me say it?" Ramiel grated.

"Yes."

"She loves you." Ramiel exploded from his chair. He hurled his goblet across the room. Glass and red wine splattered the brilliant white floor. "She loves you." Ramiel's shoulders slumped. "She stays out of a loyalty to me that reflects far better on her than it does on me." He pressed his thumb and forefinger into his eyes. "But she does not love me. Anymore. She has a new love."

Like he was frozen, Wrath sat there and stared at Ramiel. He hadn't known what to expect when he came here, but he had come prepared to do whatever it took to get Haziel to hear him out.

Although he stood as tall and proud as ever, there was a brokenness to Ramiel that Wrath recognized. It was only when a being was brought face to face with their own failures that they truly experienced the depth of who they were. And Ramiel had failed. Not because Haziel loved another being, but because his own flawed love had made him act in a manner that he couldn't be proud of. It had been the fire that forged Wrath, and he hoped that Ramiel found it the same. "She has not said that she loves me."

"But she does." Ramiel straightened his shoulders. "And may the heavens help the two of you, because you still have to get the gathering to agree to let her be with you, but I will not oppose you."

"As much as I appreciate that"—Wrath stood—"those are words that need to come from Haziel. We are not able to sit here and discuss her future as if we have the right to do so. I am here because I love her. It rests with her what to do with that knowledge."

FORTY-ONE

Haziel stopped in the middle of her training session with the younger angels and lowered her sword. For a minute there, she felt sure she could feel Wrath, but that couldn't be. Wrath rarely came to Ramiel's demesne, and it was merely wishful thinking on her part.

Zephon winged into the training ground, looking like he was ready to rip heads off and apologize later. She wasn't in the mood for one of Zephon's tantrums, so she turned her attention back to her trainee. Taking him by the hand, she shifted the dagger in his clasp. "Like this. You keep holding it the other way, and it's too easy to knock out of your hand."

"Yes, Haziel." He nodded and gave her his shy smile.

His smile reminded her of Issy, the sick human girl, and the promise she had made. She would need to journey to the earth plane and fulfill her promise soon. Not that she foresaw any issue getting permission from Ramiel. He was contorting himself to make her happy, and it made her feel a bit guilty. Not guilty enough to stop taking advantage of the situation, but she did feel a mite of pity for him. After all, very few knew as well as she did the constant pain of unrequited love.

Her own feelings had shifted so suddenly that she might be accused of being fickle. But then she remembered Wrath and all the things that made her heart beat faster. It was more than his raw, primal beauty. It had to do with his quiet sense of humor, his intractable honor, the way he cared so deeply for those he loved, and his strength and determination. These were all qualities she'd seen in Ramiel, only to discover that they existed in her imagination.

"Fucking hell prince." Zephon thwacked a small bush with his sword. "They have no rights here."

The hair on Haziel's nape stood on end. Her pulse throbbed erratically in her throat. Could she have felt Wrath?

She turned to Zephon. "There is a hell prince here?"

"As if you don't know." He sneered at her. Her fellow seraphim had not been happy about her association with Wrath and were keen to share that opinion with her. She didn't care about the opinion of beings who swaddled themselves from experiencing the life they had been created to preserve.

But Haziel did care, very much, about the possibility of Wrath being there. She cared so much she might hang around in the background to catch a glimpse of him. He wouldn't have come here for her. She'd left him and followed Ramiel. Despite what her stupid heart wanted to believe. "Is Wrath here?"

Zephon turned his back on her.

Now that was just plain rude and fucking annoying. Launching herself at him, Haziel struck him with her full body weight between the shoulder blades.

He hit the ground with a grunt.

Haziel still had her trainee's dagger in her hand, and she pressed it against his throat. "I asked you a question politely."

She spoke directly into his ear. "And I will get a polite response."

"Fuck, Haziel." Zephon squirmed beneath her, trying to free himself. He was welcome to try. She was Ramiel's second, and her power was part of the reason she'd been granted that position.

"I'm going to ask you again." She applied a bit more pressure with the knife. "Is Wrath here?"

"Yes," Zephon snarled. "He is with Lord Ramiel."

Every part of Haziel softened as she absorbed that news.

Beneath her, Zephon managed to wriggle free and toss her off him.

She barely even noticed him as she sat with her ass on the ground and tried to get her mind to work. There was every possibility that Wrath was here to talk about the issue with the seals, or the mixed demon hordes. Maybe he had new information he needed to share with Ramiel. But then surely he would call a gathering and share it with all the others at the same time.

She didn't want to think impossible things. Wrath had made her no promises, as she had made him none. And in the end, he would see what she had done as the same abandonment and rejection he had suffered from Rosabella.

But Wrath was here, and she wanted to see him with every functioning part of herself.

"Haziel." Her trainee crouched in front of her. "Are you all right?"

Was she all right? Haziel stared at his pretty, eager young face and had no idea how to answer that question. She was suddenly laughing with no idea why or how to stop it.

"Get a hold of yourself," Zephon snapped, dabbing at the small nick she had given him with his forefinger. "Your behavior is setting a poor example to the young."

She barely heard him. Would Wrath want to speak to her before he left? She was too terrified to even entertain the hope. And what would she even say to him if he did? That she was sorry, but she had given her word to Ramiel that she would leave. That she would do it again if it meant Ramiel would help Wrath heal his daughter.

"Haziel." Ramiel appeared through the door leading into the palace. "I need to speak with you."

She clambered to her feet, keenly aware of how hot and sweaty she was. Her hands shook so badly that she handed the dagger over to the trainee. Now was not the time to entrust her with a weapon.

Ramiel's expression was unfathomable as she approached him. He motioned her to follow him inside. "You've heard."

It was not a question. "Yes."

"He is here for you." Ramiel stopped and faced her. The open longing in his green eyes made her heart constrict. He was hurting, and despite everything, she didn't want that for him. "And you, my sweet Haziel, have a decision to make."

She shook her head and her throat constricted as she said, "No, I don't."

Pain shadowed Ramiel's eyes. "It shall be as you want."

"Thank you." Now she needed to hear the words from Wrath.

"Oh, and Haziel." Ramiel smiled. "You could say that I did you an unintentional favor by insisting you return here with me."

This she needed to hear. "And how is that?"

"Now you know, without doubt, how much you mean to him."

WRATH FELT as nervous as a stripling as he waited for Ramiel to fetch Haziel. He should have prepared a speech and not flown up here with no clear intention other than to get his female. He should have asked Vexia to give him some talking points, or better yet, Shade. Shade knew how to speak to someone you desired. He should have worn something other than fighting leathers.

And then she was there, standing in the open doorway. Light glanced off her dark hair, and all the white was a perfect setting for her warm skin. She approached him slowly, the cloth of her wide-legged pants floating around her legs. "Wrath"

"Hi." In terms of a great beginning to the most important conversation of his life, it was a failure.

Her lips quirked. "Hi, yourself."

She looked so beautiful it felt like his heart had stopped. How had he forgotten how vivid and alive her big, green eyes were? Forgotten how good she smelled. Forgotten how being close to her made something tight and hot unravel in his chest and make it feel like he could breathe again. "I came to ask you something."

She stopped a foot in front of him and peered up at him. "So ask."

Sensation torpedoed him. The challenge in her beautiful eyes, the soft almost smile lurking at the corners of her full mouth, the warm amber of her skin, everything about her that fanned the spark of life to a conflagration within him. And he said the first thing that came to mind, "Come live with me and be my love?"

"Christopher Marlowe?" She chuckled.

He couldn't prevent his answering grin. "He was a close personal friend. Actually, I gave him those words."

"Liar." Eyes twinkling, she shook her head at him.

It seemed like forever since he'd gazed into those eyes. "Maybe." He closed the small distance between them. "So, will you?"

"I'd like to." The heat radiating off his big body called to her. "But I need some other words first."

Dammit! Words were not his strength. "Like what?"

"Like why you want me to come with you." She jammed her hands on her full hips.

"Because I love you." Unable to resist touching her, he slid his arms around her waist. "Because I am a miserable bastard without you."

She held her body stiff. "You seem to have arrived at this decision rather suddenly. When last we were together you were warning me that you couldn't promise me anything."

"And then I nearly lost you." Those terrifying moments when he'd been unable to stop the pull of the horsemen. That horrible death knell of a moment when she'd told him she was leaving. "And then I did lose you."

"What about Rosabella?" She allowed him to inch her forward.

"I loved Rosabella." But the sting had not been within him for some time. Wrath couldn't say when it had stopped, just that living with her rejection had become an uncomfortable habit. "But not in the way I love you."

She narrowed her eyes at him. "Explain."

"Hell's teeth, female." How many fucking extra words did she want from him? He'd covered the most important ones.

Haziel stared at him, demanding he answer.

"With Rosabella, it was like hankering for something that I could not have. The further it went, the more I wanted it. It was the wanting more than the thing in the end. Rosabella is not you. She lacks your warmth, and your vitality, your kindness, and your loyalty. She doesn't make me a better version of myself."

Her eyes softened. "And I do?"

"Yes, Haziel. You most certainly fucking do." He dipped his head toward her, and then stopped. "And why am I the one doing all the explaining?" He didn't bother to conceal his hurt from her as he said, "You left me."

"I did." Tears gleamed in her lovely eyes. "I didn't want to, but I had promised Ramiel that if he helped you heal Eddie, I would separate myself from you."

Her gaze begged him to understand, and he wanted to end Ramiel all over again. The archangel had bartered for his daughter's life to get his love away from him. "And you never break a promise." It was one of the things he valued about her, her integrity.

She crinkled her nose. "Not deliberately, but I kind of broke my word when you followed me to the horsemen."

"Nah." That memory was one of the sweetest of his life. "And you didn't know I was coming, so technically you didn't do anything wrong." Then he got to the crux of the matter for him. "If you hadn't promised Ramiel, would you have stayed?"

"Yes." No hesitation and no doubt.

And that was enough talking for him. "May we get to the kissing part of the making up now?"

"Just one more question."

He groaned aloud. "What?"

"How will this work?" She slid her arms over his chest and around his nape. "I am a seraph, and you are a hell prince. There has never been a coupling like us before."

"And Nephilim were considered abominations and killed before," Wrath said and pulled her hips flush with his. The sweet feel of her body against his almost brought him to his knees. "But you will find that I don't give a fuck about any of that."

"Wrath." She giggled. "You know that we need permission from a full gathering."

"Haziel." He touched his lips to hers. "A full gathering will not keep me away from you."

"Oh, Wrath." And she softened against him. Raising her head to his, she kissed him.

The taste of her hit him anew, and he wanted more, all of her. But not here, not beneath Ramiel's nose. Despise the fucker as he did, he knew too well the agony of watching another male leave with your female. Unleashing his wings, he flew them up and out of Ramiel's throne room.

FORTY-TWO

Gabriel tapped at her cursed tablet as she glared at Haziel and Wrath across the greenroom. "It's unprecedented."

"But there is no rule against it, per se," Ramiel said and winked at Haziel. Their new relationship left her feeling odd. The power balance had shifted between them, and she had to suppress the desire to pander to Ramiel. After all their time together, it had become reflex. She really did wish him happiness.

Wrath took her hand and kissed her knuckles.

"Where is Lucifer?" Haziel looked around the greenroom. All the archangels were here, and the other six hell princes. Ava had given her a hug when she'd walked in and whispered, "Bring him to his knees, sweetheart."

Well, Haziel was not so sure she wanted to do that. Although Wrath had proven to be rather inventive on his knees. Once this gathering was over, she was planning a replay.

They'd flown to the earth plane and the theatre. She hadn't

been able to resist showing him how powerful seraphim wings really were. From the grin Wrath had shot her, he'd enjoyed it as much as she had. Despite her desire to be alone with him, he wanted this final hurdle dealt with before they went to his demesne.

Eddie grinned at them from where she was tucked beside Shade. Those two looked to be growing closer, and she wished for them all the joy she now felt.

"I support them." Ramiel leaned against the wall beside the door.

"I don't care either way." Michael punched one fist into the opposite hands. "We have much bigger issues to deal with than one seraph coupling with a hell prince."

The guardians were excluded, because according to Wrath when he'd called the gathering, nobody really gave a shit what they had to say about this situation.

"Let's vote on it." Raphael held up his hand. "All in favor."

Shade's hand shot up almost faster than Wrath's.

"I don't think you can vote," Gabriel glared at Wrath.

Wrath shrugged. "Just did."

"Before we vote, there is a more important issue to consider." Cassiel smiled at her apologetically. "There is the balance to consider. Haziel may remain Ramiel's second, but we still are short one powerful being in the heavens."

Shade kept his hand in the air. "Haziel is not actually going to be Wrath's second, so how is that a problem?"

Azrael pursed her lips. "That's not how it works."

"One more for our team seems a great outcome for us." Ava put her hand in the air. "Besides, Haziel is awesome. She fits right into hell."

"Cassiel and Azrael make an excellent point." Gabriel handed her tablet to a hovering Raguel. "In all things, there must be balance."

"I don't give a fuck about balance." Wrath stood and held his hand out to her. "I am taking Haziel to my demesne, and not one of you is going to stop me."

"Sit down, Satanus," Michael snapped.

And, predictably, Wrath snapped back, "Make me."

Haziel felt the hell gate surge.

Beside her, Wrath tensed and looked at the door. "What the fuck?"

The others felt it too, and all gazes swung to the door.

Haziel tried to get a power read on the being who had stepped through. She had half been expecting Lucifer, but this being felt like...wrath?

"What?" Eddie must have picked up on the tension because she looked to Shade for an answer.

"A being just used the hell gate," he murmured. "Not one of mine."

"She's mine." Wrath frowned. "And I don't know what she's doing here."

"Uh-oh," Belle murmured from her position near the microwave. "We don't need any more bad news."

Dressed in fighting leathers and exuding badassery, Vexia strode into the greenroom. She bowed first to Wrath and then to the other hell princes and finally, the archangels.

Shade whistled. "Vexia," he drawled. "Looking like two of my favorite things, sin and violence." He caught Eddie's gaze and flushed. "I mean, two of my former favorite things."

Laughing, Eddie patted his thigh. "She looks hot."

"Vexia?" Wrath narrowed his eyes at his second. "Is there a problem?"

"No, my lord." Vexia raised her chin. "But I believe I have a solution to your current situation."

Dee smirked. "Atta girl, Vexia."

"Greetings, Deandra." Vexia smiled and then returned her

attention to Wrath. "The archangel Ramiel's second is returning with you to the wrath demesne, correct?"

"Yes." Wrath nodded.

"Then perhaps the archangel Ramiel will accept me as a replacement."

Wrath gaped at her. "Eh?"

"There's no procedure for this." Gabriel snatched her tablet back and jabbed at it with two fingers.

Haziel caught Wrath's slight flinch and stood beside him. She wrapped their fingers together as she asked Vexia, "Why?"

"In all things, there must be balance," Vexia said. "I am Wrath's second, and you are Ramiel's second. If we traded places, the balance would be maintained."

A low murmur of conversation broke out in the greenroom.

Wrath stared at her. "Are you not content in your position?"

"Lord Wrath." Vexia's smile was almost maternal in its tenderness. "There could be no greater honor than serving you. And in serving you, I seek only your happiness."

"But Vexia." Ava stood and twitched her breastplate into place. "Do you really want to go and live with these stuffed shits in heaven?"

Shade grinned at her. "I believe the expression is stuffed shirts."

"I said what I said." Ava grinned back.

"Must you?" Michael grimaced at Ava. "Must you always be so provocative?"

"Hmm?" Ava cocked her head and tapped her forefinger against her mouth. "I mean, if you want to get technical, I don't suppose I must." She threw him a glittering grin. "But it's so much fun."

Ramiel had gone still as he studied Vexia. Haziel knew him

well enough to know that he was giving the suggestion serious consideration.

"Absolutely not." Gabriel tossed her tablet to Raguel, who caught it one handed. "The solution to one irregularity is not another."

"Excuse me." Raguel raised his hand. "But I do believe there is precedent for such a trade."

Gabriel glared at him.

Raguel tossed Haziel a quick wink. "If we were to consider it in the light of a trade agreement, a sharing of resources?"

Opening her mouth, Gabriel stopped and then snapped it shut again. "I mean, there was that time...back in..." She turned to Raguel. "When was that?"

"The eighth human century," Raguel replied. "Then again in the sixteenth. Also during the wars of—"

"Good thinking, Raguel." Shade gave a slow hand clap. "A trade of skills and resources to facilitate overcoming our present difficulties. There is plenty of precedent for that."

"All in favor," Azrael grinned and called.

All hands shot up. Except for Ramiel, and Haziel held her breath as she watched him.

Ramiel gave Vexia a thorough once over. "I accept."

The greenroom breathed a collective sigh of relief.

Wrath's hand tightened over hers. "Time to leave, angel."

HAZIEL WAS ALMOST sure Wrath was nervous as he led her into his castle fortress. The first thing that struck her was all the color. Rich creams, deep umbers, and colorful mosaics. The next thing that struck here were all the demons. Despite the thinning of his horde, there were still many demons around the castle, and they all seemed to be staring at her.

Holding tight to her hand, Wrath led her up a sweeping cream and ochre staircase. "Normally, Vexia would do this part." He shrugged.

"She loves you, Wrath." Haziel hated to think of Vexia leaving as hurting him. "She did this for you."

He grimaced. "I hope you're right about that."

Haziel had been second for long enough to know what she said next to be the absolute truth. "And maybe she also wanted the adventure. We don't get much of that as seconds."

"Huh." Wrath glanced at her. "I suppose I never considered that." Then he chuckled. "Anyway, Ramiel's in for a hell of a shock. Vexia may look all demure and self-effacing but she's my best warrior, and there's a reason she's considered strong enough to be my second."

The Vexia at the theatre had looked neither demure nor self-effacing, and maybe someone less accommodating would be exactly what Ramiel needed.

Wrath led her down a long, light corridor to a large set of wooden doors at the end. He threw them open to reveal an expansive, airy sitting room filled with comfortable furniture. "And these are my chambers."

Glass doors all along one side were thrown open to catch the refreshing breeze and provided a panoramic view of grassy plains rising into craggy, tree covered mountains.

Haziel took a deep breath of the balmy air. This was to be her new home.

"Do you like it?" Wrath watched her as if he was holding his breath.

"I love it." She smiled at him. "Now show me the most important part."

"Which is?"

She cocked a hip and met his stare. "The bedroom."

"Angel." Wrath's eyes gleamed. "That smart mouth of yours is going to get you into all kinds of trouble."

She giggled. "That's what I'm counting on."

Wrath lunged and swept her over his shoulder. "Don't say you weren't warned."

Viewing her new bedchamber from upside down was a novel experience. She got a fleeting impression of polished wood floors with bright rugs and a massive four poster bed in the center.

And then she was tossed into the middle of a fur-covered bed, and the time to appreciate her surroundings was over. The time to appreciate her hell prince, however, was just getting started.

Wrath followed her down, pinning her beneath his weight.

Part of her couldn't believe she was actually here with him like this. She'd woken this morning prepared to go through the routine of another day in Ramiel's realm, and now she was here, with Wrath's strong, hard body pressing her into the bed.

"Hey." He framed her face with his hands. "Regrets?"

"Not a one." She wrapped her arms around his neck. "Except for the time it took you to come and get me."

"Never again," Wrath growled. "You are mine, and by my side is where you will stay."

And then there was no more talking. What started as a slow exploration, quickly escalated into a desperate need for hands, mouths, and bodies. It felt as if neither of them could get close enough, as if they both sought to erase the time they'd spent apart.

Haziel gloried in their joining, a celebration and a beginning, and a promise of so much more to come.

EPILOGUE

Isabella Grace Henshawe was buried on a bright, Highveld winter day. The air was dry from the winter, the grass beneath the feet of the mourners yellow and sparse. Issy had always hated winter, and they'd so hoped she would be with them to see one more spring. Bare Jacaranda trees ringed the quiet, secluded cemetery behind the Anglican church. In a month or two, their branches would be heavy with the violet, trumpet-shaped flowers that only appeared in the spring. But Issy wouldn't be here to see them.

One more year, one more month, one more spring—the perpetual bargain for more time. Until time had run out and Issy had left them. Issy's mother stood alone beside the coffin. A heavy arrangement of white lilies perfumed the air, their sweetness turning her stomach. She'd known since Issy's first diagnosis three years ago that this was coming, but she'd kept hoping the doctors were wrong, that Issy would beat the odds and be that rare miracle.

Her husband and mother were waiting for her in the car. People would be gathering at their Parkhurst home to mourn with them, with her. Her mother had given her a pill from the doctor this morning to help her through the funeral, but she hadn't taken it. Her pain was hers, and blunting it even slightly felt like a betrayal to the child whose life had been cut so short. Parents shouldn't outlive their children. It was wrong, unnatural.

Movement flickered out of the corner of her eye, and a bird alighted on the coffin. She lunged to chase it away, but something stopped her. Another four birds joined the first, the bright morning light catching the brilliant blues, russets, and yellows of their plumage. Her heart stopped, and her breath caught in her throat. European bee eaters, not due back yet from their annual winter migration. Issy's favorite bird. They'd started bird watching together as a way to pass the time when Issy was no longer well enough to go to school. It had become their special thing.

Tears blurred her vision, and she could have sworn the bee eaters cocked their heads as if watching her.

"Issy," she whispered.

The bee eaters stretched their wings and took to the air. Spring was coming. The seasons would roll forward. Life would go on. Without Issy, but life would go on.

Another Epilogue

Lucifer tracked the lingering essence of Ashe to a small village over his border in Ava's demesne. The slippery fucker was long gone, the tavern all but deserted except for a table of low order demons who eyed him with suspicion.

"I'm looking for a high order demon," he said to the tavern keeper.

The tavern keeper spread his hands on the counter and eyed Lucifer from beneath the overdeveloped ridge of bone over his eyes. "You might be lost. We don't get many of those in here."

Lucifer reached for whatever claim on patience he could manage. It had never been much, and his long hunt had whittled it down to a nub. "Which is why you would have remembered one."

"Begging your pardon, your lordship." The tavern keeper's knuckles whitened under the nervous press of his hands into the bar counter. "But we don't get many of your kind either. Unless you're here by invitation of our prince."

Not many demons would challenge a hell prince, and Lucifer gave the demon points for courage. Or was that stupidity? The two were remarkably intertwined, with the difference often lying in the outcome of said courageous or stupid act.

The barkeeper was clearly loyal to Avarice and was questioning his right to be in this demesne. Lucifer had ripped demons apart for lesser offences, but with Ashe's betrayal burning a hole in his belly, he had to admire the keeper's loyalty to Ava. "Mammon would have no issue with me being here. I am on business that affects all of us."

The keeper nodded and licked his lips, no doubt relieved that Lucifer had decided not to hand him his ass.

The lower order demons at the table had stopped their dice game and were watching the conversation with avid interest.

A mahogany woodland gnome raised his hand. "Excuse me, Lord Lucifer." He swallowed, his huge black eyes darting around his companions as if waiting for support. "But would that be Ashe you were looking for?"

The name surged through Lucifer on a wave of victory. At fucking last, he was getting somewhere. Stalking over to their table, he loomed over the quaking demons. "Tell me what you know of Ashe."

Looking like he regretted opening his mouth, the gnome quivered and squeaked. "Uh...er...um...I don't know much, my lord."

Weeks of frustration from hunting down his traitorous second gripped Lucifer as he thundered, "Tell me."

The gnome's eyes rolled back in his head, and he slid off his chair and dropped in a dead faint. His body hit the floor with a *thud*.

Fuck!

The gnome's imp companion squealed and made a dash for the door.

"Not so fast." Lucifer caught the imp by the pink horn and dragged him back. "It appears that your friend is unable to answer my questions at the minute. Why don't you tell me what you know?" It was not a request.

"Lord Lucifer." The troll lumbered to her feet. "Leafrot knows him best." She indicated the still unconscious gnome. And Blot over there don't know anything."

"She's right." The imp wriggled. "Nothing. I know nothing."

"You're also an imp." Lucifer gave Blot a small shake. "You could be lying."

Blot grimaced. "You got me there, my lord." Then he brightened. "But I'm telling the truth. This time."

Lucifer stared at the downed Leafrot and ground his teeth. The gnome could stay that way for weeks, and he didn't have days, let alone weeks. With the horsemen waking, the rebellion spreading across hell, and the seals weakening, he needed answers now. And he was very much looking forward to extracting them from Ashe.

"I know a little something," the troll said.

Lucifer's bad mood hovered on the edge of a slight improvement. "Tell me."

"Ashe has folk near here," she said. "Or, at least, he used to have." She nudged Leafrot with an enormous, dirt-caked toe. "Leafrot was friends with one of the family."

Ashe had come to Lucifer fully formed, and not as one of the demons he'd raised. He'd never thought to ask where the fucker hailed from. There was a lot he'd never thought to ask the lying shit, and he was paying for that oversight now. "You said Ashe's folk used to be from around here? Where are they now?"

The troll shrugged. "Don't know. They was three females

and two males as far as I remember. Leafrot could tell you for sure, but they aren't here no more."

This would be going so much better if Leafrot would wake the fuck up. He made a mental note to remove the gnome's ability to go dormant and asked, "So if they're not here, where did they go?"

"Dunno." She flinched in anticipation of him not liking her answer.

He hated her answer, but he wasn't going to punish the troll when she was trying to be helpful.

"I do know that they disappeared a while back," the troll said. "Leafrot went to visit them, and they were gone. He said they just disappeared. Dishes still on the table. Wash hanging on the line. Wouldn't shut up about it." She stared down at Leafrot. "I know he don't look like it now, but he's normally a talkative sort."

"I remember that," the tavern keeper chimed in. "Several of my customers were speculating about what had happened to them."

On his hunt, Lucifer had learned not to dismiss even the most innocuous sounding gossip. "Any conclusions reached in their speculation?"

"Most believed they'd upped and legged it," the keeper said. "But they never could say what from. Others thought they'd been taken."

Taken or told by Ashe to disappear and do it fast? Ashe knew him well enough to know he would punish disloyalty and might have wanted to make sure he got his folk out of the way before he turned traitor.

"Leafrot always said Ashe took care of them," the troll said. "Used to come here on days he wasn't working for you. Sent goods and food. That sort of thing." She frowned and clicked her tongue. "There was something wrong with one of them.

Couldn't work. So the others had to watch them." The troll sighed. "Honestly, my lord, that's all I remember. Leafrot's a big talker." She glanced down and winced. "I don't always listen to all he says."

Lucifer made another design adjustment to future demons he might raise, better listening skills for trolls and less bullshit spewing for gnomes. Clearly gnomes needed some rethinking. If Ramiel could slap a truth telling imperative on his seraphim, there was no reason why they couldn't make a few tweaks to demons. If he'd thought to do to Ashe what Ramiel had done to Haziel—made it impossible for the seraph to lie—he wouldn't be in this position now.

"Anything else?" He took in the troll and the tavern keeper. A jolt along his arm reminded him that he still had Blot suspended by the horn and he lowered the imp to the floor.

"I remember something." Blot patted his horn as if to reassure himself it was still attached. "It was only the offspring," he said. "The sire and dam were ended a long time ago. Back before I was born."

As imps had as much value for the concept of time as they did for truth, that could mean anything from a day to a millennium.

"Mixed couple is what I heard." The keeper took a tankard from the shelf behind him and ambled over to a large keg mounted on the bar. "Dam was from Gluttony and sire was one of yours."

Mixed couples in the demonarchy often denoted a pair who originated from different demesnes as much as it did a cross demon breed pairing. Strange that Lucifer had never picked up anything but his own power signature in Ashe. Although it looked like he could write a book about all he hadn't known about Ashe.

An odd twisty sensation tightened through his chest. It

wasn't a feeling he was accustomed to. It had happened a few times around his brother, Wrath. He felt...hurt, rejected and not good enough. Not that he would let either Wrath or Ashe in on his dirty secret. Those fuckers didn't deserve his wounded feelings.

Of course, the problem might be hunger. It had been weeks since he had last sought sustenance. Hell princes didn't have the same pressing needs as humans, especially not whilst in hell, but they did have them. And he really enjoyed a good feed. Not as much as Zeb, obviously, but a great meal went a long way to soothing a hell prince's rough edges. And while he was thinking about his rough edges, it had also been a while since he had enjoyed the company of a bed mate. All this running around after Ashe was seriously compromising his self-care regimen. He needed to find the fucker, end him, and get on with the business of being the king of hell.

Miraculously, Leafrot twitched, and his eyelids flickered open. He fastened his gaze on Lucifer and his eyes rolled back in his head.

"No." The troll kicked him, and not gently. "You're not doing that again."

Lucifer smirked. It was such a burden to always be the big bad. It was nice when someone else stepped up as the villain.

The troll crouched beside Leafrot. "Lord Lucifer has questions, and you're going to answer them for him."

"He didn't end you?" Leafrot blinked at the other tavern occupants.

"Not yet." Blot beamed at Leafrot. "But he might change his mind if you don't tell him what he needs to know."

Wincing, Leafrot struggled into a sitting position. He probed the back of his head with his fingers. "Did nobody think to catch me?"

Lucifer crouched beside him. "I understand you are acquainted with Ashe's folk."

The summoning hit him like a wave of icy water through his body. Gritting his teeth, Lucifer ignored it. He was finally getting somewhere in his pursuit of his missing, traitorous second. No fucking human witch was going to summon him now and drag him out of hell. "When was Ashe last here?"

"Hmm?" Leafrot tapped his temple with his forefinger.

Lucifer suppressed the urge to bellow at him to hurry up before that fucking witch had another go.

"I don't rightly remember, but it was a while ago," Leafrot said. "He didn't get here as much as he liked because..." Leafrot started guiltily and averted his gaze.

"Because he was busy following my orders." Lucifer finished for him. "Give me some idea of what a while ago means."

The summoning hit him again, harder this time and fastening around his being like invisible manacles.

Lucifer leaned into his power and refused the summoning. "Ashe." His voice grated as the summoning heaved at him and he fought it. "When did you last see him?"

"I'm not sure." Leafrot whimpered. "Don't end me, lord. I'm thinking."

"Think faster." The summoning pulsed stronger, urgent and demanding. It tore into his muscles and sinews and insisted he obey.

"It was after his folk vanished." Leafrot clicked his fingers. "I remember now because he looked so shocked when he found them gone. Also, he looked sad, but not shocked sad, kind of like he knew that they were gone, and now he had to do something. He said—"

The summoning snatched Lucifer into the abyss and sent him hurtling through the hell gate. He bellowed his rage as he journeyed. Some fucking human witch was going to rue the day she'd summoned him.

The Hell Bound continue their mission in Pride. And this time Hell Prince Lucifer must do his part.

**Buy your books directly from me at
Sarah Hegger Books**

For first dibs on news, deals, giveaways, and so much more, join the @Home Collective

Or if Facebook is more your thing, join the Sarah Hegger Collective

Anything and everything you need to know on my website http://sarahhegger.com

About the Author

Born British and raised in South Africa, Sarah Hegger suffers from an incurable case of wanderlust. Her match? A hot Canadian engineer, whose marriage proposal she accepted six short weeks after they first met. Together they've made homes in seven different cities across three different continents (and back again once or twice). If only it made her multilingual, but the best she can manage is idiosyncratic English, fluent Afrikaans, conversant Russian, pigeon Portuguese, even worse Zulu and enough French to get herself into trouble. Mimicking her globe trotting adventures, Sarah's career path began as a gainfully employed actress, drifted into public relations, settled a moment in advertising, and eventually took root in the fertile soil of her first love, writing. She also moonlights as a wife and mother. She currently lives in Ottawa, Canada, filling her empty nest with fur babies. Part footloose buccaneer, part quixotic observer of life, Sarah's restless heart is most content when reading or writing books.

ALSO BY SARAH HEGGER

Sarah Hegger also writes as Sarah Edwards

Paranormal Romance

The Hell Bound Series

Lust

Wrath

Pride

Avarice

Envy

Sloth

Urban Fantasy

The Cré-Witch Chronicles

Prequel: Cast In Stone

Vol l: Born In Water

Vol ll: Purged In Fire

Vol III: Raised In Air

Vol IV: Cradled In Earth

Vol IV ½: Forged In Fate

Vol V: Joined In Spirit

Sports Romance

Ottawa Titans

Roughing

Contemporary Romance

Passing Through

Drove All Night

Ticket To Ride

Walk On By

Ghost Falls

Positively Pippa

Becoming Bella

Blatantly Blythe

Loving Laura

Willow Park Romances

Nobody's Angel

Nobody's Fool

Nobody's Princess

Medieval Romance

Sir Arthur's Legacy

Sweet Bea

My Lady Faye

Conquering William

Defying Roger

Henry's Honor

Love & War

The Marriage Parley

The Betrothal Melee

Western Historical Romance

The Soiled Doves

Sugar Ellie

Standalone

The Bride Gift

Bad Wolfe On The Rise

Wild Honey

PRAISE FOR SARAH HEGGER

Drove All Night
"The classic romance plot is elevated to a modern-day, wholly accessible real-life fairy tale with an excellent mix of romantic elements and spicy sensuality."
Booklife Prize, Critic's Report

Positively Pippa
"This is the type of romance that makes readers fall in love not just with characters, but with authors as well."
Kirkus Review (Starred Review)

"What begins as a simple second-chance romance quickly transforms into a beautiful, frank examination of love, family dynamics, and following one's dreams. Hegger's unflinching, candid portrayal of interpersonal and generational communication elevates the story to the sublime. Shunning clichés and contrived circumstances, she uses realistic, relatable situations to create a world that readers will want to visit time and again."

Publisher's Weekly, Starred Review

Hegger's utterly delightful first Ghost Falls contemporary is what other romance novels want to grow up to be." – Publisher's Weekly, Best Books of 2017

"The very talented Hegger kicks off an enjoyable new series set in the small Utah town of Ghost Falls. This charming and fun-filled book has everything from passion and humor to betrayal and revenge." – Jill M Smith, RT Books Reviews 2017 – Contemporary Love and Laughter Nominee

Becoming Bella
"Hegger excels at depicting familial relationships and friendships of all kinds, including purely platonic friendships between women and men. Tears, laughter, and a dollop of suspense make a memorable story that readers will want to revisit time and again."
Publisher's Weekly, Starred Review

"...you have a terrific new romance that Hegger fans are going to love. Don't miss out!"
Jill M. Smith – RT Book Reviews

Blatantly Blythe
"Ms. Hegger has delivered another captivating read for this series in this book that was packed with emotion..." Bec, Bookmagic Review, Harlequin Junkie, HJ Recommends.

Nobody's Fool
"Hegger offers a breath of fresh air in the romance genre." – Terri Dukes, RT Book Reviews

Nobody's Princess

"Hegger continues to live up to her rapidly growing reputation for breathing fresh air into the romance genre." – Terri Dukes, RT Book Reviews

"I have read the entire Willow Park Series. I have loved each of the books ... Nobody's Princess is my favorite of all time." Harlequin Junkie, Top Pick

www.ingramcontent.com/pod-product-compliance
Lightning Source LLC
Chambersburg PA
CBHW051134300726
48978CB00011B/271